MAKING *the* MARQUESS

BROTHERHOOD
OF THE
BLACK
TARTAN
BOOK 4

NICHOLE VAN

Fiorenza Publishing

Making the Marquess © 2021 by Nichole Van Valkenburgh
Cover design © Nichole Van Valkenburgh
Interior design © Nichole Van Valkenburgh

Published by Fiorenza Publishing
Print Edition v1.0

ISBN: 978-1-949863-10-9

To Shannon
For being such a gloriously unexpected light.

To Dave
For always lighting my path.

PROLOGUE

YORKSHIRE, ENGLAND
ON A ROAD NORTH OF RIPON
JULY 7, 1817

King Louis the XIV had arrived to deliver the baby.

Lottie feared she was hallucinating.

And then, just as quickly, she feared the opposite. That the gentleman racing toward her in the antiquated purple justacorps, white-powdered wig, and rouged face paint was *not*, in fact, a figment of her imagination.

After all, the man clutched a doctor's bag in his hand, and their footman, Danny, was at his heels.

How could this gentleman possibly be a physician?

Lottie's sister, Margaret—Lady Frank Fulton to the world at large—moaned and gasped her way through another labor pain, her hand squeezing Lottie's in a vise.

"I think the doctor has finally arrived, Margaret dearest," Lottie murmured, wiping perspiration off her sister's forehead.

"At long last!" Margaret groaned, her blue eyes fluttering open. "He will be a most welcome sight!"

Lottie wondered if her sister would feel the same in five minutes when the physician and Danny reached them.

The men had left their horses back on the roadway and were hopping the hundred or so yards across the boggy meadow toward the tree where Margaret lay. Danny carried a pile of folded linen under one arm and a bucket of water in the other.

The doctor, for his part, struggled to jump from clump-to-clump of dry grass, as the flared skirt of his long justacorps obscured the view of his boots. The curls of his enormous peruke extended nearly to his waist, sending white puffs of hair powder aloft with each lurching leap. And . . . was that a mole-patch on his cheek?

Regardless, the doctor's clothing was a solid hundred years out of fashion—ancient attire for a man who appeared far younger.

Was this the medical care one received so far out in the country? Or was this more a case of beggars-not-choosers?

Lottie was unsure.

She had never assisted a sister in giving birth atop carriage blankets under a sprawling oak tree.

She squinted as the men bounded closer.

But if not a physician, who was the man? A costumier? An asylum fugitive? A masked-ball enthusiast?

Hmmm.

Hallucination was still a possibility. The situation certainly had a dreamlike quality.

A grunt of distress had Lottie turning back to Margaret. Her sister lay with her eyes closed, panting and whimpering through yet another labor pain. Lottie dabbed Margaret's brow again with a handkerchief, hating that she was so helpless in the face of her sister's suffering.

This was certainly not how her sister had envisioned bringing her second child into the world. Margaret had despaired for years, believing herself barren. She had been overjoyed to be increasing once more.

Of course, Lottie considered it decidedly ironic that the actual child-birth had come upon them so unexpectedly. But, alas, babies had much in common with time and tides—they waited for no man.

Lottie was encouraging Margaret through her labor pain when a doctor's case landed near her elbow.

She glanced up. The doctor stood over her, rimmed in light and appearing like a ghostly apparition of centuries past.

"Good afternoon, ladies," he said. "I see ye are in a wee spot of trouble."

The doctor's commonplace words were a sharp contrast to the chaos of his attire. Moreover, his voice sounded so . . . prosaic, laced with a doctor's forced cheeriness and threads of Scotland.

He dropped to his knees beside them, the curls of his peruke swinging forward.

Margaret opened her eyes at the movement, met the doctor's gaze, and promptly recoiled in horror, a startled shriek on her tongue.

Definitely not a hallucination then.

"Who the *bloody hell* is this?!" Margaret screeched, reaching for Lottie's hand and attempting to scrabble backwards. Her cumbersome body resisted, barely moving.

Ah, yes.

Lottie had noted the rather illuminating expanse of her older sister's vocabulary over the past several hours.

"He's the doctor, dearest," Lottie explained, silently praying she was correct.

The doctor directed Danny to set his armful of linens on the carriage blanket beside Margaret and the bucket of water beside it. The footman bowed and beat a hasty retreat, heading back to the horses.

Pulling off his black riding gloves, the doctor opened his case, retrieving a small amber-colored jar.

He was young. Even through the face paint, Lottie would hazard the man had not seen a day above thirty.

That said, he radiated competence. He situated a few more jars and then pulled out a pocket watch.

Margaret shrank from him, yanking her wrist out of his hold as he attempted to monitor her pulse.

"I don't want this doctor, Lottie." Her eyes turned pleading. "You must find me another one."

"Now, Margaret—"

"I have waited too long for this child to have it delivered by a . . . a . . . foppish *lothario*." Margaret grabbed Lottie's hand. "Can you imagine Frank's horror?"

The good doctor's face devolved into pure granite as Margaret spoke—the expression utterly incongruous with his absurd attire.

"I assure ye, this is my idea of a nightmare, as well." The doctor's tone was starkly dry.

The mole-patch on his right cheek slipped downwards, as if finally ascertaining that it was far too frivolous for his stern face.

The doctor startled and swiped at the patch—much like one might swat a mosquito—smearing a bright streak of rouge down to his jaw. He stared at the pink staining his fingers, as if both perplexed and horrified. Lottie had seen that look before on her cousin Gabriel's face after one too many glasses of brandy.

It was the expression of a man with regrets.

But the blush climbing the doctor's neck implied that he was not immune to embarrassment.

"I was led to believe your situation was more dire than it appears at present," he continued. "But now that I am here, I promise that ye and your unborn babe are in capable hands, Mrs. . . ." His voice trailed off, waiting for Margaret to provide her name.

"*Lady* Frank Fulton," Margaret said, emphasizing her title.

Lottie knew her sister to be kind and generous, but she was perhaps slightly less so with those she viewed as being beneath her.

The doctor did not blink at her tone.

"Lady Frank, my apologies. I gather that we both have a tale to tell." The doctor pulled a cloth from his case and proceeded to wipe the rouge from his hands with jerking motions. "For yourself, it will be how a finely-bred lady ended up here, atop carriage blankets beneath a tree, ready to give birth—"

Margaret groaned again, eyes closing in pain and turning Lottie's fingers purple with the strain of her grip.

"—and for myself, it will be how I arrived dressed as ye see. This is *not* my habitual apparel." He waved a hand up and down to indicate his old-fashioned dress, eyes rolling in frustration. "I ken that this entire situation appears untoward. But a wee bairn cares naught for propriety and will come into this world in the manner it chooses. We must merely make do with the hand God has dealt us."

Lottie smiled.

It might have been the exhaustion and stress clouding her thinking, but Lottie decided then and there she liked Doctor King Louis the XIV.

Sunlight filtered down through the oak tree overhead, dappling the carriage blankets atop the spongy grass. Margaret continued to moan, her back arching, her breaths coming in short gasps. Lottie mopped the perspiration from her sister's forehead.

The doctor opened the small jar and stirred a spoonful of powder into the bucket of water.

"Chlorinated-lime," he said, noting her questioning look, "to ensure everything is disinfected. I'm an oddity among physicians, I know. But I believe in the importance of cleanliness when dealing with patients, particularly during childbirth."

He dipped both hands into the mixture, rubbing them thoroughly. Shaking his hands dry, he unfolded one of the bedsheets the footman had brought and draped it over Margaret's legs.

"I need to check the progress of your bairn, Lady Frank, so please forgive this indignity." The doctor's tone was soft and gentle. "You will only feel a slight pressure."

Lottie's eyes widened.

Gracious, childbirth was proving a cleansing experience—scrubbing their lives of decorum and catapulting them into a sort of reluctant familiarity.

The doctor lifted the sheet, gently pulling on Margaret's ankles to open her knees. The curls of his periwig dragged across Margaret's calves, causing her to shriek once more and jerk her legs away, pushing her feet into the blanket, as if to sit up.

The doctor sighed, rocking back on his heels, hands atop the satin justacorps covering his thighs.

"I am truly here to help." His voice held a decisive bite this time. "But in order to help, I must determine the position and progress of your bairn."

Margaret raised her head and glowered at him, hair sticking to her damp cheeks. "I want a proper physician. Or, at the very least, a competent midwife."

The doctor closed his eyes, perhaps praying for patience.

Though, in this, Lottie could understand Margaret's reluctance. The necessary intimacy of this situation *was* shocking.

"I *am* a proper physician," he said through clenched teeth. "I graduated as a fully-fledged Doctor of Medicine from the University of Edinburgh just three years past."

Lottie swallowed. The doctor was as young as she had supposed.

Margaret turned weary eyes to Lottie. "Was there no other doctor in town?"

"Believe me," he interrupted, "I dinnae want tae be here anymore than yerselves. But your choices, my lady, were myself dressed like this or one of the other three physicians in town who are currently drunk as wheelbarrows. Proper roaring *fou*, they are."

"Are you quite sure you are not drunk yourself?" Margaret flicked her eyes over his gaudy attire.

"My lady, I am dressed like this precisely *because* I am sober, not the other way around." He sighed, leaning forward and sliding his hands down to his knees. "My story is quite simple. I was returning to Edinburgh and stopped in Ripon to visit a school chum who has a surgery there. My friend wished to celebrate my return to Britain, as I have been abroad for a pair of years. He invited his friends and proposed a drinking game. He would add something vile to each finger of brandy, and the man who refused a drink had to don another piece of this monstrosity." The doctor swept a hand down the front of his violet justacorps. "I dinnae drink alcohol. Therefore, I lost every round."

"How can you be a gentleman—a *Scot* no less—and not drink—" Margaret cut off mid-sentence, her body arching in agony.

Lottie shook her head. "Please forgive my sister, sir. You are not seeing her at her best." She mopped Margaret's face once more. "We have had a trying afternoon."

"Aye. I think we all have." He managed a grim smile.

"The lack of propriety for this situation has been a shock," Lottie said. "We all supposed Margaret would be in the privacy of her own boudoir when she gave birth. Not atop a blanket beside a boggy meadow."

Poor Margaret was lost in her pain, curses dropping from her lips, breaths coming in short pants. The doctor slipped his hands under the sheet, and this time, Margaret allowed him to examine her progress.

"Ye are coming along nicely, my lady. I can just feel the baby's head beginning to descend in earnest, though it is not quite yet crowning. It shan't be more than another hour or two, I reckon. I see no point in moving you and attempting to reach habitation. How came you to be here?"

"'Tis a bit of a tale." Lottie wiped Margaret's brow. "We left London three days ago to return to my sister's home outside Darlington to begin her confinement. We spent last night in Ripon but were two hours on the roadway this morning when her waters burst. The pains came hard and fast, and we were attempting to return to town, but poor Margaret could not tolerate the jolting and rocking of the carriage. We stopped and she paced her way across the boggy meadow—" Lottie motioned to the marsh before them. "—and then did not have the wherewithal to return to the carriage. The servants brought blankets and rushed to fetch a doctor."

The doctor dipped his hands into the lime mixture to wash them, frowning as the cuffs of the justacorps dragged in the water. "Is this Lady Frank's first child?"

Margaret grunted, moaning and cursing again. Her labor pains were certainly lasting longer with less time between them.

"'Tis her second, sir," Lottie answered. "Her first is a sweet girl, Anne, who is at home with her nurse. But it has been nearly six years since my sister last gave birth. We had supposed her barren, so this child is truly a gift."

"I'm grateful, then, tae be part of this joyous occasion." The doctor nodded and took a seat on the opposite side of Margaret, settling onto the blanket there.

The sun had passed its zenith and was heading toward late afternoon. But as they were approaching the summer solstice, sunset was still half a day away.

Margaret's labor pain eased.

The doctor smiled at her. "Second deliveries are usually much quicker than first, Lady Frank. Rest as much as ye can."

Margaret whimpered and closed her eyes, face exhausted, a hand pressed to her swollen belly.

"Thank you for being here, Lottie," Margaret murmured, eyes still closed.

"Hush. There is nowhere I'd rather be than here. Rest." Lottie pressed a kiss to Margaret's forehead.

For his part, the doctor began digging his fingers into his scalp.

"Hairpins," he said, as he noticed Lottie noticing. "My drunken friends insisted upon it, which is why I havenae removed this dratted wig. I couldnae locate them while following the groom on horseback." He pulled out a hairpin and set to finding more.

The man was a conundrum, Lottie decided. Underneath the face paint, the doctor was a subdued kind of handsome with a rather Grecian nose and sharp jawline. Lean and clean-shaven, he exuded a quiet competence. As if the world could go topsy-turvy, and he would simply roll-up his sleeves and set-to, cleaning up the mess.

But most significantly, he had kind eyes—slate-gray and soulful, calling to mind the sky on a cloudy winter's day. The promise of better things to come.

He pulled out a final hairpin and dragged the offending wig off his head, revealing tousled brown hair. Leaning to one side, he scrubbed a hand through his hair, shaking loose the remaining traces of powder and coaxing it into some semblance of order. His hair obeyed with remarkable alacrity, falling into well-behaved straight lines. He then dipped a handkerchief in the lime water and began wiping the cosmetics off his face.

"I'm Dr. Alex Whitaker, by the by," he nodded, swiping through the rouge. "Likely should have introduced myself afore now."

"Dr. Alex *Whitaker*?" Lottie grinned. "I am Lady Charlotte Whitaker. Did you hear that, Margaret?" she asked.

Her sister opened her weary eyes.

"The doctor's surname is Whitaker, just like ours," Lottie repeated. "Perhaps he was fated to be here with us today."

"Our surname is hardly uncommon." Margaret rolled her eyes. "I fear sometimes you live too much in books, dearest." She closed her eyes, signaling she wanted nothing to do with this conversation and preferred to rest.

Mmmm.

Margaret considered Lottie something of a bluestocking.

Well, Lottie *was* something of a bluestocking, she supposed.

Hadn't Grandmère said as much last week?

Our Lottie could hold her own in a meeting of the Blue Stocking Society, c'est vrai. *But I find it* odieuse *that the term 'bluestocking' is now considered so derogatory. An educated mind is an elegant thing.*

Granted, Grandmère's opinions were decidedly *un*-English, having been formed in the salons of Paris in decades past.

Lottie rubbed Margaret's hand and turned her attention back to the doctor with a wry smile. "Margaret is likely correct. Besides, surely you spell your last name differently from ourselves. My family are Whitaker with one 'T,' not two."

Dr. Whitaker rinsed his rag, brows drawn. "My family uses only one 'T' as well."

Lottie laughed. "Next, you will say you are related to the Marquess of Lockheade, and I shall perish from astonishment."

The doctor's brows drew down further as he continued to wash his face clean.

Margaret's eyes snapped open, her attention piqued.

"The Marquess of Lockheade?" Dr. Whitaker parroted. "Aye. We do have a connection with the family. My great-great-grandfather was the third Lord Lockheade."

"In truth?" Lottie nearly crowed with delight. "My father is the *seventh* Lord Lockheade. Why . . . Dr. Whitaker! We're *cousins!*"

Margaret frowned, staring at the doctor as if searching for a family resemblance. "I am not entirely sure I trust that claim, Doctor."

"Upon my honor as a gentleman, I have not lied about my connection with Lord Lockheade, my lady." The doctor frowned.

"Margaret . . . ," Lottie began, a hint of reproach in her voice.

"Lottie, 'tis absurd!" Margaret turned to her. "An unknown doctor shows up dressed like he is fit for Bedlam. And then—low and behold!—he abruptly declares himself to be a long-lost cousin—*oof!*"

Margaret cut off abruptly as another labor pain hit, her hand clenching Lottie's in an attempt to transfer some of the agony. Given the painful throbbing in the tips of Lottie's fingers, her sister's plan was effective.

Lottie shot the doctor an apologetic look.

The doctor appeared unconcerned over Margaret's objections. Instead, he stood and began shrugging out of the purple satin justacorps. The long coat was truly ridiculous, with miles of silver braiding and tarnished buttons. He tossed it aside.

Hmmm.

Lottie surveyed him, as if finally seeing the true Dr. Whitaker. Which, she supposed in a way, she was.

The remnants of the previous century were now gone.

He wore a fine waistcoat of dark-green silk with brass buttons over buckskin breeches and a pair of Hessian boots. His cravat was fashionably tied and his shirt neatly laundered.

All in all, Dr. Whitaker appeared a man who could be her distant cousin. In her mind, Lottie labeled him as such—Cousin Alex.

Cousin Alex rolled up his shirt sleeves. He washed his hands and checked Margaret again. "Not much progress."

Margaret nodded, panting through another labor pain. Lottie wiped her sister's face yet again. Margaret kept her eyes closed, her hair disheveled and sticking to her neck.

Lottie bit her lip. How much more could her sister withstand?

The doctor sat back on the opposite side of Margaret, tugging a watch from his waistcoat pocket and checking Margaret's pulse.

"Thank you, Doctor," Lottie said. "Despite my sister's misgivings, I believe you when you say we are cousins. My father always says we must value family above all else—*Familae primum semper cognosce.*"

"Think first of family." Dr. Whitaker translated the Latin phrase.

Lottie beamed at him. "Exactly! That is what we Whitakers do."

Think first of family was the motto for Lottie's life. She had even taken to stitching it into the corners of the handkerchiefs she embroidered for Papa, Cousin Gabriel, and little Anne.

Family was everything, was it not?

Margaret opened her mouth, perhaps to object again, but she abruptly cursed and began wheezing through another labor pain. The pains were coming faster and faster now.

The doctor checked Margaret's progress once more, but the baby was slow in descending, he said.

Margaret closed her eyes, exhausted, conserving her strength for panting through each labor pain.

Lottie took it upon herself to entertain them all.

The sheer absurdity of the situation struck her anew—a babe about to be born, an unknown cousin found, and Lottie conversing as if she were having tea with the vicar.

She began by telling the doctor about Frome Abbey—the family seat in Wiltshire. That led to describing her French grandmother, the Dowager Lady Lockheade. Grandmère had stepped in to raise Lottie and Margaret when their mother had died young. Somehow that hared off into a discussion of Cousin Gabriel and his artistic talent.

"He is the most remarkable painter." Lottie couldn't keep the pride from her voice. "Cousin Gabriel continually pesters Papa to finance a trip to Rome so he can study further, but Papa will not hear of it. He says he does not wish his heir to be so far away—"

"Gabriel is a harebrained idiot," Margaret muttered.

"Tush, Margaret. You love Gabriel just as much as I do."

"Of course, I do, but we can all call a spade a spa—" Margaret left off, gasping in agony as yet another labor pain rolled over her. Cousin Alex frowned and reached for his pocket watch, timing Margaret's pulse again.

Lottie wiped a cool cloth across her sister's brow.

"You would deeply miss Cousin Gabriel were he to leave for Rome, Margaret," she murmured to her sister. "Besides, Cousin Gabriel must remain here for my wedding."

That got Cousin Alex's attention. His gaze snapped to Lottie's as he released Margaret's pulse. "Ye are tae marry, my lady?"

"Yes," Lottie nodded. "I am betrothed to Mr. Theodore Lancet. We are to marry next spring."

Margaret's labor continued on. Between her sister's moans of pain and Cousin Alex's ministrations, Lottie found herself telling the whole of her history with Theo, from meeting him at her come-out ball in London to fainting over nerves when he proposed.

"Ye fainted, my lady?" Cousin Alex appeared concerned. "Is that a common occurrence for ye?"

"Not particularly."

"What about Lady Lewis's ball last year?" Margaret reminded her.

Lottie sighed. "I guess there was that, as well. But the evening was unbearably hot, and I had neglected to eat—"

Margaret gasped and arched her back, letting loose an agonized scream. She pulled at her clothing and half rose, clutching Lottie's hand and squeezing her eyes shut, as if pushing.

"I need this baby out! Now!" she cried. "I need to push!"

Instead of showing alarm, Cousin Alex appeared pleased.

"Excellent!" He sent his hands under the sheet again and smiled. "I think it is time to bring this babe into the world."

He positioned himself between Margaret's legs and crooned encouragement.

Margaret screamed and cursed God, her husband, and the doctor in equal measure.

Cousin Alex merely smiled and complimented her on her creativity.

Margaret swore at him.

For her part, Lottie held her sister's hand, alternating between horror at Margaret's behavior, wonder at Cousin Alex's calm demeanor, and terror that she herself would likely go through this one day.

The process went on and on. The sun dipped toward the horizon.

Margaret's energy waned.

"So close," Cousin Alex coaxed, his tone honeyed encouragement. "One more push. Ye can do it, my lady. Ye've shown plenty of heart up tae now. Dinnae fail me."

Margaret lifted up her exhausted head, clenched Lottie's hand, screamed, and pushed.

And pushed. And pushed.

"Good, lass! Ye can stop now." The doctor was busy holding something beneath the linen sheet.

A sharp cry rent the air.

Margaret gasped and lay back down, sobbing in relief.

Lottie found tears streaming down her own cheeks.

"Congratulations, Lady Frank," Cousin Alex smiled, lifting the squalling babe aloft. "Ye have a fine son."

"Oh!" Margaret cried, pressing a kiss to Lottie's hand. "I have a son! Did you hear that, Lottie dearest?! A son!"

Cousin Alex wiped off the baby with a spare corner of a sheet, handling the screaming red infant with competent, sure hands, flipping him this way and that. He wrapped the tiny baby tightly with another ripped section of fabric, instantly soothing him.

From his place at Margaret's feet, the doctor extended the small bundle to Lottie, nodding for her to pass the boy to Margaret.

With breathless awe, Lottie carefully took the swaddled babe and looked down. The newborn stared up at her, wide and wondering, his eyes pools of soft gray.

And in that moment . . .

Lottie fell instantly, irrevocably, eternally in love with her nephew.

She pressed a kiss to the baby's head and laid him gently into her sister's arms.

"He's beautiful," Lottie whispered.

Margaret nodded and stared at her son, rubbing the back of one finger across his cheek.

"He is, isn't he?" Margaret's voice held a sort of awed wonder. She touched her son's tiny, perfectly-formed hand that had crept out of his swaddling.

Margaret lifted her brimming eyes to smile at Lottie. She reached up and pulled Lottie's wrist, encouraging Lottie to lie down on the blanket.

Lottie smiled and stretched out beside her sister, the wee babe between them.

"Thank you, dearest." Margaret appeared exhausted yet euphoric. "This has been a most trying day for you—"

"Don't be a goose."

"No, do not dissemble. I have treated you horridly, but I could not have managed without you." Margaret smiled. "Thank you, sister dearest."

Lottie swiped at her own wet cheeks, pressed a kiss to Margaret's forehead, and then placed another on the baby's cheek.

Familae primum semper cognosce.

Think first of family.

Lottie wrapped her arms around Margaret and her newborn nephew before stealing a look at Cousin Alex washing his hands once more.

Her heart ballooned in her chest.

Family could be grander than she had ever supposed.

DOCTOR KING LOUIS THE XIV—the man who had become Cousin Alex one memorable summer day in Yorkshire—held fast in Lottie's memory. He was an unexpected golden apple on a distant branch of their family tree.

And Cousin Alex had helped bring her favorite person—Frederick George *Alexander* Fulton—into the world.

Margaret insisted that the *Alexander* in Freddie's name had nothing to do with Cousin Alex.

"It is an old Whitaker family name, dearest," Margaret said several weeks later, her expression patient. "That doctor is no real relation."

Lottie, of course, did not point out the faulty logic in her sister's statement. That Cousin Alex had likely been named Alexander for the same reason as Freddie—because it *was* an old family name.

Of course, Lottie told her betrothed, Theo, about Cousin Alex when next she saw him in London.

It was a gloomy day in October when the clouds hung low in the sky, threatening rain but never quite delivering it. She and Theo braved a walk through Hyde Park, as it had been months since they had seen one another, much less talked.

"Dashed bit of rum business, I say, this doctor claiming to be a supposed cousin." Theo mumbled the words as was his habit, his eyes on the ground and then on the trees and finally stopping on the swans in the Serpentine. Anywhere but on her.

Lottie frowned. "Did you not hear what I said? I believe he *is* a cousin, regardless of Margaret's suspicions. He stated his last name before I stated mine. He was not attempting to ingratiate himself—"

"Yes, but the whole affair scarcely matters," Theo interrupted, bending to toss a pebble into the water. "Once we are married, you will become part of my family and leave yours behind. We shan't spare a thought for your distant cousin."

"Pardon?!" Lottie froze in place, her heart tumbling in her chest. The wind tugged at her new bonnet and billowed her Paisley shawl. She clutched both tighter to her body.

"You know what I mean, Charlotte." Theo finally looked at her directly, his expression baffled. "When we marry, you become part of my family. You will scarcely see your own anymore, thank goodness. I know I shall be glad to have less contact with Lady Frank. Your sister can be rather overbearing in her opinions."

Lottie's jaw dropped. "How dare you speak of Margaret in such terms!"

"You were literally just blistering my ears about her! I am merely agreeing with you."

"*I* am allowed to complain about my sister from time to time, but I still *love* her. And she loves me. She will forever be a significant part of my life—"

"Truly? I had anticipated that you would see little of her once we were married."

If Theo had delivered a blow to Lottie's solar plexus, she could not have been more winded. "Pardon?! Why would I ever—"

"You must see it is for the best."

"No. No, I truly do not."

Theo's expression was thunderous, likely a reflection of her own.

"It is what a wife does," he said, his voice heating. "A wife leaves her family and cleaves unto her husband."

"Leaving my family to live with you does not mean I desert them entirely!"

"I knew all your reading had led to expansive ideas about marriage—"

"Pardon?! Are you referring to Wollstonecraft? I have been reading such things for years. How can you only object *now*?!!"

How could she be having this conversation? She *knew* Theo, did she not? She had known him for years.

And *this* was his true opinion? That she abandon her family? Abandon educating her mind?

"I cannot marry a man who expects me to forsake my family. One who does not see me for the person I am." She forced the words out. "I cannot, and *will* not, choose between a husband and my family."

He stared down at her, his chest heaving with emotion. "I cannot marry a woman who will not ally herself entirely with me."

And that was that.

Oh, they carried on for another month, but it was all a sham.

Something had irreparably broken between them.

Six weeks after their conversation in Hyde Park, Lottie sent Theo a letter, officially breaking off their betrothal. She simply could not marry a man who would force her to make such a choice.

Familae primum semper cognosce.

Lottie held firm to the family motto.

But Theo's perfidiousness was only the primer—the first painful cut into the fabric of her life.

More losses followed.

The following year—right after Lottie's twenty-first birthday—Cousin Gabriel prevailed on her father to study under the 'gaze of the Masters' in Rome. Papa was fiercely proud of his nephew's artistic talent and eventually that pride overwhelmed the potential ache of Gabriel's absence.

And so, Gabriel quit Frome Abbey for a palazzo in Rome.

But they all missed him terribly.

That was the problem with their motto, Lottie decided.

Thinking first of family was all fine and well when they were about. But when Margaret, Anne, and little Freddie departed for Lord Frank's estate near Darlington—or when Papa remained in Town for Parliament, leaving Lottie and Grandmère at Frome Abbey—the *thinking* became more razor-edged.

But at least such departures rested on the promise of a return.

Others, however . . .

The summer of Lottie's twenty-second birthday, Anne and Freddie caught a severe chill from a negligent nurse.

Freddie, miraculously, survived.

Anne . . . did not.

Lottie held Margaret as her sister sobbed over her daughter's lifeless body. Only Lottie's gentle but firm voice persuaded Margaret to relinquish Anne for burial.

The shock of Anne's death rippled through the family.

Margaret sank into a deep melancholy of spirits.

Lord Frank was at turns inconsolable and then, just as quickly, spry and falsely bright.

Papa retreated into hunting and tromping over the estate grounds.

Even Grandmère walked the parterre garden with red-rimmed eyes.

For her part, Lottie had scarcely begun facing the day without tears when news arrived from Rome—

Gabriel had become drunk and taken a dare to row a skiff across the Tiber from Castel Sant'Angelo.

He never arrived on the opposite bank.

His body was retrieved days later and miles downstream.

The loss of Cousin Gabriel scraped Lottie raw.

The feeling crested when Papa died not four months later—the twin grief of losing Anne and then Gabriel had been too much for his body to bear.

"Papa literally died of a broken heart." Margaret dabbed away her endless tears.

The word *broken* hummed in Lottie's brain. Was that what they all were now?

Lottie feared grief had ruptured the palette of her world, turning the vibrant colors of life to ashy grays and blacks.

After Papa's funeral in April, Frank disappeared to London, staying with his father, the autocratic Duke of Ferndown.

Margaret tried to appear resigned to her husband's absence, but Lottie saw the tenseness of her eyes and heard the snip in her voice when addressing the servants.

What would become of them all now?

An answer to her question arrived a month later when Frank returned, a group of stern-faced solicitors and his father, the Duke of Ferndown, accompanying them.

They gathered as a family in the drawing room to listen as a stern solicitor read Papa's final will and testament.

Despite the grimness of the situation, Lottie couldn't help but feel a thread of joy that they were together once more.

After all, they were still family, were they not?

The solicitor droned on. The dense language of the legal documents caught in the gears of her mind, forcing Lottie to dissect it.

Her father was dead.

His heir, Gabriel, was dead.

There were no other direct male heirs.

Neither daughters nor the children of daughters could inherit.

The marquisate would revert to the Crown.

With every dry word out of the solicitor's mouth, Lottie frowned, the dismay in her chest rising higher and higher, until it had nowhere else to go but out her mouth.

"Pardon?" Her voice cut through the solicitor's monotone words. "I do not understand."

Every head in the room turned her way, eyebrows raising in surprise. Grandmère in her widow's weeds and Margaret with her melancholy eyes. Frank with an annoyed eye roll and the Duke of Ferndown with a scowl.

"Yes?" The gray-haired solicitor looked over his spectacles at her, clearly exasperated.

Perhaps the Lottie of years past would have retreated from such unspoken censure.

But the Lottie of *now* was different.

Grief and pain had carved new channels in her heart.

She forged ahead. "There are no other heirs, you say?"

"None."

"But . . ."

Her frown returned in force.

She saw all-too-clearly in her mind's eye a country doctor in shirt-sleeves, lifting a squalling newborn Freddie, a joyful smile on his face.

"Lady Charlotte, have you anything to say?" the solicitor asked, a snap to his words.

"Yes." Lottie straightened her spine and looked the man in the eye. "What about Cousin Alex?"

EDINBURGH, SCOTLAND
OCTOBER 12, 1820

D r. Alexander Whitaker disliked surprises.
He particularly disliked surprises that altered carefully laid plans and strictly measured time. The sort that threatened to upend his life.

Surprises precisely like the shock of this moment.

"P-pardon?" Alex stuttered, washing blood off his hands before reaching for a towel. "Could ye please repeat that last wee bit? I cannae have heard ye correctly."

Mr. Carter—a man whose card proclaimed him to be a solicitor with Carter, Mason, & Smith LLP of London—shifted his bag from one hand to the other.

They stood in the consultation room of Alex's surgery on King Street in New Town, the room awash in the pale morning light. Muted traffic sounded from the road outside.

"As I said," Mr. Carter replied, "you are the sole surviving male descendant of the Lords Lockheade. The title and its extensive entailed holdings have devolved upon you."

A long pause.

The solicitor's eyes dropped to the blood splattered on Alex's surgical apron. The man swallowed, face paling.

"Surely there has been a mistake." Alex's pulse raced, a precursor to full-out panic.

"I assure you, there has been no mistake." Mr. Carter offered an anemic smile. "I and my colleagues are nothing if not meticulous in our research. I would not be standing here were there any doubt as to the validity of the claim. You are indeed the heir to the late Marquess of Lockheade."

Alex shook his head. Tossed the towel upon the washbasin. Spun in a circle, eyes inventorying the bottles of paregoric, calomel, and wormseed oil. Did he need to talk with the apothecary about—

He stopped right there, forcing a deep, slow breath.

In. Out.

A scream sounded from the hall beyond the closed door, causing Mr. Carter to flinch. Alex's partner, Dr. John McNeal, was seeing to a young groom who had come in with his arm hanging at an unnatural angle.

"I am an *English* marquess?" Alex asked again. Was that an appalled catch in his voice?

"We Englishmen are not all a bad lot, I assure you." Mr. Carter's expression turned wry.

Coals settled in the grate, the red-hot glow pulsing in the dim light. The clock over the mantel struck the hour, reminding Alex that he did not have time for a life-altering crisis.

He was a doctor, dammit, not some pampered English aristocrat.

Mr. Carter had arrived not thirty minutes' past, part of an entire phalanx of solicitors and clerks, primed to storm the bastion of Alex's surgery. Alex hadn't bothered to count them all, as he had been focused on stitching up a cartwright's bleeding scalp.

What did one call a group of solicitors anyway? Were they a *pride*, like lions? A *murder*, like crows?

Several of Alex's closest friends were naturalists. He should have a clever answer for this.

A *quarrel*, perhaps?

Regardless, Alex had made the Quarrel of Solicitors choose an emissary for parley, and Mr. Carter had been selected, thrust from their midst, a black brief-bag clasped before him like a shield—

Alex was mentally babbling.

It was just . . .

Och! For heaven's sake!

He was . . . *flustered*.

Alex did not *do* flustered.

Not agitated or shaken or unsettled or rattled or . . . babbling—

Definitely not babbling.

This had to stop.

He turned back to Mr. Carter, shrieks echoing once more down the hall.

"I appreciate that this is something of a shock." Mr. Carter swallowed, darting a wide-eyed glance at the door and commotion beyond. "Unfortunately, before we progress in our discussion, I must tell you that the matter is not entirely straight-forward."

"Nothing ever is, is it?"

Snick.

Doctor McNeal opened the door, poking his head into the room.

"Terribly sorry to interrupt," he said, giving Mr. Carter an apologetic smile, "but I need assistance to set this lad's arm, Whitaker. The break is somewhat severe."

"I'm coming," Alex said.

McNeal nodded and shut the door.

Alex looked at the clock above the mantel again.

"Clearly we must discuss this, Mr. Carter," he said, "but as I explained earlier, ye have caught me in the middle of a busy day. I have appointments 'til supper. Perhaps we could postpone until the week's end—"

"This cannot wait. We are to return to London tomorrow afternoon."

"Yes, well, my patients' health cannae wait either." Alex gritted his teeth and, this time, consulted the watch in his waistcoat pocket. It indeed matched the clock on the mantel. He needed to hurry. "I have an arm to set and house calls to make."

Mr. Carter sighed. "I shall accompany you and speak between patients, then."

The solicitor settled into a chair, holding his official-looking case on his lap. His expression was best described as *resolute*.

Alex nodded, grinding his teeth. He didn't even have the time to argue.

Instead, he left to help set the poor lad's arm, his thoughts a buzzing hive.

An *English* marquess? *Him?!*

In McNeal's examination room, Alex held the young man steady— offering calming words as McNeal pulled the lad's arm straight—but his mind was miles away.

Was it too much to hope that the lacking straight-forwardness of the matter would provide a loophole? A way for Alex to prove this was merely a legal misunderstanding?

He had no desire to be the Marquess of Lockheade. Surely, the demands of a marquisate would require he quit his profession as a physician.

Alex *liked* being a physician. He felt bone-deep satisfaction in helping others and had committed his life to doing so.

After setting the arm, Alex spoke with the young man's employer, giving care instructions, before returning to the consultation room and Mr. Carter.

"Please. Help me understand this situation." Alex washed his hands again and swapped his bloody apron for a tailcoat. "How is this matter of the marquisate not straight-forward?"

Alex consulted the clock over the mantel and then his watch, just to be sure. Damn. He was going to be late.

He hated being late.

Alex snatched up his hat, gloves, and doctor's case before stepping out the front door of his surgery. Mr. Carter followed.

"Typically, situations like this are quite simple." The solicitor paused as Alex hailed a hackney cab. "The heir presumptive presents his credentials and petitions the Committee on Privilege to issue a Writ of Summons which orders the new Peer to take up his seat in Parliament. English laws of primogeniture are inviolable. One cannot renounce a title nor choose where to bestow it. An heir may shirk the responsibilities of the title, but no true gentleman would do such a thing, as it would cause needless suffering to his dependents."

Alex nearly stumbled as a hackney stopped at the kerb.

One cannot renounce a title.

Was that his answer, then?

He gave an address in Greenside to the driver and then ducked into the carriage, Mr. Carter following and sitting beside him.

Alex stared ahead, fingers drumming a militant tattoo on his knee.

Mr. Carter glanced at Alex's nervous tapping. "I appreciate that this is a lot to take in."

"That is a modest assessment of my current mental state, yes." Alex instantly regretted the terseness of his tone.

Mr. Carter was simply the messenger.

Alex ordered his fingers to still, with only middling success.

Why was the hackney so small? Why did the pressure in his chest feel akin to the sensation of drowning?

He was panicking.

The medical part of Alex's brain knew this.

And yet—

What else was he to do?

This was a most *panickable* turn of events!

Yes, two of his best friends—Sir Rafe Gilbert and Andrew Langston, Lord Hadley—were members of the English peerage, but it did not follow that Alex wished to emulate them.

Besides, both Andrew and Rafe had been raised to fulfill the duties their stations required. They'd had year upon year to adjust to the expectations, to mold their lives around the weight of their responsibilities, to the way of life it dictated.

No true gentleman would cause such needless suffering.

Alex had devoted fifteen years of his life to alleviating suffering—to become a physician, to spend his days tending to others' ills.

More to the point, Alex had sacrificed much to achieve this goal.

He had been cast off by his wealthy father for his *ungentlemanly* pursuit of medicine. Though impoverished, Alex had forged ahead with his studies, living off meager funds. He had subsisted on dry bread and salted pork, memorized Latin by guttering candlelight, and used blankets instead of coal to ward off the winter frost.

When his older brother, Ian, had died six years ago, his father had demanded Alex abandon his studies and assume his place as heir to the family horse-breeding business.

Alex refused.

He had made his choice, and the decision was inviolable.

He would be a physician—full stop.

His father had been incensed and turned to whisky to numb his pain.

If such events could not convince Alex to give up medicine, then a London solicitor and a distant marquisate hadn't a prayer of doing so.

"Before you leap to conclusions, allow me to finish my explanation." Mr. Carter shifted in his seat, his brief-bag balanced on his knees. "As you are most likely aware, titles generally pass to the highest-ranking male member of a family. If there is no male heir, the title reverts to the Crown. The late Lord Lockheade had two daughters but no sons."

Alex nodded, looking out the hackney window as the carriage crawled through traffic on Queen's Street. He well remembered his encounter with Lady Charlotte Whitaker and her elder sister, Lady Frank Fulton.

The entire sequence of events still set a blush to his cheeks. Even three years on, he could recall the horror on Lady Charlotte's astonishingly-pretty face as she realized that the man in a dreadful justacorps and powdered peruke would be delivering her sister's baby.

Lady Charlotte was likely married with children of her own by now.

Mr. Carter continued, "The title was to have passed to a cousin, Mr. Gabriel Whitaker. Unfortunately, Gabriel Whitaker drowned in Rome last autumn."

Alex tapped a foot. As was typical of a solicitor, Mr. Clark was taking forever to get to the point. "You said the matter was not straight-forward. How so?"

Mr. Carter nearly sighed. "As you can well imagine, the late Lord Lockheade was distraught over Mr. Gabriel Whitaker's death. As his lordship was unaware of your existence, Lockheade assumed that his title would go extinct. Therefore, his lordship did what any responsible lord would do—he planned. His elder daughter is married to Lord Frank Fulton, second son of the Duke of Ferndown—"

"Ferndown. Frank. Fulton," Alex interrupted. "That's a tremendous amount of alliteration."

"Gossip has it that Ferndown and his children are fond of the letter 'F.' Case in point, Lord and Lady Frank's son was christened Frederick."

Ah. The very child that Alex had helped bring into the world.

Alex placed a steadying hand on the door as the hackney rounded St. Andrew's Square and carried on toward Greenside Place two streets beyond.

"The Duke of Ferndown—Lord Frank's father and little Frederick's grandfather—sits on the King's Privy Council and has His Majesty's ear," Mr. Carter continued. "Last January, Lockheade and Ferndown submitted a formal petition to the Crown, requesting that upon Lord Lockheade's death, Parliament should bestow the title and its entailed properties on their lordship's joint grandson, Master Frederick Fulton. This is a common practice in such situations. The Crown likes to see properties and titles stay within the bloodline whenever possible."

"That makes sense." Alex leaned back against the carriage squabs, still drumming his gloved fingers against the wooden seat. "Why allow the title tae veer off to an unknown Scot who's never lifted a finger in support of the marquisate?"

"Yes. The problem, as I stated earlier, is that English law does not allow a parent or grandparent to choose an heir to a title willy-nilly. In this case, Lord Lockheade passed away before any decisions had been made. Ferndown took control of the affair at that point because, well, he is a duke and they tend to assume control of things that affect them. And then your existence was brought to the Crown's attention."

The carriage rocked to a stop before a modest townhouse at the base of Calton Hill. Alex excused himself. Mr. Carter nodded and indicated he would wait in the carriage.

This was Alex's first home visit of the day—Mrs. Stewart and her affliction of diabetes. She liked to be bled every Tuesday. Alex obliged, as most medical professionals still considered bleeding to be an appropriate treatment for *diabetes mellitus*. However, he had found a restrictive diet to be more effective in reducing the sugar in urine and alleviating the symptoms. Not that Mrs. Stewart listened to him, no matter how many times he urged her to give up shortbread biscuits.

Regardless, he bled a half pint of blood and listened to her heart with his *stethoscope*, a newly-arrived device from Dr. Laennec in Paris. The instrument was rather ridiculously named but effective. He smiled as she told him about her grandson, and he asked polite questions about her daughter's health. Alex privately believed that Mrs. Stewart, like many of his patients, benefited from kindness and a listening ear.

He made notes in his physician's log, checked his watch, and returned to the hackney cab thirty minutes later, giving the driver an address on West Bow in Old Town.

Mr. Carter continued on, as if they hadn't been interrupted. "As I was saying, the history of your branch of the family is important to this case. Your great-grandfather, Lord Colin Whitaker, joined the Jacobite rebellion of '45 and was part of the Duke of Perth's personal retinue. Fortunately for him, Lord Colin was abed with fever when the Jacobites fell at Culloden. Unfortunately, the fever did not prevent Lord Colin from being accused of high treason. His father called in favors in Lords and had his son's name removed from the list of traitors in the Act of Attainder of 1747."

"Aye." Alex knew much of this history. "But I fail tae see how this impacts us at this juncture?"

"Ferndown and his son are determined to see the late Lord Lockheade's wishes made a reality." Mr. Carter shifted the case on his knees. "They feel strongly that a second incarnation of the Marquesses of Lockheade should be created with Master Frederick as the first heir."

All the pieces slotted into place.

"They wish tae see my branch of the family attainted." Alex nodded slowly. "If my great-grandfather is formally declared a traitor for siding with the Jacobites and conspiring against the Crown, his entire family line will be disinherited."

Mr. Carter's eyebrows ratcheted up. "Precisely. A Writ of Attainder against Lord Colin Whitaker would effectively dismiss any claim your family line had upon the marquisate. High treason is the *only* way a man can lose a title he was rightly born to bear. Ferndown argues that Lord

Colin was declared a traitor at the time—even if his actual name was removed from the Act of Attainder of 1747—and that Lords should now formally recognize the verdict."

"But . . . *I* am not a traitor." Alex frowned. "And declaring a dead man a traitor nearly eighty years after the fact is unusual, particularly when Parliament at the time chose not to attaint him."

"Correct. It is unprecedented." Mr. Carter's expression could best be described as long-suffering. As if this idea had already been discussed *ad nauseam*. "Parliament has not issued a single Writ of Attainder since that mess with Lord Edward Fitzgerald over twenty years ago. Lords is strongly inclined to mend fences at the moment, not burn them down. In fact, they have begun *forgiving* the Writs of Attainder from '47 and reinstating lands and titles. So it seems almost comical to think that this petition will get anywhere. But as I said, Ferndown is powerful and has the King's ear."

Alex stared at the city passing by as Mr. Carter spoke. They were crossing over the Earthen Mound and climbing into Old Town proper.

He could feel Mr. Carter's eyes on his shoulders, measuring the breadth of him, surely wondering how the flower of English aristocracy had devolved upon a Scottish physician.

Alex turned back to Mr. Carter beside him. "If this all happened last Spring, why am I only now being informed, six months on?"

"Well," Mr. Carter sighed, "neither Lord Frank nor Ferndown had any obligation to inform you. And the Courts had not insisted upon it, so nothing was done until now. All of which explains our presence here—myself and my colleagues."

"What happens now?"

The carriage rocked to a stop in front of a small door on West Bow. Mr. White and his gouty leg awaited Alex on the second floor.

Mr. Carter was still meandering to the point.

"Myself and my colleagues have been sent as representatives of the Crown to present all this to you. The Committee on Privilege is strongly split on what to do in this instance—award the marquisate to yourself or to young Master Frederick Fulton. Both sides have made a compelling case. So the decision was made to seek your own wishes in this matter."

"Pardon?" Alex reached for the door handle.

Mr. Carter managed a weak smile. "Unlike most titled peers, you now have a choice before you—do you wish to contest the posthumous Writ of Attainder on Lord Colin and fight to succeed as Lord Lockheade? Or will you accept the Writ of Attainder on behalf of your ancestor and permit yourself and your descendants to be disinherited?"

ALEX MOVED THROUGH THE NEXT few days in a blurry haze—bleeding patients, stitching wounds, prescribing medicines.

His mind was fixated on Mr. Carter's visit.

The solicitor had made matters clear before he left:

If Alex contested the Writ of Attainder, it was plausible that Lords would side with him. If, however, he declined to contest it, Lords would likely award the marquisate to wee Frederick Fulton.

The Committee on Privilege needed Alex to make a decision.

However, some on the Committee—those opposed to Ferndown—were worried that Alex, as a Scottish physician residing in Edinburgh, did not understand what he might be accepting or rejecting.

Therefore, they had invented an unusual plan to match this unusual circumstance.

Mr. Carter would prepare a detailed account of the marquisate's properties and enterprises for Alex to peruse. Then after the New Year, Alex would visit Frome Abbey, the seat of the Marquess of Lockheade. He would spend several days there, surveying the estate and speaking with the steward. He would be encouraged to assess the marquisate holdings and ask questions. The goal was for him to understand the responsibilities and privilege entailed upon assuming a marquisate.

Basically, dipping his toe into the business of being Lord Lockheade.

From there, Alex would journey to London, present himself before the Committee on Privilege, and inform them of his decision.

It was all a pointless exercise.

Alex had already made his decision.

He would renounce the title.

The words *English* and *marquisate* and *Dr. Alexander Whitaker* simply did not belong together.

He had asked Mr. Carter if he could reject the title immediately and be done—no trip to Frome Abbey and London needed.

But Mr. Carter made it clear that if Alex declined to follow the outlined plan, the Committee on Privilege would not consider his disavowal to be binding. In short, Alex would likely be awarded the title and lands.

If that happened, Alex could choose to neglect the title and continue on with his life as a physician, but doing so would cause endless suffering for the thousands of tenants who lived on marquisate lands. Alex was too much a gentleman—too much a healer—to deliberately cause such harm.

He had to go through with this whole charade and then sign the declaration, agreeing to the writ of attainder on Lord Colin Whitaker.

Part of him grimaced at the thought of permitting his ancestor to be attainted, but, in all truth, a traitor in England was often a hero in Scotland. Besides, his sister, Catriona, would understand and support him, if and when he told her. Both their father and older brother, Ian, were dead. There was no other living member of his family to object.

And much as it pained him, he would *not* tell his closest friends—members of the Brotherhood of the Black Tartan—Andrew, Rafe, Ewan, and Kieran. They would try to talk him into accepting the marquisate, to become a member of Lords with Andrew, to rub elbows with Rafe and Ewan at *ton* events in London. But Alex would refuse, no matter how convincing their arguments. Telling them would only serve to drive a wedge between himself and his friends.

And Alex could not bear to do that.

THREE DAYS AFTER MR. CARTER'S VISIT, Alex was applying a poultice to an ugly burn on a blacksmith's arm when voices sounded in the hallway.

Alex instantly recognized them both.

One belonged to the housemaid.

The other—

"Alex!" Master Kieran MacTavish burst into Alex's consultation room in a billow of sea air and deck tar.

"Kieran!" Alex looked up, smiling despite the interruption. "Your carcass is a sight for sore eyes. Where have ye been?"

Hallelujah! After disappearing without a word over three months ago, Kieran had returned.

His timing, however, left something to be desired.

"Wait. Dinnae tell me quite yet. Let me finish with this gentleman." Alex nodded toward the blacksmith, shooting the man an apologetic smile, as he continued to wrap the inflamed arm.

"I'm staying right here." Kieran took a seat opposite, doffing his top hat and holding the brim with one hand atop his bouncing leg. About Alex's own height and build, his friend exuded an endless, exuberant energy. "If I wait until ye aren't with a patient, I'd never speak with ye."

The blacksmith snorted and then winced as Alex continued to bind the poultice.

Alex sneaked a glance at his friend.

Despite his energetic greeting, Kieran looked . . . tired. His pale blue eyes were bloodshot, and his skin held a sallow pallor. But the acrid smell of stale whisky no longer clung to him.

Kieran was, thankfully, sober.

"Keep it dry," Alex instructed the blacksmith once he had finished binding the wound, "and have your wife change the bandage every evening. Cleanliness is the most important thing at this point."

"Thank ye." The blacksmith stood to leave, testing his newly bandaged arm. "The lads at the *howff* werenae lying when they said ye were the best doctor in the city."

The man tipped his hat and slid past McNeal who appeared at the door.

"Do ye have a minute, Alex?" McNeal asked.

"Och, ye cannae have him, Dr. McNeal." Kieran waved a hand toward Alex. "I've come tae kidnap him and force him to eat a warm meal for once."

Alex grimaced and checked the mantel clock. He would actually welcome the chance to talk with Kieran but, "I have a full slate this afternoon. McNeal knows I dinnae have time for a warm lunch—"

McNeal looked at the clock. "Nae, my words can wait. Ye have nothing for at least an hour, Alex. And if something comes up, I can cover for ye." His partner snorted. "Go with yer friend. He has the right of it. I dinnae think ye've had a warm meal since my wedding."

Once upon a time, Alex had shared his townhouse with his sister, Catriona, who ensured he had hot meals and a cozy fire in the sitting room. That was until the day, six months prior, when she announced that she and McNeal had fallen in love and were to marry.

Now when McNeal went home to his comfortable house, he had Catriona and all her warmth, too.

"Come along, Alex." Kieran started for the door. "Ye need to stop measuring your life by your watch. Relax. Maybe even attend a ball. Dance with a bonny lass—"

"What would I ever do with a bonny lass?"

"What would ye do with a lass?!" Kieran gave a bark of shocked laughter. "If ye are asking me that, then you're worse off than I thought."

"Do ye need us to explain it tae ye?" McNeal shot Alex a ribald wink. "I'm sure I have a medical book with some helpful diagrams."

Kieran laughed.

Alex sighed and went for his hat and coat, his friends' teasing voices chasing him down the hallway.

His life was too frenetic to worry about courting a lady or, heaven forbid, marrying.

And now this business with the marquisate.

Och. It was all a mess.

But Kieran had returned—sober and smiling—and that was a bonnie thought.

"We've missed ye," Alex said as he and Kieran left the surgery and turned left onto the bustling street. "Now tell me—where have ye been?"

"Glasgow and Bristol mostly. Asking questions." Kieran shoved his hands into the pockets of his greatcoat. A few curls of his inky-dark hair slipped out from his hat, clinging to his temple.

"What kind of questions?" Alex asked.

"Questions about Jamie. About us all."

Kieran continued to talk as they walked, detailing his travels.

Rain had begun to fall—typical for Scotland in October. No one bothered to carry an umbrella. In Edinburgh, rain tended to fall more sideways than down. Umbrellas were merely one more thing for the Scottish weather to wreak havoc upon.

Alex lifted his eyes to the battlements soaring above the rooftops. Edinburgh Castle seemed the only thing indifferent to the constant onslaught. Perched atop Castle Rock—a dramatic stone outcropping which jutted skyward in the middle of the city—the fortress loomed overhead just as it had for centuries. Impervious. Unmoving. Predictable.

Alex loved the castle for its constancy.

They reached a nearby public house and secured a secluded table. After ordering haggis and neeps-n-tatties, Kieran finished describing how he had spent the past three months.

"I have tae know exactly what happened to her . . . my Jamie. Ye ken that, right?" Kieran's eyes pleaded for understanding.

Alex nodded, scrubbing a hand over his face.

He and Kieran were members of the Brotherhood of the Black Tartan, a group of five men who had met aboard the frigate *The Minerva* nearly six years ago.

Their trip began as a voyage of scientific discovery to the South Pacific but ended in tragedy—the Brotherhood being marooned on Vanuatu and *The Minerva* sinking a short time later, all hands going down, including Jamie Fyffe, Kieran's bride.

Jamie had come aboard *The Minerva* disguised as the carpenter's mate, James Fyffe. But Jamie was actually Eilidh Fyffe, James' older sister. Kieran had uncovered Jamie's true gender—though the name, Jamie, had stuck—and the two had fallen deeply in love. They had married through a private handfasting ceremony in Sydney before the ship left for the New Hebrides. By the time they dropped anchor in Vanuatu, Jamie was increasing—a fact Alex found out much later.

When she and her unborn babe had gone down with *The Minerva,* Kieran had been nearly mad with grief. It had taken nearly four years for Kieran to begin to heal from the loss.

Then last year, the Brotherhood discovered that Captain Cuthie and his first mate, Robert Massey, had survived the wreckage. They claimed that the ship had not accidentally shattered on a reef as previously thought but had been intentionally blown up.

The knowledge that others had survived the wreck, but not his Jamie, had sent Kieran into a steep decline, drinking heavily. He was dismissed from his ship for excessive drunkenness. Alex still recalled his own panic at hearing this news.

He had already lost too many loved ones to despair and addiction. Kieran's name would *not* be added to that list.

Alex spent two days, going pub to pub in Leith and Edinburgh, finally finding his friend drunkenly passed out in the dim light of Anchor Close. Alex had taken Kieran to his own flat and nursed him back to health, attempting to wean him off the whisky bottle.

A few months later, Kieran had disappeared entirely.

But he was back now, looking worse for wear, but blessedly not drunk.

"Did ye find what ye seek?" Alex asked.

Kieran let out a long breath, fingers tapping atop the table. "Nae, not yet. Cuthie and Massey have gone to ground. They're still prowling around the Caribbean last I heard. Moreover, I saw this in the paper this morning."

Kieran pulled a folded copy of the *Edinburgh Advertiser* from his coat pocket and slid it across to Alex. A notice was circled.

> *The sinking of* The Minerva *must be more fully examined. Gross crimes were committed, and those responsible have yet to be brought to account. Do not allow this debt to go unpaid.*

"Another one?" Alex shook his head, setting the newspaper down. "This is the third notice in little over a year."

"Aye, and they are all similar, demanding that those who survived the wreck of *The Minerva* must pay some debt. I'm assuming we still dinnae know who is posting them?"

"No. Cuthie and Massey have both insisted they have no part in these notices." Alex tapped the newspaper. "The fact that both men are currently abroad—and have been for the better part of a year—confirms it."

"Aye, I thought the same. In the past, we have assumed that the notices must refer tae the Brotherhood somehow, as we are the only ones who survived. But have we considered that the notices might be referring to Cuthie or Massey instead?"

Alex lifted his eyebrows. "Nae, I hadnae considered that, to be honest. I'll have to mention it tae Andrew and the rest. Or perhaps ye can do it yourself, assuming ye're back in Scotland to stay for a while?"

"Nae, I'm for Spain in a week's time. A retired captain is said to know something."

"About Jamie?"

"Something of the like. He supposedly tells tale of fishing an English woman from the waters of the South Pacific. This might be the information I've been seeking."

Oh, Kieran.

And what would become of his friend when this rumor, like all the others, came to nothing? Would Kieran return to the bottle to drown his grief?

Something of Alex's dismay must have shown on his face.

"Haud yer wheest." Kieran held up a hand, palm out. A bleak sort of determination in his jaw. "I ken that I've been a wee bit crazed over this, but I will find out, once and for all, what happened tae Jamie. I cannae move on 'til I know."

"Kieran . . . ," Alex began, "how many times must we all say it—if Jamie were alive, she would have contacted us by now. She loved you too much to not fight for ye. It's been nearly five years since *The Minerva* sank—"

"Please, Alex. I need your help in this." Kieran sat forward, his eyes pleading. "I need answers. I need tae know if my Jamie is dead or alive. I keep looking but all I'm finding are more questions, more hints that all is not as it seems. This captain in Spain may know something helpful."

Alex scrubbed a hand over his face.

He knew Kieran's expression all too well.

It was the look of a man begging for one more bottle of laudanum, one more glass of whisky, one more pipe of opium. One more venture into the sludge of appetite and addiction.

A bone-deep weariness pressed on Alex's skull. Why did he feel as if his life's work was simply to free others from the quagmire of their darkest habits?

Worse, with this tangle of the marquisate looming over him, Alex didn't have *time* to monitor Kieran, ensuring that he didn't slip into yet another cycle of destructive grief.

"I'll help," Alex agreed, barely stifling a sigh, "but only if ye promise to not turn to whisky if this all goes to pot. You'll stay sober and you'll write us regular-like. Your word."

"I'm not going back to the bottle, Alex. I'm no help tae my Jamie if I'm soused. I ken that now."

Alex stared at him for a heartbeat.

Kieran's gaze was steadfast and resolute.

That was good. But would it last?

"What do ye need from me?" Alex asked.

Kieran smiled, a bleak thing. "A loan of fifty pounds and a promise ye'll keep my whereabouts from the others."

Alex pressed two fingers to his forehead.

Well, considering that Alex intended to remain mum about his own issue before the Committee on Privilege . . . he supposed adding more secrets to the list did no harm at all.

2

THE LONG GALLERY
FROME ABBEY, WILTSHIRE
JANUARY 15, 1821

Cousin Alex had come at last.

Lottie watched him climb the front stairs, her body partially hidden behind the Florentine damask curtains Grandmère adored.

She had been keeping vigil since daybreak. Lord Frank said Dr. Whitaker was to arrive today, but the lack of *when* had haunted her. She had tried to lose herself in a recent translation of Mr. Immanuel Kant's celebrated treatise *Logic*, but philosophical reading was slow going at the best of times. When waiting for a potentially life-altering visit, absorbing subtle inflections of logical thought was nearly impossible. She had given up after reading the same page for the fourteenth time.

But now, well past luncheon, Cousin Alex had finally come.

Lottie had been unsure what to expect. The Cousin Alex of her memory was soft. Kind eyes. Kinder voice. A gentleness to his hands that belied the no-nonsense economy of his movements. A healer.

But the man climbing the steps below her did not appear soft. The rigid lines of his caped Garrick coat and the gleaming shine of his Hessians matched the tense set of his jaw beneath his top hat. He appeared to be less a healer and more a knight preparing to storm the enemy's keep.

In short—Cousin Alex had come ready for combat.

Which, all things considered, was a somewhat apropos tactic, she supposed.

But she still felt a pang for the gentle doctor of her memory.

"Who the man, Tottie?" Freddie asked.

Lottie smiled, never tiring of hearing herself called Tottie—an elision of *Aunt Lottie*—in Freddie's lisping three-year-old voice.

Her nephew slid a sticky hand into hers. Lottie darted a glance down to his fingers. Why were children's hands always so distressingly sticky? It was an eternal mystery.

Regardless, she clasped his fingers and smiled at Freddie's blond head. "That is our cousin, Dr. Alex Whitaker."

"Mmmm. Papa no like him." Freddie pressed his small face to the glass, attempting to watch Cousin Alex enter the house below. As was typical of a three-year-old, he became distracted by the sensation and instantly stuck out his tongue.

"Frederick Fulton! Gracious! Windows are not to be licked!" Margaret's voice cut through the room.

Freddie jumped back.

Margaret met Lottie's gaze with an exaggerated shake of her head that said *I cannot believe the things I say as a mother.*

Lottie smiled in return. She pulled Freddie away from the window before the servants or Cousin Alex noticed his wayward antics. What would this stern version of Cousin Alex think of such behavior?

She urged Freddie to sit on the floor and play with his toys. Of course, he would have none of it until Lottie sank onto the rug with him.

Freddie immediately climbed into her lap and reached for the onyx beads around her neck. Lottie dodged his (still sticky) hands and handed him a clever mechanical soldier, which Freddie set to dismantling. She pressed a kiss to his rumpled curls before leaning back on her hands, fingers sinking into the lush pile. Thank goodness, Grandmère preferred the softness of Savonerrie carpets over the short nub of an Aubusson rug.

Grandmère and Margaret were at the opposite end of the room before the roaring fire, embroidering small stitches while verbally unstitching one another.

Lottie's grandmother and her sister were often at loggerheads. *They are far too similar to get along,* Papa had often said. *Both too stubborn and firm in their opinions.*

"Dr. Whitaker is rather late in his arrival." Margaret stabbed her needle through the crimson silk, her blond ringlets bobbing with the motion.

Lottie empathized with her sister's frustration over the unsettled and precarious nature of their current situation. So much now hinged on Cousin Alex's choices. Margaret's grief over her daughter's death had morphed into a grim determination to see Freddie well-settled.

"Was the doctor to have arrived sooner?" Grandmère's question, though mild, came out rimmed with Gallic disdain.

"Yes. In his last letter to Frank, Dr. Whitaker indicated he would be here in the morning. And yet, here we are, well after luncheon." Margaret stabbed her thread more forcefully. Unfortunately, embroidery, as a means of venting anxiety, was woefully inadequate. "If the doctor had any courtesy at all for the distress of this situation, he would have arrived at daybreak, seen to this nonsense the Committee on Privilege have concocted, and taken himself off before supper."

Grandmère arched a single eyebrow at Margaret's tone.

The effect was rather dramatically scathing.

Judgmental eyebrows, Gabriel, with his artist's eye, had been wont to say. He was not incorrect.

Grandmère's brows were dark, elegant slashes in her pale skin. They slanted downward even in repose, giving her grandmother's calmest words a sharp bite.

"That was not what was agreed upon," Grandmère tutted, that censorious eyebrow hiking higher, her Parisian-accented English swallowing her words. "The doctor is to stay *trois jours*—just three days. He will dine. He will speak with us and see the estate. Then he will decide."

Margaret was not one to be intimidated—not by Grandmère's formidable eyebrows or Cousin Alex's potentially earthquaking presence.

She, Freddie, and Frank had been living at Frome Abbey since last summer, when the Committee on Privilege had named Frank as temporary guardian of the marquisate, pending a decision.

The Duke of Ferndown was also in residence. His Grace had come down from London specifically to oversee Dr. Whitaker's visit and encourage the doctor to agree to the attainder. The duke was not the paterfamilias for the Whitaker family, but as an old friend of Lottie's father and relation-by-marriage, he had taken on the role. It was a duke-ish thing, Lottie supposed.

"It is distressing that circumstances have devolved to this," Margaret said. "This is not the outcome Papa would have wished."

Lottie tucked Freddie closer, remembering Papa lying so still in his bed that final night.

Preserve my legacy, he had begged all of them—Lottie, Margaret, Grandmère, Frank, and Ferndown. *See that my lands and people are secured. Promise me.*

They had promised.

And it was a promise Lottie intended to keep.

Except her family now felt she had betrayed them.

"Why d-did you open your mouth, Lottie?!" Margaret sobbed afterward. "That d-doctor is likely not our cousin. He was merely ingratiating himself with a p-pair of women far above his station."

"Perhaps," Lottie replied, defending herself against the sting of Margaret's words. "But it would be dishonest to hide his existence if he does turn out to be a cousin."

"What about the honor owed to your family? To Papa's memory? Ferndown says that Papa wished Freddie to inherit—"

"But I did not know that, Margaret! By mentioning a potential heir, I thought to save the marquisate from oblivion. Besides, Parliament would likely have uncovered Dr. Whitaker's existence regardless. Can you not see?"

"A Scottish doctor was not what Papa meant when he asked us to secure his

legacy! He wanted Freddie to inherit. My Freddie! He specifically said as much to Ferndown."

"But you just said the doctor is likely not our cousin, so the entire matter will be moot—"

"But what if he is?!"

"Then we have behaved honorably!"

Lottie took a deep breath.

Of course, now it had all gone sideways.

The doctor *was* a cousin. He *was* the heir presumptive. Freddie likely *would* be disinherited.

Because what man would relinquish the coronet of a marquess?

Guilt ate at her, particularly in the dead of night when darkness pressed in and anxiety creaked and rattled.

In her attempts to be helpful, Lottie had inadvertently betrayed Freddie. She had added to Margaret's worry and distress.

The Duke of Ferndown was confident that even if Lords awarded the title to Cousin Alex, they would give some portion of Papa's entailed estate to Lottie and Margaret. But that was all still milling around in some hypothetical *if.*

Heavens, but it was all such a jumble.

Lottie pressed another kiss to Freddie's head, needing to reassure herself more than anything.

He leaned away, all boy, with a whispered, "No kisses, Tottie. I no baby," under his breath.

He was growing up too quickly.

What would become of Freddie? What would become of her?

"I hope the doctor does not wish to meet with us before dinner." Margaret looked at the clock above the mantel. "I imagine he is eager to survey the contents of Frome Abbey for himself."

Grandmère's eyebrow made a dramatic appearance at Margaret's acerbic tone.

Margaret willfully ignored it.

"I hope that you will make yourself agreeable to Lord Nettlesby at dinner, Lottie dearest," her sister continued. "He leaves tomorrow, and you have not spent more than five minutes in his company."

Lottie barely stopped a grimace.

Margaret was being rather dense to the obvious—Lottie had manipulated events to ensure she only had to endure Lord Nettlesby's presence for five minutes at a time.

Nettlesby was an old school chum of Frank's who visited with more regularity than Lottie would have liked.

She had not been to London in over two years, not since breaking her betrothal to Theo. After all, little Anne had died. And then Cousin Gabriel. And then Papa. And Lottie couldn't shake the bleakness from her heart.

So because Lottie refused to go to London, Margaret and Frank kept bringing London to her, inviting lordlings to visit with hopes that Lottie would take a liking to one of them. Her sister had particular expectations for Lord Nettlesby.

Lottie hadn't the heart to tell Margaret that his lordship was decidedly *not* for her.

"Would you mind ringing for the nurse, Lottie?" her sister asked. "I think it time for Freddie to return to the nursery."

Freddie instantly devolved into wails of despair at being dismissed, clamping his sticky hands around Lottie's neck.

"I'll take him, Margaret." Lottie struggled to her feet, Freddie clinging barnacle-like.

"Be careful not to wrinkle your gown, *cherie*." Grandmère raised her lorgnette. "That child has no care for your toilette."

Lottie managed a smile as she left the room carrying Freddie, though she could feel her sister's troubled eyes following her out the door.

ALEX WARMED HIS HANDS OVER the fire and attempted to ignore the sumptuous bedchamber around him.

It was rather difficult.

He had arrived at Frome Abbey, been greeted politely by the butler, and shown to his suite of rooms to 'warm up and refresh his person' before joining the family for dinner. *Who* that family would be, Alex could not say with any certainty. Lord and Lady Frank—the parents of young Frederick—most likely. What other family would there be? Lady Charlotte and her husband? He hoped the man she had married was a good sort. Alex had been taken by her ladyship's warm vivacity. Enough so that he remembered Lady Charlotte even three years on.

He rubbed his hands together before the fire, the crackling flames enveloping him in a cozy warmth. But glimmers of plush fabrics and luxurious furnishing danced in his peripheral vision.

The room was well-appointed, as befitted a guest bedchamber of a marquess. Expensive silk hangings draped the poster bed and thick Savonerrie carpet sank like spongy moss with every step. Two over-stuffed wingback chairs flanked the hearth.

A repast of hot tea, warm scones, and roast beef sandwiches had been laid on a small table between the wingback chairs. Hot water sent up a ribbon of steam from the pitcher on the wash stand in one corner.

Every luxury.

It wasn't that Alex was a stranger to affluence. He had been raised a gentleman, and he stayed with Andrew often enough to appreciate the elegant trappings of extensive wealth.

It was simply . . . he didn't wish to find any part of this life alluring.

And yet the *whole* of it was bloody-well enthralling.

His journey from Edinburgh had been tedious and yet not.

The Committee on Privilege had insisted that Lord Lockheade's estate send a carriage to Edinburgh to retrieve Alex. He had ridden the length of the Isle of Great Britain in grand style.

But no matter the luxury of the carriage, travel was still . . . travel.

Day upon day of bone-rattling roads through the desolation of the Scottish Borders morphing into the muck and grime of the Midlands only to reach this lush corner of the world—the rolling hills of Wiltshire and an endless parade of charming villages.

The contrast could not be more pronounced.

And then the grandeur of Frome Abbey itself, nestled into the land-scape and glinting in the icy winter air as if it were some priceless jewel.

That Alex had even experienced such a florid thought upon first seeing the house was irritating.

That he found the expanse of the entrance hall fascinating and the view from his bedchamber idyllic only increased his ire.

Everything in the room beckoned for him to stay, to allow the comfortable chairs to massage his weary muscles, to sip his tea and read a book just . . . because.

When had he last read a book just . . . because?

He frowned.

He had long ago eschewed such ephemera. If life was to be meaningful and purposeful, it could not be experienced from an armchair, resting on one's laurels.

But that was exactly what being a marquess entailed, did it not? Resting on laurels? In this case, the laurel leaves of a titled coronet.

He gritted his teeth and turned, placing the fire to his back.

Thankfully, no one knew he was here.

He hadn't even told Catriona or McNeal. The truth had simply stuck in his throat.

In the end, Alex had rattled something about a personal matter in London before kissing Catriona goodbye and handing McNeal a sheaf of notes, detailing his patients' care while he was away.

Perhaps part of his reluctance had been tied to the portfolio of documents he had received from Mr. Carter, describing the marquisate's extensive holdings.

Alex supposed most men would be awed by the list. The whole read like an inventory of Aladdin's Cave of Wonders.

Frome Abbey with its twenty thousand acres of arable land.

Three other large estates in England with a combined total of another thirty thousand acres.

Over ten thousand tenanted structures in total between all estates and over *fifty* thousand tenants.

A hunting lodge in Aberdeenshire.

A townhouse in London.

A vast sugar and tobacco plantation in the West Indies.

Two large woolen mills in the Midlands and a slew of profitable interests in shipping and coal mining.

The catalog was extensive. Page after page of items.

The marquisate was not just a title.

It was an empire.

No wonder the late Lord Lockheade had an entire office of solicitors at his beck and call. Alex wouldn't even know where to begin to oversee such diverse interests, even with a team of experienced clerks and secretaries.

More to the point, he didn't *want* to oversee it all. He had trained to be a doctor, not a man of business. Had he wanted a life of estate issues and horse breeding, he would have taken over the family's enterprise as his father had begged him to do after Ian's death.

The Committee on Privilege had appointed Lord Frank custodian of Frome Abbey and the marquisate holdings until the title succession was settled. As far as Alex was concerned, Lord Frank was welcome to the task long term.

Alex would fulfill the requirements the Committee on Privilege demanded, travel to London, sign what needed to be signed, and wash his hands of all this.

Until then . . .

He glanced at the clock on the mantel and then compared the time with that of his pocket watch.

Och, even the marquisate's clocks were delightfully punctual.

Servants had brought in his small trunk and traveling desk, setting the latter on a table, ready for use. Pulling up a chair, he opened the inlaid wood writing slope and retrieved a letter. It had arrived right as he was leaving Edinburgh, and he simply had not had a moment to respond.

Alex snapped the letter in his hand.

Dear Dr. Whitaker,

Forgive this intrusion on your time, but I have a matter of some sensitivity which I would like to address. It has come to my attention that you were aboard The Minerva, *the private vessel that sank in the South Pacific in '16. I wish to consult with you about a medical matter which relates peripherally to The Minerva and her wreckage. However, the issue must be attended to with some delicacy. I would require that any discourse between us be held secret under your Oath to Hippocrates as a medical physician. Moreover, I currently reside near Wetherby in Yorkshire and, though I occasionally travel for business, I am never in Edinburgh. Do you ever pass through this area?*

Alex pursed his mouth.

His brain had passed the hours of his journey musing upon the letter's clues and his own time aboard *The Minerva*.

Alex had come on ship as a personal physician to the gentlemen financing the trip—Andrew Langston, now the Earl of Hadley, and Sir Rafe Gilbert. It was common for wealthy men such as Andrew to bring their own physician when traveling abroad.

On a whim, Alex had replied to the advertisement for a physician. He had just completed his studies at the University of Edinburgh, passing the brutal series of exams required to become a fully-fledged Doctor of Medicine. The exams were so taxing that less than one out of five students passed them. But Alex had been granted a mark of high distinction.

And then Ian had died.

As ever, Alex mentally shied away from thoughts of Ian, the gaping emptiness left by his supportive, kind older brother. He recognized that Ian's death would always loom as a seminal event, the sort of chronic wound he had to be excessively careful not to jostle.

A point forever dividing *before* and *after*.

In the months after Ian's passing, their father had gone nearly mad with grief. Alex, mourning and desperate to escape his father's angry recriminations, responded to Andrew's advertisement for a physician. He had been thrilled to be hired on.

Their trip had been relatively uneventful until they reached the islands of the New Hebrides, northwest of Australia. There, Captain Cuthie had betrayed them, destroying a native village and nearly killing Andrew and Rafe in the process. Only Alex's expert medical skills had saved their lives.

In the chaos, Cuthie had sailed out of the harbor with Jamie still aboard ship, marooning the Brotherhood on the island. Kieran had been inconsolable.

A Portuguese whaler had sailed into the island's harbor a month later, telling tales of floating through the wreckage of *The Minerva*. They surmised the ship had broken apart on a shallow reef. All hands aboard were assumed lost, Jamie included.

And now this unexpected letter arrived from some Mr. S. Smith, raising the hackles on Alex's neck.

Most significantly, how did this man know that *Alex* was a survivor of the wreck? That information had never been made widely known. Andrew and Rafe were the more public figures connected with the wreck. But the information was no secret, either. A determined person *could* learn of Alex's presence aboard the ship.

The missive was signed 'Mr. S. Smith' which, as a name, was so common, it could belong to hundreds of thousands of men. Alex remembered several sailors by name of Smith aboard *The Minerva*.

What did S. Smith know? Was he another survivor of *The Minerva*? Or a family member of one of the crew?

The handwriting—assuming it was Mr. Smith's own and not that of a local vicar acting as a scribe—was that of an educated man: an elegant copperplate of neat strokes and swooping flicks. Among those who had been aboard *The Minerva*, only Alex, Andrew, and Rafe had such educated penmanship.

The letter yielded few other clues. The return address provided was an inn in Wetherby that likely took in post, as well as saw to travelers and the like. Nearly all postal offices in England were extensions of some other business. In this case, the innkeep would simply hold onto a letter for S. Smith until the man himself turned up to retrieve it.

The larger question—

Was the issue truly related to *The Minerva*? Or was S. Smith simply using that fact to get Alex's attention? Had the recent notice in the newspaper jarred this man loose?

But again, how had he known to contact Alex?

And, most importantly, would Alex tell the rest of the Brotherhood about this?

This was the problem. Every additional piece of information that surfaced—the captain and first mate had survived, the ship had exploded—

sent Kieran into another downward spiral of fevered hopes that ended in dashed dreams.

A year ago, Kieran had been a man on the brink.

"I cannae sleep," Kieran whispered, clutching Alex's coat, whisky soaking the air. "I keep hearing Jamie screaming my name as the ship explodes, the flames crawling over her—"

"Ye are driving yourself insane with such thoughts, Kieran." Alex lifted his friend, attempting to coax his fevered body back to bed. "Ye need rest and warm food—"

"I need more whisky!" Kieran shouted, pushing Alex back. "I cannae bear the pain! Ye dinnae comprehend what it's like, tae not know what happened tae your own wife!"

"I may not understand, Kieran, but I know that whisky isnae the answer!"

"Like hell, it isnae!"

Alex hated this. The situation was too much like Ian. Too much like his father. He would not lose another person he loved—

Alex shook off the memory.

Kieran was doing better. He was. Their conversation in Edinburgh last autumn and Kieran's subsequent letters convinced Alex of this.

The missive from S. Smith would likely come to naught, and Alex would tell no one about it until he had more information.

Regardless, meeting with the man was of the utmost importance. Fortunately, it would be a small matter to divert to Wetherby on the way back to Edinburgh. He should be able to meet with this Mr. S. Smith before a week was out. In the meantime, he would at least ask for more information.

Another glance at his pocket watch showed that he still had an hour before needing to dress for dinner with his Whitaker cousins.

Alex pulled out a fresh sheet of foolscap and began writing his reply.

In the end, Freddie's sticky hands had rendered Lottie's frock equally sticky. So after delivering him to the nursery, she summoned her maid and changed into a silk dress of deep lavender.

Lottie knew she needed to leave off the blacks and grays and lavenders of mourning. Margaret had cast off her dark colors before Christmas.

"Between Anne's passing and Papa's death, I've been in mourning for nearly eighteen months," her sister had said as a maid tied the tapes of a red satin gown. "I still have a husband and a son who live, and I shall cease being a black rain cloud and wear color for them, if no one else."

But for Lottie, who had no husband or child, the blacks and grays reflected the shade of her heart—the hovering weight of loss. The endless sting of Papa's passing and Gabriel's tragic death and little Anne's absence.

She simply could not bear to don colors. Not yet.

To be quite honest, she wasn't sure if life would ever again paint itself in bold hues. She felt too raw and tumbled to tolerate such chaotic vibrance.

Lottie stepped down the central staircase of Frome Abbey, a muted Paisley shawl wrapped tight around her shoulders to ward off the January chill.

As the name indicated, Frome Abbey had begun its life as a Cistercian monastery. The Reformation had seen it awarded to the third Baron Lockheade and transformed into a Tudor country estate.

A century later, the second Viscount Lockheade had renovated the property, adding an impressive Baroque facade to the south entrance reminiscent of the grandeur of Versailles. Or so Grandmère claimed, as she was the only one of them who had seen Versailles firsthand.

The grand staircase zigzagged through the center of the house, its marble steps cantilevered out from the wall with no central supporting pillars. A skylight—added by her father—illuminated the whole from above.

The portraits of ancestors watched Lottie descend each step. She lifted her eyes mid-way down the flight of stairs and stopped.

Cousin Alex stood on the landing below her—hands clasped behind his back, face in profile—studying the painting on the wall. He had shed his caped overcoat and top hat, obviously. But his green clawhammer coat and black woolen breeches, though simple, were impeccably tailored.

He appeared younger than her memory of him. Here . . . he was merely a gentleman come for dinner.

He turned his head toward her and froze.

Oh.

He might seem younger in appearance, but his eyes . . .

She did not remember them being so . . . so . . . *seeing.*

He had ancient eyes. Slate gray, no trace of blue or green.

Eyes that perhaps had seen too much of life—too much death, too much suffering, too much helplessness—and were honed sharp in their refusal to tolerate others' twaddle.

Had he always had such a gaze? Had she, in her youth and naivete those years ago, simply not noticed it?

Or, like herself, had Life knocked him about since then?

Those ancient eyes watched as she descended the final few steps to him.

Lottie curtsied.

"Dr. Whitaker," she murmured, saying nothing of their cousin-ship. He did not *feel* like Cousin Alex anymore.

"Lady Charlotte." He bowed. It was a precise, courtly motion.

No matter his current occupation and the absurdity of their previous encounter, Lottie was confident Cousin Alex—*ehr* . . . Dr. Whitaker— had been raised a gentleman.

As he raised his head, his eyes flicked to her bare hands. As they were to dine *en famille*, Lottie had not donned gloves. Given how his gaze lingered there for a moment, she had to wonder if he condemned her small lack of decorum—

The thought evaporated as his gray eyes lifted and again locked with hers.

Steely eyes. Battle eyes.

The sort of gaze a soldier might see right before his own demise.

Lottie swallowed.

Like with his peruke and justacorps those years ago, Dr. Whitaker was once again rendering her maudlin.

He was not her adversary. She *knew* this. The man was no more guilty of his parentage than she was of hers.

And yet, somehow, Fate had landed them on opposite sides of this quarrel. A quarrel she had opened her mouth and created.

And now, holding his gaze . . .

He was handsome, she realized with a startled blink.

No.

Attractive.

He was *attractive*, which wasn't quite the same thing as handsome, but infinitely more troubling.

Handsome . . . one could simply admire.

But attraction—

Attraction was fraught.

His beauty was that of a blade, sharp lines and broad strokes. The bold slash of his nose. The acute angularity of his jaw. The sleek shine of his mink-brown hair. The coiled strength in the lean lines of his body.

This was a man who knew his own mind.

The sort who, when he committed to a woman, would devote his entire self.

I would welcome such devotion.

The thought rocketed through her before she could call it back.

And on its heels, that dratted attraction fluffed and stretched, expanding in her chest.

An onslaught of unwanted and objectionable physical responses immediately followed.

A sharp tang of awareness, a catch in her lungs, an abrupt flush of blood beneath her skin.

He was a physician. Surely he had studied such phenomena. Could he discern her thoughts from observation alone?

Oh, heavens. Was she going to blush?

Donotblushdonotblush.

Lottie forced a slow breath in through her nose and out her mouth.

Enough. You have not been so long out of company that this man will render you mawkish.

"I trust ye are well?" Dr. Whitaker asked.

Scotland rolled off his tongue in a smooth brogue. It brushed up against her Englishness, as alluring as it was unsettling. Though she supposed the sensation summed up a thousand years of Scottish and English history.

"Yes, quite well." She pulled her shawl tighter around her shoulders, as if it could protect her from the onslaught of . . . *him.* "Thank you."

What did one say to the man who could decide her future? Who felt like he could be . . . *more* . . . and yet was clearly in the box labeled *Enemy—Do Not Fraternize?*

A plain *Good day, sir* felt . . . anticlimactic.

But then falling to her knees and begging him to sign the attainder so Freddie could inherit the marquisate would likely be deemed overly dramatic.

Besides, was it her imagination or did his eyes continue to linger on her? And if so, why? Though she wanted to fidget, she met his gaze instead.

He startled, as if embarrassed to have been caught staring, and abruptly turned back to the painting he had been contemplating.

Ah, yes. She had nearly forgotten the painting.

She could feel the questions crowding his tongue.

His first was predictable.

"Is this meant to be your . . . family?" His eyebrows raised.

"Yes. Myself, my sister, and my father. My mother passed away long ago."

"Ah."

"It is one of Cousin Gabriel's pieces," she offered.

He shot her a sideways glance. "The cousin who died in Rome?"

"Yes."

"It is certainly . . . unconventional." Dr. Whitaker studied the painting for another moment. "Did your family request this . . . ?" He waved a hand in a circle.

"No. It was all Gabriel's doing."

Though Dr. Whitaker said nothing more, Lottie could hear his unspoken criticism.

She supposed he would judge the painting harshly. His ancient eyes likely had no patience for such frivolity.

She stifled a sigh.

Very well.

The painting *was* absurd.

There. She could admit as much.

Her family treasured all of Gabriel's works, but it was obvious why this one did not have a place of honor in the drawing room.

"He painted ye as dogs." Dr. Whitaker spoke the words flatly, as if not sure what affronted him more—the offense to good taste or the offense to canines.

Another moment of fraught silence.

"Why would he paint ye as *dogs*?" The doctor's brow furrowed. "I cannae fathom it."

The painting truly was awful. There they were— she, Papa and Margaret—painted with normal human faces but each sporting a canine body. They looked as if they had each donned a dog suit, complete with fluffy ears and a tail.

Papa stood proud. Margaret sat in a chair staring boldly out at the viewer. Lottie lounged on a rug before them.

It was bizarre.

Papa was an enormous gray mastiff, secure and strong, the powerful muscles of his haunches carefully rendered.

Margaret was a King Charles spaniel, a sweet natured and pampered pet.

But Lottie . . . she was painted as a common shepherding dog with ginger and white hair, lolling at the feet of everyone else.

"I suppose in painting us as dogs, Gabriel thought . . ." Lottie paused and then shrugged helplessly. There would be no hiding Cousin Gabriel's eccentricities from Dr. Whitaker. "Gabriel thought to be *clever*, you see. The family coat of arms features a wolf, and Papa commissioned Gabriel to paint a family portrait that captured our sense of allegiance to our family heritage. Gabriel took the injunction quite literally."

"Are ye . . ." Dr. Whitaker's brow furrowed further. He leaned forward. "Did he paint ye as a *collie?*"

A beat of silence.

"Yes," she nodded. "Yes, he did."

Gabriel had painted the family portrait on the heels of her broken betrothal, right before his departure for Rome.

Collies are the most loyal of dogs, he had told her, grin stretching wide. *And you, with your lovely loyal heart, chose our family over Theo.*

"Cousin Gabriel felt that I am loyal in my affections, like a collie," she continued. "However, my sister thinks that Gabriel should have painted me as a more exotic canine."

"Aye." His eyes flicked sideways to her—up, down, raking from head to toe. "Bit of an understatement that."

A COLLIE?

Alex nearly laughed again at the absurdity of the painting. What would Ewan with his artistic eye think of it?

He darted another look at Lady Charlotte and then forced his eyes away.

She had descended the stairs in a flutter of jasmine and rustling silk. A glittering jewel, sending his wits scattering like spillikins.

Like everything else in this rarefied world, Lady Charlotte was alarmingly alluring. Blue, blue eyes wide-set in a fine-boned face framed by golden hair and a pert chin. The woman was nearly a parody of genteel feminine beauty, so perfect were her manners and comportment.

Had she been this handsome before? He couldn't recall. To be sure, the Lady Charlotte of his memory was a bonnie lass.

But this woman—

This woman was staggeringly beautiful.

The sort of elegance that spoke to centuries of Anglo-Saxon nobility and gentility.

The sort of lovely that turned heads and led people to whispering once she had passed.

The sort of beauty that could easily dissuade him from his chosen course.

It annoyed Alex to no end.

The turmoil in his chest set him to clenching and unclenching his fists, as if a bout of fisticuffs could ward off her charms.

He resisted the urge to look at her fine-boned hands again, specifically the bare ring finger on her left hand.

She was unmarried. No highborn lady would be seen out-and-about without her wedding ring.

How was it possible she was unwed? In his memory of that afternoon together years ago, she was betrothed. What had happened?

She seemed the sort to be settled with an indulgent husband who lavished her with gifts. Instead, she appeared unattached and entirely too captivating.

He swallowed and forced himself to study the painting, which in all truthfulness, was perhaps a mistake.

It truly was bizarre.

Though, silver lining, not *everything* in this house spoke of perfection.

He could think of no one *less* like a sheep-herding dog than Lady Charlotte.

An elegant *bichon frisé*? Absolutely.

A primped pomeranian? Of course.

But a collie?

They both contemplated the painting for a beat. The dog with Lady Charlotte's face and a collie's body, tail in the midst of wagging excitedly.

Alex unclenched his fists and clasped his hands behind his back, refusing to allow his eyes to drift back to the living Lady Charlotte beside him.

Despite her porcelain beauty, she did not strike him as spoiled and vain. Instead, a painful sort of earnestness laced her words. Which when combined with her ethereal loveliness, simply made the entire situation all the worse.

He did not wish to like her. Not in any whit.

Admire from a distance. That was *all* he intended to do.

She turned from the painting, as if willing it away. "I trust your journey was not too arduous?"

"It was as passable as a journey from Edinburgh can be."

"Ah," she said. "I would imagine that translates as *tedious* and *long*."

Her words surprised a smile out of him. "Ye are not wrong, my lady."

She smiled in return, soft and wan, her crystalline beauty all the more striking against the backdrop of her care.

His heart made a tumbling sort of lurch in his chest.

No.

This would not do.

Like everything else in this aristocratic world, Lady Charlotte was far too compelling for his peace of mind. Glittering Diamonds of the First Water were not for the likes of him.

The very thought of Lady Charlotte with her fine manners and porcelain beauty traipsing through his medical practice in Edinburgh was ludicrous.

More to the point, such a highborn lady would never stoop so low as to become the wife of a Scottish physician.

The very thought was absurd.

And he, himself, was too sensible to become infatuated with a beautiful woman who would turn the head of any man.

Yes, that was how he must think of it.

Lady Charlotte was akin to one of his late-father's prized mares. A unique horse that was the product of impeccable bloodlines, years of care, and extensive training. One would never hitch a horse like that to a farmer's wagon.

No. Such a filly was far too scarce a resource to be wasted on menial labor. She was meant as a show horse, a symbol of status.

Lady Charlotte was of the same vein.

That wasn't to say that he did not take a moment to admire such beauty in either form—horse or woman.

Granted, he was quite sure Catriona would box his ears to hear him compare a woman to a horse.

Everything about this venture was primed to addle his wits.

The sooner he fulfilled the requirements of the Committee on Privilege, the better.

4

"Pardon?" The venerable Duke of Ferndown lifted his eyebrows and scrutinized Alex sitting partway down the dinner table. "Did you truly just say you do not drink wine?"

"Aye," Alex replied, barely maintaining a stiff smile on his face. "I dinnae drink alcohol of any sort."

Silence hung in the room, as if Alex's assertion were so traumatic, it required a moment of deathly quiet in order to properly mourn it.

"And yet, you consider yourself a gentleman?" His Grace peered down his aristocratic nose at Alex, tone utterly baffled.

"I was unaware that imbibing alcohol had been added as a requirement of gentility?" Alex kept his voice even, but sardonic humor hummed through his words.

Given how thoroughly the duke's expression froze, His Grace was *not* amused.

Dinner had been a wee bit of a disaster.

The Duke of Ferndown sat at the top of the table, as his rank dictated. Though well into his fifth decade, the duke was still a large, athletic man, bringing to mind an aging monarch—autocratic and fussy but ready to ride to hounds at any moment. Granted, this sense was helped along by His Grace greeting Alex and then launching into a twenty-minute lecture on grouse-versus-pheasant hunting.

His Grace did nothing by halves. His opinions, his side whiskers, and the boom of his voice were all duke-sized. Everything about him saying, *I am supremely confident of my place in the world.*

As well he should be, Alex supposed. The man was a duke, after all. Such men were the center of their own universe.

His Grace's son, Lord Frank, sat beside his father, an uncanny copy of his sire. Seeing the two men together was like watching Time in action. Though on Lord Frank, the duke's bombastic personality became more supercilious than supremely confident. Lord Frank, after all, was a second son, not the duke's heir, and gave every appearance of feeling that lack keenly.

Lady Frank sat opposite her husband, on the right-hand of the duke. Pretty and delicate like her sister, she was much as Alex remembered. But a haunted melancholy clung to her, a lingering pain that he did not recollect being there before. The family had seen death in recent years. Alex's presence alone testified to this. Both Ferndown and Lord Frank sported mourning armbands on their evening coats, as if to loudly proclaim their continued grief over the family's losses.

At the other end of the table, the Dowager Lady Lockheade was a force to be reckoned with. French wit laced her English, and she had a shrewd gaze which Alex suspected missed nothing despite her advanced years.

As for Lady Charlotte, she sat opposite Alex. She smiled and said little, but her inquisitive eyes hinted that her thoughts were legion. Mostly, she parried the conversational thrusts of the man at her elbow, Lord Nettlesby.

Nettlesby, introduced as a close friend of Lord Frank, had instantly set Alex's teeth on edge. The gentleman clearly had designs on Lady Charlotte. He monopolized her attention and laughed like a braying donkey at every third thing she said.

To her credit, Lady Charlotte's reaction to his lordship could best be described as 'long-suffering tolerance.'

Clearly no one, including himself, wished to be here tonight.

But the assembled company was attempting to behave civilly toward Alex. After all, no one wanted to so thoroughly offend him that he chose to fight the attainder strictly on principle.

Had Alex been in a more agreeable frame of mind, it might have even been amusing to watch so many entitled aristocrats attempt to walk that fine line.

Or, rather, stagger up the path like a passel of school chums three sheets to the wind.

Case in point—

"The ability to discern a fine drink is the hallmark of any refined gentleman," Lord Frank said, eyes narrowing.

"Hear, hear." Nettlesby raised his wine glass in approval and shot a daft grin at Lady Charlotte, as if looking for her approval.

"Well said," Ferndown boomed. "A full day of hunting needs to be finished with a stiff drink. There's nothing more bracing for the constitution."

"Exactly, Father," Lord Frank agreed, turning to look at Alex. "But as Scots regularly imbibe whisky, perhaps the sense of nuance is lost on your race, Dr. Whitaker. Bit of a hammer to the senses, scotch." His tone implied that *Scotsmen* themselves were included in that sentiment.

Alex kept his polite smile firmly in place.

As he had noted, the duke, Lord Frank, and Nettlesby had been walking the line between civility and boorishness like roaring *fou* sots.

For example, Lord Frank remarked that Alex's evening attire was 'surprisingly elegant for a Scotsman.' Nettlesby agreed and laughed that Alex was more 'literate' than he supposed a Scot to be.

Edinburgh University led the world in medical studies, and Alex had graduated as a full MD with highest distinction. How did Nettlesby think that had come about? That Alex had merely slept on his medical textbooks for a few years and magically woken one day knowing all the information inside?

Of course, when Alex had politely pointed this out, Nettlesby and Lord Frank had changed tactics. They moved on to discuss hunting and riding to hounds, now assuming that Alex was a milksop and a polymath, and therefore incompetent when it came to sporting activities.

Honestly.

Alex was intelligent enough to understand what was going on here. The gentlemen were flaunting a hauteur that glittered as sharply as the polish on the silver.

All in an effort to proclaim, *You will always be an outsider.*

Part of Alex seethed that their blatant efforts at manipulation were so bloody effective. His competitive spirit wanted to rise to the bait and blast them all with a similarly cutting politeness.

Another part of him simply didn't care. He merely wanted done with this blasted business.

Thankfully, Nettlesby would be departing in the morning. Ferndown and Lord Frank would be leaving in two days for a meeting with the Committee on Privilege in London. His Grace had mentioned more than once that the King required their presence in London.

"Dr. Whitaker, I remember your aversion to strong spirits." Lady Charlotte lifted her blue eyes to his from across the table. "It is why you were the doctor who arrived to assist us with Freddie. We were ever so grateful."

Was that an apology in her eyes as she attempted to turn the conversation?

"Aye," Alex replied. "I was the only sober physician for miles that day."

"I say, Lady Charlotte." Lord Frank shot his sister-in-law a stern look. "Talk of childbirth is hardly the done thing over dinner."

Color flushed Lady Charlotte's cheeks. Candlelight flickered from candelabra on the table and bounced from mirrored sconces on the walls, bathing the lady in glimmering light.

Another stab of annoyance jabbed at Alex's chest.

First, the act of childbirth was a natural thing. There was no shame in discussing it.

Second, he disliked the sense that Lord Frank felt the need to silence Lady Charlotte's voice. As if she were to be pretty and nothing else.

Third, Lady Charlotte blushed most becomingly, and the sight affected Alex's breathing, as he suspected that nearly every expression appeared graceful and elegant on her.

He mentally shook away the florid thought.

He did not find Lady Charlotte charming.

He did not find this dining room with its gilt ceiling and velvet draperies beautiful.

He did not find the roast beef on his plate delicious.

And if he kept telling himself that, perhaps it would be true.

Just get through dinner.

The Dowager cleared her throat at the bottom of the table, reaching for her own wine glass. "As a French woman, I cannot agree with your opinion on alcohol, Dr. Whitaker. A fine wine, after all, is as French as beautiful silks, exquisite food, and clever conversation."

Ferndown chuckled. "You are correct, as usual, my lady."

"*Merci*, Duke." Her ladyship nodded her head in acknowledgment. "However, I must respect your *ténacité*, Dr. Whitaker. You are like our Charlotte, *mais non*? She will not eat meat. You will not drink wine. You are together in *solidarité*." The Dowager lifted her glass in a salute.

Against all his better judgment, Alex smiled. He met Lady Charlotte's gaze across the table, darting a glance at her plate that was, indeed, free of meat.

"Is this true, Lady Charlotte?" he asked. "Ye dinnae eat meat?"

"Yes. It is true." She nodded, blushing again.

Alex had many follow-up questions.

Why did Lady Charlotte choose not to eat meat? Was it simply the taste?

Or did Lady Charlotte harbor more philosophical reasons for her decision?

The thought intrigued him.

After all, such an attitude implied mindfulness, a sense of self-awareness and intelligent idealism that he considered at odds with such porcelain beauty.

But . . . why? If she had been plain, would he have felt the same?

The thought shamed him because he wasn't sure he knew the answer, and what did that say about him? Had he not mentally castigated Lord Nettlesby not ten minutes past for similar behavior?

More to the point, he disliked that he was pondering Lady Charlotte's inner life in any way, weighing it against his own idealism, wondering at her possible philosophical thoughts.

Enough. Dinnae let the bonnie lass distract you.

Complete this visit, sign the papers in London, and resume your life.

He picked up his knife and fork, contemplating the roast beef on his plate. It tasted delicious, but if he viewed it as the flesh of a once-living thing . . . the whole did become rather unappetizing, he supposed.

He raised his eyes back to Lady Charlotte. "I agree with your grandmother, Lady Charlotte. Refusing to eat meat would take fortitude—"

"*Bah!* It was not meant as a compliment." The Dowager gave a decidedly Gallic wave of her hand. "Were dinner left to you both, it would be a tasteless expanse of vegetables and bread washed down with water. The very thought is utterly depressing. Life is meant to be lived in full. Not rationed into petite morsels of joy."

Nettlesby frowned. "I say, how have I never noticed that you don't eat meat, Lady Charlotte?"

The *look* Lady Charlotte gave Nettlesby—eyebrow raised, lips pinched—had Alex swallowing back a laugh.

She might as well have said aloud, *You haven't noticed, Nettlesby, because you see me as a prize to acquire rather than a person.*

Nettlesby rattled on, however, confirming his obliviousness. "How can a beautiful woman such as yourself decline to eat meat?" His lordship's frown deepened.

Och.

This gentleman.

Alex was helpless to stop his sardonic tongue. "I am sure that Lady Charlotte possesses a great many admirable qualities *beyond* beauty."

The Dowager gave a startled burst of laughter, nursing her wine glass as if delighted.

Alex looked at Lady Charlotte across the table. "I have read Mr. Percy Shelley's pamphlet defending a vegetable system of diet and found his ideas interesting."

Lady Charlotte sat straighter in her chair, her eyes lighting with the first sign of true interest he had seen from her.

"Yes," she nodded, "I have found all of Mr. Shelley's arguments in *A Vindication of Natural Diet* to be most compelling—"

The Duke of Ferndown cleared his throat. Loudly.

Ah.

The duke did not wish to have a philosophical discussion about the virtues of a vegetal diet. And as Ferndown *was* a duke, he got his way.

Conversation stalled.

Lady Charlotte met Alex's gaze across the table.

An almost uncanny unspoken flurry of thoughts passed between them.

The sense that she *did* have deep-seated reasons why she chose not to eat meat. Likely reasons as formidable as his own for not drinking alcohol. And because of this, he sensed that he and Lady Charlotte would see eye-to-eye on a great many things.

Perhaps it was this sense of kinship that had him opening his mouth further.

"I will stand in solidarity with ye, Lady Charlotte." He pushed the beef to the side of his plate and reached for a tureen of sauteed winter spinach.

"Thank you," she smiled and then motioned for a footman to remove her wine glass. "I will return the favor."

Lord Frank rolled his eyes. Nettlesby lifted his wineglass for a footman to refill, his expression still puzzled.

"Well," Ferndown sighed, reaching for his own glass, "at least we can all enjoy dessert."

Alex froze in the process of wiping his mouth. His panicked gaze met Lady Charlotte's.

"You have the look of a man who has been found out, Dr. Whitaker," the lady laughed, a delighted tinkle of sound. "Is dessert also forbidden you?"

Alex set down his fork, a rueful grin on his lips. "Aye. I dinnae eat sweets, either."

Lord Frank shook his head with a groan. "Do you have any vices, Dr. Whitaker? Or are you determined to strip every last ounce of enjoyment from life?"

Lord Frank, Alex supposed, was perhaps a wee bit too attached to his moniker. His words were as frank as his name.

"Surprising as it may be, one can live a full and contented life without alcohol and sugar." Alex only barely managed to keep the sarcasm from his voice.

Silence greeted him.

"Ah," Lady Frank said, swirling her wine glass, "but now I raise the most critical question—will Lottie abandon her pudding?" She raised her eyebrows toward her sister, a wry smile on her lips.

Lady Charlotte laughed. "In that, I must disappoint. My sense of fairness and solidarity does not extend to giving up flummery and fairy cakes."

Lady Charlotte fair sparkled at the words. Charming. Dazzling.

Alex detested how his heart flipped in his chest.

He was not this man.

A bonny English lass would not turn him into a love-sick welp.

No, she would not.

Thankfully, Ferndown cleared his throat again, even more loudly this time. His Grace took back the reins of the conversation, and the remainder of dinner devolved into an argument between Lord Frank and Nettlesby on the possibility of pheasant hunting even in January.

"WELL, THAT WAS A RATHER excruciating evening," Margaret said. "Dr. Whitaker is not quite as genial as I remember."

Her sister looped her arm through Lottie's as they left the drawing room, intent on the central stairs.

Lottie pinched her lips shut.

Margaret was not wrong.

Dinner had been . . . frustrating.

But her sister was also mistaken.

Given the situation, Dr. Whitaker's behavior had been remarkably patient and restrained. After all, every word and glance had been calibrated to snub and wound the doctor. Their poor cousin who had done *nothing* wrong, except be born and outlive every other heir.

Dr. Whitaker had endured the lot with the sort of *sang-froid* she imagined men took to the guillotine, alternating between glacial silence and gallows humor.

Despite the family's opinions, Lottie was not convinced that Dr. Whitaker intended to contest the proposed Writ of Attainder. He looked upon each room—and each of them, to be honest—with a sort of muted horror. As if he were almost crawling out of his skin, racing to see the backside of this venture. He was a dragon eager to return to his own lair, not one intent on pillage and conquest.

Or perhaps she was merely projecting her own wishful thinking.

"I do not wish to offer censure, Lottie, as we are all under a great deal of strain," her sister continued. "But you were rather too forward in your manners with the doctor tonight."

"Pardon?" Lottie stopped at the base of the staircase, her sister's words causing her brow to furrow rather dramatically. "I do not understand your meaning, Margaret."

"You are far too intelligent to misunderstand me."

Lottie waited.

Margaret finally rolled her hand.

"*I will return the favor, Dr. Whitaker,*" Margaret repeated, her voice lightly sing-song. "*My solidarity does not extend to fairy cakes.* Dearest, you were all but flirting with the man."

Lottie swallowed, tamping down the roil in her stomach.

"I was *not* flirting," she sputtered, but her words lacked conviction.

Perhaps she had enjoyed the brief interaction with Dr. Whitaker, sensing a kindred mind.

Perhaps she had liked watching those steel eyes spark with humor.

Perhaps she *had* been flirting.

Or, perhaps, she simply wished to nettle . . . Nettlesby.

After all, it had been *so* long since she had conversed with a truly intellectual man.

Margaret merely gave her a disappointed look—her sister excelled at them—not believing Lottie's words any more than Lottie herself did.

"Lottie, I know the goodness of your heart, but you simply cannot treat that man with kindness." Her sister's eyes were gentle but firm. "Dr. Whitaker is a bachelor and a physician and poor. He is employed in *trade*. He has nothing to recommend him to those of our set."

Given the quality of Dr. Whitaker's attire, Lottie was skeptical that the man was truly impoverished. His manners and address spoke of money somewhere along his lineage. And a physician could still be a gentleman.

More to the point, he had much to recommend him.

I am sure that Lady Charlotte possesses a great many admirable qualities beyond beauty.

Did the doctor know how much she appreciated that simple sentence? Lottie had always found compliments about her physical appearance puzzling. As if her beauty were something she had created. As if it were more than simply an accident of birth.

That he would see such a thing—and defend her—said loads about his character.

She had the presence of mind to avoid saying as much to Margaret, thank goodness.

"You know what is at stake here, Lottie." Margaret was not done saying her piece. "It's *our* future. *Freddie's* future. If Dr. Whitaker fights this attainder and triumphs, Lords could decide to award the entirety of the entailed estate to him. *Freddie* would get nothing. You know that Frank's portion is small. Freddie will need more if he is to live the life of a gentleman."

They stared at one another for a moment.

It was so strange, Lottie thought. How she could feel such an odd combination of outrage and shame all at once.

Outrage that Margaret and the rest disdained Dr. Whitaker for no other reason than the accident of his birth.

Shame that she might have inadvertently flirted with Dr. Whitaker and, thereby, encouraged him to wish a closer connection with her.

"First think of family. Remember where your loyalties lie, dearest." Margaret looked pointedly up at Gabriel's absurd painting hovering above the landing. "There is nothing wrong with being as faithful as a collie in this particular situation."

Margaret turned on her slippered heels and walked back toward the drawing room.

For her part, Lottie climbed the stairs, past Cousin Gabriel's wretched depiction of the collie dog, the eyes of the painting following her the entire way.

5

The next morning, the Duke of Ferndown and Lord Frank were waiting in the stable yard.

Alex pulled up short when he saw them.

The only part of the venture Alex had *not* been dreading was today's excursion. He was to ride out with the estate steward, Mr. Warden, to view the home farm and visit a few tenant houses. The intention was to show Alex what being a landlord and marquess would entail.

Alex had come to the stable to collect a horse and meet Mr. Warden in front of Frome Abbey, the two of them riding out together.

But that, apparently, was not to be. His Grace and Lord Frank were dressed for riding, as well.

Ferndown was pacing in a greatcoat and well-worn buckskins, a riding crop in one hand and a gleaming fowling piece in the other. The same mourning armband from the evening before peeked out from the duke's sleeve underneath his greatcoat.

Lord Frank was equally dressed for a morning of hunting, his Garrick coat swirling around his Hessians. He held a modern half-barrel fowling gun in his hand, likely the work of Manton, if Alex were to guess.

Both men's breath puffed white, sending glittering crystalline clouds into the January air.

Why were they here, as if waiting for him? If the men wished to hunt, they did not need Alex's company to do so.

Had the father-and-son pair not had their fill of quizzing Alex the night before? Long after the ladies had retired, they had devolved deeper and deeper into their cups, regaling him with tales of hunting red deer in the Scottish Borders and shooting grouse on the Duke of Marlborough's estate. Lord Frank had continued his argument with Nettlesby, insistent that one could hunt pheasant in January.

Alex had sipped his tea and pondered the mind-numbing boredom of aristocratic life.

"My lord. Your Grace." Alex bowed, in greeting.

Neither Ferndown nor Lord Frank returned the sentiment, their cool nods calibrated to emphasize the vast difference in their stations in life.

"Thought we'd join you this morning, Doctor." Ferndown snapped his riding crop against the side of his coat.

"Always nice to go for a ride," Lord Frank agreed, hefting his gun. "Besides, I have to prove Nettlesby wrong and attempt to scare up some grouse or pheasant. Pity he is too hungover to join us."

"Hear, hear," the duke nodded. "We leave for London tomorrow, but it seems a shame to return to Town without at least having a go at a hunt. You don't mind, do you, Doctor?"

Alex shook his head.

Of course, the two men could come along. Alex could deny them nothing. Their rank and station made it so. It was merely a gentlemanly sense of fair play that Ferndown asked for 'permission.'

It was, in some ways, comical to witness—a duke and his son contorting themselves to both underscore the power of their social positions and yet, simultaneously, persuade Alex that he wanted no share in that power.

Were this a play and not his life, Alex would laugh.

"I am happy tae have you both along," he said, stopping beside them. "Provided neither of ye is planning on dispatching me back to my Maker this morning."

He motioned toward the fowling guns in their hands.

Ferndown grinned, though the smile didn't quite reach his eyes. "Only if you decide to be a pheasant, Doctor."

"Or get in the way of my gun," Lord Frank said, far too cheerfully.

Bloody hell.

A look passed between the father and son.

Alex's eyes narrowed. Were they up to something then? With *guns*, no less?

Fortunately, the pepper shot of a fowling piece was unlikely to be lethal unless fired at close range, but it jangled his already frayed nerves.

The warm scent of hay and manure and horse wafting out from the stables wasn't helping.

It was a common enough smell. But something about the crisp morning amplified its sense of *home*.

A wave of unexpected emotion rose up, hitting Alex with all the subtlety of a sledgehammer—homesickness and crushing grief.

His father should be here.

Ian should be here.

Why *now* of all times? He hadn't felt maudlin about the past in . . . *years*.

Had this situation with the marquisate simply had him dwelling more on his family? On his upbringing in a similar landed estate?

Or was it the thought that his father or brother should be standing in this stable yard, not him? Or that they would expect Alex to reach for the marquisate with both hands?

Both men should have inherited this lot before him. Alex could almost hear his father's astonished laughter at finding himself the heir to an English marquisate.

It'd be a lark, aye? Ian would chuckle, nudging their father. *You . . . a marquess. Show them English what a Scot is made of, Da.*

Alex swallowed back the ache in his throat.

The sense of disorientation and nostalgia only increased as grooms led three mounts out of the stable block.

Two of the horses appeared calm enough.

But a groom struggled to tame the third horse—a high-spirited stallion with a glossy chestnut mane that shimmered in the light.

Alex barely suppressed a gasp.

Have I been hurtled through time? Are Da and Ian here then?

But, no . . .

Alex stared at the chestnut stallion as if seeing a long, lost friend. Which, in a way, he supposed he was.

He recognized the sleek lines of the horse's legs, the curve of its haunches, the spring in its step.

This was a McPherson-bred horse. A colt of King Arthur, the prized Thoroughbred stud.

Alex's past rose up to meet him.

Scampering after his father in the early morning mist, pockets bulging with apples for the horses in their stalls.

His father training King Arthur in the main paddock, carefully guiding the high-strung stallion through a series of measured jumps.

The field of pregnant mares on their estate, McPherson Farms, heavy with the next year's colts and fillies. Horses that were prized by wealthy men throughout the country.

And that last ghastly argument with Ian. His brother ripping off his peg leg and throwing it at Alex, cursing the loss of his limb. Alex's pitiless actions and scalding words—the last he'd spoken to his brother and ones he wished more than anything he could take back.

It was savage, this feeling of worlds colliding and intertwining. Alex's senses reeled from the ambush.

Of course, a part of him babbled. *Of course, this would happen.*

Everything else about this experience had been tortuous. Why not resurrect every ghost that haunted him?

Ferndown laughed, a jarring boom of sound. "Ha-ha!"

Lord Frank joined his father. Another guffawing *ha-ha!*

Alex flinched, the noise so unexpected.

He turned to see the gentlemen wreathed in smiles, like naughty schoolboys.

There was *nothing* funny about this situation. Only a pair of heartless bastards would *laugh*—

"You should see your face, Doctor. You've gone pure white." The duke continued to chuckle.

"Scared witless!" Lord Frank joined in. "I'm guessing you are not of a mind to ride Galahad out this morning, then?"

Their smiles faded slightly as Alex continued to regard them in wide-eyed horror, mind scrambling to piece together the bizarre cruelty of the situation.

"Father and I thought to play a bit of a prank, is all. Show you what a real horse looks like," Lord Frank explained, expression still gloating. "I'll have the grooms saddle a more docile hack for you. Galahad can be a bit much."

Alex stared, chest heaving, eyes blinking.

Oh.

They don't know.

They truly, honestly had *no* grasp of the mean-spirited viciousness of their 'prank.'

How could they not know the basic history of Alex's family? That his father had bred the horse before them?

But then, upon further thought . . . why *would* they?

Alex hadn't volunteered the information.

Ferndown and his son were too self-absorbed to ask.

Lord Frank chuckled, as if Alex's pale face were all that he had hoped for.

"Let's get another mount for the doctor, shall we? Galahad isn't for the faint of heart." Ferndown waved toward the stallion. "But he should suit me, I think."

Still chuckling, Lord Frank strode forward and took Galahad's lead from the groom, pulling on the bit and likely bruising the animal's mouth.

The horse reared.

Bloody idiot.

Lord Frank. Not the horse.

Horseman, my arse.

Only a fool would handle a prized stallion like Galahad in such a cavalier manner.

Galahad tossed his head high, tearing the halter out of Lord Frank's hands and nearly pulling the man off his feet. Lord Frank staggered back.

Galahad reared again and then bucked, whirling as if looking for an escape route through the gathered men.

Instinct took over. Alex rushed past the grooms and made the shushing, clicking noise all McPherson horses were trained to respond to from birth.

Galahad instantly paused, backing up, snuffling and whinnying in agitation.

Alex changed the shushing-click to a low whistle . . . the command going from *calm down* to *come here*.

Galahad neighed and trotted to him, obedient as a dog. Alex caught hold of his halter, rubbing his forelock. The horse nudged his chest.

"There now. There's a good lad," Alex crooned a greeting. "I ken who ye are. Ye know who I am, too. Wish I had brought ye a carrot or two."

He continued to scratch Galahad's nose and then patted his neck.

Alex had chosen medicine over horse-breeding years ago.

But he had never stopped loving horses. And seeing Galahad, despite the ambush of painful scenes . . . it was like greeting a long-lost friend.

Given how the horse responded, the feeling was likely mutual.

Rubbing the stallion's withers, he quickly checked the girth and stirrups. Satisfied, he pulled himself up into the saddle, Galahad dancing beneath him. He could feel the tensile strength in the horse's muscles, the power in its hind legs.

The horse felt just like King Arthur.

Memories washed over him again. A thousand moments with his father and that prized stallion.

Clenching his jaw against the tidal surge of emotion, he pivoted the horse with the barest touch. Galahad responded effortlessly.

Bloody hell.

How could he have forgotten the sheer pleasure of riding one of his father's horses?

He whirled Galahad around to face Ferndown and Lord Frank. Their wide eyes and slack jaws were worthy of a Drury Lane play.

"I think Galahad will do just fine," Alex said, words clipped.

He saluted the men and nudged Galahad into a canter.

He could exit through the open gate.

But Galahad was restless, and it was infinitely more enjoyable to urge the stallion to soar easily over the paddock fence.

Leaving Ferndown and Lord Frank to gape after him.

FERNDOWN AND LORD FRANK CAUGHT up with Alex ten minutes later in front of Frome Abbey.

Mr. Warden awaited them there. The steward raked Alex with a disapproving frown on his thin lips before effusively greeting the duke and his son.

The three other men immediately launched into a discussion of the possibility of finding pheasants about in January. Alex listened politely as they set off cross-country toward the home farm.

Given the sullen expression on Lord Frank's face, his lordship was seething over Alex's behavior. Alex allowed Mr. Warden and Lord Frank to ride ahead, hoping some space would help Lord Frank cool his temper.

Ferndown, however, held back his mount, riding alongside Alex.

"You didn't tell us you were a horseman," the duke said. His first words since the paddock.

"Ye didnae ask, Your Grace," Alex replied. "Ye simply saw a doctor and made assumptions."

Any bonhomie he felt toward the older man was long gone. Duke or no, Alex had no intention of dancing to this man's tune.

"No, I didn't." The duke paused, his voice quiet, and then said, "You handle Galahad like a professional."

I am a professional, Alex wanted to say. But to what end?

"What did you say your father did?" the duke asked.

It was on the tip of Alex's tongue to reply, *I didnae.*

Instead, he sighed.

Ferndown was attempting to mend a fence. He was apologizing as much as a duke ever would. The man was being a gentleman and attempting to treat Alex as more of an equal.

Alex could at least be a gentleman in return.

"My father was Mr. Callum Whitaker, late owner of McPherson Farms."

A long pause.

A *weighted* pause.

A pause that said the duke understood much of the implications of the statement.

They rode through the silence of the frosty winter morning. Alex breathed in deeply, the icy air cleansing cobwebs from his lungs. Ahead, Lord Frank and Mr. Warden were motioning toward a thicket of brush. It appeared that Lord Frank thought there might be some pheasants hiding there and was lamenting the lack of a hunting dog at the moment to flush the birds out.

"I heard about that affair with your brother," the duke finally said, voice low. "It was . . . unfortunate."

Unfortunate? That was a mild way of putting it. But life went on.

Alex knew that better than most.

"Yes," he said, "it is all years past now. However, it explains why I was so thrown off in the stable yard. I didnae expect to see one of my father's horses here." Alex leaned down and patted Galahad's neck. "I would know a colt of King Arthur's anywhere. Galahad is the mirror of his sire. Do you own him?"

He dared a glance at Ferndown, rocking easily in his saddle. The duke's side-whiskers were growing frost in the cold air. His Grace appeared intent, as if weighing his next move on the chessboard.

Clearly, the entire Ferndown/Whitaker clan wished Alex gone as ardently as he wished to *be* gone.

"No, Galahad is not mine," Ferndown said, mouth twisting as if the admission cost him. "He was the pride and joy of the late Lord Lockheade."

"Ah. He's part of the estate then? Part of the marquisate?" Some devil likely made Alex say it. To hint that Galahad might be a swaying factor.

Or perhaps it was just the rawness of his senses. That feeling of having been scraped so thin that polite niceties were abruptly beyond his ken.

Lord Frank and the steward had stopped, Lord Frank prevailing on Mr. Warden to act as the hunting dog. The steward had dismounted and was working his way through the brush, clapping his hands and shouting.

Alex and Ferndown stopped to watch the proceedings—the steward stomping through the ice-crusted grass, and Lord Frank, gun in hand, calling directions from horseback.

Ferndown grunted and then turned in his saddle, his own fowling piece held loosely across his pommel.

"As you seem to be a sporting gentleman, let me come straight to the point, Doctor," the duke said, staring at Alex. "Lockheade wanted the marquisate to go to his grandson. To Freddie. It was his dying wish. The last promise he wrung from me."

"You promised him?"

"Yes. I swore him an oath that I would see Freddie inherit. You see . . . I considered Lockheade the best of friends." The duke studied him and then sighed, as if relinquishing a strip of his pride. "Lockheade and I met at Eton as young lads and that was that. There's a reason why our children married. They were thrust together from a very young age, as Lockheade and I lived in one another's pockets over the years. Frank and Margaret's marriage rendered Lockheade and myself family in truth. We both grieved when little Anne died, Frank's oldest daughter." He paused, his eyes looking off. He swallowed and when he continued, his voice was gruff. "And then Lockheade, himself, of course."

He had lost a granddaughter, this man. He had lost his best friend. Moreover, the duke still grieved for them. The black armband peeking out from his greatcoat truly represented mourning.

The knowledge humanized the duke in a way that ruffled Alex's composure.

He wanted to think of Ferndown as one-dimensional—haughty and aristocratic and thoroughly selfish.

But the duke's eyes were those of a man who had suffered much loss over the past few years. And who now faced yet another disaster—losing the estate and title of a dear friend to an unknown upstart.

No wonder the duke and his cronies in the Committee on Privilege were doing everything they could to revoke Alex's right of primogeniture in this instance.

Lord Frank yelled more commands, encouraging Mr. Warden. The steward shouted in return, hands on his hips, finally casting doubt on the likelihood of pheasants in January.

This, of course, simply further motivated Lord Frank to prove everyone wrong.

Alex watched the back-and-forth with pained amusement. Regardless of the unforeseen depths in his father, Lord Frank was the very epitome of spoiled *noblesse oblige*.

Ferndown shook his head.

"I'm not sure where you stand at the moment with the marquisate, Doctor," the duke continued. "But I can sense that you are a fair man. You've chosen a career in medicine, though if McPherson Farms was your family's legacy, I'm guessing you do not need to work. You likely have sufficient funds to live as a gentleman."

Alex sat very still. Ferndown was also more intelligent than he had supposed.

Lord Frank continued to yell orders. Mr. Warden shouted back, finally losing patience with being treated as a hunting dog.

"Give this up." The duke looked at him then, waving a hand toward the fields around them, glittering rainbows of frost. "*Please* give this up. For this family who has known so much loss. For a cousin, the late Lord Lockheade, who you never had the chance to know but who was the very best of men. Please allow this all to stay within our bloodline. I am asking you, one gentleman to another. Please."

Ferndown's expression was open and painfully honest.

Alex took in a long breath.

To use his father's beloved Scottish expression—*wow*.

Wow.

This was close as an English duke would ever come to begging.

"I am prepared to make it worth your while," the duke continued.

"Pardon?" Alex frowned. "Worth my while?"

"Yes. I know the Crown's solicitors prepared a portfolio of the marquisate's holdings for you, so you have seen the wealth on offer. I understand that in letting go of the title, you are releasing a significant source of income. You are, after all, technically the legal heir. I am prepared to offer you the sum of thirty-thousand pounds to quit the field and sign the Writ of Attainder. Thereby, allowing my grandson to inherit this lot." Ferndown shot Alex a wry smile. "If it would sweeten the pot at all, I can also see that Galahad is thrown into the mix."

Alex blinked, positively winded.

Thirty. Thousand. *Pounds.*

It was a king's ransom.

Enough, that when added to his already large reserves, he could live well for the rest of his life. No work needed, should he choose, and without the pressure of a peerage on his shoulders.

Alex didn't require the funds.

But Ferndown was not wrong. Money and Galahad—yes, he would be taking the horse, too—did indeed sweeten the pot.

"Shake hands on it now," Ferndown continued, extending his palm. "Come with us tomorrow to London. We'll have it all settled in a trice. You with your money and us with the signed affidavit saying you will not contest the Writ of Attainder."

It was on the tip of Alex's tongue to agree. To shake hands and give his word as a gentleman.

It was what he wanted, after all.

Everyone won.

But before he could reply or raise his hand, a shout from Lord Frank drew his attention.

A brace of pheasants burst from the brush, badly startling the poor steward who fell backward, arms wind-milling.

Lord Frank swiveled in his saddle, tracking the birds with his gun, not paying attention to Alex and Ferndown who were forty yards behind him.

Lord Frank fired, his aim too close to where Alex sat atop his horse.

Galahad squealed and startled, jumping sideways.

Had that damn idiot just grazed his horse with bird shot?!

That was Alex's first and last thought, as Galahad instantly bucked, then reared, and then took off at a gallop, racing straight for the cover of a clump of trees.

Only Alex's instinctual expertise as a horseman kept him in the saddle.

But as Galahad barreled into the forest, Alex realized that he would have been better off to allow the stallion to throw him.

Skilled horsemanship was useless against the forest itself.

Branches whipped him and tugged at his coat.

A low, wide branch jutted across the path, right at chest height.
Galahad was moving too quickly for Alex to react in time.
In one wrenching motion, Alex was swept clean off Galahad's back.
Alex spun and tumbled before hitting the ground. Hard.
The forest went black.

6

They brought Dr. Whitaker back to Frome Abbey on a litter.

Lottie directed the four footmen carrying each end of two poles up the front stairs. The doctor lay slung between—bloody, battered, and teeth gritted in pain—but alert.

It clutched at her heart.

Of course, rumor had run ahead like wildfire.

It had started with Frank racing into the front hall, calling for the butler and explaining the situation, eyes wild and frantic.

Lottie had caught the words 'Dr. Whitaker' and 'accident' and 'badly hurt' before needing to clutch the banister for support.

Frank disappeared into the study with his father, defending his actions in a loud voice that carried throughout the house.

"How was I to know the doctor would be unseated so easily!" Frank roared.

"You shot toward a man seated on a prized stallion!" the duke roared.

"The horse is fine. Merely a minor wound on his left flank—"

"The horse is the lesser of my concerns here!"

The rest of their conversation was garbled but Ferndown's scathing tone was clear.

Margaret had gone white as a sheet and ensconced herself with Grandmère in the music room—the room closest to the study—listening intently to her husband pleading his case.

The immediate crisis of poor Dr. Whitaker's situation—lying injured on the frosty ground somewhere on the estate with only the steward at his side—had been all but forgotten.

Lottie leapt into action.

Footmen were dispatched to arrange a wagon and litter to bring the doctor back to the abbey. The head groom was ordered to fetch the local veterinarian to tend to Galahad and bind his superficial wounds.

A footman was charged with summoning the local doctor. Lottie had the presence of mind to ask the footman to fetch young Dr. Smithson, rather than the elderly Dr. Graves her late father had preferred. She suspected that Dr. Whitaker would be more likely to trust a younger man, and Dr. Smithson was reputed to be excellent.

But once the immediate hubbub subsided, a strained quiet descended on the house.

A tense waiting.

That was when servants' tongues began wagging.

Dr. Whitaker had gone on a morning ride with the steward, Lord Frank, and the Duke of Ferndown.

Lord Frank had shot at the doctor.

His lordship insisted it was an accident. A miscalculation.

But one footman muttered that Lord Frank was far too experienced a sportsman to make such a mistake. The shot *had* to have been deliberate.

Regardless, the doctor's mount had been peppered with bird shot, panicking the poor animal, and eventually sending Dr. Whitaker tumbling to the ground.

Accident or no, Lord Frank stood to gain a great deal with Alex's death. A marquisate was at stake, a position of immense power and a king's ransom in wealth.

As Lottie heard one maid whisper to another: *Many men would commit murder for such power.*

All Lord Frank had to do was make the incident appear accidental.

The butler was heard asking the housekeeper if there should be an investigation? If the magistrate should be summoned?

The worst part?

Lottie could not swear that Frank had *not* acted maliciously.

Her brother-in-law was desperate for Freddie to inherit the marquisate. He wanted his son to be the beginning of a powerful dynasty. Moreover, as Freddie's father and guardian, Frank would assume control of the marquisate until his son came of age. Frank would have nearly two decades of living with all the trappings of a marquess. He would only lack the title itself.

But would that lead Frank to attempt murder?

Lottie couldn't say.

The only thing she *could* do was that which women had done since time immemorial—wait and hope.

And so, she waited, one hand pressed to her stomach, desperately ordering her nerves to settle.

Before Dr. Smithson arrived, the grooms returned with Dr. Whitaker on the litter, his eyes open and wild. He was bleeding from a cut to his head. His greatcoat and tailcoat were torn and muddy, revealing more scrapes. But worst of all, he hissed loudly with every rock and jolt, as if there were more severe injuries that Lottie could not see.

As no one else was about to advise her, Lottie had them place the doctor in the marquess's bedchamber—the set of rooms that had once belonged to her father.

The room was large and comfortable with an excellent vantage over the surrounding countryside. It also contained the most comfortable bed.

Given how Dr. Whitaker winced and groaned as he was laid upon the feather tick, Lottie feared he might be there for a while. The misery of his situation set her heart to thumping painfully in her chest. She wanted to rush to his side and grasp his hand, lending him what strength she could.

Instead, she ordered the fire built up to roaring proportions and sent a maid to fetch the softest pillows and quilts in the house. She could at least ensure Dr. Whitaker didn't catch a chill in addition to his injuries.

The man lay distressingly still upon the counterpane, eyes closed, breaths shallow, his face drawn and tense.

Dr. Smithson arrived a few moments later.

Lottie greeted him on the upper landing.

"Thank you for coming, Doctor," she said.

"Lady Charlotte," Dr. Smithson bowed, shooting her a small grin. Even in an emergency, he was a capable, cheerful sort. "I only wish that this visit were under more auspicious circumstances. I understand a cousin was injured in a hunting accident?"

Lottie managed a faint smile of her own, leading him toward the bedchamber. "Something of the like."

She motioned for him to precede her into the room.

Dr. Smithson made it three steps toward the bed before swearing loudly and rushing to Dr. Whitaker's side.

"Alex! Alex Whitaker?! Is that you?" Dr. Smithson ran his eyes frantically over Dr. Whitaker's body. "What the hell happened?!"

Dr. Whitaker looked up, eyes bleary as he tried to focus.

"Michael? Of all the luck." He laughed, strained and bewildered. "I havenae seen ye since we graduated. You're here? In Wiltshire?"

"Yes, I took a position near to my family. You're lucky I'm here to tend to you and not the old sawbones the village calls a doctor. What happened?"

Dr. Whitaker winced. "Damned idiot peppered my horse with bird shot. Horse bolted. A low hanging branch swept me to the ground. I hurt everywhere. Cuts. Bruises. Maybe a concussion. But I've definitely broken my left tibia, damn it all. I could practically hear the *crepitus* all the way back to the house."

"Blast." Dr. Smithson set down his bag and set to.

Lottie wondered if she should summon hot water from the kitchen. Or would ice be better?

Regardless, she needed to leave.

She would leave.

She *would*.

But her heart pounded in her chest and her hands shook, and she couldn't walk back into the hall, worrying and wondering.

She needed to know.

Would Dr. Whitaker be all right?

And so she remained stock-still, standing between the fireplace and the bed, watching as Dr. Smithson pulled back Dr. Whitaker's eyelids and studied his pupils intently. The doctor probed the blood on Dr. Whitaker's head, assessing the cut there.

He then unbuttoned Dr. Whitaker's waistcoat and ripped his torn shirt from top to bottom, exposing the doctor's chest.

Lottie jumped at the noise.

Gracious!

She needed to leave. In fact, she ordered her feet to do just that.

But her stubborn legs refused to obey. All of her too riveted to move.

Though leanly built, Dr. Whitaker clearly cared rigorously for his body. His chest was comprised of defined cords of muscle, the sort of which Lottie had only ever seen in paintings.

But in this case, it was anything but art. Blood and scrapes criss-crossed the whole. Moreover, Dr. Whitaker groaned when Dr. Smithson pressed on his ribcage, probing the extent of his injuries.

"You've got a nasty but shallow cut right at your hairline," Dr. Smithson said. "Some bruising and cuts along your left shoulder and arm. Three bruised ribs, but I don't think any are broken. Your pupils are dilating normally. No signs of concussion that I can see."

"Thank my hard head for that."

Dr. Smithson smiled faintly before turning his attention to Dr. Whitaker's lower left leg. He pressed along its length. Dr. Whitaker hissed and cursed.

"I'm concerned about the leg." Dr. Smithson shook his head. "I'm going to have to cut off your fine Hessian boot."

"Lucky I was wearing boots when this happened, honestly." Dr. Whitaker grunted as Dr. Smithson gently lifted and repositioned his left leg. "I reckon the boot prevented the break from coming out my skin. God willing, it provided just enough protection to keep the bone from utterly shattering."

"We'll find out soon enough." Dr. Smithson nodded, his face grim as he retrieved a sharp knife from his bag. "I'll go slow, but it's going to hurt like hell."

Dr. Whitaker touched Dr. Smithson's elbow, drawing his attention.

"Michael, please, ye must promise me." Dr. Whitaker's voice turned hoarse, his eyes glittering in the candlelight. "*Promise* me you'll do everything ye can tae save my leg. I dinnae want it amputated."

The blood drained from Lottie's face.

Had she truly heard that correctly? The doctor's leg might have to be *amputated*?

But—

But . . . what else was to be done if the break were bad enough? The bone would be impossible to set.

She knew this and yet . . .

She hadn't thought that . . .

No!

She pressed a shaking hand to her mouth, abruptly blinking back tears.

"Alex—" Dr. Smithson's voice broke. "I promise I will do my utmost." He rested a comforting hand on his friend's shoulder. "But you and I both know that I may not have a choice. If the break is bad enough . . ."

Dr. Whitaker swallowed, his Adam's apple moving up and down in the low light. He pressed the heels of his hands to his eyes, his throat convulsing over and over as he fought some ghastly internal battle.

Yes. Lottie needed to leave.

She should not be in this room. Not while Dr. Smithson was slowly cutting off the boot. Not while Dr. Whitaker hissed in pain and sweat beaded his brow.

But . . . how could she leave before she knew?

Would they have to amputate his leg? When next she saw Dr. Whitaker, would there only be empty bed linens below his left knee?

Nausea roiled in her stomach. Her heart hurt in her chest. She rubbed the heel of her hand over her breastbone, as if she could somehow soothe it.

Would that she could soothe *him*.

It felt wrong to see Dr. Whitaker so. A weary veteran fighter out of commission, no longer able to assist in the field. He should be tending to others, not requiring healing himself.

And now to possibly face amputation?

Dr. Smithson continued working his knife slowly through the glossy leather.

Dr. Whitaker groaned and bit his lip, his hands grasping the counterpane.

Dr. Smithson paused his cutting. "I can give you something for the pain, Alex. Are you still adverse to whisky or gin?"

"Aye. No spirits."

"Laudanum?"

"Definitely not."

"Are you sure?" Dr. Smithson bent over and looked his friend in the eye. "It would deaden the pain considerably."

Dr. Whitaker set his jaw. "No. I willnae take any. No alcohol. No laudanum. Nothing."

Dr. Smithson shook his head, as if he were well-acquainted with Dr. Whitaker's stubbornness.

Picking up his knife, Dr. Smithson continued to cut through the leather.

To Lottie, it appeared as if Dr. Whitaker were desperate to remain silent through the ordeal. To bear the pain with stoic manliness. He clenched his teeth and set his jaw. But despite Dr. Smithson's slow and careful movements, the agony of it forced out the occasional grunt.

Finally, Dr. Smithson succeeded in removing the boot. He gently untied the garter, and then gently rolled off Dr. Whitaker's woolen stocking.

The doctor's calf appeared, white and covered with sparse hair. Even from her vantage point, Lottie could see the sharp musculature of his leg, the purple bruising rising.

More to the point, the right side of his calf bulged unnaturally.

The sign of a serious break indeed.

Oh no.

Dr. Smithson gently probed the injured leg, feeling along the bone.

Dr. Whitaker groaned, back arching in pain, the heels of his hands pressed into his eye sockets once again.

Lottie held her breath.

Please, she pleaded.

Please let the break be clean. Please allow him to keep his leg.

Dr. Smithson continued his examination, hands running down the injured leg.

His shoulders sagged and he leaned forward, tugging Dr. Whitaker's hand from his face.

"You can breathe, Alex. The break appears clean," Dr. Smithson said, a smile in his voice. "I'm not feeling any other fragments. It merely needs to be set."

Dr. Whitaker's chest heaved, as if he had run up a steep hill. "Thank heaven," he rasped.

Relief washed over Lottie, a pure and buoyant wave.

"Could you fetch some warm water?" Dr. Smithson flicked a hand in Lottie's direction without looking up. "I'm also going to need yards of strong muslin and several straight boards to wrap the leg once I set it."

Lottie nodded, walking to the bell-pull near the fireplace.

Dr. Smithson finally turned toward her.

"Lady Charlotte!" His eyes flew wide, voice rising a solid octave. "I didn't realize it was you here."

Dr. Whitaker raised his head, staring at her. His torn shirt slipped, revealing even more of his chest, drawing Lottie's eye downward.

She froze like a simpleton before the fireplace, one hand outstretched toward the servants' bell-pull.

"Ye shouldnae be here, lass," he gasped.

Her eyes flew to his. They were stormy and glazed, as if he were being held together by sheer grit.

"Please, this is no place for a gently-bred woman, Lady Charlotte." Dr. Smithson pointed toward the door. "Go fetch the housekeeper and a strong footman to assist me."

Lottie froze in place, unable to look away from Dr. Whitaker's tormented gaze.

"Go. Please." Dr. Whitaker slumped back, pressing his hands again to his eyes. "I didnae want ye here when Michael sets this leg."

Lottie flinched and lurched into action, leaving the room in a rustle of skirts.

She was halfway down the stairs when Dr. Whitaker's choked cry of agony reached her.

"YOU NEED TO TAKE SOME laudanum, Alex." Michael Smithson hunched over Alex's left leg, tying off the splint. "Your head injury is minor, thank goodness. The rest of your scrapes are superficial. You've the beginnings of a mild fever, which is to be expected when the body endures such a shock. But neither of us wants to see that fever strengthen and infection to set in. This means lying impossibly still, so as to not disturb your leg. But in order to do that, we must alleviate your pain."

Alex drew in a slow breath, tamping down the panic he could feel inching in.

His leg might not need to be amputated.

The bone was set. A splint had been applied. A footman had brought in a fracture box for the leg to rest in as it healed. The pain had gone from sharp and excruciating to dull and throbbing.

The worst was over.

Perhaps.

He was terrified to tempt Fate at this point.

Every time he thought his visit to Frome Abbey could not get any worse, reality managed to surprise him.

So . . . maybe he should just be grateful to be alive.

But at the moment, it was hard to see any silver linings.

No, he took that back.

There was *one* enormous blessing in all this.

He looked at his friend.

"Thank you," Alex murmured, ignoring the advice about laudanum. "Thank the Lord on High it was *you* who arrived today."

"Aye," Michael chuckled, a dry, mirthless sound. "If they had summoned Dr. Hatch, my older colleague in these parts, he would have taken your leg clean off by now."

Alex shuddered and fought against panic in earnest.

A broken leg was an unknown quantity. The bone could heal beautifully well and be as good as new. Or infection could set in, causing the leg to gangrene. The only way to save a patient's life at that point was to amputate the infected leg and pray the patient survived. The worse the break, the more likely the injury would become infected.

Consequently, many older doctors felt that amputation was the best solution for any significant break. Why risk a life-ending infection?

In an instant, Ian's leg swam before his vision, a bloody mass of mangled flesh—

Alex took in another slow breath, desperate to quell the acidic terror he could taste in the back of his throat.

But his injury was too eerily similar to his brother's. Alex wanted to laugh at the cruel irony. Worse, how was he to suppress the memory of Ian thrashing in agony—

Don't think on it.

Don't think about all that could go wrong.

But it was no use. More memories forced their way in, pushing past thoughts of Ian.

A coachman screaming as Alex amputated his infected leg, McNeal holding the man down.

A little girl drawing her last breath, skin gray and bloated, because infection from her broken arm had spread throughout her wee body.

And Ian himself, screaming and screaming, blood everywhere, Alex's hand shaking so badly he had to leave another doctor to perform the amputation—

"Stop!" Michael's sharp voice cut through Alex's thoughts. "Stop it. Stop this instant! I can practically see the gears in your head, working through every worst-case scenario."

Alex ran a hand over his face, not surprised to realize he was shaking. He took in gulping breaths of air.

Shock? Nerves?

He couldn't say.

Michael grabbed Alex's hand, holding it fast.

"Enough, Alex! You must stem these thoughts. For your very sanity, you must. We both know that the bone-healing business is a risky gamble at best. But your break is clean. The bone didn't shatter. Between you and me, you are in the best of hands. If anyone can get this bone to heal straight and strong without infection setting in, it will be us."

Alex swallowed, chest heaving.

Michael was right.

Alex knew this.

But his thoughts held a fuzzy quality, as if the trauma and stress of the day had stuffed his head with cotton.

He opened his eyes and met his friend's intense gaze. Michael released Alex's hand and sat down on a stool beside the bed, scrubbing his hands through his hair.

"I had no idea you were a relation to Lord Lockheade," the doctor said after a moment. "I'm still trying to understand how you are here. I thought your family raised horses in Scotland."

Ian's face rose again in Alex's memory. The agony of his screams. Alex's hoarse sobs. King Arthur's whinnying in distress—

Stop it. Don't dwell on it.

Alex swallowed, gritting his teeth. "They did. But I'm a distant descendant of Lockheade. My father's family renounced their English relations generations ago."

"Wait." Michael's head went back. "Are you telling me you're *that* Scottish relation? The new heir?" The doctor's voice climbed with each word, eyes wide.

"Aye." Alex was too tired to gauge if his friend was shocked or horrified. "Unless my blasted relatives finish me off first." He flicked his hand, indicating his bandaged leg.

"Lord Frank was rather distraught when I arrived."

"As well he should be." Alex snorted. "Damned idiot could have killed me."

Michael shook his head, as if tossing away some thought. His eyes focused on Alex's clenched fists resting on the counterpane.

Silence hung. The fire popped.

The scent of Lady Charlotte's jasmine perfume lingered, mixing with the woodsmoke.

She had been here.

Alex *hated* that she had seen him like this, bloody and utterly shaken.

No matter his opinion on his Whitaker relatives, the marquisate, or the aristocracy, no man wanted a bonnie lass to witness him groaning in agony.

Alex's leg had settled into a humming sort of pain. It came in waves, radiating up his thigh. It tensed the muscles in his chest and made his neck tight.

"Alex," Michael wrapped a warm hand around Alex's forearm to draw his attention. "I understand why you are loath to take laudanum. We all know its effects when used indiscriminately. We've both seen, first-hand, the horrors of an opium eater. But, my friend, the pain is making everything worse. You are too tense to relax properly. Soon, the pain will set you to moving in a sort of restless helplessness. Your body will twist and turn trying to find a way to soothe the agony. This will, in turn, jostle your fracture, perhaps jarring loose chips of bone that will lead to infection. To have any chance at recovering completely, you *must* remain absolutely still."

Alex released a slow breath, willing his muscles to relax.

It wasn't working well.

Laudanum.

The last indignity this day had needed.

His eyes stung.

Damn and blast!

Was he . . .

Was he going to *weep*?!

He placed a hand over his eyes, hating the wetness there, but helpless to stop the telltale signs of a good *greit* coming on.

He swallowed convulsively.

It was just . . .

First, this mess with the marquisate.

Second, . . . Galahad and all the haunting memories—both happy and tragic—that accompanied thoughts of his family.

Then, the accident and his injury—the unknown terror of a broken leg. The horror of his life being turned upside down in one horrifying instant.

The lovely lass *watching* him suffer. Witnessing him laid so low.

And now . . . *this*.

Bloody hell, I truly am going tae end up just like Ian.

I cannae end up like Ian.

No.

Anything but this—

He couldn't take laudanum. He simply . . . *couldn't*.

His fear of the drug was too great. His loathing and dread too strong.

He had promised himself, over his brother's lifeless body. . . Ian's eyes staring sightlessly upward—

"Look, Alex," his friend murmured quietly, "I heard enough about what happened with your brother."

Alex tensed at Michael's words, as if his friend were reading his mind. Though why Alex should be surprised, he didn't know.

Everyone knew what had happened to Ian.

The story had landed in the broadsheets, for heaven's sake. The Whitaker family's worst nightmare and deepest pain prettily packaged for public consumption. Just remembering it rendered Alex light-headed and nauseous.

"So knowing that situation," Michael continued, "I understand why you are reluctant to take laudanum. The choice is yours, obviously. But I must say two things. One, I do not think you will need to take laudanum for very long. Several days, maybe a week at most. Just long enough for the worst of the pain and swelling to subside, to ensure that your mild fever remains mild, for the bone to begin to knit. Not so long that it will become an uncontrollable habit. Second, without the laudanum, we both know that the pain will make it difficult for you to remain motionless during these first critical days. We both want that bone to set straight and true. There is also a risk that bits of bone have embedded in the leg tissue and that can lead to infection. But both problems can be mitigated if you remain perfectly still for at least the first week. Alex, I don't want to amputate your leg any more than you wish it gone."

Alex let Michael's words wash over him, dripping through his thoughts like the tears running down his temples to the pillow below.

Air left his lungs in great gusting gasps.

The worst part?

Michael was *right*.

Every word he spoke was absolutely correct.

Alex would recommend the same course of action for his own patient.

It was the *only* way.

The only guaranteed path to ensure the leg healed perfectly.

He closed his eyes and pushed thoughts of Ian back, back, back into the recesses of his mind.

He could do this.

He could.

He would.

And so, taking one last gasping breath, Alex wiped his tears away and took Shakespeare's advice:

He screwed his courage to the sticking place and nodded.

Dr. Whitaker cannot be moved for at least two months while his leg heals. That is the opinion of Dr. Smithson." Ferndown scowled from where he stood beside the drawing room mantel. "Therefore, he must remain here at Frome Abbey."

Lottie pinched her lips and cuddled Freddie closer, ignoring the flip in her chest.

Of course, the doctor could not be moved. But how terrible for him to be gravely injured in enemy territory, so to speak. To be so far away from friends and family.

Evening had fallen long ago. The uproar in the house had settled, and Lord Nettlesby had (blessedly, thankfully) departed for London.

Ferndown had called the family together. Margaret and Frank sat side-by-side on the sofa, Margaret winding a handkerchief round and round her fingers and Frank sipping his third glass of brandy. Grand-mère was in a wingback chair opposite them, embroidering steadily in the candlelight, reading glasses perched upon her nose, as if this were any other family evening.

For her part, Lottie sat in a chair in one corner cradling a sleeping Freddie, listening intently but knowing her opinion would not be called upon. She doubted Ferndown or Frank even realized she was in the room.

She was, as ever, visibly invisible. A pretty face to be admired but never a voice to be heard. She pressed a kiss to Freddie's head, glad of the comforting weight of his small body.

Freddie's bed routine was invariably lengthy, involving both his mother's and Lottie's presence, if possible. First, he had to collect all the soft sock animals Lottie had made for him over the years. She knitted them into fanciful shapes—a sheep, a monkey—and then stuffed them with wool. Once all the animals had been assembled, Lottie cuddled him while Margaret told him a story. If Lottie attempted to leave the nursery before he fell asleep, Freddie would reach for her with a pouting, "Tottie stay!"

But tonight, Lottie had wanted to hear what was being discussed in the drawing room. Freddie refused to stay with his nurse and allow her to put him to bed. And so they had compromised, Lottie rocking Freddie to sleep in a drawing room chair.

Lottie had risked censure and peeked into Dr. Whitaker's bedchamber as she went to the nursery to fetch Freddie. Some part of her was compelled to see how the doctor fared.

Dr. Whitaker lay motionless on the bed, his left leg in a box, cradled in a sling of leather straps. He slept, breaths rising in shallow bursts, skin pale and drawn in the flickering firelight. Even injured and sleeping, he radiated a sort of masculine intensity. The taut tendons in his neck. The acute angle of his jaw.

Dr. Smithson had advised them to give Dr. Whitaker laudanum, twenty drops every six hours. They were to allow the laudanum to wear off enough for Dr. Whitaker to eat and drink each meal. Then he was to be dosed again.

"He might fight it," Dr. Smithson had warned, "but he needs to rest quietly and pain-free for the next several days. At that point, we will hopefully have a better understanding of how his leg will heal. But if his current fever worsens, summon me immediately."

Even now, that same tightness banded her chest.

Worry, she supposed, that Dr. Whitaker would not heal properly from his injuries. That the threat of amputation still loomed large.

Fear that the doctor would decide to fight the attainder as retribution for Frank's careless actions.

Lottie pressed another kiss to Freddie's curls.

Ferndown paced before the drawing room fire.

"This is a most unfortunate turn of events." The duke pinched the bridge of his nose, shaking his head. "Dr. Whitaker was close to agreeing to sign the Writ of Attainder, I'm sure of it. Now, however, it will be several months before he can travel to London to sign the necessary documents."

Frank snorted. "Bit of a fool to get himself hurt—"

"Silence!" Ferndown scowled at his son. "'Tis your idiotic actions that landed us in this mess. You call yourself a Corinthian, and yet you were still so feather-brained as to fire toward the horses?"

It was a testament to Ferndown's displeasure that he scolded his son in front of the ladies. Frank surely felt the censure, sinking lower in his seat and knocking back the rest of his brandy. He would likely be falling-down drunk within the hour.

"The gossips . . . they will be brutal," Grandmère said, voice decidedly matter-of-fact, not bothering to raise her eyes. "They will say you tried to kill the doctor."

Her French accent stretched out the vowels—*keeel ze docteur.*

"Grandmère!" Margaret gasped.

"'Tis true, *ma petite.* They will not be kind." Grandmère raised her head and flicked her censorious eyebrows upward. "We have too much to gain from the doctor's death. It is like you English say—all is fair in love and war. We fight *une guerre* for the *marquisat.*"

Grandmère went back to stitching bright bluebells as if she were discussing weather with the vicar.

But then, her grandmother had a flair for Gallic *sang-froid.*

Lottie supposed once one had witnessed friends and family being sent to the guillotine, nothing else seemed quite as dire.

"Unfortunately, you have the right of it, my lady." Ferndown tossed back his own drink. "Once the Committee on Privilege learns the specifics of this incident, they might be swayed to side with Dr. Whitaker on principle alone—"

"It was an accident!" Frank scowled. "An honest accident!"

"But not everyone will see it that way, Frank." Margaret's hand clenched tightly around her handkerchief. "Grandmère is right. The gossip will be vicious."

Ferndown nodded. "Agreed, my lady. We must leave for London tomorrow. Frank, you have a meeting with the Committee on Privilege, and the King demands my presence. Margaret and Freddie will accompany us, of course. Oh . . . and Lady Charlotte, too," the duke replied, flicking a look toward Lottie as if only just remembering her.

Lottie gave a wan smile, swallowing. She did not particularly wish to go to London, even with Margaret and Freddie there. The thought of shedding her mourning colors and being escorted around Town . . .

"But surely Grandmère cannot be left to deal with Dr. Whitaker alone?" Margaret's brow drew down in concern. "That is asking much of her."

Grandmère raised one critical eyebrow. "I assure you, Margaret, I am more than capable of directing servants to care for the doctor—"

"Yes, but the servants may not know what is best. *We* need to be seen as caring for the doctor." Margaret twisted her handkerchief. "I should likely stay here with you."

"Nonsense, Margaret." Frank shook his head. "I need you in London to help quiet these gossips you insist will plague us."

"But, Frank—"

"I will care for him." The words were out of Lottie's mouth before she had even consciously thought them.

Every head turned her way.

Again, as if surprised to find Lottie still in the room.

Heavens, was she truly so invisible?

"Let me remain here," Lottie continued. "My absence will not be noted in London, and I can see to the care of Dr. Whitaker."

Silence greeted her words. As if the occupants of the room were startled that Lottie would yet, once more, have tossed her opinions into the middle of a family gathering. Freddie stirred in Lottie's arms.

"I like this idea," Grandmère nodded.

Margaret's distress increased. "We cannot possibly leave Lottie here. She is needed with us. Besides, she cannot be alone with Dr. Whitaker. It would not be proper."

Ferndown turned the full weight of his gaze on Lottie. "I admit to some reservations, as well—"

"Bah!" Grandmère waved her hand. "It is an excellent solution, Your Grace. I like it very much. Leave Charlotte to oversee the care of the wounded doctor. She is most capable. Besides, the doctor is a cousin—he *is* family—therefore Charlotte's reputation will be safe, particularly with myself in residence to act as chaperone. No one will consider it *de trop*."

Margaret bit her lip as if wishing to argue.

"I am most capable," Lottie rushed to say. In all truth, the more she pondered the idea, the more she liked it. "And Grandmère and I can join you all in London once the doctor is well enough to travel." She scrambled, reaching for more reasons. "Even better, I can speak with Dr. Whitaker about committing to sign the Writ of Attainder once he is well enough to travel."

More silence greeted her.

Frank snorted.

Ferndown sighed, rubbing a hand over his side whiskers.

Margaret continued to wring her handkerchief, clearly wanting to argue but not sure if it was wise.

Only Grandmère stitched away, unconcerned.

"You have volunteered, Lady Charlotte." Ferndown fixed Lottie his ducal stare. "But this is a heavy task for anyone, much less a young lady. We need Dr. Whitaker to agree to the Writ of Attainder."

Lottie swallowed, pulling Freddie's sleeping body closer. "I will see it through. I will fight for Freddie to receive his rightful inheritance."

"*Familae primum semper cognosce*," Frank murmured, eyeing his empty glass.

"Precisely." Lottie met her brother-in-law's gaze. "I will always put the needs of our family first."

"Like you did during the reading of Lockheade's will?" Frank's eyes sparked in the dim light.

Lottie flinched.

Ferndown looked between them, gaze dark and inscrutable.

"*Familae primum semper cognosce,*" the duke repeated the motto. "See what you can do to convince the doctor, Lady Charlotte. We will depend upon you."

"I'M SORRY FRANK WAS SO unbearably rude to you this evening," Margaret murmured.

Lottie stroked Freddie's soft curls. She and Margaret were nestled into Freddie's bed, his small body cuddled between them. This had been their way from that first afternoon after his birth—Lottie to one side, Margaret to the other, and Freddie snuggled between.

It was a place of comfort for Lottie. Where she and Margaret had cried their tears for Anne, then Gabriel, and finally Papa. Whenever she was sad or lonely, a long cuddle with Freddie soothed her soul.

"You know Frank is a good man. Truly, he is," Margaret continued, pressing a kiss to her son's sleeping head. "It's merely that this situation has rendered us all tense and more unkind than we should be."

Lottie knew that to be true, but Frank had never been one to mince words.

His opinions usually came out unfiltered and raw, leaving his wife to mellow their sting. Margaret spent far too much time mopping up behind her husband's thoughtlessness.

"Think nothing of it. I understand," Lottie replied because she *did* understand the fear and worry facing them all.

They rested in silence for a moment, the three of them nearly breathing in unison as a single living organism. Lottie adored this sense of closeness, of being cocooned with those she loved best.

Coal settled in the grate, sending warm light through the dim room.

"Will you be all right here?" Margaret asked. "You and Grandmère?"

"Of course. You know I don't love London." Lottie continued to run her fingers through Freddie's hair. Thank goodness he was a sound sleeper.

"Yes, but this will be our first Season in two years. I was looking forward to chaperoning you around Town again. I sense that you are not terribly partial to Lord Nettlesby, but he is not all bad."

Lottie smiled. Margaret was not subtle in her wish for Lottie to marry.

But how to let her sister down gently? "Nettlesby is a little too hunting-mad for my taste."

And too idiotic and too vain and too apt to view Lottie as a prized pig at a village fair.

She declined to add those bits.

Though given how Margaret grimaced—her face a ripple of shadow in the dim light—Lottie guessed her sister already knew.

"We will find you someone else then when you arrive in London," her sister promised. "A paragon of a gentleman who will adore you and fill the rest of your life with endless happiness."

"I would welcome such a man." Lottie chuckled.

Freddie snuffled in his sleep, tucking into a ball and burrowing into Lottie's chest.

Margaret stroked her son's cheek. "Just promise me that the man will not be Dr. Whitaker."

"Gracious, Margaret," Lottie huffed in surprise. "My loyalties are with you and Freddie. Remember, I am the collie of the family."

Margaret laughed, soft and low. "Gabriel always said you had the loveliest loyal heart."

"Precisely. I will not give my loyal heart to the doctor. Instead, I shall see the man recovered and then I will rush to join you in London. And until then, you and I will write often."

"Letters every day," Margaret promised.

Firelight flickered through the room, wrapping them in warmth. Lottie closed her eyes, breathing in the scents of her sister's floral perfume and Freddie's little-boy stickiness.

Margaret's voice reached her just before she drifted into sleep. "Protect my Freddie's future. Promise me, Lottie."

"Always," Lottie whispered in return, yawning. "Always."

8

H er family left mid-morning.

Lottie watched them hurry from the house to the waiting carriage—Margaret swathed in a voluminous cloak, a nurse scurrying behind carrying Freddie. Ferndown and Frank followed in heavy Garrick coats, a dusting of snow swirling about their boots. The carriage horses' breath drifted white clouds into the winter air.

Margaret turned before stepping into the traveling coach, making eye contact with Lottie who stood before the long gallery window. Lottie could practically *feel* her sister willing Lottie to protect Freddie's inheritance. To fight for their father's wished-for legacy.

Lottie raised a hand in goodbye, letting that simple action convey her commitment.

She would ensure that Dr. Whitaker healed.

She would do what she could to convince him that he did not, indeed, wish to assume the title of Lord Lockheade. How she was to accomplish this . . . she had no idea. But surely something would occur to her.

Margaret smiled in parting and climbed into the carriage, the nurse and men following. A footman slid hot bricks in after them to provide warmth. Lottie did not envy them the cold journey to London.

She watched until the carriage disappeared into the fir trees lining the lane.

Grandmère was still abed. Her grandmother held a Parisian attitude toward mornings—they were to be slept through or, if she chose to awake before noon, experienced in bed with a pot of chocolate and a bundle of letters from her vast circle of intellectual friends.

In short, Grandmère would not leave her chambers before luncheon.

Which left Lottie with a Scottish physician to attend.

Well, she supposed she needn't do much for Dr. Whitaker.

He was asleep, last she had asked. He had awakened earlier, eaten a bit, and then drunk down another dose of laudanum. A maid had been assigned to sit in the room, darning socks and mending clothing, keeping watch as the doctor slept.

Lottie was not needed there.

Her goal was to keep the man comfortable and healing but not keen to take up residence. Hovering and caring would be anathema to this.

She *knew* that.

And yet . . . her feet seemed incapable of taking her anywhere else in the house.

It was just . . .

Dr. Whitaker was . . . interesting.

There.

She admitted as much to herself.

He was so very different from primped dandies who swore by champagne to shine their boots. Or bucks who loudly recounted a recent carriage race. Self-important men like Nettlesby who saw Lottie as another potential accessory for their lives. A bauble to be collected.

Despite the brevity of their acquaintance, Lottie sensed Dr. Whitaker saw her as a person, unique and valued beyond her pretty face. After all, people lived or died at his hand. He *had* to see each one as an individual.

How would the marquisate fare were a man such as Dr. Whitaker at the helm? A man who had been trained to notice and heal?

Was it like Ferndown and Lord Frank claimed? That only those born and tutored in the peerage could effectively govern it?

Or did a man's innate character and competence matter more?

Logic told her that the latter was the weightier factor.

She sighed.

Such thoughts were at complete odds to her mission and goals; therefore, she would be wise to banish them.

Focus on Freddie.

Even knowing that, her feet led her up the stairs and into the main bedchamber where Dr. Whitaker lay.

Stepping into his darkened room felt a little like sneaking into a dragon's lair, the sort from a child's fairy tale. The thrilling sense of lurking danger—of reaching for something forbidden and potentially dangerous, but oh-so-alluring, it was nigh impossible to resist.

The drawn window curtains, red velvet bed-hangings, and golden lap of the dancing fire in the hearth did nothing to dispel her fanciful thoughts. The room was awash in blood red and flickering flame.

Lottie crossed to the enormous poster bed, motioning for the maid to stay seated. The girl nodded and went back to her mending.

Dr. Whitaker was still sleeping. His dark lashes were curved crescent moons above his cheekbones. His foot poked out of the blankets, splinted and elevated, carefully resting in its bone box sling.

His chest rose and fell, lifting the counterpane with each breath. He had been changed into a night shirt, the neck loose and open. Lottie could not stop herself from staring at the bit of chest exposed there. The curve of a muscle. The sparse sprinkling of hair. The image rose of that same chest, bare and arcing in pain.

It all felt piercingly intimate.

She remembered the steel-eyed man she had dined with just two days past. The man who had listened to her and defended her so forthrightly.

She sensed that Dr. Whitaker would not be pleased to know she had seen him like this—comatose and helpless. But he *was* a cousin, as Grandmère had said. There was no great impropriety in Lottie being here, particularly with the maid present.

Was his face less drawn, less pale than the night before?

It was hard to say.

She placed a hand on his forehead. He was warm. Not alarmingly so, but his mild fever remained.

Lottie frowned and sat beside his bed.

Perhaps . . .

Perhaps, she would keep the maid company.

LOTTIE SPENT THE NEXT THREE days at Dr. Whitaker's bedside.

Honestly, what else was she to do, aside from expire of boredom?

It was January. In rural Wiltshire.

Social engagements were thin on the ground. Besides, she could hardly call upon neighbors without Grandmère. And Grandmère rarely left her rooms, except to complain about the cold weather and lack of company.

Moreover, the doctor's bedchamber was by far the warmest place in the house at the moment. Lottie was simply being economical.

Hour after hour, she sat at Dr. Whitaker's bedside.

In keeping with the fey feeling of the room, she had retrieved Grandmère's well-loved copy of *Contes Nouveaux ou Les Fées à la Mode*—or in English, *New Tales, or Fairies in Fashion*.

There were plenty of weightier tomes she could be reading, but the book was a long-time favorite and one she knew the maid would enjoy. And, as it featured tales of fantastical creatures in outlandish settings, Lottie deemed it fitting for the circumstances.

She began with the story of *Finette Cendron*, an earlier version of the English Cinderella, reading it aloud, translating from French as she went. The maid gasped and sighed in all the correct places, offering commentary about the horridness of Cendron's wicked sisters and the romance of the prince searching for his lost Cendron.

Dr. Whitaker, of course, slept through it all. To be sure, he stirred from time to time, but it was only to open his gray eyes and look at her, unfocused and bleary. He ate little, the laudanum sapping his appetite. His mild fever remained, neither worsening nor improving.

It was oddly captivating to watch him sleep. As a gently-reared young woman, Lottie had scarcely ever witnessed a man in slumber. Only her father snoozing in the library or Gabriel napping on the drawing room sofa.

But even though the doctor was a cousin, it was nothing alike.

She felt like a cartographer, mapping the planes of Dr. Whitaker's face—noting the fluttering movements of his eyes behind his closed lids, the twitch of his mouth, the occasional murmured word.

She could watch him for hours.

Heavens, she *did* watch him for hours as she read.

Dr. Smithson called and declared that all was going as well as could be hoped. Lottie left the room as he and a footman changed Dr. Whitaker's bandages and saw to his needs. There was no sign of infection—the mild fever being a signal that his body was healing. Both good developments. Dr. Whitaker simply needed to eat to keep his strength up and continue to take laudanum for another couple of days.

After Dr. Smithson left, Lottie moved from Cendron to *Le Serpentin Vert* or *The Green Dragon*. Fitting, she supposed, to read about a cursed dragon while tending to a wounded one.

Not that Dr. Whitaker would ever realize that fact.

The Green Dragon was a lengthy tale, vaguely similar to Sleeping Beauty but with all the various bits of the story mixed up. In this version, the princess, Laidronette, was cursed with ugliness. She eventually meets a green dragon with fiery eyes who invites her into his home, and they fall in love. The dragon is, of course, a prince in disguise who sees beyond Laidronette's cursed ugliness to the beauty inside.

On the third day, Lottie was reading of Laidronette's woes when Dr. Whitaker wearily opened his eyes.

The bedchamber was still cave-like, the shutters shut and the heavy drapes drawn to keep out the frosty January winds. A fire roared in the hearth, casting the room in red-gold shadows. Candles flickered on the bedside tables.

Dr. Whitaker blinked slowly, as if the weight of the laudanum was impossibly heavy, but he was determined to fight it. She pressed a hand to his brow and was relieved to note that his small fever had abated almost entirely. This was good news. Assuming he would be hungry, Lottie sent the maid from the room to fetch a supper tray.

Dr. Whitaker turned toward the movement of the maid leaving, his eyes at half-mast.

He had been like this each time he stirred—awake but . . . not. As if the animal within him held sway and Dr. Whitaker himself were still asleep.

"Betty has gone to fetch some food, Dr. Whitaker," Lottie said, knowing that he likely was not quite aware enough to reply but feeling the need to be informative.

She had been watching him breathe for three days, after all. They were past the point of polite greetings and inquiries after the weather.

She met his bleary gaze. As she had done repeatedly over the past several days, Lottie found her eyes tracing his features.

His face was lean planes, almost too sharp for typical handsomeness. His brown hair, normally ruthlessly straight, was more tattered-scarecrow at the moment than elegant-gentleman-about-town.

He had a small scar near his left temple. More scars crisscrossed his hands, thin white lines here and there which testified to a life of physical labor.

She had so many questions. How had he come by those scars? Why did he dislike laudanum so vehemently, as he had said to Dr. Smithson?

Lottie set aside her book and rose.

"You've had a long sleep, Dr. Whitaker," she said, moving to stir the fire.

As with the maid, his gaze followed her as she crossed the room, his eyes glittering in the low light.

Fiery eyes.

Primordial eyes.

He tracked her as she poked at the coals. As she pulled the counterpane taut. As she ensured that his leg was secure in the bone box.

The weight of his unyielding gaze rattled her nerves and sent sensation skittering across her skin. As if he were the hunter and she, his quarry.

Finally, she had enough. She paused at the foot of the bed, meeting his stare with one of her own.

Something about the looming shadows and the sense that he was only partially awake emboldened her tongue.

"I see you watching me," she said, notching her chin. "You think to scare me, peering out with your sleepy dragon eyes. It won't work. I am made of sterner stuff, you know."

He simply studied her in return.

Of course.

That's what a dragon did, was it not? Prowled and waited for the best moment to strike and devour its prey.

Lottie disliked the sense of being prey.

She certainly should not be thinking about Dr. Whitaker devouring her. The thought was abruptly more alluring than alarming and that, well, truly terrified her.

She shook her head.

His mouth opened, as if he would speak, but nothing came out.

Frowning, she noted that his lips were cracked and dry. Was his throat similarly parched?

How neglectful of her. Dragon or no . . . Lottie was here to act as nurse.

She filled a glass from a pitcher on the bedside table.

"Here." She held the tumbler under his nose. He shied away. "It's just water. Not laudanum."

His eyes moved to her, gaze still hazy. There was none of that razor-like steel in them. Only a glittery lurking, the doctor's iron will laudanum-drunk and sleeping.

He was ignoring the water, but he needed to drink. Dr. Smithson had been most firm on that point.

"You must drink," she murmured.

She hesitated and then slid her hand under his head, the silk of his hair threading through her fingers. Leaning over, she lifted his head, encouraging him to drink from the glass.

He gave one tentative sip, tasted that the liquid was indeed just water, and greedily drank the lot.

Lottie watched as he swallowed, her head so close to his she could see the pores in his skin and feel the rasp of his whiskers against her fingers holding the glass.

How could such a small act be so intimate?

As he finished drinking, his gaze flicked to hers, his expression soft and malleable. The look of a man deep in his cups.

Abruptly, the lack of space between them sent alarm bells ringing.

She was close.

Too close.

She could count his eyelashes and see the faint streaks of lighter gray in his eyes. Her hand all but clutched his head in a lover's caress, as if she were about to bend and kiss him.

Their eyes locked for one heartbeat.

A single joint breath.

In. Out.

Lottie lurched upright, shattering the spell. She slid her palm out of his hair and turned to set down the water glass on the bedside table.

She likely should leave this room. The situation was rapidly overtaking her good sense—

His hand snared her wrist, engulfing it entirely. The abrupt contact burned, a manacle of hot iron.

Lottie bit her lip and darted a look down at her tethered hand before raising her gaze back to his.

He studied her more intently now. His mouth moved, murmuring.

"What is it?" she asked.

He tugged on her wrist, as if coaxing her closer.

Swallowing, Lottie leaned, turning her ear toward him.

"'Tis a lie," he whispered.

Lottie blinked, righting herself.

She blinked again.

Surely she had heard him wrong.

"Pardon?"

"'Tis a lie," he repeated and then took in a deep breath, those glittering eyes still hazily focused on her. "It makes me verra angry."

So . . . she *had* heard him correctly. It was just . . .

What . . . what a strange sentence.

Perhaps he was less aware than she had presumed.

"What makes you angry?" she asked.

His eyes closed for a moment, and she nearly thought him asleep again. But his hand wrapped around her wrist didn't slack.

He shook his head, rocking to and fro on the pillow.

"Ye say the princess is ugly, but that is a lie," his voice rasped, creaky from days of disuse. "The princess is . . . *beautiful.*"

He opened his eyes and fixed her with such a . . . *look.*

Haunted—

No . . . *yearning.*

"So. Beautiful," he repeated.

Lottie's brow drew down, down, down.

The man must be addled still.

"The princess in the story?" He remembered her reading?

"Aye." His squeezed her wrist where he held her, the delicious weight singeing her nerves and sending shooting darts up her arm. "Ye . . . called me . . . dragon. But ye . . . princess . . . *you* are beautiful . . . and it makes me angry."

Lottie nearly laughed in shock, his words startled her so.

He *had* heard her reading. And he thought her to be a princess?

More to the point, Dr. Whitaker considered her beautiful?

That seemed . . . uncharacteristic.

Not that she presumed to know Dr. Whitaker's preferences on feminine beauty. But he did not seem the sort for tender, soft emotions . . . for flattering a lady and openly admiring her beauty. The very idea sent her thoughts spinning into a knot.

She had assumed he saw beyond her face, that he did not consider her physical charms to be the sum total of her value.

Had she been wrong? Was this proof that Dr. Whitaker was as human as any other man?

Moreover—

"My *beauty* makes you . . . angry?" she managed to stammer.

Why was her *attractiveness* a source of anger? Was Dr. Whitaker possibly the sort of man who protected his heart by decrying feminine beauty? That seemed equally unlikely, as such an attitude did not conform to the confident, sensible man he appeared to be.

In short, his current words made no sense whatsoever.

"Aye. It's no' fair. I cannae stop watching ye. My eyes willnae obey me. They watch and want and I *hate* it." He emphasized the word *hate* with an almost comedic helplessness. "I dinnae want tae find any part of this beautiful." He stared at her again, eyes slowly blinking, as if sleep sat too heavily on his lids. "I dinnae want to fancy ye. Why cannae ye be whey-faced like the princess is supposed tae be?"

The plaintive note of complaint in his voice—the tangled frustration with being unable to stop staring—startled a laugh out of her.

As far as compliments went, it was absurd and ridiculous, and Lottie loved it more than any other she had ever received.

He watched her laugh, eyes wide and fascinated.

"Cruel," he whispered, his thumb rubbing the inside of her wrist and scattering gooseflesh up her arm. "The cruelest, loveliest thing."

She understood now . . . the softness she had seen in him.

It was . . . *wonder.*

She was the wonder.

How very astonishing.

"Dr. Whitaker—"

"What happens to the dragon?" He shifted his hold, sliding his hand down to hers and wrapping his fingers around her palm. The pressure of his warm skin set her heart to skipping. "The one in the story?"

Lottie's smile refused to dim. How stupefying this conversation had become.

"He falls in love with the princess," she told him, sinking into the chair beside him. "And the princess with him."

"Ah." A long pause. His eyes drifted shut in earnest, his breathing deepening. "A happy ending then—the dragon and the princess?"

"Yes."

He did not respond. But he *did* pull her hand onto his chest, splaying her palm over his heart and placing both his own atop it, as if cuddling her hand to him.

Lottie stared, the sensations zinging up her arm almost overwhelming. She could *feel* the thump of his heartbeat, the rise and fall of his ribcage as sleep claimed him once again.

She reached for the book—one-handed, of course, as she would not be the one to remove her hand from his.

But then his voice reached her.

"No' for me, that happy ending," he murmured. "For myself, I ken love would be a catastrophe."

9

The world came back to Alex in pieces.

The scrape of the counterpane under his hands.

The rustle of a servant stirring the fire.

The smell of wood smoke and camphor.

That odd befuddlement of his senses being heightened and yet scattered at the same time.

Memory rushed in.

Shooting. Accident. Broken leg. Rest. Heal.

Laudanum.

He had taken laudanum. And if the bitter taste in his mouth and cloudiness of his thoughts were any indication, he had taken a *lot* of it.

How long had he been asleep?

Closing his eyes, he assessed his body.

He deliberately took in a series of deep, slow breaths.

His ribs ached, but there was no sharp pain.

His broken left leg was splinted and resting in a bone box.

He opened his eyes.

He tried to lift his head to look around the room, but even that wee movement set everything to spinning.

He swallowed, fighting the nausea.

He couldn't move without help.

What was he to do now? Had he heard someone moving around?

And, if not, how was he to summon anyone?

He had never felt so helpless. Even in those dark days following Ian's death—when grief and guilt had threatened to drag him into a deep ocean of regret and melancholy—he had at least been able to do . . . *something*.

But now . . .

Alex gritted his teeth, swallowing again. This time he tasted frustration and a wee bit of panic.

The room was dark. But here and there, he could see wisps of daylight drifting through the shutters and drawn curtains.

But as it was, the bedchamber reminded him of a dragon's lair, glimmering firelight and dark gold-rimmed shadows—

No.

Wait.

He blinked and sucked in another deep breath.

Dragons.

He remembered something about . . . dragons and a golden-haired princess . . . a woman so beautiful it caused a pang in his chest . . .

He closed his eyes once more.

Damn laudanum.

He hated it.

He hated the feeling of his head stuffed with wool.

He hated the vague sense that he had said and done something ill-advised.

He hated the loss of control.

His chest constricted, frustration and panic increasing.

Once more, he forced himself to breathe in deep, filling the bottom of his lungs, then the middle, then the top, then out his mouth in a heavy rush.

He blinked.

Dragon?

Princess?

Beautiful?

Why?

Why was he thinking—

Lady Charlotte.

Had Lady Charlotte been here, sitting at his bedside? Had they spoken of . . . *dragons*?

He rubbed his brow and took in another bracing lungful of air. The deep breaths blew away the silky tendrils of laudanum that clouded his thinking and addled his wits.

But the further he awoke, the more he realized—

Everything hurt.

His leg.

His head.

His chest.

His very *skin* ached.

He was finished with the laudanum.

He would not take another drop.

Another deep breath. In and out.

His mind cleared further. This was not as fortuitous as he might have hoped.

The fleeing mental cobwebs released another fluttery stampede of panicked thoughts.

He was stuck in this god-forsaken bed, hundreds of miles from home, and bloody hell—

No one knew where he was.

No.

One.

In hindsight, he should have taken *someone* into his confidence. McNeal, at the very least.

But McNeal would have insisted on telling Catriona. And what if Catriona had fancied the idea of having a marquess for a brother?

Alex had simply not wanted anyone to pressure him to make a different decision.

But now—

Everyone would have to know. McNeal. Catriona. It was impossible to not inform them, particularly as Alex would spend the next few months recuperating a solid week's journey away from Edinburgh.

Catriona was going to be furious—understandably hurt and angry that he had kept this secret from her. McNeal, too.

Och! How would McNeal manage their practice without him? Alex was going to have to send detailed notes about patients—what to do with Mrs. Stewart's diabetes, and Mr. White's gout, and Mr. McKay's cancerous growth.

And what about Alex's friends? Damnation, he was likely going to miss the Brotherhood's meeting in March, wasn't he?

That meant he was going to have to tell them the entire sordid story.

Alex let out a low groan.

There were so many people to inform, so many angry responses to field.

But he could hardly blame his friends and family. The letters he would have to send them would be shock-inducing—

Surprise! I am currently heir to the Marquisate of Lockheade. It's a long tale, but I hope to extricate myself from having to assume the title of Lord Lockheade. Though, I must confess, this information about the marquisate is somewhat ancillary to my actual news.

In a rather theatrical turn of events, I was shot at. By a duke's son. In Wiltshire. Oh, terribly sorry. Did I neglect to mention I am in Wiltshire at the moment?

As a result of the duke's-son-shooting incident, I suffered a bad fall off my horse. I currently have a severely broken leg that I'm praying will heal correctly enough to allow me to walk normally again. Or, at the very least, won't go gangrenous and have to be amputated. But I am still alive, so . . . silver linings?

All that to say, you may not be seeing hide nor hair of me for some time to come—

Alex groaned again—the pained whimper of a wounded animal.

Snick.

The door opened.

Alex lifted his head as Lady Charlotte sailed into the room.

Her eyes instantly met his.

"Dr. Whitaker! You are properly awake!" A smile spread across her face, delighted and welcoming. "Your fever broke last evening, so Dr. Smithson decreed we should allow the laudanum to wear off today."

Alex blinked and told himself that Lady Charlotte's smile bore no resemblance to the sun, no matter how much it brightened the gloomy room.

Such unabashed cheer bordered on maniacally obnoxious. It set his teeth on edge and his shoulders to bristling.

He was in the middle of a mental existential crisis!

Had the lady no compassion?!

Moreover, what gentleman wanted a bonnie lass like Lady Charlotte to see him like this? He was as helpless as a mewling babe.

"Yes, I am awake," he replied, voice cracking. Abruptly, he realized his throat was painfully dry. "Is there any water tae be had in this house?"

"Oh! Of course!" Lady Charlotte hurried to his side—that dratted smile stretching wider—and poured water into a glass. "You must be hungry, as well. I will summon a light repast immediately. Here is the water."

Alex reached for the glass, noting that his hand shook uncontrollably.

Damn and blast this laudanum!

He gritted his teeth and wrapped his fingers around the cup, careful not to brush Lady Charlotte's fingers.

He attempted to lower the glass to his mouth, but his jittery hand caused water to slosh over the edge and down his sleeve. He grunted as the cold wet slid down his arm.

"Here." Lady Charlotte steadied the glass for him. "Allow me."

She bent over and tipped the cup to his lips.

The action brought her pert nose and elegant jawline closer, eddying swirls of jasmine around him.

Even in the low light, she glowed. Impossibly lovely and utterly enticing.

What right had this woman to be so beautiful? To cloud his thinking and scatter his wits?

A rogue surge of anger sliced through him. That he was so helpless in the face of her loveliness. That part of him longed to give in to her allure, to allow himself to fall, fall, fall . . .

He lifted his head and drank the water, guzzling it down.

A memory surfaced. Fuzzy. Foggy.

No . . . it was more a sense than actual memory.

A feeling that he had been here before.

That this same sequence had already happened—his anger over her beauty while swallowing water down his parched throat.

Again, that bizarre image of a princess and a dragon surfaced.

Why was he thinking of fairy tales?

He hated this lingering opium haze.

He finished the water, frowning at Lady Charlotte with her face of elegant hollows and graceful curves.

She moved away from him, water glass still in hand, and spoke to someone outside the room, requesting food.

He looked left to right, trying to see a clock, his watch, *something* that would at least tell him the time. But the room was too dark and shadowy to discern much clearly.

It only underscored, once more, exactly how helpless and dependent he was. He could not move. He couldn't lift his damn *head* without assistance.

He was utterly at the mercy of these strangers.

What was he to do?!

Lady Charlotte returned to his beside. "Can I offer you more water—"

"Must this room be so blasted dark?" His frustration rendered his tone snippy. But he seemed incapable of stemming it.

The laudanum appeared to have wandered off with his manners.

Lady Charlotte's smile slowly melted off her face. "We felt the shutters and curtains would keep out the chill."

"We? Is that a royal 'we,' then?" Alex had rarely felt quite such a bastard. But once loosed, his tongue took on a life of its own.

Her eyebrows flew upward. "Dr. Whitaker—"

"Do ye think if ye confine me to a metaphorical coffin that eventually I will take tae one in truth?" Alex couldn't stop the frustration spilling out his mouth. "Finish what Lord Frank started?"

It all felt phantasmal, as if his mouth and words were disconnected from the reality of his self. As if another man were castigating Lady Charlotte, and Alex merely the observer of a play.

Lady Charlotte's nostrils flared and her lips pinched shut. She set the glass down on the bedside table with a *clink* and rounded the poster bed, pulled back the heavy window curtains, and unlatched the shutters.

Frosty winter sunlight and a draft of cold air flooded the room.

"Is that better?" she asked, tone noticeably cooler now.

Regret laced through him, but Alex couldn't find the mental strength to stem the tide of his snippy words.

"Yes." He swallowed. "What is the date?"

"The twenty-second of January."

Blast! He had lost nearly a week!

He swallowed back the panic crawling up his throat.

"And the time?" he asked.

She glanced toward the fireplace he could barely see opposite the foot of the bed. "Half ten."

Alex clenched his jaw. So many days lost. He was to have returned to Edinburgh in just two days' time.

He needed to send a letter to McNeal immediately.

Lady Charlotte moved back to his side, a rustle of silk and petticoats. She paused, looking at the bedside table and shuffling something out of his vision. Books, perhaps?

Her hair shimmered in the light, so pale blond it was nearly silver. Wee tendrils of her coiffure had escaped to curl against her temple and neck.

He was trapped here. And having this impossibly-lovely woman as his jailer felt like the final indignity. The last cruel blow this farce had to deliver.

But then, he noticed it. A small mole in the center of her left cheek. It was no feigned *mouche* like those of the century past—a beauty mark artfully placed next to one eye or at the corner of a mouth.

No, the wee mole was entirely natural, stuck to the center of her cheek as if Lady Charlotte were at the end of a drunken night out and her *mouche* had slid down her face. It was faint, only a few shades darker than her skin and easily missed at a distance. But this close, it stood out, that wee imperfection.

The mole should have abated his anger over her beauty. *Look here!* it said. *This woman is not so perfect, after all.*

But it had the opposite effect. It highlighted that the lady was not to be pigeon-holed. She was not monolithic but human and approachable and mussable.

And Alex didn't wish the words *mussable* and *Lady Charlotte* to ever come near one another in his brain.

She turned back to him.

"May I read to you while we wait for Cook to send up something tempting?" she asked, lifting a book in her hands.

Abruptly, a vision flashed through his head. Lady Charlotte's beautiful head bent over a book, stories of princesses and dragons tumbling out in soothing English tones.

Or was it a memory?

"A fairy tale, I wager." His tone left little doubt as to his opinion of such a thing. "Am I tae be relegated to the nursery next? Or are ye like all pretty women and strenuously avoid words which will lead tae—heaven forbid!—thinking?"

Lady Charlotte's expression grew more and more remote as he spoke.

"May I offer you a pastime that is more acceptable then? Something more studious, perhaps?" Her words held a sharp edge.

Good. Alex wanted a fight.

"Yes. Paper, pen, ink, and a way to sit up would be greatly appreciated. I have far too many letters tae write, explaining to all and sundry my present degraded circumstances."

She tossed the book she had been holding back onto the bedside table with a loud *smack*.

"I shall see that a writing desk is brought to you immediately, then." She turned to leave, denying him the fight he craved.

"And my watch, if you please," he snipped.

She stopped and looked back at him, a question mark on her face.

"My writing desk *and* my pocket watch," he repeated.

"Of course, Dr. Whitaker. I shall see if they can be located." Her tone dripped acid. She flicked a look up and down his supine body. "Fortunately, you shall not want for time to write your letters."

Alex narrowed his eyes. Was she taking the piss out of him, now?

"Is there anyone else who could see tae my care?" he asked.

A long pause.

Lady Charlotte stared at him the entire time. He could practically see the emotions flitting across her face.

Astonishment. Outrage. Anger.

"Much as it seems to pain you, Dr. Whitaker, you have been left to my care at the moment." Her scathing tone could cut glass with its precision. "Do you have a complaint you wish to lodge? Shall I summon my supervisor?"

LOTTIE STARED AT DR. WHITAKER.

Oof!

The man was being an utter cad.

Dragon, indeed.

He had awakened determined to blaze fire and blister anyone who walked through the door. She simply had the misfortune to be the first one to brave his cave.

"Does this supervisor exist?" he snapped. "Or is it of the more metaphorical variety?"

"Metaphorical. But I am certain I could arrange something. Perhaps a polite renunciation of the hospitality found at Frome Abbey in *Cary's New Itinerary* would suffice? Something to deter would-be tourists from visiting? Even *that* should be possible for a pretty woman who avoids thinking."

Dr. Whitaker flinched at having his own caustic words thrown back at him.

Do not think me weak, Doctor, she felt like hissing.

Grandmère had not raised her to be a shrinking violet.

"Are you always such a difficult patient?" Lottie continued.

His eyes narrowed.

"I cannot say." He waved a hand at his leg. "I have never suffered such a grievous injury."

"Perhaps you should consider this episode of recovery as a physic, an antidote to help you better relate to your patients—"

"I dinnae need a pretty, feather-brained debutante tae recount how to practice my profession."

Oh!

Of all the things to accuse her of—

Lottie swallowed back the angry retort on her tongue.

She stiffly nodded her head. "I was merely offering assistance, Dr. Whitaker. But as I can see that is not wanted or needed, I will leave you to the servants. Good day."

She swept from the room, all but stomping down the stairs.

How dare he! The very nerve!

Pretty, feather-brained debutante!

She stormed into the library.

She could not help her beauty. It was an accident of Fate.

The same Fate that had taken Anne and Gabriel and Papa far too soon.

The same Fate that had rendered Dr. Whitaker the heir to her father's title.

All things that were entirely out of her control.

As for the *feather-brained* . . . *s*he had studied too long and too hard to allow such an epithet to stick.

She paced back and forth, chewing on a fingernail.

Ugh!

He was rendering her a child again, agitated and anxious.

The worst part?

She understood *why* he had lashed out at her.

He was a physician. By his own admission, the man had rarely been in the position of one of his patients. And now he was reduced to a beggar of sorts, relying on the kindness of strangers to assist him. Worse, he'd had to take laudanum, which Lottie knew he loathed.

She was seeing him at his very lowest.

She clenched her teeth, disliking that, even at his worst hour, she still understood him. The whole of him was entirely unnerving.

But still . . .

Grandmère, a woman raised in the intellectual salons of Paris, would not tolerate Dr. Whitaker's impertinence.

Lottie shouldn't either.

She knew this, but what to do?

She tapped her lips, surveying the library.

The library was cold with the damp cutting chill of January. Those weeks of the year where Lottie often felt it impossible to ever be warm again. Granted, there was no fire in the hearth, as she had not requested a fire be laid in here.

Her eyes drifted to the enormous painting over the fireplace. Gabriel's largest work. His finest, if Grandmère's opinion were to be believed.

Lottie moved to scour the books lining the walls until her eyes lit on the one she wished, snatching it from the shelf.

Then she joined Grandmère in the morning room. Here, a fire roared in the grate, the room warm and inviting. The morning room was more her grandmother's private study than anything. Grandmère had a sitting room off her bedchamber, but she had been raised in the era of the boudoir. When callers would join a lady as she conducted her toilette, engaging in banter as a maid applied cosmetics and fashioned her hair.

Grandmère had never outgrown the need to collect people around her, and so she rejected the idea of a private sitting room. She wished to inhabit a space where others would sit, too.

At the moment, Grandmère was writing a letter at her desk. She looked up as Lottie entered.

"Is all well, *ma petite*?" she asked in French, not missing the thunderous wrinkle of Lottie's brow. Grandmère rarely spoke English when with her grandchildren. Lottie had learned French along with her grandmother's lessons.

"*Non*," Lottie replied in French, pressing a kiss to her grandmother's wrinkled cheek. "Dr. Whitaker is being insufferable."

"Ah." Grandmère shrugged. "I think our dear doctor does not realize his own *éclat*. He wears the hauteur of a marquess with shocking ease."

Lottie gave an inelegant snort. "He is decidedly rude. He called me beautiful and silly all in the same breath."

Grandmère set down her pen. To her, such words were the worst of insults.

"Mmm—" Grandmère's eyebrows went from censorious to thunderous with the slightest effort. "I trust you will let Dr. Whitaker know where you stand, *ma petite*. Men cannot be allowed to think that beauty and intelligence are incompatible."

Lottie grinned and showed Grandmère the title of the book she held.

"Good girl," Grandmère smiled and turned back to her writing. "The doctor will receive a rude awakening, I think."

"I should like to borrow that, too, if I may?" Lottie pointed to a painting on the wall, another of Gabriel's works.

Grandmère lifted her head, her dramatic brows drawing into a questioning furrow.

"It is to make a point," Lottie explained.

"*Très bien.*" Grandmère nodded, turning back to her letters with another flick of her hand.

ALEX LOOKED UP AS LADY Charlotte stomped back into his bedchamber.

He was quite sure she would bristle at being accused of something so unladylike as *stomping*, but there was no other way to describe her walk.

For his part, a trio of footmen had assisted him in sitting up in bed—two to move the bone box and another to lift his body—but Alex was finally able to eat sitting up. He was halfway through a luncheon of beef broth and dry bread when the door smacked open.

Lady Charlotte clearly had not forgiven him for his harsh words earlier.

Alex knew he needed to apologize.

He *wanted* to apologize.

But just like the dry bread, the words stuck in his throat.

Instead, he said, "I am currently drafting my scathing commentary about Frome Abbey for the editors of *Cary's*."

If he thought to ruffle her with his words, he should have known better. She set several items down on a table near the side of the bed and shot him a saccharine smile over her shoulder, the expression far too sweet to be palatable.

"Does your commentary read something like, 'Frome Abbey, seat of the Marquess of Lockheade. Dreadful pile. Do not recommend.'?'" she asked.

"Not quite. I'm leaning toward 'Uncivilized hovel.'"

"Ah."

Lady Charlotte removed a perfectly innocent landscape painting of a river and trees from the wall.

A small tendril of her white-blond hair had escaped her coiffure to dangle tantalizingly down the nape of her neck. That wee lock of hair did uncomfortable things to Alex's breathing.

"Redecorating?" he asked the back of her head.

"Mmm?"

She turned her bright blue eyes on him. Robin's-egg blue. The shocking blue of a loch in mid-summer. The color of liquid sunshine.

Och! Enough with the florid thoughts!

He felt that irrational irritation rising again as he waved a hand toward the wall. "Why did you remove the painting?"

"Are you truly going to ask me questions now?" She turned fully around, a hand on her hip. "I'm quite sure the only thing you should say at the moment is, 'I do beg your pardon, Lady Charlotte. I have been an insufferable cad and wish to throw myself upon your mercy.'"

The sheer pissyness of her tone startled a barking laugh out of him.

He preferred her like this, he realized.

A princess with claws, feisty and determined.

This woman would not cower in fear.

He wanted reasons to dislike her, to cast aside his unwanted attraction.

Instead, the more he learned of her, the opposite kept occurring. Like her errant mole, her spunk and quick intelligence were unexpected.

Lady Charlotte pivoted and hung another painting in place of the one she had removed. He leaned forward in the bed in an attempt to see it, but her head and body blocked his view.

She turned back to him, a book in her hands. "I am sure chronicling your woes to all and sundry will likely take you days, but in case you get bored, I took the opportunity to provide you with some reading."

She set the book beside him, though her eyes said she would have preferred to toss it at his head.

He glanced at the title, brow furrowing. "*A Vindication on the Rights of Women?*" He lifted his gaze to hers, emotions vacillating between appalled and impressed. The book was scandalous reading for any unwed young woman, no matter how forward thinking. "I'm surprised your father allowed such things in his library. Do you think to shock me?"

"Not at all." Her eyes went wide with mock astonishment. "I had supposed Wollstonecraft to be light reading for—what did you call me? A pretty, feather-brained debutante?"

"Ye ken what I mean, Lady Charlotte. Surely, your family would be appalled to know you read Wollstonecraft—"

"Grandmère? Why . . . who do you think gave me the book in the first place?" She smiled, tight and brittle. "You accused me of loving fairy tales. So . . . I'm lending you one of my favorites to read."

"A fairy tale, is it? A treatise on the importance of educating women?" His nose wrinkled. "Are ye sure you've actually read this book?"

"Hah! You hold my personal copy." Her smile gained a hint of sardonic humor. "And, yes, the idea of girls finally receiving an education equal to that of boys often feels as unlikely as a fairy tale. Perhaps reading Wollstonecraft will enlighten your thinking on the *feather-brained* half of the human race."

Alex flinched. He felt like he just witnessed a puppy growing fangs.

"I shall leave you to your writing."

She pivoted and left the room.

The door did not quite slam behind her, but the deafening *clack* of the latch was effective nonetheless.

Alex felt positively . . . *winded*.

She was correct, of course. In every particular.

He was an absolute cad and merited each word of her censure.

Blast it all, he needed to apologize.

His eyes drifted to the painting she had hung on the wall.

He laughed, a sharp burst of sound that echoed in the room and caused his leg to twitch.

From within the frame, a dragon looked out at him, eyes ruby red, smoke rising from its mouth. The mythical animal loomed, an accusatory symbol.

Was this more of Cousin Gabriel's work then? It seemed stylistically similar to the painting on the stairs.

Lady Charlotte . . .

What a remarkable, spirited . . .

He blinked.

Admiration rose in his chest, ballooning and rising.

Dammit.

No! He wasn't going to like her.

He was not.

He simply had to keep that thought in his brain.

10

Alex forced himself to push aside thoughts of Lady Charlotte. He would apologize when next he saw her. In the meantime, he would focus on the letters he needed to write.

He had not received full marks and the degree of M.D.—*Medicinae Doctor*—at such a young age without the ability to focus his mind to a solitary task.

Though it took a surprising amount of willpower to stop Lady Charlotte's snapping blue eyes and quick wit from popping into his mind every five minutes.

He blamed the lingering effects of laudanum.

A pair of footmen arrived to assist him in seeing to his bodily functions and to serve him tea. They also informed him that Galahad had not been seriously harmed in the accident and was healing nicely in his stall.

A maid retrieved his traveling writing desk and his pocket watch. For some reason, having the watch at hand soothed him. Here, at last, was a sense of normalcy.

Setting his watch open atop his desk—for no real reason other than he liked to know the time—he wrote letters to his solicitor in Edinburgh and to the Crown's solicitor in London.

Next, he wrote to McNeal, explained the situation, and included revised care instructions for his patients. How McNeal was to manage it on his own, Alex couldn't say.

Then, he penned a separate letter to his sister. Catriona would be livid that he had neglected to inform herself and McNeal sooner. She would hopefully have calmed down before he saw her next. Regardless, he did request that she send on some of his personal effects—more clothing and few of his favorite novels to read.

Then, he was a wee bit tired. So he watched the rain patter against the window pane, and then slept, and then watched the fire burn in the grate, and then ate a snack, and then as only four hours had passed, he took some time (as he had *plenty* of it) to curse his fate once more.

Even his pocket watch had turned traitor.

For more years than he could count, Alex's life had been ruled by the ticking of the clock. By a list of places to go and people to see and things to do. How long would it take to get from Prince's Street to Castle Rock? How many minutes were required to meet with Mrs. So-and-So? How long would it take to write his medical notes and order supplies? He would rush through his day only to collapse into his bed and begin again the next dawn.

And now, everything had

Simply.

Stopped.

Days and weeks stretched before him with stark emptiness. His watch could tick out the time, but Alex would be doing nothing with it.

What was he to do? How was he to manage the sheer mental weight of his confinement?

At least his fever had fully abated. It meant his leg was healing well and infection had not set in. The specter of amputation receded. But even that bit of good news did not cast out boredom.

The arrival of the evening post helped dispel his gloom.

Letters had been sent to his solicitor who had instructions to forward all post to Frome Abbey, should Alex not return to Edinburgh in a timely fashion. It had seemed a bit of paranoia on his part to create such a plan, but it had clearly been clairvoyant.

If nothing else, it was a relief to hear from friends.

Andrew sent a thick letter. He began by writing at length about his wife, Jane, and their new daughter, Isolde. According to Andrew, Isolde was the bonniest, cleverest, sweetest wee bairn to ever grace Scotland.

Jane claims Isolde loves her best, but Isolde and I know differently. She may be four months old, but she only has to see me and she stops her girnin' straight away and smiles. I cannot wait for you to meet her properly, Alex. Though if you do not think her to be the bonniest lass of your acquaintance, dinnae tell me. I shall only think less of ye for it.

As you know, Rafe, Ewan, and I are already in London. Parliament is in session early, as there is much to sort in Lords with King George's ascension to the throne. We're still planning on holding our annual meeting of the Brotherhood of the Black Tartan in March. But could we possibly entice you to come to London for our meeting this year? I recognize that leaving your practice for any period of time is difficult, but to be very honest, it would be nice to have you here in Town. Sometimes, I fear you will work yourself into an early grave.

Alex sighed, looking up from the letter. Of course, he would be happy to meet them in London. If he were very lucky, he might even be ambulatory by then.

Andrew continued on:

I am no closer to discovering who has been placing the advertisements in the newspaper. They crop up about every six months. The adverts would be expensive to post, so whoever is doing this has funds that exceed that of a common seaman or day laborer. But why post threatening notices without demanding something in return?

That said, the latest notice in the Edinburgh Advertiser *riled up a procurator fiscal in Aberdeen. The man has asked the Judge Admiral to open a more formal investigation. I do not have to tell you how much this concerns me. As we have said from the very beginning, Kieran could be accused of mutiny, as he openly fought Captain Cuthie in his attempts to save Jamie. Of course, as long as Cuthie and Massey remain abroad, nothing should come of it. Mutiny cannot be prosecuted without witnesses. And we have always believed that Cuthie would be loath to provide evidence, as Cuthie himself is guilty of significant crimes that would come to light should this all go to a tribunal. Mutual silence keeps both men from gaol.*

Alex let the foolscap fall with a frown.

The Judge Admiral and a procurator fiscal becoming involved in this was disconcerting. There were letters from Ewan and Rafe in the pile, expressing similar concerns.

Alex pinched the bridge of his nose.

Oh, Kieran.

This was a disturbing development. Would this be the thing that tipped Kieran over the edge? Being charged with mutiny because he attempted to save his wife?

That night always hovered at the edge of Alex's dreams.

"Alex! Help! Cuthie has her!" Kieran screamed.

Alex looked up as Kieran, wet and bleeding, raced uphill from the harbor. Flames leapt from the island village below them, the fire being Cuthie's final act of cruelty.

Under Alex's hands, Andrew groaned, still bleeding profusely from his wounds. Rafe lay beside him, his cheek sliced to the bone. Cuthie and his crew had beaten them nearly to death.

"Help!" Kieran staggered closer. "We cannae let Cuthie take her!"

Ewan caught Kieran in his enormous arms before their friend could jostle Alex's work.

"The ship has already weighed anchor, Kieran," Ewan began, pointing to The Minerva *sailing out of the harbor.*

"We have tae try. Cuthie captured us, but we fought our way free. I nearly had Cuthie, but then Jamie . . . she stabbed him—"

"Who?"

"Massey! Massey grabbed me from behind as I fought Cuthie. Jamie stabbed him and then pushed me overboard, thinking to save me, the glaikit *lass. But now they have her!"*

Kieran had been inconsolable, unwilling to face what they all already understood—

Jamie likely would not be coming back.

Worse, Kieran was guilty of openly mutinying against his captain.

It had taken over three years to find and bring to justice the men behind Cuthie's vicious actions—events which had helped assuage Kieran's pain.

But Fate simply would not let their friend go.

New evidence kept coming to light, sending Kieran off on one wild-goose chase after another, hoping that the new information might lead him to Jamie. And then when it all came to naught, he sank once more into despair.

And now this . . .

Kieran had promised not to return to the bottle, but how many times had Alex's brother sworn something similar? And in the end, Ian had given in to his demons. Their father had too, for that matter.

Alex stared at his own leg in the bone box, recognizing how easy it would be to request a bottle of whisky and pass the next month in a blissful, alcohol-induced haze.

He swallowed the acrid taste of panic in his throat.

He would not end up like Ian.

Kieran would not either.

Alex would fight for them both.

He rifled through the remaining letters.

There were a few from friends and patients—Mrs. Hammond had much to say about the diet of her cat.

The Duke of Ferndown had sent a polite missive—or rather the man's secretary—wishing Alex a speedy recovery. It was distant and polite and rimmed all around with condescension. His Grace also invited Alex to dine once he arrived in London. The duke wished to further discuss his proposition regarding the marquisate.

But toward the bottom of the pile, Alex found a letter that had arrived at Frome Abbey directly.

The mysterious Mr. S. Smith had replied.

I am pleased that you will be in this area within the week as you return to Edinburgh. Please call upon Mr. Bennion, the innkeep at The George Inn in Wetherby. He will give you my direction.

Alex grimaced. Due to his accident, it would now be several months before he passed through Wetherby on his way back to Edinburgh.

Mr. Smith continued.

In regards to your other questions—Was I personally aboard The Minerva? And can I disclose the general medical nature of this consult?—I, unfortunately, am not at liberty to say. As you will be here soon, there is no need to discuss this via letter. Again, I must stress the importance of your discretion. It is a medical matter of the utmost delicacy . . .

Blast!

Given the movement on investigating *The Minerva* in Aberdeen, Alex needed to know what Mr. Smith knew. Perhaps if he wrote back immediately, the man might be more forthcoming now that Alex was unable to travel anytime soon.

Sighing, he picked up pen and paper and began scribbling replies.

He began by explaining his predicament to Mr. Smith and asking if the man were going to be near Bath or London in the upcoming months.

Then . . . three different letters to Andrew, Rafe, and Ewan with essentially the same content.

I apologize . . .

I should have written before now . . .

Lord Lockheade. Marquisate. Heir. Attainder.

Shot. Broken leg.

He left out the phrase *attempting not to despair*, but the feeling burned in his chest nonetheless.

Why was it so easy to coax and discuss and listen to others' emotional pain, but when it came to his own, Alex shied away?

More importantly, would his friends understand and support Alex in not wanting to take up the title of Lord Lockheade? Or would Andrew, Rafe, and Ewan offer kindly recriminations and beg him to join them as members of the *ton*?

He supposed he was about to find out.

Alex finished his letter writing far too soon.

It was still hours before bedtime.

Far too much time to ponder his own shortcomings.

His pocket watch ticked with agonizing slowness.

A conversation with a school chum who had spent time in India surfaced in his memory. The man had been enamored with the Hindu concept of *karma*—the idea that one's past actions, good or ill, called forth similar future reprisals.

Was Alex's current predicament the result of poor karma?

Too often Alex had dismissed the intense boredom of his patients as they recuperated, brushing it off as so much faradiddle.

But now . . . he felt chastened. Convalescence was nearly diabolical. It gave one far too many hours to ponder the frailties and hypocrisies of mortal existence.

Karma, indeed.

He glanced at the book Lady Charlotte had left, its worn cover taunting him.

He had read *A Vindication on the Rights of Women*, of course. Catriona had been most insistent. But like most important texts, it was laborious.

Alex's brain felt sluggish just pondering the idea.

Of course, one thing remained—

He needed to apologize to Lady Charlotte.

And he *would* apologize. If and when he saw her again.

He clutched his pocket watch in his fist, as if that simple act could encourage time to pass more quickly.

11

The door snicked open the next morning.

Alex raised his head, wondering if Lady Charlotte had at last returned.

But it was only Michael Smithson, doctor's bag in hand.

"How fares the patient today?" Michael's words were the very ones Alex had said more times than he could count when greeting a patient. Michael, at least, accompanied them with an ironic smile.

"Bored," Alex replied, stifling a sigh. "Likely to bite your head off."

"I have heard a similar report," Michael laughed, setting down his bag. "I'm glad to see you are honest."

Lovely.

The servants were talking.

Or worse, Lady Charlotte herself.

Shame washed through Alex. He wasn't this person.

Yes, he struggled to deal with the abrupt change his injury had brought, but there was no need to take his frustrations out on others.

Something of his thoughts must have shown on his face.

"Have a care for yourself, Alex." Michael's eyes were understanding. "You suffered a dreadful injury only eight days ago. Though, knowing you as I do, you must already be going mad with boredom."

"Putting it mildly, I should say." Alex managed a mirthless laugh. "I have come to the shameful realization that I have been abominably unfeeling toward my own patients as they recuperate."

Michael grinned and began inspecting the cut on Alex's head and the scrapes along his ribs.

"All healing nicely," he declared. "How's the leg feeling?"

"Achy. Itchy. Restless."

"That sounds about right. Your lack of fever is reassuring, too." Michael nodded. "I've been giving some thought to how to best secure your leg going forward. It would be nice to free you from the bone box. I'm sure you've heard about the bone-setting work of Monsieur Seutin during Waterloo—"

"His starched bandages?"

"Yes. A splint covered with bandages dipped in starch. It is said to provide excellent support for the healing limb. It could provide you with more freedom of movement."

"Aye, I've heard Seutin's bandage is strong but excessively heavy. I'd love to get about on crutches. But in order to do that, I need to have a lightweight, strong splint."

Michael frowned, pondering the problem.

"Have you read the accounts of Benjamin Gooch and his splint?" Alex continued.

"Gooch?" Michael sat down. "Seems like he wrote one of our surgery textbooks?"

"Aye, that too. But he developed a clever splint from slats of wood, leather, and metal bands. Basically, it creates a barrel-like cage around the leg that holds it immobile but should be light enough to hobble around on crutches. Most importantly, it can be removed to clean the leg when needed."

"It sounds fascinating." Michael folded his arms.

"I've been wanting to try it with patients for a year or two now, to see if the brace will truly hold the bone immobile enough. I'll draw up specifications for a carpenter and blacksmith to create one for me. We'll let the bone heal for another two weeks and then move me to the lighter brace and, fingers-crossed, it will work."

"Perfect. And in the meantime, we'll apply one of Seutin's bandages which will, at the very least, allow you to roll over in bed."

"That would be appreciated."

"I can imagine." Michael snorted. "We'll have you up and about and taking on the duties of the marquisate in no time—"

"Pardon?" Alex's forehead furrowed. "Taking on the duties of the marquisate?"

"Well . . . yes. That is why you're here, is it not? You are the new heir?"

"Ehr, I am, but the matter is somewhat muddled."

"Are you referring to Ferndown's meddling? I doubt anything will come of it. If you are the legitimate heir, then you will inherit the title." Michael laughed, as if any other outcome were ridiculous. "The laws of primogeniture are decidedly inflexible. Even for dukes."

"Perhaps. But I actually agree with Ferndown."

"Pardon?" Michael sat back in his chair.

Alex recounted his reasons for wishing to sign the Writ of Attainder.

He expected Michael to have a good laugh with him over the absurdity of it all and to agree that assuming the mantle of marquess was ridiculous for a physician.

Instead, the more Alex talked, the sterner Michael's expression became.

"So . . . you don't want the marquisate?" he finally asked, voice scandalized. "You will allow it to remain in the hands of Lord Frank?"

"Aye, though Lord Frank will only run the estate until Master Frederick comes of age. As I said, I dinnae want tae be a marquess. Master Frederick can have the title. I've chosen my career. I can do more real good in Edinburgh healing people than I can sitting in Lords blethering over the price of corn shares and squiring some aristocratic wife to balls in London. Can ye even imagine it?"

Michael lurched to his feet and began to pace, his brows drawn into a serious line. The man shook his head, pausing to stare down at Alex.

"I can't help but feel that is a bit . . ." Michael seemed to struggle to find the proper words. ". . . short-sighted. Are you confident the estate is being managed properly at present?"

"I assume Lord Frank knows what he's about, as he was raised to it. But I havenae yet assessed accounts or surveyed the lands myself. The marquisate holdings are vast."

"Yes, it's just . . ." Michael darted a glance at the door, as if to ensure that no one was eavesdropping. He then leaned forward and lowered his voice. "I have seen signs that everything may not be well."

A wee trickle of foreboding skittered down Alex's spine. "Signs?"

"Nothing glaringly obvious, just small indications of hardship. Tenants in worn clothing. Malnourished children. Disease racing through households, and people filling up the local workhouses."

Alex frowned. "That is disquieting. But it doesnae follow that such things are the result of land mismanagement. Life has been precarious these past five years. The end of the conflict with Napoleon and the flood of soldiers returning—combined with the Year without a Summer in '16—has created a dearth of jobs. Scotland has seen its share of suffering, as well."

"Agreed." Michael sat back, folding his arms. "And perhaps it is only my perception that such changes came on the heels of the late Lord Lockheade's death last spring. But after his lordship's death, the old steward retired. I'm not confident that the new steward, Mr. Warden, is as competent as his predecessor."

They sat in silence for a moment, Alex's thoughts a whirlwind. His frown deepened.

Finally, Michael sighed. "Look, Alex, we both wish to heal people. To give up being a physician would be difficult. But I would implore you to truly assess and examine the situation here before you walk away. You are a good man, Alex Whitaker. You save scores of lives every year as a doctor. But as Marquess of Lockheade, you could potentially save *thousands* of lives. You could heal not just people, but entire communities. You could not only alleviate suffering in the here and now, but generations into the future."

Alex shifted his gaze to look out the window, allowing Michael's words to roll over him.

Wasn't this precisely what he had feared? That once friends and family members knew the decision that faced him, they would attempt to sway his mind. They would argue and persuade.

Michael did not misunderstand Alex's silence.

His friend stood to leave. "I know there are many hurdles, Alex. I understand your reluctance, and it's to your credit that you are not seduced by the wealth and power of becoming a lord. But before you walk away from these lands and people, be the physician you are. Assess the overall health of the marquisate. Examine the living conditions and difficulties facing the tenants. Ask yourself: What good could I do here?"

SILENCE HUNG IN THE BEDCHAMBER long after Michael had departed.

Alex's leg ached, a dull throb that kept time with his pulse.

His mind, however, vibrated like a rung bell.

What good could I do here?

Alex had not anticipated Michael's argument.

That the marquisate could be ill, that it might need a healer's hand.

Bloody hell.

If this were true, was Alex now to be a savior of sorts? The person who would fix all ills and guide a sprawling empire into a prosperous future?

He was not so naive as to think the process so simple. Nor was he confident in his abilities to succeed where so many others had failed.

He pressed the heels of his hands into his eyes.

Somewhere deep in the house, a servant called out. A murmuring voice answered. A door shut with a thud. Footsteps clacked on a marble floor.

The sounds of wealth.

He didn't want this life.

He didn't want a house full of servants to wait upon him.

He didn't want to tromp through fields and inspect cattle, talking crop rotations and roof repairs with a steward.

He had roundly rejected that existence when he sold McPherson

Farms. He had *refused* the family legacy and had given up the estate with its thousand precious memories of his father and Ian.

The decision to sell had not been easy, but Alex had to make a choice.

He wanted the smell of camphor and the snip of a surgeon's stitches. He wanted banter with witty elderly women and the cry of a newborn babe.

Owning a large, prosperous stud farm did not fit with that.

Alex had made his decision then. And he would make the same choice again with the marquisate.

But now Michael had added *guilt* and *conscience* into this decision, appealing to Alex's sense of humanity. That as a gentleman and doctor, he was honor-bound to investigate and determine the true state of affairs.

How was he to do that? He was tied to this damned bed, unable to move and examine *any* of this for himself. Which meant, he would need to rely upon Mr. Warden to accurately present information about the estate.

But if Mr. Warden *were* the problem, how was Alex to assess anything? The man would be, at best, determined to hide his incompetence. At worst, he could be deliberately deceptive.

Alex stared at the shut door.

If only Lady Charlotte would return. She, at least, might have a suggestion or two.

If he apologized profusely first.

And if she were forgiving.

And if he asked nicely enough.

But those were far too many *ifs* for Alex to retain much hope.

BY THE FOLLOWING MORNING, ALEX was nearly out of his mind with boredom.

He had written all his letters.

He had sketched the brace based on Gooch's design and sent the drawings on to Michael.

His mind had looped through the potential problems with the estate until he feared he would go mad.

Finally, Alex had requested to see Mr. Warden. After all, Alex had ample time, and why not begin by discussing matters with the man himself.

"Mr. Warden is unfortunately away at the moment," a polite footman informed him. "He left for Devon to attend to estate business, but he should return within a week."

There was nothing Alex could do but bide his time and withhold judgment.

Even *if* the estate were being poorly managed and people's lives negatively affected, it didn't follow that Alex had to personally oversee their rehabilitation.

It was reductive to assume that the *only* solution to this problem—were it truly a problem—was for Alex to become Lord Lockheade. There would be solutions that would solve the problem without him having to assume the title of marquess. For example, Alex could insist that an entire panel of regents be appointed to oversee the marquisate's lands until the wee heir in question reached his majority.

But for now . . . Alex sat and waited, the ticking of his pocket watch the only accompaniment for his thoughts.

Wind whistled outside his bedroom window. The footmen who came to build up the fire and assist him in sitting up for the day said there might be snow by nightfall.

An hour later, Alex finally received a brief reprieve from his boredom in the form of a visit from the Dowager Lady Lockheade.

Her ladyship swept into the room in a rush of heavy silk and Parisian perfume.

"You appear well enough," she said by way of greeting, lifting a rather judgmental eyebrow. "Given the tales I have heard over the last several days, I feared you might have developed distemper. I wished to see for myself if your wounds had turned rabid."

Her ladyship's blunt words startled a laugh from him. "Nae. There is nothing medical to blame my churlish behavior on. I fear I owe an apology or two."

"*Oui*. I do not disagree with your assessment." The reproving slant of her ladyship's eyebrows was at odds with the humor in her gaze. "You have been most ungallant to our Lady Charlotte."

Her ladyship's frankness was as breathtakingly brisk as the winter wind gusting outside.

"Aye. I have," he agreed. What else was he to say? The Dowager spoke truth. "I havenae been given the opportunity to apologize, however, as I cannae quite manage walking." He nodded toward his leg, still in its bone box. "I have tae wait for Lady Charlotte to come tae me."

The Dowager pursed her lips, studying his leg. "It is quite the dilemma."

A brief silence ensued.

Alex swallowed. Her ladyship's eyebrows were truly formidable.

"Could I perhaps enlist your ladyship's aid in this?" he asked.

Her eyebrows winged upward. "I have found patience and resourcefulness to be useful traits in a gentleman. I would never dream of interfering with their development."

Well then.

Their conversation moved on, and her ladyship departed after another fifteen minutes.

Leaving Alex once more to stare out the window, helplessly bored.

His leg ached. Not a sharp pain, but a slow, dull throb. Of course, with nothing to take his mind off his injury, he focused on every wee sensation.

His eyes landed on the book that Lady Charlotte had left him.

Had the Dowager truly been the one to encourage Lady Charlotte's reading of it?

And was Alex himself so bored as to read Wollstonecraft again?

He rather thought not, but his hand reaching for the book said otherwise.

He would just read a few passages. It would likely render him sleepy, and a nap would pass a few hours, would it not?

He opened to the first page and frowned.

Neat handwriting dotted the margin.

Was this Lady Charlotte? Had she written this?

He flipped through pages in earnest.

Nearly every page had underlined bits of text and scribbled notes, all in the same precise hand.

His eyes lit on one passage that had been underscored twice:

> *In literature, as in life, women are to be leveled into one charac-*
> *ter of yielding docility and gentle compliance. A wife must be an*
> *angel, or she is an ass.*

Scrawled in the margin beside it, the sentence *Better to be an outrageous ass than a docile angel!* leapt out at him.

He laughed, a crack of startled surprise.

This *had* to be Lady Charlotte.

She had said this book was one of her favorites, had she not? Vividly, he remembered the impassioned words she had lobbed at his head before storming from the room, leaving the painting of a smoldering dragon looming over him.

He glanced at the dragon still hanging beside his bed, its ruby-red eyes drilling into him.

Why this painting?

Was she calling him a dragon with it? Or was she perhaps wishing to give him a not-so-subtle reminder of her own fighting spirit?

Regardless, Alex flipped back to the beginning of the book and began reading in earnest, eagerly devouring Lady Charlotte's commentary in the margins.

He read for hours, the pain in his leg forgotten. The sun set, a maid lit candles and stoked the fire, a footman brought dinner and helped Alex see to his physical needs.

And still Alex read on. He laughed at the sardonic tone of Lady Charlotte's witticisms and nodded in agreement with her opinions.

It was as if the entire exercise cracked her head open and allowed Alex to see the mechanical workings inside.

It was utterly captivating.

Worse, he intrinsically understood her points, the manner at which she had arrived at her conclusions. Often, he would think a thought and find she had written the exact same idea in the margin.

Somewhere around midnight, he snapped the book shut, mind racing, heart whooshing in his ears.

He had come to a rather alarming conclusion—

Lady Charlotte's interior thoughts were as beautiful as her exterior.

It seemed unfair somehow. That she should be graced so thoroughly.

Shame instantly surged in behind.

As Wollstonecraft argued again and again: Women were more than the aggregate of a pretty face and genteel manners.

And what had he done to Lady Charlotte?

He had assumed that her lovely exterior appearance was her only dimension. Not that he didn't appreciate her considerable external charms . . .

But if her scribbled notes were any guide, Alex suspected that Lady Charlotte's external beauty was the *least* interesting of the two attributes.

Ah, bloody hell.

There it was.

Against every ounce of his better judgment—

He *liked* her.

What a *fascinating* woman.

More importantly, he needed to apologize.

Grovelingly, abjectly, submissively.

Tomorrow, if possible.

12

"You wished to see me, Dr. Whitaker?" Lottie walked into the dragon's bedchamber, stopping at the foot of his bed.

She had avoided the doctor for three days.

Three days of mentally constructing sharp retorts to hurl at his snapping eyes.

Three days of watching snow fall out the windowpane and listening to Grandmère's drowsy snores.

Three days of sitting in the library, studying a treatise on the moral importance of a vegetal diet, and trying not to think of the good doctor lying in bed above her head.

She had steadfastly refused to visit him.

I dinnae need a pretty, feather-brained debutante tae recount how to practice my profession.

He clearly thought little of her, and she did not wish to give him the opportunity to abuse her sensibilities once more.

She had almost spurned his request to speak with her on principle alone.

But it seemed as if boredom propelled her to his room. Though she took a leisurely amount of time to do so. No need for the man to think that she had been waiting for him to snap his fingers.

She would not jump to his bidding.

Dr. Whitaker looked up from the bed, a relieved smile on his face. As if he were . . . *pleased* . . . to see her.

His eyes, however, held a wary hesitance.

Abruptly, he seemed akin to the doctor of her memory.

More Cousin Alex and less fiery dragon or stern Dr. Whitaker.

Had the strain of his visit and the distress of his injury altered his demeanor so thoroughly?

And was it only now, nearly two weeks after his accident, that the man was coming back to himself? To the man she met on that road so many years ago?

Granted, his leg was no longer in the bone box, so perhaps that lifted his mood? Earlier that morning, Dr. Smithson and two footmen had wrapped the injured leg with starched plaster bandages. Now the leg rested atop pillows as the bandages dried, looking like a white bale of wool.

Additionally, someone—a footman, if she had to guess—had assisted Dr. Whitaker in donning a banyan and scraping his jaw clean of whiskers and taming his hair.

Though, his hair perhaps wasn't as tame-able as she supposed. At first glance, it appeared sleek and straight, like a mink's pelt.

But mixed into the brown were strands of caramel and ginger, as if it struggled to commit to any one particular color. And there was one rogue lock near his right ear which curled defiantly against his temple.

Dr. Whitaker appeared so decisive, but his hair was fence-sitting, unsure which pose to strike.

"Thank ye for coming, Lady Charlotte. I regret that I cannae rise tae greet ye." He smiled a bit wider and nodded toward his leg. "It goes against every last lesson my mother and tutors drilled into me as a lad. Will ye have a seat?" He motioned to the chair beside his bed.

Lottie stared for a moment.

"I prefer to stand," she said.

It was truth. She liked that he had to look up at her.

"Your reticence is only to be expected." His smile turned uncertain at the edges.

He touched his pocket-watch which rested beside him on the counterpane.

"I . . . I owe ye an apology, Lady Charlotte. I . . ." He trailed off.

The fire popped.

He swallowed and ran a hand through his hair, setting it all askew.

"You . . . ," she prompted.

He cleared his throat.

"I . . . behaved like a . . . bumbling, *glaikit* oaf," he said and then continued on, phrases spilling like a burst dam. "My sharp words were inexcusable. I assure ye there was no truth to them. Just my foul temper blowing hot air. I hope that with enough groveling on my part, ye will find it in your heart to forgive me."

He said nothing more.

Lottie rocked back on her heels, her senses as startled as her equilibrium.

First, that he would apologize so promptly upon seeing her.

But, second, that he offered up no excuse. No litany of reasons *why* he behaved as he did.

The laudanum addled my wits.

I was struggling to adapt to new circumstances.

Both reasons were true.

He said none of it.

He accepted that he had done wrong and asked for her forgiveness.

No excuses.

How very . . . mature of him.

Lottie was, in a word, *astonished*.

And what did it say about the men in her life when a heartfelt apology felt like an earthquake?

"Apology accepted, Dr. Whitaker."

They stared at one another, as if the ceasefire had been brokered, but now neither army knew what to do.

Lottie nodded her head and then pivoted, intent on the door.

"I read your commentary." His words stopped her.

She looked back at him.

"Pardon?"

He lifted her copy of *A Vindication*, which she only now noticed had been beside him on the bed.

"I read your commentary. I assume this is your hand in the margins." He opened the book and pointed to the ink scrawling down the sides of each page.

"Yes." She rotated to face him again, wary. She had nearly forgotten about her fervent reactions to Wollstonecraft.

Or, rather, it had never crossed her mind that he would actually *read* them.

"I greatly enjoyed your droll insights," he continued.

Was he being condescending now?

There, there, pretty, feather-brained debutante. How marvelous that you have an intelligent opinion.

Lottie edged away from the door and waited.

He studied her with those slate eyes. "I meant that sincerely. Perhaps *droll* is the wrong adjective. I should have said *brilliant.*"

A breath snagged in her throat. Had he plucked the very thoughts from her brain?

She darted a glance at the door. She really should leave. No good would come of talking with him. Not really.

He *was* her adversary. He was the one who could snatch away Freddie's future.

She would do well to remember that.

But . . .

"Which observation stood out to you most?" she asked, her tone frosty.

The faintest bit of humor touched his expression.

"Just one?" he asked.

Her eyebrows lifted. "For the now."

"Very well."

He flipped the book open.

Heavens. He had torn slips of paper and used them to mark pages, scribbling his own thoughts on them, engaging in a vigorous conversation with her.

The sight should not have lit a glowing coal in her chest.

It was just . . .

In French, the word for mind and spirit was the same—*l'esprit*. And so, for her, ideas and soul were locked into the same box.

When someone listened to her thoughts, they were also hearing the sound of her soul.

He had . . . listened.

Abruptly, she wanted to listen, too. To hear what his spirit had sensed of hers.

She sat in the chair beside his bed, hands clasped in her lap, her back straight.

His head was still bent over the book, that rogue lock of hair curling onto his forehead. He pushed it aside absently, as if vanity were too trivial a thing.

"This right here," he said, pointing to a page. "Wollstonecraft says that Society calls a gentle, innocent female an angel but yet," he continued, reading directly, "'*they are told, at the same time, that they are only like angels when they are young and beautiful. Consequently, it is their persons, not their virtues, that procure them this homage.*'"

Lottie stilled. She remembered that passage well. It was a particular favorite.

Her scribbled thoughts peppered page after page—hundreds of ideas and words scrawling like the ravings of a lunatic at times.

And yet . . . he had effortlessly pinpointed the one theme in Wollstonecraft's writing that had resonated within her—that a woman's worth should be measured by her inner beauty.

"I agree with Wollstonecraft's ideas." He lifted his head. "But I admire even more what you wrote in reply. Do you remember?"

Lottie nodded, that warmth in her chest glowing hotter. "Being born with beauty is the opposite of riches. Every passing moment of a beautiful woman's life is spent becoming a little bit poorer."

He snorted, low and soft, a finger dragging across her writing in the page margins. Gooseflesh skittered up her arms, just as surely as if he had drawn that finger along her skin.

"I love how ye phrased it here, though," he continued. "You said, 'A lovely woman begins life as a wealthy angel and ends it, if she clings to vanity, an impoverished fiend.'"

"Yes. It went something like that, I suppose."

"It's a powerful observation." He grinned at her then, and the rushing brightness of it fanned the low flame beneath her sternum. "The concept of physical beauty as a commodity that is spent over time."

Lottie swallowed.

Truculent, frustrated Dr. Whitaker was easy enough to brush aside. He was a breathing dragon, after all, laying waste with his fiery words.

But this version of the man—this kind gentleman who owned his actions and apologized with sincerity and took time to *hear* her—*this* man was harder to dismiss.

She clenched her hands into fists, as if that could stem the potency of him.

He continued to smile at her. "I admire your intellect, my lady. Ye mentioned that your grandmother saw to your education?"

"Yes. She did."

"It is unusual, to say the least. Did your father not object?"

"No. Not really. Not that I suppose Grandmère ever asked for anyone's permission."

"She is a wee force of nature, I've noticed."

"Grandmère is that." Lottie finally smiled in earnest. "Papa told stories of Grandmère as a glittering hostess in the salons of Paris during the reign of Louis XVI. My grandfather acted as a diplomat for the Crown in Versailles for much of their early marriage. In fact, my father was born in a chateau outside Paris and grew up in France until he left for Eton. He adored his mother, so Grandmère definitely shaped his views on women and education, ensuring they were perhaps more tempered than those of a typical English nobleman."

Lottie paused, not sure she wished to say more.

But the doctor leaned forward, gaze intent and sincere, that ridiculous lock of hair curling onto his forehead once more.

"I think Grandmère saw my predilections early on," she continued, slowly unclenching her hands. "I remember the moment quite clearly. I was only eight years old, and Grandfather had just died. I think Grandmère was somewhat lost without him. I recall her watching as a nurse berated me for being so unladylike as to crouch and examine a line of ants carry bits of leaves back to their nest, dirtying my frock—"

"Ants carrying bits of leaves?"

"Of course! It was utterly fascinating!" Lottie laughed. "Grandmère took my hand and walked me to the library. I thought I was in for a scolding. Instead, she sat me upon a chair and told me to look around the room. She said, 'Because of your face, your name, and your family . . . attention and accolades will come to you on a platter. And it will feel as if you merited them somehow.' And then she paused and looked me straight in the eye and said, 'But that will be a lie. You must become more than the sum of your birth. Educate your mind. Enlarge your thinking. Make your inside as blessed and comely as your outside was gifted to be. Happiness will only ever come from within.'"

Part of Lottie marveled that she was telling all this to Dr. Whitaker, of all people.

Wasn't the man more nemesis than friend?

But the more they spoke, the more he reverted to Cousin Alex. To the kind gentleman of her memory.

More to the point, he *felt* like a friend. Or at least, he had the potential to become one. A friend and confidant, much as Gabriel had been.

"*Happiness will only ever come from within,*" he repeated. "The world would be a much brighter place if more of us understood that."

Cousin Alex kept a steady gaze on her, the steel in his eyes softening, as if he found her impossibly fascinating.

And not for the golden color of her hair or the fine texture of her skin or the 'harmonious radiance of her face,' as one gentleman had once described her.

No. Cousin Alex admired the parts of her that *she* had cultivated and curated and rigorously nourished.

A painful sort of pleasure suffused her.

"I cannot imagine that many are . . ." He paused, as if hunting for the right word. ". . . *accepting* of the depth of your education."

Lottie smiled. "You mean, do gentlemen understand that I crossed the *pons asinorum* like any other thirteen-year-old?"

She was referring, of course, to the Fifth Proposition of the first

book of Euclid—if two sides of a triangle were equal, the angles opposite these sides also were equal.

The theorem was nicknamed the *pons asinorum* or 'Bridge of Asses' as
lack-wits often had difficulty 'getting over' it.

Cousin Alex gaped at her and then devolved into delighted laughter.
The motion wrinkled his cheeks and sparked a flame in his slate-gray
eyes.

Heavens above! His laugh was a glorious thing. It fanned a corre-
sponding flame in her chest and sent something flipping in her stomach.
She pressed her hand there, warning the treacherous emotion to stay put.

He clutched his side. "Ye cannae make me laugh like that, lass. My
poor bruised ribs cannae take it."

She grinned, his laughter utterly infectious. "You should have seen
poor Theo's face—he was my betrothed several years ago—when he
heard me quote Euclid for the first time. He spluttered like a simpleton.
He could not comprehend how I grasped the Fifth Proposition, as he
had struggled for months over it."

Cousin Alex wiped mirth from his eyes.

They smiled at one another for a heartbeat. And then another.

The sensation left her breathless.

Lottie looked away first and smoothed a hand over her skirts.

"I have told you much about myself, but I do have a question of my
own. One that has weighed upon me." Lottie paused and then, when
he nodded his assent, she forged ahead. "Do you intend to assume the
marquisate? Will Freddie be disinherited?"

To his credit, he didn't blink at her question or the abrupt manner in
which she asked it.

Instead, he studied her . . . pondering.

"I cannae say for certain about the marquisate." He glanced at the
window, the snow piling in tiny mounds upon the pane. "I have heard
some worrying reports about potential problems. That perhaps Mr.
Warden as the new steward isnae quite as competent as his predecessor.
That tenants are going hungry and are, therefore, more prone to disease.
That the local workhouses are stuffed with new arrivals, indicating a loss
of livelihoods." He waved a hand toward his injured leg. "And here I am,
unable to investigate such claims. The reports could be nothing more

than the ebb and flow of Fortune. Or they could be an indication of mismanagement and cruel measures."

Was this true?

If so, Lottie was instantly ashamed of her own neglect. Hadn't she promised Papa?

Preserve my legacy. See that my lands and people are secured.

She had been so focused on Freddie, that she had forgotten that simple injunction.

"I am a doctor by trade, Lady Charlotte," he continued. "I have dedicated my life tae easing the suffering of others. Ye ask, do I intend tae assume the marquisate? The answer is . . . nuanced. Do I *wish* tae assume the title of marquess? No. Emphatically *no!*" He shook his head. "But I also cannae allow my fellow human beings to suffer, particularly when I can do something to alleviate it. I believe Cicero when he said, '*Non nobis solum nati sumus.*'"

"Not for ourselves alone are we born," Lottie translated.

He nodded.

The problem, of course, was that she *did* understand him. Intuitively. His words caused something to thump and pang deep within. A phantom sense of hearing her own desires reflected in his words.

Lottie lifted her thumb to her mouth, her teeth automatically sinking into her nail.

Oof!

Nail-biting was an abominable habit. She thought she had conquered it years ago, but anytime anxiety raised its head . . .

She dropped her hands, but her fingers still twitched. She clenched her hands into fists, tucking her thumbs tight against her palm.

Cousin Alex, however, read her silence as disagreement.

"What say you? Have ye noticed anything amiss around the estate, Lady Charlotte?"

Lottie folded her arms, further restricting her thumbs, mind whirring.

"I cannot say that I have," she said. "I certainly haven't noticed anything unusual in the village."

But even as she said the words, memories of the last six months surfaced.

In October, she had all but stared at a beggar in Frome while visiting the milliner. A ragged woman carrying a babe and a smaller child clinging to her skirts. The woman had her hand out, importuning passersby.

Lottie had never seen a beggar in their small village.

And then there had been an odd conversation between Frank and Ferndown that she had overheard. Frank had been insisting to his father that they needed to dismiss Mr. Argent, her late father's man of affairs.

"Mr. Warden can oversee it all, Father," Frank had said. *"I have every confidence in his abilities."*

"Are you sure, boy?" Ferndown had asked. *"It's an impossible amount of work for one man."*

"Mr. Warden assures me he has a plan."

"You have gone rather silent, Lady Charlotte," Cousin Alex said.

Lottie relaxed her arms, releasing a breath. "I was merely thinking. Lord Frank dismissed my father's man of affairs last summer—Mr. Argent. I cannot imagine my father would be pleased with that, were he still alive."

"Why do you say that?"

"My father always described Mr. Argent as indispensable. The marquisate is a far-ranging enterprise, as I am sure you are well aware. Mr. Argent was the man who oversaw the whole. The estate stewards and others would report to Mr. Argent. Mr. Argent, in turn, would make decisions and deal with matters that did not require my father's input. Father always said that having a competent man of affairs was the first priority of any wealthy lord."

"But Mr. Argent is no longer with the marquisate? Was he replaced?"

"No. I think Mr. Warden has been asked to fulfill that role."

Cousin Alex's forehead furrowed. "He is managing the affairs of the *entire* marquisate? In addition to being the steward over Frome Abbey itself? That is far too much work for one man."

"I agree." Lottie nodded.

"Aye. And with Mr. Warden gone for the rest of the week, I cannae ask him."

"Though it does perhaps explain why he is away. He has other interests to see to."

"Agreed, Lady Charlotte."

"Cousin Lottie." The words tumbled out of her before she could call them back.

"Pardon?"

"We are cousins, after all. Why not call me Cousin Lottie? Cousin Gabriel always did."

"Perhaps." He paused. "But it's a rather distant relationship, our cousinhood."

"Yes. But it exists nonetheless. And if you call me Cousin Lottie, then I can call you Cousin Alex."

"Very well . . . Cousin Lottie." His smile faded slightly. "I genuinely do not wish tae assume the title. And if Mr. Warden is incompetent or overworked, surely more helping hands can be hired." He stretched out his hand, as if to assure her, resting it atop the counterpane. "We are *not* at an impasse. We are not."

Lottie stared down at his outstretched hand.

It was not the soft hand of a gentleman. His palm was worn in places and those white scars stood out as stark sentinels.

It seemed to be a pact, his hand.

Take it, he urged. *Let us reach our goals together.*

She paused . . .

. . . and then slid her hand across his.

His skin was warm and his callouses rough underneath her palm.

The action should not have been momentous.

It should not have sent gooseflesh flying to attention along her spine nor skittering sparks up her arm that detonated in her chest like fizzing fireworks on Guy Fawke's Night.

But . . . gracious heavens.

Lottie looked into his steely, dragon gaze and saw . . . turmoil.

As if he, too, had felt something similar and found it just as astonishing and perilous.

Lottie didn't quite snatch her hand back, but the wish was there, no matter how demurely she removed her fingers from his.

And as soon as he turned his head to pick up *A Vindication,* she rubbed her palm against the wool of her skirt, as if desperate to expunge the feel of him.

It was no use, of course—the touch of his skin on hers lingered, a humming thrum of sensation.

Such nonsense.

Lottie was not this kind of woman—prone to fits of vapors or the excesses of sensibility.

And yet, hours later as she lay in her bed, the feel of his hand in hers still burned.

13

The following morning, the post brought Alex a flurry of replies.

Heavens, he knew the Royal Mail could be efficient when one was this close to London, but even so . . .

He was impressed that his letters could arrive and a reply be sent back in so short a time.

Would an update from McNeal on his patients arrive as quickly? Would Catriona send additional clothing swiftly, too?

Alex certainly hoped so. He itched to read how his patients were fairing. And he wished to wear more than a shirt and banyan while doing so.

He opened the first letter from Andrew.

> *You mean to tell me that this madness with Lord Lockheade is you?*
> *You are the long-lost heir that Ferndown is trying to attaint?! And you*
> *didn't think that I, one of your closest friends (and soon to be fellow*
> *Peer in Lords), would care to know this?*
>
> *Truly, Alex, I should be furious with you. And maybe part of me is*
> *hurt that you didn't feel you could tell me. But it would be a wee bit*
> *hypocritical, as I do understand your reluctance. I kept my own heritage*

from you all for years, so I can hardly castigate you now. Though I was never granted a chance to choose whether or not to inherit, I struggled to want to sit in Lords, to be surrounded by English condescension.

There is much I wish to say on this subject, but I will forebear for the now. We shall speak of this at length when we next see one another. I sincerely hope you will be well enough to meet with us in London in March. Kieran should be returned by then, and I hope to have more to report regarding the notices in the paper and the concerns of the Judge Admiral in Aberdeen.

Until then, I wish you a speedy recovery. You are in the best of medical hands (i.e., your own). I would simply urge you to not abandon entirely the idea of accepting the title of Lord Lockheade. But know this, no matter your decision, I will support you in it.

Alex set down the letter, a tightness banding his chest. He pressed the heels of his hands to his eyes.

He should have anticipated Andrew's kindness. How could he have assumed that his friend would react in anger or hurt?

Andrew was the very best of men.

The next letter was a response from this unknown Mr. S. Smith regarding his wish to consult on a medical matter related to *The Minerva.*

I am most sorry to hear about your injury. Though I reside in York-shire, I will be traveling to Plymouth and London on business the last week of February. I should be passing along the stagecoach route between Bath and London. Could we possibly meet at The Dancing Bull outside Chippenham along the way? The coach breaks there for an hour for luncheon, and I could use the time to consult with you.

Alex frowned, thinking.

If this S. Smith did indeed have new information about *The Minerva,* Alex needed to do everything in his power to acquire it.

Though the distance was not far—less than two hours via carriage—he could not make such a journey with his leg in its current state. However, the date Mr. Smith mentioned was still a few weeks off, as they were only just barely into February. Once Alex was able to graduate to the

Gooch-designed leg brace, it was possible he would feel equal to such a brief journey. He could ensure his leg was thoroughly cradled and cushioned throughout the ride.

He knew he was placing too much hope on this proper leg brace. Was he being naively optimistic, looking for anything to shrink the time of his convalescence?

Or would *karma*, in the end, demand he languish in bed for months to come?

FORTUNATELY, MR. WARDEN RETURNED THE following day, easing Alex's boredom.

Alex had many questions for the steward.

Why had Mr. Argent, Lockheade's former man of affairs, been let go? And why was Mr. Warden tasked with the man's duties?

Managing the marquisate was surely akin to ruling a small country—a sprawling enterprise of lands and buildings and industries. Frome Abbey with its thousands of acres, tenants, and structures was just one cog in the larger machinery of the title. Acting as steward over the estate was already a monumental task. But then adding the management of the entire marquisate, in addition?

Madness.

"I will not prevaricate; my tasks are numerous," Mr. Warden said when Alex questioned him on the matter. "But I am confident in my abilities."

Mr. Warden was precisely as Alex remembered from the ill-fated impromptu shooting party—thin-lipped, thin-haired, and Alex suspected, rather thin-skinned. The steward clearly did not like the insinuation that he might be in over his head.

"I do not doubt it." Alex used the voice he reserved for placating patients who balked at a required treatment. The tone that said, *Please do not make me escalate this situation.* "But what tasks do you feel could use another helping hand?"

"With all due respect, Dr. Whitaker, my hands are more than capable of fulfilling everything I have been hired to do." Mr. Warden folded his arms, his entire body a wall of defiance.

Alex sighed inwardly. Escalation, it seemed, was Mr. Warden's preference. Given that Alex might very well become this man's employer, Mr. Warden was being rather recalcitrant.

"Thank you, Mr. Warden." Alex nodded. "I would appreciate having the estate ledgers brought up. I wish to look them over."

Mr. Warden's demeanor became even stiffer. "I cannot imagine that is necessary, Dr. Whitaker. I will need to clear the matter with Lord Frank."

"Lord Frank has no authority in this, Mr. Warden." Alex set his jaw. "His son is merely a claimant, just as I am a claimant. As such, I was tasked by the Crown to familiarize myself with the inner workings of the marquisate. That is what I am doing. Had I not been injured, I would have perused the books weeks ago."

"The ledgers are merely an endless list of numbers, nothing to interest a medical man. They will bore you silly."

Alex nearly laughed. "I assure you, Mr. Warden, that the estate books could hardly be more boring than staring out the window, willing my leg to heal faster." He spread his arms wide, indicating his leg in a cast and his confinement to the bed. "Please see that the ledgers are brought up as soon as possible."

Mr. Warden glared, but as he had no ability to refuse, he nodded curtly and left the room.

The estate ledgers arrived in Alex's bedchamber an hour later—seven volumes that spanned the past five years.

The steward had not been wrong. They were mind-numbingly tedious. Endless entries of rents received, repairs authorized, and expenses paid, all neatly tallied and summed.

Alex checked a few pages and all appeared in order. The numbers added up correctly. The rents collected were consistent. There were no large nor unexpected expenditures.

Did he need to survey *all* the records?

Alex wasn't sure he had the willpower to recalculate the thousands of transactions, line by line.

If anything, staring at the estate ledgers merely confirmed, yet again, why he did not wish to assume the title of Lord Lockheade.

OF COURSE, EXPLORING THE ESTATE'S issues was a minor distraction from Alex's other all-consuming thought—

Lady Charlotte Whitaker.

Or, rather, Cousin Lottie.

Over the following week—once she genuinely believed his apology—a tentative friendship grew between them.

He found her a fascinating conundrum.

Heart-stoppingly beautiful and fiercely intellectual.

Quick to be his angelic caretaker, but just as ready to slice his logic with her wit.

Eager to read a French fairy tale or argue Greek sophistry.

And as her ladyship spent a good portion of her waking hours at his bedside—discussing philosophy, telling stories—it made thoughts of her rather difficult to corral.

"Is that better?" Lady Charlotte asked one afternoon a week later as she helped him adjust the pillow beneath his leg.

Alex was sitting upright and was dressed in a waistcoat and loosely-tied neckcloth. His clothing had finally arrived from Edinburgh with a lovingly chastising letter from Catriona. Alex was so grateful, he had only smiled at her cross words. Moreover, McNeal had not disappointed and sent a long letter, detailing every patient and their current course of treatment, as well as ending with an injunction to "stop fussing over us all like a mother hen."

Alex's leg had begun to heal in earnest. The dull aching pain had subsided, along with most of the swelling. There was still no trace of heat or fever, so Alex was hopeful that it would, thankfully, heal perfectly.

Even better, the starched bandages allowed more freedom of movement. He could now sit up unaided. But the stiff splint was heavy, and malaise from sitting so long in bed had set in. His back ached, and he feared he was developing pressure sores from being forced to remain in the same position. Alex wanted out of this bed, but his leg needed at least another week of healing before he attempted the Gooch-designed splint.

Until then, he had footmen place sheepskins underneath his sheets, as he had found the soft wool helped to wick away moisture and provide softer cushioning.

But sometimes the strain on one particular place began to feel like too much.

"A wee bit higher, if ye can," Alex murmured, pressing his hands into the mattress and lifting his weight upward.

Cousin Lottie moved the pillows beneath his knee, relieving pressure on his leg muscles. Alex tried very hard not to think of her fine-boned hands just inches from his thigh, about the jolt that would scour him were she to inadvertently touch him.

"Is that better?" She stood upright.

Alex relaxed back, testing the position.

He nodded. "Thank ye."

Cousin Lottie walked around the large tester bed and sat on the corner opposite from Alex, her back resting against the bedpost, her legs curled underneath her. It was a shockingly casual pose and one that suited Lottie enormously.

She wore a lavender gown that magnified the blue of her eyes. Alex surmised it was a favorite gown as it showed signs of wear. An equally worn Paisley shawl wrapped around her shoulders. The cloth of both was expensive—the cut immaculate—but the garments were obviously well-loved, the fabric rubbed to a soft nap. Items that spoke of comfort, not vanity.

Lottie sat on his bed because, in her words, it was something she had often done with Cousin Gabriel, and it felt cozy when winter raged outside.

Alex did not point out that they were well into February now and winter was on the wane.

Moreover, Lottie clearly thought of Gabriel as more of a brother, so sitting on *Gabriel's* bed was not beyond the pale.

Alex, however, did not fall into quite the same category of close cousin. He was fairly certain that sitting on *his* bed was not entirely proper.

But he enjoyed Lottie's company too much to say anything. And they both ensured that the door to the bedchamber remained open.

Vividly, the lingering weight of Lottie's hand resting on his, days before, flitted through his mind. Had she touched Gabriel so casually?

Mmmm, it seemed likely.

The thought that her feelings for him were similarly platonic rankled.

Though, thinking of Gabriel . . .

"Ye have yet to tell me why Gabriel favored such paintings." Alex waved a hand toward Gabriel's dragon still hanging on the wall beside his bed. "The dragon looks like a cross between a deranged lizard and an adder. Did Gabriel have a preference for painting mystical animals?"

"Like half-human dogs?" A smile touched Lottie's lips as she reached for a loose pillow at the bottom of the bed, stuffing it behind her back. "No. His subjects ranged widely. His finest painting hangs in the library. It was also his last work, arriving only a month before his death."

"What is the subject of the painting in the library? More dragons?"

"I would never spoil the surprise. As soon as you are able to move, I will show it to you." Lottie smiled in earnest, a wicked glint touching her blue eyes. Wisps of silvery hair had escaped her chignon, ringing her head in a soft halo. She was shades of blue and gold.

I could look at her for days on end and never tire.

The thought bolted in and out, no less true for its brevity.

Did Lottie truly view Alex in the same fraternal light as she had Gabriel?

Because his thoughts of her were decidedly *not* cousinly. He could scarcely think of her as *Cousin* Lottie.

Instead, she was this . . . this. . .

Och, blast it all.

He genuinely, thoroughly liked her.

No. It was more than that.

He was well and truly on his way to being smitten.

"I should take the dragon painting back to Grandmère," Lottie continued. "It is her favorite. She feels that it encapsulates the passion that Gabriel had for his art."

"And not my vile temper while under the influence of laudanum?"

She chuckled. "I'm not entirely sure the two are as different as you suppose them to be."

Alex laughed, the motion jarring his bruised ribs. But the catch in his breath felt vital somehow, the cleansing act of laughter worth the wee stab of pain.

Their conversation roamed after that.

Alex described his practice in Edinburgh.

Lottie expressed her disgust with the current state of child labor laws.

Alex loved listening to her, he realized. The rasp of her voice as she outlined her goals.

He recognized himself in her words.

The fire within. The idealism. The deep-rooted need to alleviate suffering.

All the things that drove him to medicine in the first place—

To make the world a better place for him having walked through it.

Surely, he was not the first man to recognize Lottie's internal magnificence. How was it she remained unattached?

"I wonder that you are not married, Cousin Lottie." The words tumbled from him, as if his tongue were helpless to stem the tide of his own curiosity.

Her eyes widened, and she paused, head tilted to the side.

It was an exploring sort of expression, as if she were ascertaining the seriousness of Alex's question.

Alex realized he was, in all truth, deathly serious.

Why wasn't this exquisite, clever, witty woman married?

"Must I be married in order to have worth?" She turned the question back on him. "Is my only value that of an accessory to some gentleman's life?"

She did not hide the disappointed reproof in her tone.

He heard them . . . the words she did not say.

I thought you saw beyond my surface.

I thought you valued me as more than an ornament.

"My apologies. I should have been more clear." He shot her a wry smile. "In my memory, you were betrothed the day of Master Freddie's birth."

He remembered that distinctly.

She paused at his words. They were not *quite* a question, Alex realized, but ringed with expectation of a reply nonetheless.

She turned and looked out the window. The snow had melted—it never lasted long in England—and now the world hung with a gray weariness, as if Mother Earth were too exhausted by endless winter to lift her head.

But even the tired light loved Lottie. It tripped down the gentle slope of her nose, across the fine pearl of her cheek.

Blast. The woman would turn him into a poet yet.

"Yes, I was betrothed," she said, turning her head back to him. "Sometimes . . . you can know someone for years—be betrothed to them for months—and, yet, not really know them at all."

Something hitched in Alex's chest. "Familiarity is not the same thing as love."

"No . . . it is very close to love, but one does not necessarily lead to the other." She paused. "I was *familiar* with Theo—with his moods, his actions—but I realized too late that I did not understand him. He never shared his innermost self with me, and I never shared mine with him, mostly because he never asked. Instead, I took our comfortable companionship and labeled it love."

"Ah. And why did ye break off your betrothal, if I may ask?"

"He was of the opinion that a wife must leave her own family for her husband's. He wished me to cease all but the most necessary contact with my family." She looked at the counterpane, picking at the fabric. "I refused to do so. Family is important for me, and I did not appreciate the binary nature of the choice Theo presented."

"Aye, that was wise of ye, lass. No man who truly loved a woman would force her to make such a decision. Families join *together* when a couple marries."

"You understand." She shot him a wan smile. "With hindsight, I realized that Theo liked the idea of me more than the reality. If I am being truthful, I think he found the weight of my love onerous—both my love for my family, as well as my love for him."

"Love should always be viewed as the treasure it is."

"Precisely." Her jaw flexed and fire flashed in her blue eyes. "My family is not a weight to be tolerated. My love is not a nuisance to be borne."

Alex frowned. "Doesnae Wollstonecraft say something similar? I cannae recall—"

"She does." Lottie scooted up the bed and grabbed the copy of *A Vindication* off the bedside table nearest her.

Instead of retreating to the foot of the bed, she leaned back on the pillows beside him.

It was a shocking breach of propriety.

But if she truly thought of him in the same brotherly way as Gabriel, then perhaps she thought nothing of it.

Alex, however, struggled to breathe.

Not that he wanted her to leave. He liked having her near . . . perhaps too much.

The scent of jasmine swirled around him, the heat of her body sending his thoughts tumbling and his heart to thumping.

She was a siren. Resisting her charms required a herculean strength Alex was unsure he possessed.

But, no, she took no notice of him, flipping through the book, unconcerned about their physical closeness. She scanned the pages, her lips pursed into a decidedly kissable bow. He noted the wee birthmark on her cheek, so close he would only have to lean to press his lips there.

Alex swallowed and forced his eyes away.

"This here," she finally said, leaning so close, her shawl draped over his arm. He could feel the puff of her breath on his neck.

The onslaught of sensation rendered him light-headed.

She pointed to a page.

"I love how Mrs. Wollstonecraft describes the importance of women being educated." She skimmed a paragraph with her fingertip. "She basically asserts here that a man who does not have an equally educated wife forgoes the greatest gift of all—of being loved by one who could understand him."

Alex read the words her finger traced. "'*As in the society of his very wife, he is still alone.*'"

Lottie nodded. "Can you imagine choosing your spouse as one might select furniture?" Her voice dropped, doing a credible imitation of a London buck. "'Dash it! I daresay this lady will do. Her temperament matches the drapes well enough, and she should wear well over time.'"

Alex chuckled. "You have a rather low opinion of gentlemen, Cousin."

"Are you saying that Wollstonecraft is wrong?"

"No. Of course not. I am merely stating that not all men feel this way. I know I do not."

She lifted her head to meet his gaze, only to pull back as if startled to find him so close.

Me too, my lady, he thought. *Me too.*

He expected her to scramble back to the relative safety of the foot of the bed, but she did not. Instead, she stared at him from a mere two feet away.

"What are your thoughts then?" she asked.

He darted a glance down at the book still open in her lap.

"Only that I agree with Wollstonecraft. My future wife, whoever she should prove to be, will never be decoration for my life. She would be the very dearest of friends. The one to whom I could turn with any idea, any problem or thought, and she would nod and say, 'I understand. I hear. I see.'" He paused before continuing more quietly. "And I would know that I was not alone."

Her eyes skimmed him, landing on his lips, his chest, his hand resting on the counterpane.

She swallowed and pressed her own hand to her stomach.

"How do you do this?" Her words held a nearly plaintive tone. "You pluck the very thoughts from my brain."

"Me?" Alex barely stifled a surprised laugh. "I would have said the same thing about yourself. Though I think there is another truth here. That just as ye can know someone for years and never understand them, the opposite can also occur. Ye can know someone for only a wee while and feel a deep connection."

Her eyes locked with his, holding for the space of three heartbeats.

One.

Two.

Three.

She looked away.

Alex feared for his veins. He could nearly hear the blood whooshing through his body. He could certainly feel it in the pulse points on his neck and thumb and chest.

He longed to pace the room, to somehow diffuse this energy within him. He settled for shifting upward in the bed.

She looked back at him, brows instantly drawn in concern.

"Are you comfortable?" she asked, her hand already reaching for the pillows behind his neck.

The motion brought her that much closer to him.

She rose to her knees and pulled on a pillow or two, as if moving so close to him were an utterly natural thing. The heady scent of her perfume engulfed him.

Alex nearly forgot how to breathe.

She froze at eye-level.

Her hand slid from the pillow behind his head to rest on the crook of his neck, the weight of her palm searing even through his neckcloth and shirt.

She filled his vision.

It was too much, he realized.

Too much for him to assimilate.

Too much for him to resist.

She canted forward, leaning onto her hand, putting pressure on his shoulder.

And then . . .

. . . she kissed him.

LOTTIE HAD NOT MEANT TO kiss Cousin Alex.

Truly, she hadn't.

It was just . . .

Her feelings for him were decidedly not cousin-ish. And talking with him was so effortless, so easy and natural.

He felt like the very best of bosom friends. The kind that would always listen without judging. The sort that knew all your faults and foibles and still adored you.

Sitting beside him had been the most natural thing at first—like all those afternoons spent talking with Cousin Gabriel—but the air between them had quickly turned spiky and charged.

And then, of course, the sensation was too delicious, too dangerous to want to move.

It was just . . .

He was this *blade* of a man—strong, keenly clever, and sharply attractive.

And eventually the weight of that attraction was simply too heavy, and she could no longer remain upright.

Pressing her mouth to his seemed the only way to support herself.

The fleeting touch of his lips jolted her. She should have jumped back. Leaned away. Pretended like the faint kiss had not happened.

But, no.

The sensation was too heady. Too astonishing.

She could no more pull away than she could cease breathing.

And so, she kissed him again, more earnestly this time.

She caught his surprised gasp in her mouth, thrilling at her sense of power.

She had kissed Theo, obviously. They had intended to marry, after all.

But comparing the touch of Theo's lips to Alex's was like equating a candle to a bonfire.

One was merely a pleasant point of light.

The other . . . a consuming conflagration.

Heat licked between them, curling her toes in her slippers and sending a cascade of sparks shooting through her chest.

His lips were a brand, marking her as his own.

Alex pulled back first, eyes glazed and stunned. His chest heaved under her hands.

"Why do you kiss me?" he whispered, brows drawn and baffled.

Oh!

The truth fell from her before she could catch it.

"Because my head was too heavy to resist gravity—" She paused, and then continued on a sigh. "—and I needed your lips to pillow my fall."

14

Was it possible to die from mortification?

Lottie feared it might be.

Worse, the one person she could pose the medical question to—namely one Dr. Alexander Whitaker—was the very source of her embarrassment.

How could she have kissed him? Why had she done it?

She had rushed out of his bedchamber as if her skirts were on fire. Which, given the heat of her skin in that moment, was a legitimate concern. She took supper in her rooms and then lay awake for half the night, marinating in acidic mortification.

What should she do?

She could not avoid Cousin Alex forever.

Or, rather, she did not *want* to avoid Cousin Alex forever.

But she did need a small amount of distance.

Time to clear the darts of attraction and temptation from her brain.

Time to sort through the wonder of their conversation and wrangle her wayward emotions into order.

She tossed and turned in her bed, unable to fall asleep. The clock in her bedchamber struck two.

As was typical in the middle of the night, her thoughts twisted through strange paths.

She mourned Papa and Gabriel and little Anne. She never forgot them.

Some days, she still expected to hear Papa call out to her—*Lottie-love, have you seen my spectacles?* Or to feel the mattress sag as Anne sneaked into her bed for a cuddle. Or to watch Gabriel layer paint on a canvas.

Their absence was a gaping hole, and Lottie struggled to rebuild the shambles of her life around the chasm of their loss.

Of course, pondering her ever-present grief did not logically follow from her mortifying kiss.

However, they *were* connected for her.

It was the oddest thing. But after nearly two years of pain and grief, melting into embarrassment over an ill-advised kiss felt almost . . . normal.

As if the very act of kissing Alex had awakened something within her. Something that longed to stretch its wings and truly *live* once more.

She laid on her side, cheek resting on her palm. The pulsing glow from the banked fire painted the room in quivering shadows.

The beginnings of that kiss had likely been kindled when Cousin Alex had listened.

What had she said about Theo?

He found the weight of my love onerous, both my love for my family, as well as my love for him.

Theo had only heard what *he* wished in her words, the bits that corroborated with the life *he* wanted to lead. He gave every appearance of listening, yet had not, in fact, heard her.

But Cousin Alex was Theo's opposite in this, was he not? When she spoke, Alex listened, hearing meaning even in the words she did not say.

Somewhere in the middle of all this . . . she finally fell asleep.

She woke to fitful sunlight slipping through the shutters.

Mortification still fluttered in her chest.

But somehow part of her was freer.

For once, she didn't wish to don black or gray or even lavender. She was ready, she realized, to let go of her mourning colors. It was time to move onward.

Her maid blinked in surprise when Lottie asked to wear a favorite cornflower-blue frock from years past. But the girl quickly smiled and rushed to press the dress.

Now Lottie merely had to sort what she was to do about the situation with Cousin Alex.

Fortunately, Dr. Smithson had arrived to check on his patient. Therefore, Lottie did not have to actively find reasons to avoid Cousin Alex's room.

But by afternoon, she was nearly twitchy with nerves.

She and Grandmère were in the morning room, Grandmère embroidering and Lottie making a show of replying to her correspondence.

Margaret had written a comical letter about an ill-advised trip to the Tower of London and Royal Menagerie. Freddie had begged for nearly two weeks to see the lion and other exotic animals housed there. So an outing had been planned.

But sweet Freddie took one look at the mangy lion and burst into tears, begging his mother to purchase the poor animal and set it free.

I fear he has inherited your soft heart, Lottie dearest, Margaret wrote. *Freddie speaks of nothing now but freeing the lion. He is far too young for such vigilante thoughts. How shall we ever manage him in a decade's time?*

Normally, Lottie would grin and savor every last flourish of Margaret's loopy handwriting. But a riot of regret crashed through her chest, squelching her joy.

Familae primum semper cognosce.

Lottie certainly hadn't been thinking of her family when she kissed Cousin Alex.

Margaret would be aghast were she to learn of Lottie's behavior. She would view it as fraternizing with the enemy and would be understandably hurt.

But . . . if Cousin Alex was intent on renouncing the title—as he repeatedly asserted—then perhaps it wasn't *too* much of a betrayal?

Lottie nibbled on her thumbnail, worried that perhaps she was merely looking for reasons to justify her poor behavior.

Oof!

Enough.

She would apologize to the doctor and promise to never kiss him again.

Yes. That was what she would do.

No kissing.

But she would retain her friendship with him. There could be little harm to Freddie and Margaret in that.

Dr. Smithson had left hours ago. The silence pressed on her, each tick of the fireplace clock ringing in her ears like a gong.

Should she check on Cousin Alex then? Apologize right now—

"You look lovely in your frock, *ma petite*." Grandmère raised her head. "That color has always suited you. Will you be setting aside your mourning colors in earnest now?"

"Yes." Lottie nodded, hoping her flushed cheeks were not too obvious. "I think it is about time. I've put it off long enough."

"Mmmm." Grandmère bent back over her embroidery. "Does the presence of a certain doctor factor into this in any way?"

Lottie's blush deepened. She kept her face averted, as if looking over her writing. "Whatever do you mean, Grandmère?"

"Only that you have been spending time with him. And now, today, *poof!* You are here, wearing colors, and feigning ignorance. Is there a *raison* why you are no longer keeping the doctor company, *ma puce*?"

Lottie could feel the bristling force of Grandmère's gaze pressing into her shoulder blades.

She darted a glance at her grandmother.

"Out with it, Charlotte. You are the color of a Burgundy grape. Something has happened, and I would hear the tale."

"Grandmère, there is nothing to tell—"

"Bah!" Grandmère made a beckoning motion with her hand. "You know I will always ferret out a secret. Come. What has happened?"

There was no help but to confess the whole.

After a brief hesitation, Lottie said, "I kissed the doctor."

Grandmère looked up from her embroidery, her eyebrows winging upward.

A bit of a pause.

"Was the experience unpleasant?" Grandmère asked.

Lottie barely held back a huff of surprise, her blush somehow intensifying.

Trust Grandmère to take a decidedly French view of the situation.

Should she tell the truth? That the kiss had been transcendent? That she could scarcely think of anything else?

Though given how Grandmère scrutinized her face, Lottie rather thought her grandmother had already deduced that last bit. Another hallmark of her Grandmother's French blood.

"If you enjoyed the kiss, then I do not understand why there is anything to fuss over. The doctor appears to be a sensible fellow—very eligible—and you are wise to permit him a liberty or two."

"Grandmère!" Lottie gasped.

"You are far too English, *ma petite*. You must think like a Frenchwoman. You are not meant for the life of *la vieille fille*."

"I am not quite a spinster yet, Grandmère."

"No, but you adore Freddie, and I can see that your heart aches for children of your own."

Lottie fell silent. Grandmère spoke truth.

"I will be honest with you, in ways I have not been with your sister," her grandmother continued. "The doctor is likely to inherit the title. The odds are not in Freddie's favor. Government dislikes moving against the tides of precedent and history. So why not allow the doctor to kiss you? Why not encourage his affections and take my place and your mother's as Lady Lockheade?"

The bald shock of Grandmère's words pushed all the air from Lottie's lungs in a giant *whoosh*.

"Grandmère! How could you suggest such a thing? The next Lady Lockheade will be Freddie's wife! I cannot rob Freddie of his inheritance. I cannot betray Margaret's trust. The very idea is heretical. Besides, I must disagree with you. Dr. Whitaker has said he does not want the marquisate. He will sign the attainder as soon as he is well enough to journey to London. The very thought that he . . . that I . . ." Lottie tossed up her hands in frustrated bewilderment.

"Then why the concern with letting the doctor kiss you?"

"I kissed *him*, Grandmère." Lottie tapped her chest. "*I* took the liberty."

Grandmère's censorious eyebrows climbed even higher.

"Well," Grandmère paused, setting down her embroidery, "did the doctor return the favor?"

"What do you mean?"

Grandmère rolled her hand. "Did he kiss you in return?"

Lottie's face burned brighter.

Why do you kiss me?

His plaintive words still rang in her ears.

Did he kiss her in return?

Oh, gracious.

"I do not know, Grandmère!" Lottie pressed her hands to her fiery cheeks. "How can I not know? I kissed him and, well, I lost my head a bit."

Grandmère's expression softened. A faint smile appeared.

"*L'amour* has a way of doing that, *ma petite*."

"I am not in love with Cousin Alex."

"Oh! Cousin Alex is he now."

"Grandmère!"

"*Pfft.*" Grandmère waved a dismissive hand. "You modern girls. You take *l'amour* far too seriously. So you kissed him? Apologize if you must."

Sometimes Lottie felt like her English heart would never understand her far-too-French grandmother.

Lottie rose and made for the door.

"But Lottie—" Grandmère waited for Lottie to turn around before continuing. "If you enjoyed his kiss—and the doctor is amenable—no need to be shy in encouraging him to kiss you again. You have my blessing, at the least."

LOTTIE FOUND COUSIN ALEX IN his bedchamber.

Of course. Where else would he be?

But he was not, for once, lying in the bed.

"You are upright!" she exclaimed. "You are walking!"

"I am!" he returned, eyes lit with an exuberant warmth.

He was indeed standing upright in the middle of the marquess's bedchamber, a crutch under each arm and a complicated-looking brace wrapped around the lower half of his left leg. It looked as if a cooper had made a strange barrel with metal bands and leather straps holding the vertical wooden slats together.

"Do you like it?" Cousin Alex lifted his leg for her inspection. "Dr. Smithson and I finally deemed my leg healed enough to use the brace."

He grinned at her, the stern lines of his face morphing into an endearing sort of boyishness.

Lottie had seen Cousin Alex serious, angry, confused, stern, thoughtful, and contemplative.

But until this very moment, she had not seen him . . . happy.

Happy was a transcendent look on him. He should wear it more often.

"It's marvelous," she said, momentarily forgetting that she was supposed to be mortifyingly embarrassed in his presence.

"It is, isn't it? I can even walk with the crutches."

He demonstrated by swinging through the room, his crutches moving in an arc as he easily hopped back and forth on his whole leg, keeping his injured leg bent at the knee.

"See?!" He grinned again, the expression so infectious, Lottie couldn't stifle her laugh.

He took another lap around the room.

Lottie knew she needed to leave. Even with the door open, she should not be in his bedchamber.

When he had been bedridden, her sense of decorum had been muted. After all, the man was injured and helpless.

But *this* Cousin Alex was anything but helpless. He crackled with a fiery energy.

More to the point, he was in breeches and shirtsleeves. No waistcoat. Certainly, no tailcoat. Heavens, the man was not even wearing stockings!

Instead, he swung around the room on his crutches, his bare toes digging into the thick carpet pile.

Lottie dragged her eyes away from the doctor's feet. She truly had to doubt her sanity when the arch of a man's foot set her heart to thumping.

Running her eyes up his body did nothing to distract her thoughts. His shirt was of the finest cotton lawn which rendered it rather see-through. She could see the flex of muscle in his upper arms, the ripple of solid-looking planes across his stomach.

Of course, Cousin Alex cared for his body well. She knew this. He viewed it as a machine of sorts. No sugar. No alcohol.

It was such a *Cousin Alex* way of living. To allow nothing unhealthy or mood-altering to pass his lips—

Oh, no.

Lips.

Her eyes darted to his mouth.

I kissed those lips yesterday.

The thought charged through her brain before she had a chance to chase it out.

A blush scalded her from slippered toes to the roots of her curled hair.

I forced my lips on his, was how that thought should have gone.

The strength of her mortification must have affected the very molecules in the air, as Cousin Alex paused mid-swing to look at her.

His steel eyes were far too *seeing*. She could only hold his gaze for three seconds before looking away.

"Ah," he said.

It was a rather telling *ah*. The non-verbal equivalent of saying, 'Why, yes, I do remember what happened yesterday, and I do believe you have every reason to be mortified for your behavior.'

Ah, indeed.

Lottie swallowed.

Just apologize and be done with it, she told herself. *You cannot go back to being friends until you do.*

She pressed a hand to her midriff and straightened her spine.

Grandmère had not raised a milksop.

"I owe you an apology, Cousin Alex." Once she managed that much, the words spilled out in a rush. "I should not have behaved as I did. I shall not excuse my behavior, as it was reprehensible, but I only wish to—"

"Reprehensible?" he interrupted.

Somehow, Lottie's biology found a way to fan the flames of her blush even hotter.

She pressed harder on her stomach, as if that simple act could keep her embarrassment from exploding.

Was he going to make her say it?

The pinched brows over his gray eyes said that, yes, perhaps, he was.

Lottie closed her own eyes and whispered, "I kissed you."

Silence.

And then again—

"Ah."

Her eyes flew open.

Cousin Alex looked at her with . . . amusement? fondness?

She didn't know.

"I noticed," he continued. "The kiss, I mean."

Oh. Let me die now.

Lottie swallowed.

"I apologize," she whispered.

"Apology accepted," he nodded.

And then he turned and made another lap around the room.

As if, truly, they had just put the kissing incident behind them.

As if . . . that was it.

Done and dusted.

Lottie blinked.

Huh.

Men.

Lottie would never understand them.

Worse, what did it say about her that she was . . .

Well, that she felt . . .

Oof.

She was . . . *disappointed.*

Had the kiss been as uneventful for him as he implied?

She still thrummed from it nearly a day on. But Cousin Alex appeared utterly unaffected.

Again.

Men.

He stopped in front of her after another circuit of the room, that impish grin still in place.

"I feel like I'm a prisoner set free. Giddy on power and not sure what thing I wish to do first," he said.

Right.

Their kiss was to be forgotten.

They were to be friends and nothing more.

That was good.

That was right.

That was the loyal-to-her-family thing to do.

Lottie nodded and shooed away the flutter of disappointment in her chest.

"Where would you like to go?" she asked.

It was February, after all; the ground outside was a boggy swamp.

"Not too far," he said. "I hear tell of a painting in the library that is most lovely."

"Lovely?" she repeated and then laughed. "I think I shall have to allow you to be the judge of that. But, yes, the library is an excellent choice for an excursion."

LOTTIE KISSED HIM.

She kissed me.

Instead of counting sheep the night before, Alex had fallen asleep with *that* thought leaping fences over and over in his mind.

At the moment, Lottie had quit his bedchamber so Alex could finish dressing and join her in the library.

A footman helped him don a waistcoat and banyan.

All the while, Alex struggled to puzzle out—

Why had she kissed him?

Was it truly as she asserted? That Newton's Third Law of Motion compelled her lips to meet his?

But . . . certainly there was more at play here than mere gravity.

He didn't know.

No woman had ever seized the initiative and kissed him first.

Was she simply bored and curious and his lips were convenient?

Or did she like him as *more* than a distant cousin?

He wished to ask Lottie about it, but her blush and discomfort had been so acute as she apologized, he couldn't bring himself to linger on the subject.

Unfortunately, the problem-solving portion of his brain was rather desperate to sort the puzzle.

And if his current torment was akin to how a woman felt after a man kissed her, he had been doing the female population a terrible disservice. It was rather unnerving, on the whole.

Naturally, another question lingered—

Did he wish to kiss her again?

Och!

Was the sky blue? Was the pope Catholic?

Of course!

O'course, he wanted to kiss her again.

What red-blooded male subject of King George would *not* want to kiss a lass as lovely as Lady Charlotte Whitaker?

But . . .

. . . *would* he kiss her again?

That seemed unlikely.

Kissing Cousin Lottie was a complication that he simply could not allow.

As a gentleman, kissing a woman led to commitment.

But Lady Charlotte was a marquess's daughter. And the daughter of a marquess would not marry a Scottish physician.

The reasons were legion.

Alex's life in Edinburgh was spartan compared to the luxury of Frome Abbey. Moreover, as a lowly physician's wife, Lady Charlotte would no longer be received in London society. She would be cut off from friends and family. And Lady Charlotte had proven with her first broken engagement that she would not contemplate marriage to a man who would come between her and her family.

Of course, if you became the marquess, many of these problems would evaporate.

Alex pushed the idea aside.

No.

He would not assume the marquisate to woo a woman. No matter how much he liked the lady. No matter how egalitarian and accommodating she might be.

Besides, were he to claim the marquisate, Lady Charlotte would be devastated. She would still reject his suit, as she wished the title to go to her nephew.

So . . . no.

There would be no more kisses.

Any romantic entanglement between them could only end in heartbreak.

Alex was a man used to corralling his appetites. He gave up sugar and whisky, for heaven's sake.

He should be able to forgo kissing one charming, aristocratic lass.

Besides at the moment, he faced a more perilous question—

How was he to navigate the main staircase on crutches?

The brace was nothing short of miraculous. His leg continued to ache, but the brace held it steady and firm, finally allowing him to stand upright and move unaided.

He hadn't been exaggerating when he said he felt like a prisoner set free.

But learning to move smoothly on crutches was going to take practice.

Alex swung down the hallway to the main staircase, surveying it as a mountaineer sussing out the best way to climb a munro in the Cairngorms.

Well, as with climbing a mountain, he supposed one simply had to take the first step.

With two footmen watching and ready to help if needed, Alex descended the stairs, hopping down them one at a time. It took a ridiculously long time, and he was inordinately proud of himself when he reached the bottom. The footmen clapped their approval, so perhaps he was not alone in celebrating the wee accomplishment.

Cousin Lottie was waiting for him in the library, looking even lovelier than normal in an embroidered blue frock.

He couldn't squelch the grin on his face as he came to a stop before her.

"Impressive," she said. "You make locomotion via crutch appear effortless."

"Thank ye." He looked around the room with its expanse of bookcases. "Now where is this masterpiece of Cousin Gabriel's I was promised?"

She waved a hand behind him. "You are going to have to turn around."

Alex pivoted and looked up. And up. And up.

He stared in absolute silence.

The painting was enormous. Easily twelve feet tall and nearly as wide, stretching high above the fireplace.

"As I said yesterday, Father kept begging Gabriel to come home from Rome, saying he missed him. Gabriel sent this instead."

"This precise painting?" Alex surveyed the canvas.

"Yes."

The painting was done in a neoclassical style, focusing on sharp, realistic details. A figure angled through the frame edge-to-edge, his unclothed body facing the viewer straight on, his limbs and torso painted with clear muscular definition. Enormous feathered wings floated above the figure's shoulders and a halo rimmed his head.

Alex squinted. "What does it say across the bottom there?"

"*When this you see, please think on me,*" Lottie recited at his side, a hint of laughter in her voice. "In case you were wondering, it is indeed a self-portrait."

"Pardon?!" Alex looked at her and pointed back to the enormous canvas. "That's a self-portrait?"

"Yes."

"Your cousin painted a portrait of himself as the Archangel Gabriel?"

"*Our* cousin," Lottie leaned her head toward him. "It's the family's pride and joy."

Alex blinked. The sheer scope of the vanity on display in the portrait was . . .

He stared, lost for words.

"I understand the feeling of being overwhelmed by its . . . uh . . . majesty," Lottie said, her tone rather gleeful.

"But . . . he painted himself . . ."

"Nude? Why, yes, he did. As unclothed as the day he was born."

"It's a lot to take in," Alex replied, voice faint. "So much skin. It must have required a lot of . . . paint."

"Mmmm, yes. But I don't think an excess of paint was the reason Margaret nearly fainted when she first saw it."

"I can empathize with her turmoil. Though, I suppose Gabriel's attention to detail is to be commended," Alex managed to say. "The painting could be used as a medical textbook drawing of masculine musculature."

"Possibly. Though Margaret felt that Gabriel was overly-optimistic in his appraisal of his own physique. For my part, I am eternally grateful for that strategically-placed bit of ribbon there." Lottie pointed. "If Cousin Gabriel had to choose only *one* time to show a hint of modesty, he chose well. Some family secrets should really just remain . . . secret."

Alex shook his head. "And he thought this was what his family would want? A nude self-portrait as a winged archangel?"

"Well, he always claimed he was named Gabriel for a reason. Grandmère, of course, wept with joy to see it hung here. She quite doted on Gabriel." Lottie cleared her throat. "She can be rather French and has, therefore, called Margaret a prude for finding it anything other than glorious—Grandmère's exact words."

"That is . . . telling."

"Shall I have a chair arranged just here, so you can enjoy the painting all afternoon? It is Grandmère's favorite angle." Lottie's eyes held a teasing glint.

Alex pivoted on his good leg, turning back to her and leaned forward, resting on his crutches. "I shall have to defer for now. I am afraid I have already experienced as much glory as I can handle."

"Handle?"

"Uhmm, perhaps *stomach* might have been a better word. As much glory as I can stomach."

"Ah."

"Are there other oddities to explore?"

Lottie smiled. "Follow me."

THEY SPENT AN HOUR CHASING Gabriel's paintings around the main floor of the Abbey.

Well, not so much 'chased' as 'hobbled-sedately,' Alex supposed.

Gabriel was prolific. Some of his work was traditionally staid, like a view of the Palantine Hill and another of the newly-uncovered ruins in Pompeii.

Other works were more . . . eccentric.

One painting featured the Emperor Napoleon as a centaur—"Part of Gabriel's human-animal-amalgamation phase," Lottie explained.

Another showed miners as ghouls, swinging pickaxes underground in funeral shrouds—"My ravings about the working conditions of Welsh miners likely played a part in that one."

They stopped from time to time as Alex had to rest his leg or his arms. It was appalling the muscle strength he had lost after only a couple weeks of inactivity.

In the end, they circled back to the library, eating a hearty luncheon and playing chess under the lofty gaze of a winged Gabriel.

Alex still longed to return to his earlier musings—*why* had Lottie kissed him?

In fact, he ruminated too long and found himself in dire straits on the chess board.

Bloody hell but this lass was good at chess.

The fact that Lady Charlotte Whitaker excelled at chess was not shocking.

Rather . . . it was the *way* she played.

Given her external serenity and fierce intelligence, he would have assumed her to be a measured player. The kind to thoughtfully weigh each move and consider its ramifications.

Instead, Lottie dashed into the game. Recklessly. Fearlessly.

Her pawns stormed and her knights laid siege. Her bishops conspired while her queen slashed and plundered.

Her strategy of play could be summarized as *breathless defiance*.

He had vastly underestimated her.

As usual, Lottie's external harmony led one to assume that her inner life was similarly peaceful.

But like the mole on her cheek, her small outer imperfections were wee emblems of the riot of living inside her head.

And, in the end, wasn't that the answer to his question—

Why had she kissed him?

She had kissed him because Lady Charlotte, despite her demure princess-like appearance, was herself a dragon.

And perhaps in that breathless moment when her lips touched his, she had unleashed the fire to live her life as boldly as she checkmated his king.

15

A lex awoke the next day to sore muscles in his arms and chest from using his crutches. He clearly needed to strengthen his upper body.

Letters arrived. The day and time were now set for Alex to meet with Mr. S. Smith outside Chippenham. As the date was still a week off, Alex was cautiously optimistic that his leg and body would be up to the strain of the coach ride.

In the meantime, being mobile again meant Alex could more actively explore Frome Abbey and its lands. He wasn't quite up to traveling out to survey the estate himself, but he could at least track Mr. Warden down on his own two legs.

Consequently, the steward continued to be grudgingly helpful. Alex supposed Mr. Warden relayed every one of their interactions back to Lord Frank, not that there was anything untoward about that. Alex couldn't fault Lord Frank for being watchful.

But Mr. Warden was fiercely loyal to the man who had hired him. This was problematic on multiple levels. The steward wished to show his employer in a positive light; therefore, any of Lord Frank's bungled errors would be swept under the rug. Moreover, Mr. Warden wanted to appear competent and knowledgeable himself, so any mismanagement on his part would also be well-hidden.

Alex came to the conclusion that he needed to be methodical about his perusal and go through every aspect of the marquisate's finances and management with a fine-tooth comb.

After all, he had the time.

Consequently, he set aside two hours every morning to review the estate ledgers and make his own tallies of the figures. He also asked for the reports and correspondence sent by other managers and understewards. It wasn't much to go on, but it was a beginning.

Of course, skimming through page after page of estate reports and figures brought back a host of memories of his youth—his father, Ian, and McPherson Farms.

As was Alex's wont when such memories assailed him, he busied his hands to still his mind.

LOTTIE FELL INTO AN EASY friendship with Cousin Alex.

The topic of their kiss did not come up again, and for that, she was simultaneously grateful and frustrated.

For his part, Alex quickly became adept at maneuvering with his crutches. He traversed stairs with ease and even began to make brief forays into the gravel-lined paths winding through the abbey's formal gardens. The wiry physical strength and stamina of his body was truly astonishing.

She learned inadvertently from the butler that Alex spent an hour every morning working through a series of 'Greek' exercises with a pair of dumb-bells Dr. Smithson had sent up. Alex said the exercises were intended to maintain strength in the upper body and other limbs while his leg healed.

From the housekeeper, Lottie heard Alex had spent two afternoons seeing to the medical needs of the estate staff, speaking with each one personally in a small room beside the butler's pantry.

In short—Cousin Alex was a whirling dervish of energy.

Keeping track of him felt a little bit like trying to corral Freddie when he had been a toddler. Her nephew had been prone to disappear the second eyes were not upon him.

Alex was cut of the same cloth.

Did he ever sit still, Lottie wondered? Was his life as a physician also one of constant motion?

Lottie paused at the thought, as she wasn't entirely sure. She supposed being a doctor could be rather frenetic at times.

But she wanted to know.

She wanted to know . . . *everything.*

How he spent his days in Edinburgh with patients. How he passed the evenings. How he dined and conversed and worked and would it be possible to envision herself in those scenes with him?

Such thoughts were unhelpful.

Particularly as word of Alex's never-ending busy-ness even reached London.

Margaret wrote in one of her weekly letters—

Mr. Warden informs Frank that Dr. Whitaker is moving about readily now. Will the man remove himself from Frome Abbey soon and come to London to sign the writ, do you think? Mr. Warden has expressed concerns that Dr. Whitaker is prone to seeing problems where none exist. Frank and Ferndown worry that the longer Dr. Whitaker lingers, the more he will wish to govern the whole of Frome Abbey himself. But the King and Committee on Privilege have made so many demands, Frank cannot spare the time to travel to Frome Abbey and force the issue himself. What is your opinion of the situation?

Please write soon. I am missing your company here in London, and Freddie keeps asking when Tottie will come . . .

Lottie sighed.

What *did* she think about Cousin Alex? He was scarcely five weeks into his recuperation.

But Margaret was not wrong.

Alex was decidedly mobile.

But mobile enough to withstand a lengthy carriage journey? First the three-day journey to London to sign the attainder? And then the even longer trip back to Edinburgh?

That . . . she was less sure.

Fortunately, she felt like they were good enough friends at this point that she could simply ask him.

Lottie ran Alex to ground in the stables.

"There you are," she said, peering over a stall door.

Alex was grooming Galahad. The stallion had been her late father's pride and joy, so Lottie was pleased to see that the horse's injuries had healed entirely. Alex had a crutch under one arm and a brush in the other. "I did not expect to find you doing a groom's work."

He shrugged. "I like to stay busy."

"I hadn't noticed," she said, her words holding a desert of dryness.

He chuckled.

"My family wonders how much longer you will be with us now?" she continued, getting straight to the point.

"Och, anxious to be rid of me?" Alex arched his eyebrows.

"Not for myself." Lottie shook her head and gathered her cloak tighter around her shoulders to ward off the chill. "You are an economical guest. Our stores of sugar and French wine have never been more secure."

Alex smiled. "Not to mention meat."

"That, too."

Alex brushed Galahad, his hand moving in confident strokes. "I cannae say I plan tae quit the estate for another pair of weeks at the least. My leg still aches and here I can easily rest when I tire."

"*Do* you tire?" she asked with a laugh.

"A wee bit in the evenings." He shrugged, continuing to brush Galahad's flank.

Lottie knew this. He never complained, but he elevated his leg after dinner and massaged his thigh muscles, grunting occasionally as if in pain.

"I am cautious and careful with my injury," Alex continued. "As long as the bone remains well-supported, it will continue to heal whether I lie abed or make myself useful."

"You are like Cox's timepiece—a perpetual motion machine. Always moving, never at rest."

As if proving her point, he did *not* pause. Instead, he continued to brush Galahad's coat, hopping and leaning on one crutch.

"I shall go mad if I sit," he said, voice quiet. "Besides, as Galahad was involved in my injury, I did not want to wait to confront him." Alex raised his head and looked at her. "I'm sure the servants or Dr. Smithson or someone has given ye a synopsis of my family's history."

"Not as such, actually," she replied, dredging up what little she had heard over the past weeks. "Just that your family owned a large stud farm in Scotland and that Galahad came from there."

She said nothing about the other rumors she had heard the steward whisper to the butler, something about Dr. Whitaker's brother and a tragic incident.

But she sensed the history lingering there, in the air between them.

Alex continued grooming. "When ye train horses, the first thing ye have tae learn is how tae fall without breaking your neck. The second is how to get right back on the horse, no matter what has occurred. I cannae get on Galahad quite yet—" He stood upright and waved the brush at his leg in its brace. "—and so I'm settling for tending to him instead. Besides, Galahad is a welcome bit of home."

Alex set down the brush. Galahad nudged Alex's pocket. With a smile, Alex withdrew several sugar cubes, offering them to the horse.

"So Galahad is allowed sugar but not yourself." Lottie shook her head.

"Something of the like." Alex gave Galahad one last pat and reached for his second crutch, hobbling his way over to her.

Questions crowded Lottie's tongue as he unlatched the door and stepped out.

You only speak of your sister. What happened to the rest of your family, particularly your brother?

What drives you to never sit still?

Why won't you eat sugar?

She suspected that the answers would reveal painful wounds, deeply gouged and perhaps still festering.

Hence his silence.

And hers in questioning him about it.

But the more she came to know him, the more she wished to ask.

Lottie watched as he set the brush in the tack room, his body swinging easily on his crutches to return to her.

Instead of poking directly at his pain, she asked, "Why are you a doctor in Edinburgh and not the owner of a prosperous horse farm? You have an obvious affinity for horses."

Very well, it was still obliquely related to her *true* questions.

A lady had to try, after all.

"My father often asked me that exact thing. '*Why medicine? Why cannae ye be content with horses?*'" He snorted. "The honest answer is the simplest—medicine fascinates me in a way that horses never have. I love animals and wished my family every success with their endeavors. But Ian, my older brother, was always destined to inherit the estate and stables. I would only ever be a hired hand. I didnae want that for my future. And so, I enrolled at university."

They fell into step, moving out of the stables and toward the parterre garden without either of them needing to direct the other.

Lottie tucked her hands into her muff and buried her face into the collar of her cloak. Alex appeared less affected by the cold—though his nose was decidedly red—looking out over the bare trees and brown earth.

"And your father supported you attending university?"

"Och, no!" Alex rolled his eyes. "My father was livid. I may have been his youngest child—the spare, not the heir—but that didnae mean his expectations were any different. It was only Ian's pleading that stopped my father from disinheriting me entirely. But my da cut me off financially, refusing to support my education. A wee inheritance from my mother and the occasional guinea from Ian were what saw me through my medical studies."

Lottie could imagine it. This man with such drive to excel, living in near poverty, scrimping by on meager rations, so doggedly determined.

Did he understand how attractive she found his idealism? How it called her, a song of competence and caring?

And so, naturally, she wanted to understand the forces that had shaped him—who loved him and who he loved in return, how he had come to move through the world.

"No wonder sitting still is difficult. I'm guessing you haven't stopped moving in decades."

"If Catriona is to be believed, I was born running."

Lottie smiled into the wool of her cloak.

"My father was not the most . . . understanding of men," Alex continued. "Dinnae misunderstand me, he was a good man but very much a man of his time." A long pause. "He took Ian's death hard."

Silence.

The gravel crunched underneath their feet.

They looped through the leaf-bare garden, Lottie's hands chilly despite her fur muff. The wind cut through her cloak, the air holding a bleak reminder of winter.

And yet, here and there she could also see the very beginnings of snowdrops coming up, the faintest hint of Spring.

The promise of better things to come. A reminder that life could blossom after a winter of suffering and sorrow.

She would be wise to remember that for herself.

And perhaps remind Alex of it, too.

"I would know how he died, your brother, if you would tell me the story." Lottie dared a brief glance his way.

Silence again.

The kind that stretched and pulled like taffy.

She should let the matter drop.

But . . . she could *feel* his grief, his suffering. It fairly pulsated around him.

And so, she said, "I am not a doctor, but I understand that sometimes lancing a wound helps to relieve any infection that may . . . fester."

The silence continued to lengthen.

She almost thought that he would not tell her. That she had crossed a bridge too far.

Finally, he sighed. "Ye are correct, of course, lass. All ye have to do is ask anyone who read the broadsheets seven years ago, and ye would have the whole sad tale. It isnae a secret, in the end. It's just . . . most already know, and so I dinnae bother to repeat it."

Ah.

"I would hear it." She glanced at him again.

His Adam's apple slid up and down his throat.

"It is a grim tale." His voice held a note of warning.

"Ah, well, I *must* hear it now."

He snorted, a smile ghosting over his lips.

The world was winter-still. Only the sound of their footfalls on the pebble path and the far-off lowing of cattle interrupted the silence.

"You must understand Ian was the best of brothers," Alex said into the quiet. "Many men complain about their elder brothers, how they teased and tormented. But not Ian. Even though I was six years his junior, he always welcomed me following him about the estate, helping with the horses. It is not too far to say that I worshiped Ian as a lad. Even after my falling out with my father, Ian regularly wrote and visited me in Edinburgh. He gave me a portion of his monthly allowance, anything to help me meet my ambitions."

He swallowed again.

Lottie sensed that he needed a moment, a brief space to gather his thoughts, to remember the good and not dwell too long on the bad.

"Two years before I graduated with my medical degree, Ian suffered a horrific injury. King Arthur, Galahad's sire, was a temperamental beast at best. A magnificent stallion but difficult to manage. The stallion kicked Ian, breaking his arm and shattering his right leg."

"Oh, gracious!"

"Aye. We were all panic-stricken, worried that Ian would die. But he was always a fighter, my brother. His leg had to be amputated—"

"Oh, Alex! How awful!" She pressed a hand to her mouth. "No wonder you were so distraught over your own injuries!"

"The similarities were terrifying, I willnae lie," he chuckled, dry and mirthless. "As you can imagine, Ian's recovery was long and painful. His arm was slow to heal, and the pain from his phantom missing leg was agonizing."

"I have heard of this. That after an amputation, it can feel as if the limb is still there and hurting."

"Exactly. In order to bear it all, Ian turned to laudanum in heavier and heavier quantities." Alex paused, leaning on his crutches, looking sightlessly over the dead garden. His eyes darted to hers. "I should tell you that the men in my family display a predilection toward excess. My father was prone to drunkenness. I am sure ye can see where this sad tale is headed. It did not take long for my brother to find himself in the thralls of opium."

"He became an addict?"

Alex nodded. A slicing up-and-down motion. "He devolved into an opium eater. Have you read De Quincey's *Confessions of an Opium Eater*?"

"Yes. It is rather engrossing."

"It is, but do not let De Quincey's whimsical narrative persuade ye into thinking that such a habit is not devastating. Everything I loved about my brother disappeared into his addiction. He became sullen and morose, his moods swinging wildly between euphoria and melancholy. I was in my final year of university, and—here I must admit to some shame—I did not fully appreciate the extent of Ian's crisis. I was too busy in my studies to give my brother the attention he needed. My father did what he could to help, but he had his own demons to fight . . ." Alex drifted off.

Lottie easily filled in what he did not say. If his brother was struggling, then his father had likely turned more and more to the bottle to deal with the stress.

"The business began to suffer. Even though he was mobile with a peg leg, Ian began to make costly mistakes. His moods were frightening, the laudanum addling his thinking. Over the Christmas holidays, Father begged me to speak with Ian, to see what I could do."

Alex leaned on his crutches and looked away, eyes glassy.

Lottie stretched out a hand, as if to . . . what? Wrap her arms around him in comfort? Stroke his face and to tell him that she didn't need to know, that he didn't need to expose his pain?

But they had removed that physical realm from their relationship. Touching him was a forbidden land she didn't dare trespass upon.

She let her hand fall.

He looked back to her.

"Dinnae look like that, lass." He smiled gently, eyes still unnaturally bright. "Ye were right. I ken that speaking of Ian *does* help the wound heal a wee bit more each time. But like all effective medicines, it tastes right terrible in the moment." He shook his head. "Let me finish this. I found Ian in the stables. He was clearly in the middle of an opiate fit, waving a dueling pistol round and round. I tried to speak with him, but it all went south. He was out of his mind, shouting that King Arthur needed to share in his misery. He shot the stallion in the leg with his pistol. Then he pulled the second dueling pistol from his pocket and, looking me in the eye, turned the gun on himself."

Lottie gasped, the air simply whooshing from her lungs.

She closed her eyes, as if somehow she could take the memory from his sight.

To *watch* a beloved brother take his own life in such a fashion.

To live with the grief and memory of it, again and again, every day.

To worry, endlessly, that the weakness of such excess ran in his own veins. That the slightest slip in himself might lead to a similar end.

"Oh, Alex," she whispered, opening her eyes and looking into his, trying to communicate her empathy in ways that words failed.

He nodded and leaned more heavily on his crutch.

"You can imagine the aftermath, I am sure. King Arthur had to be put down. My father . . ." Alex clenched his jaw and looked out over the fields. "My father did not cope well. *I* did not cope well. Nightmares still plague me from time to time."

He said nothing for a while. Lottie's heart thumped in her chest.

The horrors this man had endured.

He looked back at her. "I did not magically acquire a love of horse farming after that, no matter how my father pleaded and begged me to take over the family business. It was his dying wish, actually. But I simply could not. I realized that I loved horses because *Ian* had. Without him . . ." Alex drifted off with a shrug. "So you see, if the pain of my own family's history could not dissuade me from being a doctor, the demands of a far-off marquisate never will."

16

A lex had not lied to Lottie.

There *was* relief in talking about Ian, in reliving those painful, fraught memories. In speaking with her, he had felt something loosen within him. Some dread or tightness or *something* that had been stiff and sore had simply . . . melted.

He found himself falling into an easy rhythm, spending hours each day in Lottie's company.

He told her of the aftermath of Ian's death—his almost compulsive need to leave Britain and how that led him to respond to an advertisement for a physician aboard *The Minerva*.

He spent hours recounting his travels. He told her about Andrew, Rafe, Ewan, Kieran, and Jamie, as well as their journey to Sydney and then the New Hebrides.

He described their time in Vanuatu and Cuthie's perfidy in attempting to take the villagers there as slaves. The horror of Rafe and Andrew being beaten nearly to death for their refusal to cooperate. Ewan and Kieran, along with the villagers, freeing their friends only to be marooned on the island. The ship's subsequent destruction and Jamie's supposed death. Their eventual rescue by a Portuguese whaler and their year-long return to Britain.

He told her of his efforts in recent years to build his medical practice and his pride in what he and McNeal were accomplishing in Edinburgh.

She listened and exclaimed and Alex had never felt so thoroughly understood. The sensation was a host of adjectives—novel, cleansing, redeeming.

In turn, she told him about her father and their close relationship. How wee Anne's death had nearly broken them all, particularly as both of Margaret's pregnancies had been so hard won.

Mostly, her expression nearly glowed as she spoke of Freddie and what a healing light he was for all of them.

"It's why we must ensure that the estate is well-managed," Lottie said several days later as they sat in the library. "I wish everything to be passed along intact to Freddie."

"Aye," Alex agreed. "But let's face facts—we are making no headway with Mr. Warden."

Mr. Warden, when he was at home, remained recalcitrant. However, the man traveled incessantly.

"How can Mr. Warden possibly see to the needs of Frome Abbey, as well as the marquisate as a whole?" Lottie asked.

"The man is far too busy. He seems to be doing the work of a wee army single-handedly."

Lottie nodded. She turned sideways in her chair, one arm draped across the back.

Weak February sun poured in from the windows beside them, washing her face from left to right and burnishing her silvery hair. She was dressed in soft green wool, a colorful shawl wrapped around her shoulders and gray knitted half-mitts on her hands for warmth.

As usual, the force of her beauty caught Alex unawares. Often now, he thought of her as simply Lottie, the woman who was his friend.

But moments like this caught him out, where he realized, yet again, how staggeringly lovely she was.

Sometimes the sheer pull of his attraction to her frightened him.

Case in point—he avoided even *thinking* of kissing Lottie again.

A wise man knew his limits. When it came to Lady Charlotte, the tether of Alex's control was far too frayed for his liking.

It was likely for the best he was leaving to see this Mr. S. Smith in the morning. He had already made arrangements with the coachman and ensured that the interior of the carriage was well padded.

The time away from Lottie's cheery smile would hopefully allow for clearer thinking.

"How was the estate managed before Mr. Warden, I wonder?" Alex asked, forcing his eyes away from her lovely face. They had a tendency to linger and stare.

Lottie tapped her bottom lip. "We should ask."

"Pardon?"

"We should ask my father's former man-of-affairs. I would wager that I could find an address for Mr. Argent in my father's study. At the very least a former address that we could apply to for information."

"I am an *eejit* for not thinking of this before now." Alex nearly laughed at his stupidity. Granted, he had been wanting to avoid entangling himself in the affairs of the marquisate. But that ship had long sailed.

"I'll fetch pen and paper." Lottie rushed from the room.

Alex watched her leave, trying to decide what concerned him more—

The fact that Mr. Argent would thoroughly enlighten him as to the problems with the marquisate.

Or the realization that Lady Charlotte took the sun with her whenever she left a room.

ALEX ARRIVED EARLY TO MEET Mr. S. Smith.

He procured the finest private parlor The Dancing Bull had to offer—which was a wee, shabby space off the main dining room—and ordered up a selection of cold meats, cheese, and tea. He checked his pocket watch.

Mr. Smith was to arrive with the London-bound coach around noon. The stagecoach would break for an hour for passengers to lunch and would then be off again, with Mr. Smith aboard. Alex would only have one hour to discuss Mr. Smith's medical issue and his connection with *The Minerva*.

Who would this Mr. Smith turn out to be?

Clearly he wasn't so ill as to be unable to travel long distances. The journey from Yorkshire to Plymouth and back was not for the infirm.

Alex longed to pace as he waited, but the jostling of the two-hour journey to the inn had set his leg to aching. Servants had piled the interior of the carriage high with pillows and blankets to cushion his leg, and though the coachman had driven at a snail's pace, the jolt of the rutted road had been unpleasant.

He had settled into a chair as soon as he arrived, propping his leg atop a footstool with relief. The twinge was a good reminder that no matter how recovered he felt, his leg was still healing.

And so instead of pacing, he was left to obsessively consult his watch and compare its time against that of the aged clock sitting atop the fireplace mantel. The simple act brought up a surge of familiar memories—wiping down his surgical table between patients, the smell of chlorinated lime, McNeal's laugh echoing down the hallway.

Bloody hell but he missed his life in Edinburgh.

Soon, he promised himself. Soon he would be well enough to travel. Just a few more weeks.

And what about Lottie? a quiet part of his heart asked.

Alex swallowed. He didn't have an answer to that, and the thought made him tetchy.

He checked his pocket watch again.

Where was the blasted coach?

After nearly an hour's wait, the stagecoach rattled into the coaching yard. A few minutes later, Mr. Smith entered the parlor with a quick rap.

"Dr. Whitaker, I presume?" the man asked, removing his hat and fixing Alex with a rather stern look.

Mr. Smith was a wiry man who appeared determinedly sparse in everything—height, hair, bonhomie.

More to the point, Mr. Smith was more appropriately referred to as

Reverend Smith. The man's cassock coat and stiff collar loudly proclaimed his profession. The threadbare nature of both testified of his poverty.

"Aye." Alex nodded. "Forgive me for not standing tae greet ye. My leg wasnae keen on the journey here." He waved toward his propped foot.

"Ah." Reverend Smith dragged his gaze over Alex's injured leg, studying the wood-and-metal brace for a moment. "A lack of manners is to be expected with such an injury, I suppose."

Alex barely stopped his eyebrows flying upward in surprise.

The reverend's tone was unexpectedly combative.

They settled into eating their luncheon.

Or, rather, Alex asked questions while Reverend Smith ate with single-minded focus and gave predominantly monosyllabic answers.

Yes, the weather was fine.

Yes, his health was excellent.

No, he did not wish to discuss, at the moment, why he was in this corner of England.

The man's accent was an indiscriminate sort—educated enough to make pinpointing his exact origins difficult. Moreover, the reverend appeared to be sizing up Alex's person, as if weighing the value of him. The man might be a vicar, but Alex had met card sharps with a less calculating demeanor.

On the whole, the meeting was jarringly unexpected.

After fifteen minutes, Alex glanced at his pocket watch yet again and recognized that he had, perhaps, been had for a fool.

How could this impoverished cleric have any information that was worth the effort and pain Alex had gone through to be here?

And why would the man wish to consult a doctor? If his appetite were any indication, Reverend Smith appeared hearty and hale.

"Ye said in your letter that ye wished tae consult with me about a medical matter?" Alex finally asked, shifting his aching leg with a wince. "I am eager to get on with the purpose of this meeting."

"Yes." Reverend Smith drank his tea with gusto. "The medical matter is not for myself, you see. It pertains to a friend."

Of course.

Alex all but sighed.

It did appear that he had been grossly mistaken in Reverend Smith's intentions.

Alex had been so caught up in his own desires to uncover more information about *The Minerva* that he neglected to carefully scrutinize Reverend Smith's bonafides.

"It is rather difficult to assess a patient who is not present," Alex replied, a hint of exasperation creeping into his tone.

If he noticed, Reverend Smith did not show it.

"I'm not sure if questioning the patient will help, to be honest," the man replied.

"Yes, well, only a qualified physician should be allowed to make that decision," Alex said, growing snippier.

"Perhaps." Reverend Smith poured himself more tea, insensitive to Alex's rising frustration.

The man seemed careless and haphazard. And yet, there was an air of deliberation about him that rendered Alex wary. A sense that the reverend could be either friend or foe, and Alex had no idea where the man would land in the end.

Reverend Smith fixed Alex with a pair of intelligent eyes. "To be brief, a friend of the family suffered a severe blow to the head several years ago, resulting in a total loss of memory of all events for months prior to the injury."

"I see," Alex said, "and ye wish tae know if this individual's memory will heal in time?"

"I cannot assume that my friend's memory will heal. It has been years since the injury." Reverend Smith reached for another slice of cold ham. "Rather, if this friend is healthy otherwise, would it be ill-advised for them to undertake a rigorous journey?"

Alex frowned. *This* was the question Reverend Smith had been desperate to have answered? It seemed a rather paltry thing.

"Without seeing and speaking with your friend in person, I cannot give a definitive medical opinion," Alex replied.

Reverend Smith took the words in stride. "Does your opinion remain the same if I am concerned that the journey might bring back unwelcome memories?"

Alex's frown deepened. "Unless the injury happened due to a similar sort of journey in the past, I cannot envision why such travel would incur a risk of jarring memories loose. But, again, without speaking directly with the patient—"

"And if the injury *did* occur during a similar journey?"

Alex blinked, sitting back in his seat.

What was this man's game? What was he about?

Why go to so much effort to ask *Alex*, of all people, these questions?

Alex drummed his fingers on the table. "I repeat, without seeing the patient, I can say nothing definitively. Hypothetically, the end results of what you describe could be unpredictable. Monsieur Sauvages classifies many types of amnesia, but generally, once a memory is lost, it is considered lost for good. The mind *can* heal over time, but a complete recovery of erased memories almost never occurs. Any restoration is fragmentary, at best."

"Ah." Reverend Smith leaned back in his own chair.

That was all the man said.

Simply, *ah.*

Maddening.

Alex fixed the reverend with a stern look.

"Ye said this matter related to *The Minerva* in some way," Alex said, the bite in his voice more pronounced. "I would like tae know how."

He followed this by pointedly checking his watch, making it clear that the reverend was running out of time.

Reverend Smith smiled, as if he found Alex's frustration . . . amusing.

"I have received funding from a generous benefactor to undertake a mission to preach Christianity to the heathen tribes of the South Pacific," the man said, patting his stomach. "That was my business in Plymouth. I was finalizing details for our journey to Sydney, Australia."

Alex let out a slow breath, hunting through the reverend's words, deciding which thread he wished to tug first.

"*Our* journey?" he asked.

"Myself and my wife. Four other couples from my congregation. And possibly this family friend."

"And ye wish tae ask about my own journey there?" Alex glanced at the clock on the mantel. The man's stagecoach departed in less than fifteen minutes. "I would need hours to recount it all."

Reverend Smith stared at him for a long moment, that same *calculating* look on his face.

"Ye seem tae be dancing around the issue, sir," Alex said. "Perhaps ye could spare my guesses and get to the point."

The reverend laced his fingers together. "It has come to my attention that there was a woman aboard *The Minerva*."

The words were an ambush.

Alex hissed in a breath, his jolting reaction nearly visceral.

Reverend Smith's impassive face said he had *expected* as much.

Alex's heart leapt into his throat, his mind racing.

How could this man know about Jamie Fyffe? It seemed almost impossible—

"Your silence, Doctor, is telling," the reverend continued, his expression hardening into firm resolve. "You sit here in your finery and gentility and pretend to be a man of honor. But I know that you sanctioned men keeping a helpless woman aboard *that* ship. You aided them in using that poor creature for their . . . their *base* pleasures."

Alex's mouth, quite literally, dropped.

His jaw flapped open, words unequal to the sheer depravity of this accusation.

"*Pardon?!*" he gasped. "What in damnation—"

"Though not a lady by birth, Miss Eilidh Fyffe"—the reverend stretched out her first name, *AY-lee*—"most certainly did not deserve to spend her days forced to act as a *harlot.*"

Alex struggled to form words, but the horrific shock of such allegations had sucked all the air from his lungs.

Reverend Smith continued on, "You are a doctor. You have *promised* to care for those in need. And yet, you stood by and allowed this poor woman to be cruelly abused. How can you live with yourself? How can you think to stand before God and defend—"

"Bloody hell, man!" Alex all but shouted, air whooshing back into him. "Miss Fyffe was *never* forced to use her body for men's pleasure. She was a dear friend. I protected her—"

"That is not what I have heard."

"Who told ye this?" Alex pounced. "Who has been filling your head with such lies?"

Very few people knew that Jamie Fyffe was actually Miss Eilidh Fyffe. The reverend stared at Alex in frosty silence.

"Who told you?" Alex repeated. "Was it Captain Cuthie? Mr. Massey? Some other person who survived?" Alex snapped his fingers. "This man with memory loss. Was he aboard *The Minerva*, too? Does this brain injury stem from when the ship sank? Does *he* have memories of Miss Fyffe? Memories that appear incomplete?"

The stagecoach horn blared, the sound jolting through the room.

"I best be off." Reverend Smith stood, gathered his items, and lifted a hat to his head.

"Ye cannae leave! I have far too many questions!" Alex struggled to his feet, wincing as his leg throbbed, reaching for his crutches propped against the wall. "Miss Fyffe was a dear friend. I have mourned her death most keenly. Please! Stay! I would hear what you know. I will pay for your transportation back to Yorkshire."

That got Reverend Smith's attention. His eyes glinted at the mention of money.

"What if I asked for a significant contribution to our trip to the South Pacific?" the man asked.

Alex paused. "Such an outlay would depend upon the information provided," he hedged, mind scrambling. This man knew something. And as Massey and Cuthie had gone entirely to ground, the reverend might be their best source of information. "But anything that would help me understand what happened to my good friend, Miss Eilidh Fyffe, would have monetary worth. Stay. Let us discuss it. Perhaps you know something of these notices in the newspaper, as well."

The reverend studied him, as if weighing the worth of the information he possessed.

Alex had to convince this man to spill what he knew. Not just for Jamie, but for Kieran, too. With the procurator fiscal making noise in Aberdeen, Kieran's life could be in danger. The Brotherhood needed every last scrap of information.

"Stay," Alex repeated. "*Please.* I would hear what you know of Mis Fyffe—"

The stagecoach blew a second warning.

The reverend shook his head.

"I must away." He turned for the door.

"Wait—"

"You will hear from me, if and when I decide that you are worthy of the information I know," the reverend said, one hand on the door knob. "Good day, Doctor."

Alex struggled to move with his crutches in the small space. He couldn't even round the table before Reverend Smith was out the door.

Alex truly had been taken for a fool.

Just not in the way he had thought.

ALEX WAS STILL STUNNED AND fuming when he arrived back at Frome Abbey two hours later.

His leg throbbed, a pulsing arch of pain that had kept time with every jolt of the carriage.

He could scarcely force his exhausted body up the stairs to his bedchamber.

Reverend Smith was long gone, off to London and Yorkshire.

Had Alex been capable, he would have hired a horse on the spot from the inn's stables and taken after the stagecoach, determined to demand the entire story from the man.

Alex would almost believe the man an opportunist—a fraudsman out to extort money from the Brotherhood for baseless accusations.

Was the man even a pastor? Or was his clothing a lie, as well?

But . . .

Reverend Smith had known that Miss Eilidh Fyffe had been aboard *The Minerva.*

That was a closely-guarded secret.

The good reverend had to have learned it from a survivor of the wreck.

Cuthie and Massey had been gone from British soil for over a year, as far as Alex knew. Were they Reverend Smith's source of information?

Or was this mysterious man with a missing memory another survivor then? And, if so, who was the man?

For the briefest moment, Alex pondered that perhaps the person with the missing memory was Jamie herself.

But . . . no. To report such a tale, Jamie would have had to have forgotten them all . . . even Kieran.

Particularly Kieran.

Such an idea stretched the bounds of credulity—that Jamie would remember her own identity but not that of her husband. She had loved Kieran too fiercely for that memory to have been utterly wiped from her mind.

Alex collapsed into his bed, exhausted.

But before succumbing to sleep, he managed to lift pen to paper and scribble out a letter.

> *Dear Andrew,*
>
> *What are the chances Jamie could have forgotten about Kieran . . .*

17

Fortunately, Alex did not have to wait long for Andrew's reply. It arrived a scarce four days later:

> *What the bloody hell! Your tale certainly throws a spanner into the works. I cannot imagine a situation where Jamie would have forgotten about Kieran, no matter the injury. I will hire a Runner from Bow Street immediately. If this Reverend Smith is a man of God, it should be simple enough to track down his location and verify any potential ties to Cuthie or Massey. Surely, he learned of Jamie from them and is now looking to profit from the information.*
>
> *In other news, how goes your appraisal of the marquisate? If your leg is healed enough to withstand travel to a coaching inn, I assume you have managed shorter journeys around the estate to see matters for yourself?*

Alex nearly sighed. Those were good questions.

The journey to the coaching inn had taken a toll. He had lain in bed and moved little for two days afterward, allowing the ache in his leg to subside before even considering a larger venture. Lottie had kept him company for an afternoon of his recovery—a maid in the corner as a chaperone—reading a dry medical treatise to him and asking frighteningly intelligent questions.

Fortunately, the journey did not appear to have hampered his leg's healing. Once the pain retreated and Alex dared to stand again, he felt no lingering twinges. In truth, the bone grew stronger and stronger with every passing day. He wore the brace obsessively—and would for at least another month—but provided he was careful, he was confident of a full recovery.

Andrew was correct, however.

Alex needed to inspect the estate for himself.

In the days following, Alex felt well enough to begin forays out to assess the estate with his own eyes. He still couldn't ride or drive himself, but as long as the coachman drove at a sedate pace to minimize jarring, Alex fared just fine.

Unfortunately, his journeys around the estate lands did nothing to stem his concerns.

Fields needed to be modernized, their drainage improved before crop yields would increase.

Fallow land needed to be converted to pasture, and current livestock improved with heartier breeds that would bring in better revenues.

Tenanted properties showed signs of disrepair.

Overall, there was a general lack of activity, even for February.

It was hard to determine if Mr. Warden was incompetent or simply too over-taxed to properly address problems. Alex suspected it was likely a combination of both. Would hiring a more capable steward and a separate man of affairs be sufficient to address the issues?

Alex didn't know.

They hadn't had a reply from Mr. Argent, the former man of affairs for the marquisate.

And until then, Alex would simply continue to gather evidence.

DAYS PASSED AND FEBRUARY MELTED into a blustery March.

This year, however, Lottie's heart no longer drowned in grief and mourning. Spring loomed like sunrise, a glorious awakening she couldn't wait to greet.

Granted, Alex contributed to her sense of optimism. Somewhere over the weeks, their tentative camaraderie had become a deeply-satisfying friendship.

At times, Lottie feared she viewed Alex as considerably more than a friend.

Would a mere friend occupy so much cranial space in such a short period of time? Truthfully, what had she spent her time pondering before his arrival?

Now, she replayed their conversations over and over. The hoarse timbre of his voice as he spoke of his brother's horrific death. The way his eyes crinkled at the corners when he laughed.

The soft pressure of his lips when she had kissed him . . .

"What would it take for you to eat some sugar?" Lottie asked him one particularly-dreary Friday in early March.

Alex looked up at the question.

They were sitting side-by-side at a large table in the library, both replying to correspondence in companionable silence. Rain pattered against the windowpanes.

Dreich weather, Alex called it.

"Why would I eat sugar?" A smile tugged at Alex's lips. "That's a rather odd place to begin a conversation."

Lottie sat back in her chair and indulged in the simple joy of staring at him.

Alex lounged beside her with coiled strength, his braced leg extended. His shoulders amply filled out his tailcoat and the muscles in his upper arms pressed outward on his sleeves.

Heavens but he was a finely-formed man.

She particularly liked watching him write, the way his long fingers held the quill pen, the flex and ripple of tendons across the back of his hand. He had even walked her through the names of said tendons once, holding out a fist for her to examine as he pointed and labeled each one—*pollicus longus, extensor indices, extensor digitorum, digiti minimi.*

The sight of Alex dragging a pencil across the back of his hand, naming tendons, should *not* have set her heart to pounding and yet, *everything* about the man was a hammer to her good sense.

"I was merely pondering the idea of sugar," she said. "You allow Galahad a bit of sugar and yet not yourself."

He shrugged. "Why eat it?"

"No, I think the proper question is *why not?*" She grinned. "Why not eat sugar in moderation? It is hardly deleterious like strong drink or opium."

"Why do ye eschew meat?"

Lottie smiled broader. If he thought to trip her up, he should have known better by now.

"We've touched on this before. I choose not to eat meat because I cannot abide the thought of ingesting another living thing. I agree with Mr. Shelley and others that our practice of consuming our fellow creatures is cruel and unnecessary. An animal is capable of affection and kindness; the least I can do is not eat them in return. But I do not see the same ideological restriction applied to sugar."

A grin touched his lips.

Lips I've kissed.

Lottie batted away that unhelpful observation.

"Perhaps," he said. "Though I am sure ye are aware that sugar is often produced on the backs of slave labor."

"Of course. It is why I insist that we only purchase sugar that was grown and milled by freemen. Such things exist."

"Too much sugar is not healthy for the body, particularly one's teeth." he countered.

"Excess of anything is not advisable, I agree. But surely between eating mountains of cakes and biscuits every day and never putting even a grain of sugar in your tea, there is a happily-lived middle place where sugar and health can reside in harmony?"

His smile broadened, as if he sensed she was prepared to press him further.

He was a wise man.

"Of course, the occasional wee bit of sugar doesnae a habit make, nor do I think it will adversely affect an otherwise healthy person." He extended his braced leg, stretching it out and massaging the muscle in his thigh. "I wish I had a grand answer for ye, but the truth is banal—I stopped eating sugar years ago and have simply never reconsidered it."

"You have *never* reconsidered it?"

"I hear the oblique censure in your words." He laughed, hooking a nearby footstool with his good leg and tugging it under the table. He lifted his braced leg to rest on it. "Ye perhaps wonder if I shun anything that I find too enticing? That after the experience of my father and brother, that I fear losing any part of myself to appetites I cannot control?"

"You *do* deny yourself most of life's pleasures." The words fell from her lips before she could catch them.

Now she was censuring him in truth.

And perhaps reminding him of her own indiscretion in kissing him. After all, he had not sought a chance to revisit their kiss.

But if he found offense in her words, he did not show it.

"I have already asked Cook to make fairy cakes tomorrow," she continued. "Will you accept a dare and eat one with me?"

Alex appeared to contemplate it.

He looked down at the table between them, a long finger idly tracing the wood grain. Lottie stared at the flexing tendon—*extensor digitorum*.

She laid her palm on the table just to be that much closer to him.

"I will accept your dare." He lifted his eyes to hers, but not before they snagged on her hand resting beside his. "But I would ask for a truth in return."

She stilled and then laughed. "You require a truth from me in order to perform a dare? I am not entirely sure you understand how the game works, Cousin Alex."

He smiled, his eyes meeting hers with a peculiar sort of look. As if he found her wondrous.

"Have you never played Truth or Dare?" she continued.

"I am familiar with the game, yes."

"Mmmm," she mused. "If you have a question, you can simply ask it of me. No need to hide behind games."

He went back to tracing a finger on the table, as if her reply left him vaguely nonplussed. Was his hand now wandering closer to hers? And how absurd that the very thought set a pulse drumming in her wrist.

"I have been wondering . . . and not to dredge up past, erhm, *conversations*—" He leaned on the word, giving it levels of meaning. "—but why when we, or rather, when you leaned in and—" He cleared his throat, as if unequal to saying the words *kissed me*. "Why did ye say that your head was so heavy?"

Lottie could feel a blush creep up her cheeks as he spoke. Perhaps her earlier words *had* sparked his memory after all.

How to answer that question?

You deny yourself every sweet thing, but I clearly do not.

Your lips looked too delicious to resist.

Mmmm.

"What is so heavy in your life that you require assistance to catch it?" he continued, words flowing better now. "Isn't your life unencumbered? Is that not the goal of every gentleman? To shelter and support the women in his life? To ensure that they never know such heaviness?"

Lottie's heart lurched.

She found her eyes lingering on his finger still tracing the wood grain, close but never touching her hand. Her own fingers tingled with each pass of his, so near and yet . . .

Abruptly it was a metaphor for herself and Alex—close but never *together*.

She swallowed, dragging her gaze off their hands and back to his face. "I would counter and ask—why must I be so sheltered from life? If we are dredging up the remains of past discussions, let us return to Wollstonecraft. Men feel lonely in marriage—that they lack a true partner—*because* of this societal wish to keep women innocent."

"Innocent?" His brows drew down. His finger stilled. "I'm not sure I follow."

"Well, that is the result of sheltering a young lady, is it not? A sheltered woman is an innocent one. Truthfully, it is the stupidest thing."

He laughed, a startled sound.

"You may laugh," she continued, "but you know I speak truth. Why must women remain innocent? What are men afraid of? That once a woman knows better—once she experiences even a bit of the world—she won't want a life with the man in question? And, if that truly were the case, then what does that say about . . . well, *everything*?"

"I see your point. I suppose such sheltering goes back to the antiquated idea that women are less capable of dealing with the sheer ugliness of life."

Lottie leaned into the back of her chair, her fingers now drumming the table beside his, expression likely as indignant as she felt. "You and I both know that is simply preposterous."

"It is."

"Men go off and have grand adventures—like yourself with your overseas voyage—and then come home and expect to marry a woman who has never done anything, either with her brain *or* her life. But such a marriage is hopelessly imbalanced—he has lived too much of life and she . . . not enough. So as a result, both parties end up unhappy and betrayed. I have seen it too often in aristocratic marriages."

"Your parents, as well?"

"I cannot say on that account," Lottie said. "My mother died when I was too young. But my father never remarried, so that speaks to his devotion to my mother. I do vaguely remember my grandparents' marriage, however, as my grandfather died when I was eight. Theirs was a marriage of equals. Grandfather was always delighted to be in Grandmère's company, even after thirty years of marriage. Which, of course, merely proves my point. Grandmère is a well-educated, erudite, and sophisticated woman of the world."

"Ye would like such a marriage?" He had gone back to idly tracing the wood grain again.

"Yes. Yes, I would like that very much." She looked as his finger circling her hand. "So, you will eat a fairy cake with me tomorrow then?"

"Perhaps."

He paused and then ever so softly pressed a fingertip into the back of her hand where it lay on the tabletop.

It burned her skin.

Lottie forgot how to breathe.

"But in true philosopher form," he continued, "ye still haven't answered my question—why is life heavy for you?"

The room settled into quiet, as if everything awaited her answer.

His finger drew a slow line down the back of her hand. Was he now tracing the blue of her veins?

She forced her eyes to remain on his face and not the sensation scattered up her arm.

"I suppose . . ." She licked her lips. "I suppose I never understood the weight of my words until someone truly listened to them."

She did not add a second truth to her statement—

That she had been falling, falling, falling for the past two years. Losing Anne and Gabriel and Papa had sent her tumbling headlong into a vast chasm.

But then this man had appeared. And he heard her.

And in that simple act, he had given cushion to her fall.

THE NEXT DAY, ALEX ATE a fairy cake.

It was pink and feather-light and unutterably sweet.

He immediately reached for a second.

He tried for days afterward to banish the glow in Lottie's eyes as she watched him swallow, a decidedly-kissable smile on her lips.

She was wrong, of course.

He did not deny himself every sweet thing. If he did, he would have banned himself from her presence weeks ago.

But instead, day after day, he sought her out, desperate for her company.

I never understood the weight of my words until someone truly listened to them.

Her insight was a punch to his senses.

Because, heaven help him, he wanted to be the one who caught her words.

Every last one.

18

A return letter from Mr. Argent finally arrived ten days later.

Lottie was the first to see it. Mr. Argent's reply was nestled under a letter from Margaret asking, yet again, when Lottie would leave for London.

After all, her sister wrote, *the doctor is quite recovered. He has been journeying all over the estate, from what I hear. Mr. Warden is of the opinion that Dr. Whitaker should have quit Frome Abbey a fortnight ago. To be quite honest, your insistence that Dr. Whitaker does not wish to assume the marquisate is the only reason Frank hasn't ordered Mr. Warden to evict the doctor entirely. More to the point, you are no longer needed there. Yourself and Grandmère are sorely missed. Please write back and tell me you will be coming soon.*

Sigh.

Lottie needed to join her family in London. She knew this.

But neither she nor Alex were eager to quit one another's company.

And given the weight of Mr. Argent's letter in her hand, there was still the state of the marquisate to consider.

Her father's final injunction weighed upon her. She had made a promise, but what did it mean, in the end, to 'ensure his lands and people were secured'? Was it simply an extension of his request to have Freddie inherit the title, as he specifically instructed Ferndown? Would Papa have wanted Freddie to inherit, no matter the cost?

Lottie had no answers.

"Look what has arrived," she said to Alex as she set the letter before him in the library. "I am eager to know its contents."

Alex set down his quill and motioned for her to read the letter with him.

Its contents did not disappoint.

After a brief greeting, Mr. Argent got right to the point.

I must be honest with you, Dr. Whitaker. I was stunned to be let go. I spent over twenty years as man of affairs to the prior Lord Lockheade and grieved his loss. Being dismissed so quickly after his death was a second painful blow. I am even more appalled that my position has not been filled.

As I am sure you are aware, the marquisate is a sprawling empire of lands, estates, and people (both tenants and employed workers). Overseeing it effectively was a busy job for myself and the other six men on my staff. However, at Lord Lockheade's passing and the subsequent confusion over the succession of the title, the Committee on Privilege made several decisions. They appointed Lord Frank Fulton as the interim regent for the estate and charged him with maintaining it. The assumption being that as his son stood to inherit, Lord Frank would be motivated to deal honorably with the land and people. As a check against any greed, however, all estate monies were frozen. Beyond the reasonable allowance given, Lord Frank cannot access any of the deeper funds of the marquisate.

I have come to understand that myself and my staff were let go in an effort to economize. I hear rumors that Lord Frank has accumulated large gambling debts and had hoped to use the wealth of the marquisate to assist in settling them. When those funds were denied him, he looked to other options. By casting off myself and a score of other staff, Lord

Frank thinks to skim funds. I surmise that this is not the only cost-cutting measure Lord Frank has employed.

My cousin, Mr. John Bartlet, lives on the Frome Abbey estate and has been a source of much of this information. He could likely give you a more accurate picture of what specifically is happening. My information is second- and third-hand, at best.

I currently reside with a sister in London as I continue to seek another position. If you wish to speak in person, please call upon me . . .

"I dinnae ken what to make of this." Alex dropped the letter onto the tabletop and pinched the bridge of his nose.

Lottie released a slow breath.

"It could be nothing," she murmured and then wondered if she said the words for Alex's benefit or her own.

Would Frank do such a thing? Skim profits off the marquisate to line his own pocket? As much as Lottie would like to answer *No!*, she could not say for certain. There was a certain doltish pig-headedness in Frank. So much so that she could imagine him stooping to such a scheme in panic.

"Even if it is something," Alex replied, "it doesnae follow that I must assume the marquisate in order to repair the problem. I am sure the Committee on Privilege would not uphold such an egregious abuse of power on Lord Frank's part. I can request that Mr. Argent and his staff are rehired. They will be able to repair the damage and set the marquisate to rights in no time."

Lottie could practically hear the cogs in Alex's brain sifting through all possible scenarios.

"We shall have to visit Mr. Bartlet," she said, looking out at the pattering rain.

"Aye." Alex agreed. "Until then, I am withholding judgment."

IT WAS TWO DAYS BEFORE the elements permitted a journey to Mr. Bartlet's cottage, leaving Alex feeling antsy.

It didn't help that he received a letter from McNeal detailing the health woes of their patients. Mrs. Hammond had taken a turn for the worse, and Mr. McKay's cancer was rapidly progressing.

Alex wanted to be done with this whole mess, dammit. His patients needed him.

But the more Alex learned of the marquisate, the more uneasy he felt. He was still determined to not take on the title himself.

But if people were suffering . . .

At a certain point, Alex's own wishes *would* be sacrificed for a greater good. That had always been his way.

Right now, he only wanted to prove Mr. Argent's words wrong, return to Edinburgh, and stop the endless vacillation of his emotions.

But first, he needed to speak with this Mr. Bartlet.

The weather remained dreich and dreary, the incessant rain turned land into rivers of mud. So even when the sun appeared again, they had to wait another day for the roads to dry enough to make them passable.

Mr. Bartlet's cottage was in a corner of the estate that Alex had yet to visit. He had asked Mr. Warden about this cluster of houses on the map weeks before, and the steward had described them as 'a neat row of cottages of weavers and other tradesmen.'

Lottie, of course, accompanied him on this visit. They *were* cousins, so publicly visiting tenants together was not deemed improper. Alex found this humorous, given his decidedly *un*-cousin-like feelings toward her.

Case in point . . . the coach ride was torturous. They sat beside one another, tucked under the same carriage blanket for warmth. Each bump of the road caused another part of her to press into him—a hip, a shoulder, an arm, a thigh.

It drove Alex to the brink of madness.

Thankfully, he received an early reprieve, as the coach was forced to stop at the top of a long lane down to the houses, the carriage wheels unequal to the mud.

Alex all but scrambled out.

He and Lottie picked their way down the muddy lane. The going was treacherous, forcing Alex to focus on each step, further distracting him from his wayward thoughts.

For her part, Lottie carried a laden basket from the kitchen larders on her arm and a smile that would charm their way into any tenant household. How could anyone turn away a woman as radiant and genuine as Lady Charlotte Whitaker?

Alex stole a glance at her. The sun chose that moment to burst through the winter gray and turn her hair to glittering diamonds of light. She glowed, incandescent.

How could I not fall for such a lass?

The idea flitted in and out so quickly, Alex scarcely had the presence of mind to forcibly evict it.

The truth was stark.

He was falling . . . hard and fast.

The signs were all there.

The swoop in his stomach when he saw her. The ping in his chest when she laughed. The incessant ache to hold and listen and simply *be* where she was.

And like the worst of addicts, he found himself returning again and again to her. Desperate for that rush of emotion, for the elation that filled him only when she was near.

Bloody hell.

Falling in love with Lady Charlotte would be the final death knell to his former life, would it not?

He looked back at the muddy road, focusing on his next step. He should have quit Frome Abbey a week ago. Every day that he lingered it became that much harder to leave.

Alex and Lottie rounded a bend, both coming to a stop.

The scene before them was anything but Mr. Warden's bucolic description of a 'neat row of houses.'

The cottages were in a sorry state. Several roofs needed re-slating. The exterior lime had crumbled in multiple places and needed to be re-plastered. Mud ran right up to the door of each house. The stench was equally shocking—refuse and animal dung.

"I had no idea the cottages had decayed so," Lottie murmured. "I remember visiting with Margaret several years ago and all was in a decent state."

"Something has clearly happened." Alex shook his head.

They approached the houses and were directed to the one of Mr. Bartlet.

Mrs. Bartlet answered the door, hands twisted in a dirty apron. She bobbed a curtsy and offered profuse apologies for her husband, insisting he was too ill to greet them. The educated diction of her accent indicated that she had, indeed, fallen far in life.

"Please," Alex said, "we come with word from his cousin, Mr. Argent."

Mrs. Bartlet darted a look between Alex and Lottie and finally nodded her head.

The interior of the cottage was even worse than its exterior—damp and lit only by the dim flame of a weak fire.

Children's heads poked out from various nooks around the room. Alex counted seven pairs of eyes looking at him.

So much suffering packed into one wee space.

How many other families were in similarly dire straits? How many cottages had been neglected? How could Mr. Warden or Lord Frank sanction this level of suffering on the estate?

It was unconscionable.

They had a responsibility to their tenants, to ensure certain standards of living were met.

But that had clearly not happened here.

Mrs. Bartlet led them through a doorway to a small bedroom where Mr. Bartlet lay in a disheveled bed. The man struggled to his feet, listing heavily to his left and using the wall for support.

"Have ye hurt your hip?" Alex asked, hobbling forward on his own crutches.

"Aye. I was trampled by a bull last year," Mr. Bartlett replied, nodding a greeting and wiping at his brow as he pushed himself upright. "The bone didn't set right."

The doctor in Alex took over. He had Mr. Bartlett lie back down. A quick examination showed Alex that the damage was significant. The bone and joint had been badly hurt and had healed poorly.

"There wasn't the money for a doctor, you see," Mr. Bartlet explained, pulling himself to standing once more.

"We couldn't even afford a bone setter," the wife chimed in, hands twisted again in her apron.

Mr. Bartlet managed to limp his way into the main room.

Alex hated his own helplessness. The sense that his efforts here today would be little more than a bandage on a gaping, festering wound.

Lottie said nothing, but Alex could feel her dismay, the sense that her own offerings were similarly paltry. Her smile was strained as she unpacked the cheese and bread in her basket, setting it on the table. She handed apples to the children who snatched them eagerly.

These people needed significant care, not just a bandage to stop the bleeding.

Mr. Bartlet winced as he eased himself into a chair. "Pardon me sitting down, Lady Charlotte. My leg cannot bear my weight for long."

"I do not insist on convention, Mr. Bartlet." She offered him a wan smile.

"You said you had word from my cousin? From Mr. Argent?" Mr. Bartlet turned to Alex.

"Aye," Alex nodded, leaning his weight on his crutches. "We have concerns about Mr. Warden and his stewardship of the lands."

Mr. Bartlet's face twisted into a grimace at the mention of Mr. Warden and then darted a wary glance at Lottie.

"I don't want to speak ill of your friends or family," Mr. Bartlet said, tone diplomatic.

"Please do not hesitate, Mr. Bartlet," Lottie answered the man's unspoken question. "I would rather the truth than some banal platitude."

"Mr. Argent is of the opinion that Mr. Warden and Lord Frank are wishing to skim profits from the estate." Alex saw no point in dancing around the central issue. "Your cousin pointed us in your direction as someone who might be able to lay out the true state of affairs."

Silence hung in the room for a moment. Mrs. Bartlet looked anxiously at her husband, darting a glance toward the door, as if fearing someone might overhear them.

Alex frowned.

Didn't the lady's reaction, in and of itself, say much about the state of things?

"I would ask that my identity as the one who told you this be kept secret," Mr. Bartlet said, gaze intent. "Your word as a gentleman."

"Of course," Alex nodded. "I will protect ye."

"Well," Mr. Bartlett released a slow sigh. "Mr. Argent is right. I was an overseer for the previous steward before my accident last year. It's been particularly difficult to watch both my fortunes and the estate crumble."

"What has happened with the estate?" Lottie asked.

"As you likely know, Lord Frank cannot access the bulk of the marquisate's wealth. All he can do is squeeze the land more and skim the excess. Therefore, rents have been raised and many laborers dismissed. Those that remain have seen their wages cut. Many necessary jobs on the estate are therefore being neglected. Worse, I hear tell that Mr. Warden has been making trips to negotiate with a prison governor in Devon to purchase the labor of the convicts. I don't have to tell you how that will further undermine local workers."

Alex hissed in sharply. He knew this was a common practice in other places in the British Empire, but he had not known it to happen on English soil. Hiring convicts was not illegal, but it undoubtedly showed a certain level of callousness.

"As you can imagine," Mr. Bartlet continued, "the use of convict labor has many tenants concerned. Convicts are more akin to slave labor than anything. They will leave many on the estate out of work, even for cut wages. But most of us have signed leases on our homes. So we will be in the position of needing to pay our rents, but having no employment."

"How terrible," Lottie murmured. "My father would never have approved of such a scheme. Tenants were like family to him."

"Just so, my lady." Mr. Bartlet nodded gravely.

Alex swallowed. "So Mr. Warden is doing this with Lord Frank's approval?"

He had to know where the problem lay. Was this a case of Mr. Warden acting without Lord Frank's full knowledge?

"It is my understanding that Mr. Warden was hired *because* he was unscrupulous enough to agree to Lord Frank's schemes." Mr. Bartlet gave Lottie an apologetic look. "Again, I do not wish to speak ill of your family, Lady Charlotte, but Lord Frank's reputation among tenants is low."

Alex took in a long, slow breath.

It was simple to replace Mr. Warden. That Alex could insist upon.

But as things were, Lord Frank would be part of the estate for another twenty years. Even if someone else were appointed as regent over the marquisate—which would be highly contested given Ferndown's power—Frank would still have complete control over *Freddie's* life. He was his father, after all.

There was no easy way to award the title to Freddie *and* protect the marquisate from Lord Frank's grasping hands.

"Unfortunately, the scheme with the convicts is just one of many problems," Mr. Bartlet continued. "I heard through a friend that Lord Frank wishes to return the West Indies plantations to using slave labor."

"Pardon?!" Lottie's voice rose an octave. "My father spent a small fortune to free all his slaves nearly thirty years ago! It was one of the first things he did when he assumed the title. He was an ardent abolitionist."

"I know, my lady." Mr. Bartlet agreed. "Your father insisted on paying his laborers a fair wage. But the free men who now work on the plantations definitely cut deep into profits. Your father considered it a welcome compromise. Lord Frank, however, sees it as an opportunity."

Lottie pressed a hand to her abdomen, a sure sign of her distress.

"I cannot countenance it," Lottie almost whispered. "I cannot believe that Lord Frank would betray my father's memory so."

Mr. Bartlet shrugged. "I am only reporting what I have heard, my lady. You would be well to confirm this through your own sources. All I can say is this—given the abuses that have been undertaken here at Frome Abbey, I would look long and hard at every other aspect of the marquisate. My gut tells me that if you do, you may find a Pandora's box of misdeeds."

19

Alex and Lottie took their leave from the Bartlet family a short while later.

Alex recommended some exercises to Mr. Bartlet that would improve the man's mobility. But beyond that, there was little more Alex could do to help.

The part of him that loved medicine, that could not look on suffering without *acting*, struggled to accept this.

Well, you could assume the title, a wee voice whispered. *You could become Lord Lockheade and make these people* your *people. Then there would be much you could do to help.*

He steeled himself. Though true, that wouldn't solve all problems. The Bartlets were simply one of tens of thousands of families in similar circumstances in Britain. Alex had realized long ago that he could not save everyone.

But . . . surely you can do something here, that voice insisted.

So as Mr. Bartlet hobbled toward the door using a poorly whittled branch as a crutch, Alex's heart gave a painful lurch.

"Here," Alex said, extending one of his well-formed crutches toward the man. "I'm done with this for now, and I'd like someone else tae get good use of it."

It was a bold-faced lie, but he had to *do* something.

"I can't accept your crutch, Doctor," Mr. Bartlet hesitated. But Alex could see how the man's eyes darted to it.

"I insist. Ye have given us valuable information today. And ye need something tae help ye get back on your feet properly. Someone has tae care for your weans." Alex looked at the dirty-faced children ranging behind the man. "If not for yourself, then take it for your bairns' sake."

Mr. Bartlet hesitated for a second more and then nodded, taking the crutch and thanking Alex profusely.

A few minutes later, Alex and Lottie were walking back up the lane which was every whit as long and rutted and difficult to navigate as it had been before. It was even more so with only one crutch.

Alex welcomed the challenge. He did not regret his actions.

"That was very kind of you," Lottie murmured once they were out of sight of the house.

"I hate it," he said after a moment, swinging forward one slow hop at a time. "I hate that there is so much suffering in this world. I hate that there are good people who cannot feed their bairns. I hate that there are still those who would take advantage of men such as Bartlet."

"But you did good in that house," Lottie said.

"Something is better than nothing. What of yourself? That was shocking, what was said about Lord Frank."

They walked in silence for a moment. Or rather, Alex hopped along beside Lottie.

"I'm trying to reconcile it," Lottie said. "The Lord Frank I know is a bit bombastic, even arrogant at times, but hardly cruel. He is not unkind to my sister, and he dotes on his children. You should have seen his grief over Anne's death . . ."

"But a man can be kind to his own and still ruthless in business. I've seen it enough. One set of behaviors does not inoculate one against the other, more's the pity."

"I guess the real question is what will *you* do with this information?" she asked.

Alex hobbled along, lurching forward one slow step at a time.

"I dinnae know." He answered truthfully.

He didn't know.

He could not imagine taking on the marquisate.

But he also could not fathom idly ignoring so much suffering.

He swallowed back the acidic taste of panic rising in his throat.

He simply wanted his practice in Edinburgh. The snip of scissors in gauze. The smell of camphor. The squall of a newborn babe. The soothing familiarity of things he *knew* how to do.

Not ruling a marquisate and its tens of thousands of people all looking to him for support. Not sitting in Lords and helping to rule the British Empire.

The panic rose higher, cutting more sharply.

He lurched forward another step.

"Alex." Lottie touched his elbow. "Lean on me."

He paused to look at her, his chest heaving from the effort of swinging his body up the track. At least, that was what he told himself.

"You don't have to do this alone." Her blue eyes blazed in earnestness.

Her words stole his breath.

Had she been reading his mind then?

You don't have to do this alone.

How he longed to believe her.

"Lean on me. Let me help," she continued, her gaze steady and warm. The sun peeked through the clouds, once more bathing her in golden light.

Would that I could have a lifetime with this woman.

The thought blasted into his head and left just as quickly.

But Alex was rocked in its wake.

No.

No. No. No.

He did not wish to marry Lady Charlotte Whitaker.

That was the correct thought.

He turned away from her, taking a lurching step forward. "Lass, ye dinnae have—"

"No." She grabbed his arm, stopping him. "I will not permit *you*, of all people, to decline my help. You're being needlessly stubborn."

Without another word, she lifted his free arm and draped it over her shoulders, wrapping her arm firmly around his waist.

A feeling of rightness pulled and stretched his rib cage.

Of course, he would find himself hobbling up a muddy country lane, his arm around her.

Of course, he had been hurtling toward her from that first encounter years ago.

He closed his eyes, steadying his breathing and forcing the thoughts out.

It was simply that they had spent so much time together, hours every day for weeks now. It had accelerated the rate of their acquaintance.

Once he was away from Frome Abbey, he would see this for the madness that it was, right?

But for the now . . .

Her body pressed against his side from hip to chest.

The scent of jasmine and Lottie enveloped him.

Bloody hell.

Alex was unsure he would survive this.

Swallowing, he took a step forward, leaning away from Lottie.

"Stop protecting me," she said crossly, tugging on his waist. "You are acting like I can't support the load of your crippled body."

Alex knew she could support him. But the more weight he rested on her shoulders, the more her body pressed into his. And the sensation of her soft curves molding against his side was enough to induce madness.

The sooner they arrived back at the carriage the better.

They walked in silence for a few moments, Lottie supporting him, Alex hobbling, faster and faster. His breath came in labored gulps, only some of them tied to his injured body.

With every step, he felt his irritation rise.

He knew it was illogical. That he had no right to be frustrated.

It was just . . . the entire situation chipped and chipped away at his resolve to not become involved.

He didn't want to want the marquisate.

He didn't want to want the woman at his side.

But, *bloody hell,* at the moment, he was fair desperate for both.

It had only been a matter of time, he supposed, until the weakness in his character manifested itself. Until he became so utterly enthralled with something, he could not turn away from it.

He had just never considered that his downfall would be a woman. That instead of laudanum or alcohol or tobacco, he would form a nearly unholy attachment to a lady his logical mind had no intention of ever marrying.

And day after day, he'd had to face the lush temptation of her.

Day after day, he surrendered another wee piece of his soul.

It had to stop.

But the faster he tried to move, the more she flooded his senses.

The silk of her hair brushing against his neck.

The nip of her waist against his hip.

The tensile strength he could sense within her, both literally and figuratively.

The push-and-pull was almost unbearable.

The aching desperation to run fast and far away.

And its terrifying counterpart—yearning to wrap his arms around her and never let go.

ALEX KEPT WALKING FASTER AND faster, forcing Lottie to keep up.

As if even this lane were something that had to be conquered at a run.

Why did the man never rest? Why did he insist that life was to be lived at a break-neck speed?

She could hear the harshness of his breathing.

She deliberately slowed her steps, trying to communicate her wishes to him.

Slow down. Deep breaths.

If she thought it forcefully enough, would he listen?

But it was as if he were determined to ignore her.

He continued to push his body forward, the corded muscle of his waist tense under her fingers.

He was in a full-dragon mood at the moment. Ready to trample and rampage his way through some imagined threat.

She hadn't seen him like this in weeks. But she was starting to understand that Alex Whitaker only behaved like this when something frustrated him almost to the point of madness.

Despite it all, being this close to him was a heady luxury. Her body flushed and warmed where they touched.

Part of her ached to curl even closer, to feel the support of his arms around her entirely.

Of course, in order to do that, Alex would need to stop going so fast.

"Slow down," she muttered. "This isn't a race. The carriage will wait for us, no matter how long we take."

He continued on as if he hadn't heard her.

"Alex." Her voice held a warning tone.

"I dinnae wish tae slow down." He tried to push out of her grip. "But you're welcome tae take a wee rest here. I can wait for ye in the coach."

"Stop it. I enjoy helping you." She held on to him tighter. "But you must rest sometime. Life is meant to be balanced. You will eventually run yourself ragged if you keep on like this."

"Lass, I've been working like this for years, and it's never bothered me. I cannae see why it should now."

"Why do you dislike stillness?"

"I dinnae dislike it. I simply dinnae ken tae it."

"Alex—" She stopped, using the weight of her body to force him to stop, too. "I am in earnest. Why won't you rest?"

He leaned away from her, dropping his arm from her shoulders, eyes steely and snapping. But Lottie refused to let go entirely. She kept a hand fisted into the clothing at his waist.

"If I didn't know any better, I would think that you were running from something specifically," she said. "Something more than just time itself."

He stared her down, chest heaving. His gaze grew darker and darker.

"I'm not running," he bit out. "As ye can see, I can scarcely walk."

"You know perfectly well that's not what I'm saying."

"Well, then what is it?"

"You have an almost obsessive inability to sit still." Lottie waved her free hand. "And it arises at the oddest moments, like this one, where you are all but racing back to the carriage. From there, you will rush to Frome Abbey where you will write letters for several hours. You will tell your friends in London what happened at the Bartlets. You will write McNeal with another list of questions about Mrs. Hammond or Mr. White or whoever. After that, you will go down to the stables to check on Galahad—who most certainly is well-cared for and does not require your hovering. Then you will take a turn in the garden, back to your bedchamber to dress for dinner—*oof!*" She all but stomped her foot. "It never ends. You go and go and go without resting. And if I ask you why, the mighty dragon appears and snaps at my head and singes me with fire—"

"Enough!" he all but roared.

Rather proving her point, Lottie thought. She at least had sufficient wits at the moment to refrain from saying as much.

"Why do you run from frustration? Why can you not . . . just . . . s*top.*"

"I cannae stop," he continued to stare at her, his jaw clenched, "because if I do . . ."

His chest rose and fell.

"Because if you do?" she prompted.

He shook his head. "Because . . . if I do . . . I will do this."

With his weight balanced on the single crutch, Alex wrapped his free hand around her waist and pulled her to him, snugging her body flush against his.

Lottie caught the flame of light in his eyes before his head descended and his mouth claimed hers.

Their first kiss had been accidental, a haphazard encounter between two bodies.

This kiss, however, was incendiary. A collision of two forces that had been hurtling through Space and Time at destructive speeds.

There was nothing tentative about him.

No mercy. No clemency.

Only a hungry taking.

Her wits scattered.

Oh, heavens.

Gracious.

More.

She wrapped her free hand around his neck. The other clutched tighter at his waist.

His arm was a steel band around her.

She couldn't get close enough. She was a burst dam of emotion and longing . . .

She wanted to crawl inside him, to *become* him somehow.

Words tumbled from him, a broken psalm. "Lottie. Lass. Beautiful."

If he pulled his lips away, she chased them.

If she adjusted her hold on him, he shifted with her.

Kiss after glorious kiss.

Eventually, his kisses slowed. Her own became less frenetic.

He lifted his head, chest heaving, eyes slate gray and searching.

She touched his cheek, marveling that she *could* touch him. That it abruptly felt permitted.

He turned and pressed a lingering kiss to her palm.

This man.

He knew her.

He heard the quiet thinking of her brain. The odd yearnings of her heart.

He looked at her once more and then lowered his head.

Lottie stretched upward and met him halfway.

This was deliberate now.

She appreciated that he was tall, but not too tall. He didn't loom. His height was not of the neck-cricking variety.

Just perfect for her. In every way.

EVENTUALLY, THEY MADE THEIR WAY back to the waiting carriage.

Alex *could* slow down, Lottie realized, particularly if kissing were involved. He stopped her so often for another kiss, they took an age to reach the coach.

And then once they were ensconced in the carriage, the curtains drawn, he continued his slow exploration as the coach rolled at a gentle pace back to Frome Abbey.

She had always supposed that Alex's kisses would be like every other aspect of him—timed and analyzed and, most likely, rushed.

But, no.

He leisurely kissed her jaw. He lingered on her neck and eyelids, stroking his thumbs over her cheeks.

Lottie had never felt more alive. More aware.

This is love, she thought. To have someone treasure you.

She wanted to laugh from sheer giddy delight.

Nothing much was said between them. The words would come later, she knew. The whispered confidences. The hushed laughter. The quiet plans for a future that they might embark on together.

They would talk.

For the now, it was enough to simply *be*. To exist within this cocoon of unhurried quiet.

They slid apart as the carriage rounded the last corner before Frome Abbey. Lottie pulled the carriage curtains open.

She frowned.

Ahead, two coaches stood before the main entrance to the house.

"Whoever has come?" Alex asked, leaning forward.

But Lottie recognized the carriages even from a distance.

Margaret and Lord Frank had unexpectedly returned home.

20

"How has it come to this?" Margaret shook her head, her voice hurt and bewildered. "My heart feels so . . . betrayed. We *trusted* you, Lottie."

Lottie stared into the middle distance, eyes fixed on the drawing room mantel, her own heart sinking lower and lower in her chest.

Margaret paced the floor, back and forth, stopping occasionally to stare at Lottie in wounded sadness and shake her head. Lottie found her sister's disappointment more viscerally brutal than anger and rage would have ever been.

"Really, Margaret, you are being *un peu mélodramatique*." Grandmère continued to embroider in front of the fire. "Thank goodness you sent Freddie out with his nurse. I should not like him to see us *comme ça*."

"This is Freddie's future we are speaking of, Grandmère. You both promised us that Dr. Whitaker had agreed to sign the attainder once he reached London. We trusted you. And then word of *her*—" Margaret pointed a finger at Lottie. "—goings on with Dr. Whitaker reached us."

Well, not *all* her goings on, clearly, Lottie thought.

Surely the London gossips were not quite so thorough as to glean information only an hour after it occurred.

Thank goodness.

Her lips still burned from the pressure of Alex's mouth.

Her cheeks, however, were aflame from the mortifying implications of such kisses.

She could hear a rumble of male voices next door in the library. Frank had dragged Alex there. Lottie hoped and prayed that her brother-in-law was not subjecting Alex to a similarly grueling inquisition.

The poor man did not deserve it.

Thank goodness Ferndown had remained in London, as the king still required his presence.

"It is all anyone speaks of—*Lady Charlotte and Dr. Whitaker.*" Margaret stared at Grandmère who continued to pull threads through a length of stretched linen. "I had to hear it from Lady Gardner, who, as you well know, is one of the most prolific gossips in Town. Lady Gardner begged me—*begged* me, I say!—to tell her it was true. That Lady Charlotte Whitaker had developed a tendre for Dr. Alexander Whitaker and—" Here Margaret's voice broke, becoming hoarse with emotion. "—how delighted our father would have been to have his heir-apparent marry his youngest daughter."

Margaret's unshed tears rested like an anvil on Lottie's chest.

"What could I say to Lady Gardner?" her sister whispered. "That Lottie would never betray myself and Freddie so? That such an alliance was untrue?"

Margaret had been berating Lottie for nearly thirty minutes now.

Lottie feared she herself had moved from pain and embarrassment to a sort of numbed horror over her actions.

Yes. She had forgotten her duty to Margaret and Freddie, to the people she loved longest and best. She knew from the start, did she not, that any romantic entanglement with Alex would lead only to heartache and betrayal.

What had she thought would happen? That she would kiss Alex, return home, and then curl up in her bedchamber, touching her lips and trying to understand how such a small part of her could hold so much sensation? That they could forge a future together that did not somehow impact Freddie and the marquisate?

No. That had been a fairy tale.

She had been willfully blind.

Or, at the very least, blinded by the allure of a certain Scottish doctor.

She had wanted to imagine a different life for herself, and so she had opened her eyes to the hope of Alex. But just because she had glimpsed that life did not mean she would embrace it.

She squeezed her eyes shut before Margaret could read the awful truth there.

"Heavens! Open your eyes, Lottie. You cannot hide from this," Margaret scolded, pacing before the fire again, dabbing at her eyes. "The second they heard of your behavior, the Committee on Privilege informed Ferndown that the matter sounded settled in Alex's favor. A marriage between Dr. Whitaker and Lady Charlotte neatly solves the problem, as far as they are concerned. Such an alliance allays both their concerns: it adheres to laws of primogeniture, as Dr. Whitaker is technically the heir, and honors our late father's request that his grandchild inherit his title. Completely neglecting, of course, that Father wanted *Freddie* to inherit, not an unborn son of Lottie and Dr. Whitaker—"

"There is *no* understanding between Dr. Whitaker and myself," Lottie interjected, cheeks aflame. "Certainly no talk of marriage."

Of course, even that was a bit of lie, was it not?

A lady did not spend an afternoon passionately kissing a gentleman without the thought of marriage crossing both their minds.

And now she was thinking of Alex's son. Of a small boy with his same steel eyes and mink-brown hair looking at her with solemn seriousness as he lisped a question—

"It doesn't matter what is *actually* going on—or not—between yourself and Dr. Whitaker." Margaret shook her head. "You have been seen together. Tongues are wagging. The Committee is looking for anything that will sway their votes. The process of attainting a dead man was fraught from the beginning. But it has now become doubly so, when Lords sees this acceptable alternate solution." Margaret pressed a hand to her chest, dabbing at her eyes again. "I have been at a loss as to how to proceed. How you could have so quickly forgotten *familae primum semper cognosce?*"

"I haven't forgotten!"

"Then why have you encouraged the doctor!" Margaret all but wailed, tears spilling down her cheeks.

"I haven't, Margaret. We are merely friends—"

"You arrived in a carriage together just now!"

"We are cousins. We were visiting a tenant family. There is nothing improper in that!" The denial was ash on Lottie's tongue.

Their carriage journey had been *decidedly* improper.

"Actual impropriety isn't the issue here, Lottie. It is the perception that matters. When you are seen together in such a way, others assume you are courting. Your behavior has put us all at risk. How could you care so little for our family? I consider you nearly a second mother to Freddie."

"As do I!" Emotion stung Lottie's eyes.

Voices rose from the library beyond the drawing room door.

Oh, could this day get any worse?

Frank was yelling at Alex, his voice shrill. "Did you think if you compromised my sister—"

"Sister-in-law," Alex interrupted.

"—that I would magically allow a lout like yourself to marry her?!"

"Lady Charlotte is well into her majority. And even if she were not, why would she require *your* permission to marry? You are neither a blood relative nor a former guardian."

Oh, Alex.

Lottie met Grandmère's gaze. Did her grandmother look amused or concerned? With her slashing eyebrows and the low light, it was hard to tell.

"Duping Lady Charlotte into marriage will not guarantee you the marquisate," Frank raged.

"I highly doubt an intelligent woman like Lady Charlotte could be duped into anything," Alex retorted. "Furthermore, unlike some, I do not consider financial, business, nor social advantages when pondering my future wife—"

"You will stay away from Lady Charlotte," Frank shouted. "You will not soil her with your lowliness—"

"*My* lowliness?! *I* am the one who could be a marquess. *I* am the one who could restore this estate, not strip it bare like so many bleached bones as you have done!"

"You will leave!" Even through the drawing room door, Frank's voice vibrated with anger. "I am still master here, and you will leave this house immediately!"

A moment of silence.

Another hissed exchange, too low for Lottie to hear.

And then—

"As you wish," Alex's voice rose again, "I will leave as soon as it is light enough to drive a carriage."

The men's voices faded, one of them leaving the room with a loud *clack* of the door.

Lottie pressed a shaking hand to her stomach.

She could feel Margaret's eyes on her. What could Lottie say to defend herself?

She *had* acted recklessly.

Anyone looking in at the situation would have assumed that Alex and Lottie . . .

That they were . . .

Heavens, she *herself* had thought that they might . . .

But, of course, in the glaring light of Reality, such dreams were simply . . . dreams.

"He will sign the attainder," Lottie said, her voice quiet. She dared to meet her sister's gaze. "He does not want the marquisate, Alex said as much—"

"*Dr. Whitaker*," Margaret leaned heavily on his proper name, "like most men, may have lied to ingratiate himself with you."

"No." Lottie instantly rejected her sister's words. "No, he did not. He is most sincere. He has been trying to find a way out of assuming the marquisate. You must trust me in this. We are *friends*, he and I—"

"Friends?" Margaret's voice had gone quiet. "Dr. Whitaker cannot be a *friend*. If anything, we must view him as our enemy."

"*Enemy?*!"

"Yes, Lottie, *enemy*. The situation is dire. Freddie's future—*our* future—rests on a knife's edge. I know you likely think me callous of your own wishes, but I am so terrified for my son." Margaret sat down beside Lottie, her blue eyes pleading. "Without the marquisate, Freddie's portion will be too small to provide for him. This is why Papa wanted him to inherit."

"I fear for Freddie, too." Lottie wrapped a hand around her sister's fist. "But there is a tremendous amount of suffering happening on the estate at the moment that must be addressed."

Lottie told Margaret what they had learned from Mr. Bartlet earlier that day.

If she expected Margaret to be thoroughly dismayed, Lottie was disappointed.

"So there have been some mishaps." Margaret clutched Lottie's hand tight. "Frank is still learning how to manage the marquisate, but I am sure that if given time, he will right these issues—"

"These problems are happening *now*, Margaret."

"Then I will speak with Frank." Margaret released Lottie's hand and sat back. "And if Frank will not listen to me, then we will take the matter to Ferndown. The duke is a just man, and Frank will certainly heed his father. There are many solutions here, do you not see?"

Lottie frowned. She didn't think Frank would magically stop squeezing the marquisate for profits. And would Ferndown interject himself into Lord Frank's management of the estate? She wasn't sure.

But Margaret was also correct. Even Alex asserted that there had to be other solutions.

"Please, Lottie. Trust me." Margaret continued to plead. "You must understand. The King is consumed with foreign affairs and the details of his coronation. Lords is mired in domestic issues. No one in government wants to spare the time to address our problem. Many have made it clear that they wish to side with Dr. Whitaker simply to be done with the mess. After all, awarding the marquisate to him is merely a bit of paperwork, as he is the heir apparent. Devolving the title upon my Freddie requires *two* Acts of Parliament—one to attaint Dr. Whitaker's family and another to create a second incarnation of the Marquess of Lockheade. The matter could drag on for *years*. Meanwhile, gossips like Lady Gardner are practically salivating for salacious news. Anything we do that paints us as being friendly to Dr. Whitaker could easily tip the balance in his favor. If we wish Freddie to have any chance at all to inherit, you must cease all ties with Dr. Whitaker immediately."

Lottie blinked. The truth of her sister's words cut deep.

Margaret was right.

Alex *had* to be banished, cast out of Frome Abbey.

But . . . would his leg suffer damage on the journey? And where would he go? London? And then back to Edinburgh?

Most importantly—would she never see him again?

And why did the very thought cause a jittery panic to *thump, thump, thump* against her ribcage?

But what else could she do?

"This is your choice, Lottie," Margaret said, placing a hand over Lottie's. "You can have Dr. Whitaker as a friend. Or Freddie can inherit the marquisate, as Papa intended. But you cannot have both. Any friendliness on your part will be viewed as a prelude to matrimony. I am pleading with you—sister to sister—to never speak to Dr. Whitaker again."

LOTTIE CLIMBED THE STAIRS TO the nursery an hour later, feet leaden.

She knew this heavy feeling well. It was an old friend.

Grief.

But it was all twisted this time around.

What did she grieve?

The loss of Alex's friendship, yes.

But it was more than just the immediate departure of his person, she realized.

It was a thousand future memories. Of sunrises unshared. Of words unwhispered. Of children unmade and a life unlived.

It was the death of *what if*.

But . . . what other decision could Lottie make?

She had committed—and recommitted—to her family again and again.

They—Margaret, Freddie, and Grandmère—were her constant.

She could not—she *would* not—betray them.

She had thrown off Theo for much less than this. And he had been her *betrothed*.

She was the collie with the loyal heart that beat for her own family.

Alex was simply an ethereal possibility. One, she now accepted could never be.

Lottie slipped into the nursery.

Freddie was asleep in his bed, his blond curls rumpled on the pillow. Her heart panged.

He seemed older somehow. How had it only been two months since last she saw him? It felt an age.

Even though Lottie was so silent she scarcely breathed, he still stirred, opening his bleary eyes.

"Tottie!" A smile spread across his face, and he reached for her.

"Freddie," she whispered, emotion ballooning in her chest.

She slipped into the small bed with him, wrapping his warm body in her arms, tears pricking at the scent of him—dirt and saliva and stinky little boy. She had never smelled anything more comforting.

"I miss you. London is no nice." He snuggled into her and pressed a palm to her cheek.

Of course, Freddie's hand was sticky. She bit her lip, her nose stinging. How could she have so thoroughly forgotten how vitally important his future was to her own happiness? Margaret had been so very right— she loved Freddie as if he were her own son.

How could she ever claim her own happiness on the back of his misery and penury?

"I missed you too, Freddie dearest." Lottie pressed a kiss to his curls.

She held him close, reveling in the rightness of having him in her arms once more.

She would fix her mistake, Lottie vowed. She would never again forget her duty to family.

This was where she belonged.

A few minutes later, Lottie felt the mattress dip opposite.

Margaret joined them, wrapping her arms around Freddie and Lottie, not uttering a sound.

Lottie allowed her tears to flow then, silently weeping her grief for a future that would never be, encircled in the arms of those she loved best.

21

A lex was awake and dressed by first light.
Granted, as he had hardly slept the night before, arising early posed no challenge.

The madness of the past few weeks had truly caught up with him.

What *had* he been thinking?

Lord Frank, for all his pompous, obnoxious ways, had the right of it.

If Alex even appeared to pursue Lottie—if he gave the slightest hint that they might marry—he would likely be awarded the marquisate.

How had he been so blind to that simple fact?

If he did have to assume the marquisate—and that was a giant *if*—he wished it to be his own choice. Not Lords thrusting it upon him.

He was an utter eejit.

Yes, he considered Lottie a dear friend—

Why did you kiss her then?

Och, that was the rub, was it not?

One did not kiss friends. Not if one wanted to remain friends. In his world, a female friend one kissed became one's wife.

Moreover, he had been telling himself two incongruous things.

One, that he could form an attachment to Lady Charlotte. That he could talk philosophy and kiss her and even (fleetingly, briefly) contemplate *marrying* her.

And two, that he would avoid assuming the title of Lord Lockheade.

In hindsight, of course, the goals negated one another.

In order to gain the first, he had to forsake the second. Or vice versa.

But what did that mean now? Now that he suspected Lord Frank was determined to rob the marquisate?

The previous day's revelations sat heavy. Mr. Bartlet's words would not leave him—

Given the abuses that have been undertaken here at Frome Abbey, I would look long and hard at every other aspect of the marquisate empire. My gut tells me that if you do, you will find a Pandora's box of misdeeds.

What was Alex to do?

He could not, in good conscience, sign the attainder without getting to the bottom of Mr. Bartlet's allegations.

Convicts working marquisate lands.

Tenants denied employment but still forced to pay high rents.

Slave labor being reinstated on West Indies plantations.

And as Mr. Bartlet said, those facts were likely only a sliver of the full scope of the problems.

Alex would call upon Mr. Argent once he reached London. The former man of affairs would likely know who Alex needed to contact in order to better understand where things stood.

He owed it to the tens of thousands of people impacted to fully investigate all claims. How could he sign the attainder before doing that?

The words of Hippocrates rang in his mind—

Practice two things in your dealings with disease: either help or do not harm the patient.

Walking away from the marquisate at this moment broke both vows. It did nothing to help and, if the allegations were true, damaged the 'patient'—the marquisate in this case.

More to the point, Lord Frank was acting *now*. Delays on Alex's part meant more people suffered.

And yet despite these recent revelations, Alex still could not fathom abandoning his medical practice.

It all felt impossible.

He had spent the night staring at the ceiling, feeling hopelessly trapped between dueling needs and demands.

The sleepless hours had crystallized one thought, however—

Lottie was lost to him.

If he fought to be named the marquess, she would likely never forgive him for disinheriting Freddie and denying her father his dying wish.

And even if he rejected the marquisate and allowed Lord Frank's abuses to go unchecked, why would a lofty lady like Lady Charlotte marry a lowly Scottish physician?

The very idea had been madness. It had simply been the cozy comfort of their weeks together at Frome Abbey that had forged a sense of familiarity.

Ye are a liar. Ye still burn from the lass's kisses.

He pushed the thought aside.

If some part of his soul howled at the idea of potentially losing Lottie forever, well, that would simply be another loss to bear.

He was used to losing those he held most dear.

He hobbled down the main staircase on his solitary crutch. He could see the carriage drawn up to the front door, his trunk strapped to the back. Alex had at least insisted that the most comfortable coach be supplied for his trip to Andrew's townhouse in London.

"Alex," a voice hissed behind him.

He turned to see Lottie coming down the stairs, eyes darting behind her, clearly not wishing to be caught speaking with him.

She was dressed simply, her hair pulled into a loose knot, her favorite blue Paisley shawl pulled around her shoulders.

She stopped before him, so achingly beautiful it rendered his chest tight.

"Lady Charlotte." He bowed as low as a crutch and broken leg would allow.

She winced at his formality.

Her gaze searched his. Her eyes were bloodshot, speaking to a poor night's sleep. Had his lass spent the night *greiting*?

Ah, Lottie.

She looked toward the library door and motioned for him to follow her into the room. He limped after her, helpless to do anything else. She was a siren to his weary seafarer.

She left the door ajar and turned to him.

"You are for London?" She pressed trembling lips together.

"Aye."

A long pause. He could see thoughts flit across her lovely face.

Will I ever see you again?

What will you do about the marquisate?

Her thoughts were nearly as tangible as his own.

She swallowed, looking down at her hands tangled in the soft Kashmiri wool of her shawl. "Margaret has said that we cannot remain friends."

"Yes. I fear she has the right of it."

Lottie nodded, head still bowed.

"I cannot betray Margaret and Freddie," her voice so small. "I must choose my family."

"Aye."

Another pause.

She lifted her head, eyes crystalline and blue.

"And what will you choose?" she asked.

You, a part of his heart whispered.

You, lass.

I choose you.

Instead, Alex said, "Mr. Bartlet's revelations yesterday are serious. I plan to investigate them to my fullest ability."

She pressed a hand into her stomach, a nervous gesture so familiar it tightened his breathing.

"And what if you find they are true?"

He took in a deep breath. "Then I will fight to assume the title."

Lottie gasped, her eyes flying up to his.

"No!" She pressed her hand firmer over her stomach.

"What else am I to do, Lottie?" He leaned on his single crutch. "I'm a healer. I cannae allow others tae suffer when there is something I can do tae mend it."

"But you said you didn't want the marquisate. We've had this conversation."

"Aye! But that was before I realized your brother-in-law was acting like the marquisate is his own *pirlie-pig*."

"*Pirlie-pig?*"

"His private money box to exploit. If even a fraction of what Mr. Bartlet claims is true, the marquisate is headed into dangerous waters. If the Committee on Privilege sides with Freddie, *all* the marquisate's funds will be released to Lord Frank's care. He will no longer be constrained. With more funds to hand, who knows what debts Lord Frank will accrue." Alex raked an agitated hand through his hair. "Even ye must see that, lass. If Lord Frank continues along this path, there may be little left for Freddie to inherit. It behooves us both to properly investigate this."

"The issues with Frank—*if* they prove true—can be resolved without you having to assume the marquisate—"

"How, lass? How do ye see that happening? That we slap Lord Frank's wrist and tell him to be nicer? As Freddie's father, Frank will remain his son's guardian until he is twenty-one."

"Yes, but there are other solutions. Margaret and I have been discussion options—"

"Such as?"

"I can't speak to them all right now!" Lottie all but stamped her foot. "I am simply asserting that you are creating an unnecessary binary decision here. Either Frank ravages the marquisate. Or you take it over. That is a false dilemma. There has to be a way to allow Freddie to inherit *and* the estate to be well-cared for."

Och, Alex loved debating with his fiery lass. Her quick mind always leaped ahead, finding weaknesses in his argument.

Well, except at moments like this, where he was torn between shaking some sense into her and kissing her witless.

"Ye know the situation is not so simple, lass."

"Do I?" She snatched his left hand, pressing it between her palms. The warmth of her skin on his sent a shudder up his arm. "Alex, I am asking you as a friend . . . please give this up. Go to London, sign the attainder, allow us to work out as a family how best to corral Frank's worst impulses. I am begging you. For me. For Freddie. For my sister.

For the love I had for my father and my desire to fulfill his dying wish. *Please*."

Alex looked down into her blue eyes. They were fathomless chips of summer sky, pleading. He couldn't help a lingering glance at her mouth, at those lips he had kissed and caressed and fair worshiped not even twenty-four hours previously.

The words sat there, right on the tip of his tongue.

Yes, Lottie-lass. Of course, I will do that for ye.

I would do anything for ye.

But along with the thought rose that last glimpse of Mr. Bartlet standing in his doorway, Alex's crutch under his arm. The man's ragged expression, the hollow cheeks of his children, the mud and squalor and hopelessness inside that house.

Alex had always prided himself on his steady head. On his ability to see past emotions to the bare truth of a situation.

"Lass," he whispered, something hot lodging in his throat.

He gently tugged his hand free of hers and slowly raised a finger, skimming it up the soft expanse of her cheek. He cupped her jaw, letting his adoration shine as his eyes met hers.

He expected to see hope in her gaze, hope that he would agree with her request.

But instead, her eyes filled with tears. Her chest heaved.

Ah.

She knew him so well. She knew his heart. She knew what he would decide before he spoke the words.

And wasn't that the worst of it? That he was forcing himself to hurt the woman who knew him best?

She backed away, her head shaking back and forth.

"I'm so sorry, lass," he choked out the words they both already knew. "But I *cannae* make such a promise. Not right now. I have tae investigate these claims. To do anything less would be untrue tae my very nature."

She turned away from him with a sob, pressing the back of her hand to her mouth.

Alex nearly broke.

Nearly took back his words, pulled her into his arms, and promised her the moon and stars. Anything to take away her pain.

His own vision blurred as he turned for the door, leaning on his crutch.

A rustle of fabric had him turning around.

He barely had time to gasp as she wrapped a hand around the back of his neck and pulled his mouth down to hers.

Alex banded his free arm around her waist, scooping her body into his.

She tasted of tears.

Of dreams unrealized.

Of a future lost.

He kissed her savagely.

If he thought to overwhelm her, he should have known better.

His lass would never back down.

She met his regret with her own pain, nipping at his lips until she finally pushed him away.

"Go," she whispered.

Alex nodded, blood a thumping pulse in his throat.

She stood still, fingertips pressed to her swollen lips.

Alex drank her in one last time. The wisps of silvery hair escaping to frame her face. The elegant swoop of her jaw. The endearing birthmark on her cheek. The pale pink of her bee-stung lips. The haunted pleading in her china-blue eyes.

It was too much.

He snatched her to him with a hand around the back of her neck, pressing one last plundering kiss to her mouth.

He pulled back and touched his forehead to hers.

"Goodbye, Lady Charlotte," he whispered against her lips. "It has been a pleasure to know ye."

Alex released her and backed up two spaces.

They stared at one another.

And then he nodded his head, pivoted, walked out the door, across the entrance hall, and into the waiting carriage.

He did not look back.

But the image of two tears spilling down her cheeks burned behind his eyelids all the way to London.

22

"Trust you to do nothing by halves, Alex," Rafe said, sitting back and taking a sip of his whisky.

"Aye. Ye have the right of it, Rafe," Andrew said, shooting Alex a wan smile.

Ewan saluted them all with his own glass.

For his part, Alex sighed and took a sip of his tea.

The four men were seated in the library of Andrew's Mayfair town-house in London.

The only female present was Lady Isolde Langston, Andrew's five-month-old daughter. Andrew bounced the wee babe on his knee, refusing to give her to a nurse.

I love her too much tae be parted, he had said earlier.

Isolde had adorably plump cheeks—*verra kissable,* Andrew pronounced them—and sported a shock of red hair that stuck out at all angles.

Jane cannot get it tae lay flat, Andrew had grinned with pride. *My lass's hair is just as stubborn as herself, I ken.*

At the moment, Isolde was hell-bent on sticking her father's entire thumb into her mouth. She gnawed at it with her four teeth, causing Andrew to wince with stoic verve.

Watching one of his best friends revel in his role as father amplified the emptiness in Alex's chest.

Alex had arrived three days previously, his leg aching and his heart bruised from the journey.

How could one wee woman leave such an outsized hole in him? The logic of it made no sense.

And yet the vacuum of Lottie's absence consumed an inordinate amount of his mental energy. She was a phantom limb, constantly aching and making her lack known.

"Truly, Alex, it is astonishing," Rafe continued. "Ye hide your competitive streak well, but sometimes it comes racing to the forefront."

"Pardon?" Alex looked up from stirring his tea. An agitated nervousness fizzed in his blood, lending his hands a faint tremor.

"Lady Charlotte is a renowned beauty," Rafe directed his comment at Ewan.

Alex set down his spoon, attempting to stare down his friends.

Could he get no respite from Lottie?

"Is she now?" Ewan replied.

"Aye. Staggeringly lovely."

"Don't let Sophie hear ye say that," Andrew said, shifting Isolde farther into his lap and offering the babe a rag doll to gnaw on instead of his thumb.

"Och, she would agree with me. And ye notice our Alex isn't denying it." Rafe winked at Alex.

A resigned weight settled in Alex's chest.

"Lady Charlotte is truly beautiful." He shrugged his shoulders. *In every way.* Though he did not add that second bit. "Though what does any of this have to do with me and a competitive streak?"

"My point is this," Rafe said with a good-natured smirk. "You, Alex, are rather ambitious. You have tae conquer the prettiest lass. Become the best doctor and graduate university with the highest rank. The most skilled horseman. The most accurate shot—"

"Enough," Alex groaned. "Ye know that isnae true."

"Isn't it, though?" Rafe asked.

"I think I agree with Rafe," Andrew said, pressing a kiss to Isolde's fuzzy head as she chewed on the doll's head. "Look at ye now. You're not in line for any measly barony or mongrel earldom like myself. Nae, only a lofty marquisate for our Alex."

Alex rolled his eyes, not sure what to make of the note of seriousness underneath his friends' teasing.

Tonight was not an official meeting of the Brotherhood. They waited for Kieran's arrival first, which given the details in his last letter, should be within a week or two. Thankfully, Andrew insisted that Alex stay with him at Hadley House.

They were joined by Ewan and his wife—Violet Campbell, Lady Kildrum. Lady Kildrum and Andrew's wife—Jane Langston, Lady Hadley—were undertaking the come-out of Lady Kildrum's younger twin sisters, Lady Aster and Lady Rose. The girls were to be presented at Court in three weeks' time, followed by a grand ball at Hadley House afterward to celebrate.

Andrew's Runner was still chasing information about Reverend Smith, or whomever the man might actually be. They had surmised that *Smith* was, of course, an alias—so common it was nearly impossible to trace.

But the more the Runner searched for the man, the murkier his origins became. The reverend's address at The George Inn in Yorkshire turned up nothing. Merely an innkeep who said a pastor showed up every once in a while to collect mail addressed to S. Smith. The innkeep didn't know the man at all.

They did discover that a Reverend Gillespie had returned from a mission to the South Pacific over two years ago. Was this the same man? Gillespie had led a group of over thirty men and women on a mission to convert the natives of the New Hebrides to Christianity, but he had been the only fully ordained minister in the group. They had returned to England when illness devastated their ranks.

Unfortunately, finding Reverend Gillespie was also proving surprisingly difficult. The Runner was confident that he would track down the man eventually and see what he might know. It had only been a few weeks, after all. They simply needed to be patient and methodical in their search.

Alex took a sip of tea, trying to swallow back the tightness at the back of his throat.

Why did this anxiousness weigh on him? Was it lingering worry over Kieran and how he might react to this new development with Gillespie?

Or was it more Alex's own concerns about the marquisate?

Or merely the endless energy of London bleeding into him?

Or, perhaps, a mixture of all of it?

Vaguely, he knew that this sensation was not a novel one. Wasn't this how his life *always* felt? Jittery and on the run? One more thing to be busy doing?

And yet, he hadn't really felt like this for weeks and weeks now.

Really not since . . .

He thought back.

Not since those first days after his accident.

Not since he had begun spending time with Lady Charlotte.

He had certainly been motivated to stay busy after his accident—and he had—but his habitual restlessness had somehow been . . . less.

But now, the sensation had returned in force.

"Speaking of the marquisate," Andrew said, standing to bounce Isolde and fixing Alex with a more serious gaze, "have ye further considered accepting the title?"

"Nae. My wishes havenae changed." Alex downed his tea in a rush, setting down the cup and saucer before his nerves set the china to rattling. "But the situation has developed, as ye all know. My visit yesterday with Mr. Argent was not particularly encouraging."

Mr. Argent was a capable sort. They had spoken for three hours, Alex listening as Mr. Argent expounded on the marquisate and its holdings. Alex had been impressed by the man's diligence and dedication.

At the end of their discussion, Alex had hired Mr. Argent himself. He tasked Argent with determining the precise state of affairs and giving Alex a recommended list of needed changes to Lord Frank's handling of Lockheade businesses and lands.

Perhaps with that list in hand, Alex could confront Ferndown and Lord Frank and hammer out a solution. Though he was at a loss as to how to make it binding . . .

"Before I make any decisions, I need to know all the facts," Alex continued. "I have no doubt Mr. Argent will be diligent in his recommendations."

"It is to your credit that you care so," Ewan said, reaching for another beef sandwich from a side tray. "But I know from watching my wife deal with our more modest holdings—it is not a task for the faint of heart."

"Aye. I agree with Ewan." Rafe nodded his head. "Besides, I heard today that if you sign the attainder and swear off the title, Lords will postpone resolving the matter until at least next year. No one has the energy to draft the legislation necessary to award the marquisate to Master Frederick."

"I heard the same." Andrew paused as Isolde fussed. He expertly moved her to his shoulder, rubbing her back and crooning softly.

"That is a concern," Alex agreed. "The longer this drags on, the more entrenched Lord Frank becomes in managing the marquisate. If he is behaving as we suspect, the damage he will inflict will be immense. I may not have the luxury of waiting for a resolution."

Silence for a moment.

"I know up to now I haven't said anything to try to persuade ye to take up the title, Alex," Andrew said, "as I feel like the decision needs tae be yours alone, but . . ."

"But?" Alex prompted.

"As a fellow Scot, I find it a wee bit difficult to hold my tongue." Andrew continued to rub Isolde's back, the *wean's* eyes drooping in sleep. "As Lockheade, ye could be a voice for real change in Lords. You and I, we could stand shoulder-to-shoulder in defense of our countrymen. We've spoken of this before, I know, but Scotland stands at a crossroads with England."

"Perhaps, but England has vilified Scotland for centuries." Alex took a deep breath, wishing his leg was healed enough to allow him to pace. His body nearly bounced with suppressed energy.

"Yes, but the new king has a more nuanced view of Scotland. There is even talk of him visiting Edinburgh next year."

"Aye," Rafe agreed with a nod. "After the unrest last year in Glasgow—"

"The Radical War?" Ewan asked.

"Och, that is a galling name for a civil uprising tied to unfair working conditions and low wages. Only an English newspaper would call it such." Andrew rolled his eyes. "Regardless, Westminster is eager to mend fences at the moment. It's why they have leapt onto this idea that ye might marry Lady Charlotte—"

"I'm not going to marry Lottie—ehr, Lady Charlotte," Alex interrupted.

Of course, no one missed his slip.

"Lottie?" An amused grin tugged at Rafe's lips.

"Aye." Andrew winked at Rafe. "And he admitted earlier that she's right bonnie, too."

"I give him a month." Rafe grinned wider. "A man can only deny his heart for so long."

Alex sighed, shaking his head at the teasing.

"Why *not* marry her?" Ewan asked. "It's a genuine question. Ye obviously care for the lady."

Alex did. Too much.

Trust his friends to see right through him.

Lottie had come to London with her sister and Lord Frank. That much Alex had learned these past few days. They were staying with Ferndown in the palatial ducal townhouse overlooking Berkley Square.

Alex had even driven past the house the day before. Ostensibly, he had passed Ferndown House on his way to look at Lockheade House, the townhouse the marquisate owned off Grosvenor Circle. But as the carriage slowly rolled past the gates to Ferndown House, he could not help how his gaze lingered, optimistically hoping that he might catch a glimpse of Lottie.

He was utterly pathetic.

Moreover, Alex knew that such buildings were termed "townhouses" but they were, in all actuality, wee country estates in the middle of London. Ferndown House was more palace than anything.

Lockheade House was similarly grand.

Alex had studied its elegant Palladian facade through the iron gate leading into the small forecourt. He simply could not fathom that such a building could be *his*. That he could leave the finery of Frome Abbey, and then journey in a luxurious carriage to London, only to tuck himself away from the 'rabble' in an urban palace.

Embracing such a future felt onerous. Overwhelming and exhausting. And *that* coming from a man who regularly worked eighteen hours a day.

But he remembered Mr. Bartlet's desperate expression, the wan faces of his bairns . . .

How ridiculous for Alex to be dithering, worried that luxury would be too difficult a burden while others starved.

He was being a selfish bastard.

That had to be what was driving his anxious tick—a strong desire to race from the glaring light of Reality facing him—

He was likely going to have to assume the marquisate.

He just couldn't reconcile himself with the idea quite yet. With driving that final nail in the coffin of any possible romantic relationship with Lady Charlotte.

Alex looked at Rafe. "Ye tease me that I am competitive, and yes, I was raised a gentleman. But that doesnae mean I understand how to be a lord."

"There's not much tae it," Andrew ventured, sitting back down with the now sleeping Isolde. "Ye just have tae practice giving weighted stares and making demands in a loud voice."

Alex smiled despite himself.

"Take on the marquisate," Rafe urged. "Address all its ills personally."

Alex swallowed, rubbing fingertips into his forehead. "If I do, Lady Charlotte will never forgive me for disinheriting Master Freddie and usurping her father's final request."

That was the bald, plain truth.

"Ah." Ewan fixed him with a long look. "So in accepting the marquisate, ye would be giving up two loves of your life—medicine and Lady Charlotte."

This was the problem with Ewan. His gentle heart always saw and heard more than one intended.

Alex swallowed and looked away.

Yes, he wanted to say.

But that fidgety fear closed off his throat, and he couldn't force that one simple word out of his mouth.

23

Lottie slowly fanned her face.

Voices hummed around her.

Crystal clinked. Silk rustled.

Ladies and gentlemen moved in and out of Lord Montain's elegant drawing room, enjoying Lady Montain's evening rout.

Lord Nettlesby and three other gentlemen ranged around Lottie, posturing and joking with one another.

For her part, Lottie listened with half an ear, fanned her face, and desperately wished to be somewhere else. Preferably with *someone* else.

"I say, Lady Charlotte, I was telling Peterson here that you don't eat meat." Lord Nettlesby grinned at her, motioning toward a thin dandy at his side. "He thought I was bamming him."

"Is this true?" Mr. Peterson asked, staring like she was the prettiest filly at Tattersall's, and he couldn't wait to purchase her.

"Yes, it is true." She paused to see if Mr. Peterson or Nettlesby would question her further. Any tiny tidbit that would indicate a true desire to get to know her.

But, instead, both men laughed, as if her reply were that of an adorable child.

Oof.

She had not missed London and its Marriage Mart.

She had been in London for two weeks now.

Nearly three weeks since Alex had left Frome Abbey, leaning on his crutch but head upright in determined resolution.

Three weeks without seeing him. Three weeks without his gentle laughter and thoughtful voice.

How could such a clearly measured length of time feel like a limitless eternity?

And yet, what else was she to do?

She wished Freddie to inherit.

Any interest she showed in Dr. Alex Whitaker was a barrier to that.

As if reminding her of her determined path, Lady Gardner whisked past in a blur of gray curls and expensive silk. Her ladyship darted a glance Lottie's way. Like a character in a fairy tale, Lady Gardner could grow a fantasy of scandal out of innocent beans.

Could her ladyship sense the brittleness underlying Lottie's forced cheer?

Lottie kept a bright smile on her face, determined not to give Lady Gardner even a hint of bean to work with.

Three weeks ago, Lottie had been resolute in her course.

But now . . . after feeling so keenly the pain of Alex's absence . . .

Some days she feared her heart would quite literally crack in two, divided between her love for her family and her adoration of Alex.

But how could she hurt Freddie so? How could she hurt Margaret?

The situation was utterly impossible.

"Are you well, *ma petite?*" Grandmère murmured at her elbow. "Lady Montain's routs are always a frightful crush."

"I am fine, Grandmère. It is merely stuffy in here." Lottie continued fanning herself.

She declined to mention that she had not eaten since breakfast. The strain of missing Alex and engaging in the social whirlwind of Town had utterly sapped her appetite. But she had drunk a glass of sherry upon arriving, and the wine sat heavy in her empty stomach, rendering her lightheaded.

The evening was meant to be one of laughter—conversation in one room, cards in another, while music could be heard coming from a third. A sprinkling of activities that might please everyone.

Grandmère, thankfully, had stayed at Lottie's side even as gentlemen came and went. Nettlesby was the only one who remained glued in place beside her. At the moment, their small group was standing in front of an open window opposite the doorway. The night air was only slightly cooler than the room itself, but the faint breeze was a blessing on the back of Lottie's neck.

She fanned herself, watching Frank and Margaret move through the room, greeting people. Ferndown accompanied them, currying public opinion in favor of Freddie. They stopped to speak with Lady Montain before the fireplace, all smiles and charm.

Lottie longed for the quiet of the library in Frome Abbey, Alex relaxing opposite her. He would raise those steel eyes and give her that soft look, the one that said, *Keep talking, lass. I would hear your thoughts—*

She clenched her fist, forcing the thoughts aside.

But in the same breath, some current in the air had her turning her head toward the doorway.

Some sixth sense of knowing . . .

Her eyes searching . . .

Oh.

He was here.

Dr. Alexander Whitaker.

Her Alex.

He stood in the doorway, wearing a *kilt* of all things. His leg brace was gone, and an elegant cane replaced his crutches.

Heavens!

"Well, none of us expected to see him here tonight. I do not think Frank and Margaret would have come had they known," Grandmère murmured beside her. "Our Dr. Whitaker certainly cuts a dashing figure, *mais non?*"

Lottie couldn't force a reply through her stiff lips. Her stomach swooped and dipped, her vision darkening slightly at the edges.

She should have eaten something. Anything to help brace her for the impact of seeing Dr. Alex Whitaker again.

He *did* look dashing.

Devastating, in fact.

A talented valet had taken him in hand. His dark shortcoat fit with immaculate precision, highlighting the power in his shoulders. The gold threads of his embroidered red waistcoat caught the candlelight and a gemstone winked from the folds of his starched neckcloth. His great kilt, a dark tartan shot with red and gold, draped his upper body and was belted at the waist with a leather pouch hanging in front.

On a lesser man, such finery would seem more a costume than habitual wear. But Alex carried it all with casual aplomb, using his cane to walk with ease despite a slight limp.

Given how heads turned as he made his way through the crowd toward their hostess for the evening, Lottie was not alone in her admiration. Even Nettlesby frowned at Lottie's side.

Simply put, Alex looked like a *Someone*. He always had, she realized in hindsight. He was not a man who would ever move invisibly through the world.

"Who is that with him?" Grandmère asked.

Finally, Lottie noticed that there were others in Alex's company. She recognized the auburn-haired Lady Jane, or rather Lady Hadley now. The tall man at her side must be her husband, Lord Hadley, Alex's good friend. Hadley wore a kilt, as well, in a blue-and-red tartan.

The group approached Lady Montain who was still speaking with Frank and Margaret.

A confrontation between the parties was inevitable.

"This should be entertaining," Grandmère chuckled.

"Grandmère!"

"*Beh*. You are being too English, *ma puce*. We French delight in such contretemps. If our Alex cannot surmount this situation, then perhaps yourself and the *marquisat* are not for him, *non*?"

Lottie bit back her reply that Alex had never been for her *or* the marquisate.

Frank froze, realizing Alex was approaching. Margaret was only a second behind her husband.

Her sister turned her head and sought Lottie's gaze across the room. Lottie saw it clearly in Margaret's eyes—the mother lioness. Margaret would do what she had to in order to protect the interests of her son.

Lottie nodded her head in acknowledgment.

Margaret gave her a faint smile and turned back to her husband.

Lord Hadley stopped beside Frank and introduced Alex to Lady Montain. Alex bowed.

Lady Montain turned to Frank and Margaret, presumably to introduce them to Alex, perhaps not realizing their familial connection.

Lottie knew what was going to happen even before it did.

It was what *needed* to happen, after all.

As Lady Montain spoke, both Frank and Margaret looked past Alex as if he simply did not exist.

Once her ladyship finished talking, Frank offered Margaret his arm, and they both turned and walked away without saying a word.

The cut direct.

Brutal but effective.

"I say," Nettlesby laughed at her side. "That was quite well-done of Lord Frank. No more wondering where your family stands, eh, Lady Charlotte?"

Lottie fanned her face harder. Nettlesby was correct, but the entire incident only exacerbated her unease, leaving her breathless and even faintly dizzy.

Frank's actions stated to all and sundry that a battle line had been drawn.

There would be no quarter.

No alliance between the former Lord Lockheade's family and their distant cousin, Dr. Alexander Whitaker.

Oh, Alex.

He deserved better than their scorn. It was just this impossible situation . . .

Lottie could feel eyes shifting toward her. Questioning eyes.

Were the rumors about Dr. Whitaker and herself true? Or did she share her sister's disdain?

Frank and Margaret slowly made their way over to Lottie.

Margaret gave Lottie an apologetic look, her gaze saying what she could not in front of her husband—her sister did not dislike Alex as a person. He simply was an impediment to the future happiness and financial stability of Margaret's family. Her sister would defend her tribe, as it were.

Frank, however, was pleased as Punch. He shook Nettlesby's hand, giving him a jubilant smile.

"Nicely done." Nettlesby nodded toward Alex, who continued to speak with Lady Montain.

"The first step, at least." Frank snorted and darted a glance to Lottie.

Lottie frowned. What did Frank mean by that?

"You have a prior acquaintance with Lady Hadley, do you not?" Margaret asked Lottie, stepping into place beside her.

Lottie nodded, her eyes riveted on Lady and Lord Hadley and Alex as they bid goodbye to Lady Montain and began to circle the room.

Or, rather, on Alex specifically, smiling and greeting all those to whom he was introduced.

How did he appear so effortless in her world? Did his leg still pain him? Was the bone healed now—

"You must stop looking at him so, Lottie dearest," Margaret whispered.

Lottie tore her eyes from Alex.

That was precisely how the sensation felt. As if her eyes were desperate to linger on him, and she had to forcibly cut them free.

"Pardon?" she asked, forcing herself to focus on Margaret.

Well, rather, she attempted to do so.

But as if against her very will, her eyes slowly drifted sideways, unerringly finding Alex again. Was he bowing to Miss Appleton now? Was his smile broader than normal?

He paused as he rose from his bow and then turned his head in her direction.

As if she had called to him.

As if the connection between them was too strong to deny.

His gaze instantly locked with hers.

Oh!

Electricity charged between them, an invisible looping current.

"Charlotte Whitaker!" Margaret said, perhaps a bit too loudly. Heads turned toward them.

Lottie jerked her head back with a gasp.

"Lottie, please, you must cease this," Margaret continued, frustration and hurt in her voice. "You *cannot* stare so forlornly at him. Your very face is confirming everyone's assumptions."

"Agreed," Frank cut in. "Lottie must do her part."

A churning panic roiled in her chest. "My part?"

"I think you must," Margaret nodded.

"Charlotte, you must give Dr. Whitaker the cut direct," Frank said. "Just as Margaret and I have done."

Lottie's attention snapped fully to her brother-in-law.

"The cut direct? Cousin Alex?" Lottie could not help but press a shaking hand to her midriff. "I don't . . . that is to say . . ."

Lottie could not fathom such a thing.

To announce, so very publicly, that Alex was *no one* to her.

To snub him as the elite of London watched.

A dreadful tingling sensation started at Lottie's fingertips. Yes, she really should have eaten something in the last twelve hours.

Where had all the air in the room gone? She could scarcely breathe.

Worse, the encroaching panic was the pinnacle of feminine cliches. She hated herself for it, even as hysteria flirted with the edges of her mind.

"All will be well, dearest, but you must do it." Margaret took Lottie's hand, holding it tightly. Her sister indicated the doctor across the room with a sideways flick of her eyes. "Ferndown is approaching him now. The duke will greet Dr. Whitaker. This will show the Committee that we are civilized people—that our actions are not needlessly cruel—but that we do not wish a strong acquaintance. After Ferndown's introduction, you will go and greet Lady Hadley, be introduced to Lord Hadley, and then, when you are introduced to Dr. Whitaker, you will turn and give him the cut direct. That should silence gossip. Lady Gardner will have your dismissal spread all over Town by breakfast."

Oh, gracious.

Lottie feared she was going to be ill. The tingling in her hands reached a crescendo, sending black darts across her vision.

"But—"

"For Freddie," Margaret pleaded. "For me. For Papa."

"Yes, Lady Charlotte." Frank took her hand and threaded it through his elbow. "If you wish to stand with us and show that your family truly comes first, you must do this."

ALEX FOUND LADY MONTAIN'S ROUT to be rather dull. So many people preening like peacocks, angling to see and be seen.

The hum of conversation and whirl of motion caused a twitch in his chest and increased his sense of needing to be doing, doing, doing. He resisted the urge to check the time on his pocket watch.

Only Andrew's presence at his side and the possibility of exchanging a word with Lottie made the evening bearable.

He was used to such events from his upbringing in Edinburgh society. His family had been wealthy gentry, after all. Not quite the aristocracy, but close enough that they were included in most hostesses' invitations.

Lottie, of course, glittered like the jewel he knew her to be. That first glimpse of her had stopped him cold, freezing everything into a steady focus.

Ferndown had just taken his leave of Alex and Andrew. The duke had been only vaguely apologetic over Lord and Lady Frank's actions. Alex got the sense that this entire affair was more political maneuvering than anything—an attempt to squelch rumors of Lottie and himself possibly making a match of it.

"Is that her?" Andrew murmured at his side, looking across the room to where Lottie walked on Frank's arm, greeting friends. She was impossibly lovely in a pale blue frock covered in yards of expensive lace and netting.

"Aye," Alex nodded.

Andrew gave a low whistle of appreciation. "Och, Rafe didn't lie, did he now? Ye truly do nothing by halves."

"Dinnae let Jane hear ye say that—"

"Let Jane hear what?" Jane asked, coming to stand beside her husband.

"Me admiring Alex's Lady Charlotte," Andrew said shamelessly.

"She is not *my* anything," Alex protested, for all the good it did.

"Lady Charlotte is truly lovely." Jane wrapped her hand around Andrew's elbow. "She has long been a reigning Diamond. Though I only have a passing acquaintance with her, I have always thought kindness and intellect to be her greatest virtues."

"Aye," Alex heard himself agree, his voice perhaps a tad too emphatic.

But seeing Lottie like this, watching men's heads turn as she passed, caused a yearning crack in his chest.

Did they see beyond her pretty face, these gentlemen who stared and gaped?

Did they see more than a large dowry, a titled father, and a lovely figure?

Did they hear her thoughts? Did they truly listen?

"If ye don't want tae be declared the marquess tomorrow, ye should likely stop staring at the lass like she is the beginning and end of your world," Andrew laughed into his ear.

Right.

Alex sucked in a breath and turned to his friend.

A few minutes later, though, the familiar scent of jasmine engulfed him. He heard the soft timbre of Lottie's voice behind him, greeting Jane.

"Lady Hadley," Lottie said, "it is so lovely to see you again."

"And you, too, Lady Charlotte. Hadley," Jane touched Andrew's shoulder, "permit me to introduce you to my friend."

Alex turned around with Andrew.

And there she was.

His Lottie.

His eyes snapped unerringly to hers.

He sensed that she wanted to look away from him but instead was helplessly caught in his gaze, just as he was in hers.

Had she come to give him the cut direct, as Lord and Lady Frank had done?

Would she do such a thing?

Alex supposed it would be a sensible action. Show everyone, once and for all, that there was nothing more than air between them.

He should likely bow and take his leave from her.

He should.

He *would*.

But something in her gaze would not let him go. Would not release the part of him that felt bound to her. He saw her, and the world

Simply.

Stopped.

He could feel eyes turning their way, heads swiveling.

He needed to go. They had to avoid igniting a bonfire of gossip.

Alex gave Lottie one last, intense look, committing the slope of her elegant jaw and the petal-pink of her lips to memory.

Lottie swallowed, chest heaving, blinking rapidly.

Alex paused.

And then frowned.

Something was not quite right.

She was too pale, was she not?

Lottie continued to blink rapidly, her breathing coming in quick rasps.

Wait—were her eyes dilated?

Was the flutter of her pulse in her throat too rapid?

"Lady Charlotte?" He took a step toward her.

"I think . . ." She took in a stuttering breath, lifting a hand toward him. "Alex . . ."

Her eyes rolled back in her head.

Alex barely caught her as Lottie fainted dead away.

THE NEXT DAY, LADY GARDNER eagerly sped from house to house, describing the moment to all and sundry in excruciatingly florid detail.

How Dr. Whitaker gazed upon the beautiful Lady Charlotte as if the sun rose and set on her smiles.

How Lady Charlotte—overcome at seeing her beloved and distressed by their star-crossed devotion—swooned at his feet.

How Dr. Whitaker leapt into action, attempting to revive her. The man, after all, was a doctor. One of the best, they said.

He appeared, Lady Gardner swore, to be nearly panic-stricken as he cradled Lady Charlotte's limp body in one arm and cupped her jaw with the other.

Eventually, Lady Montain produced some smelling salts, and Lady Charlotte was revived.

But not before all and sundry witnessed Dr. Whitaker clutching Lady Charlotte briefly to his bosom, as tenderly as any lover.

24

"You will never speak with him again." Frank jabbed a finger at Lottie. "Never!"

"Gracious. What a display of *l'outrage*." Grandmère murmured, calmly stitching. "And our *pauvre* Charlotte, she has scarcely had a chance to recover."

"*Grandmère*," Margaret said repressively, her presence a buffer between her husband and her family. She shot Lottie a troubled look. "I should have remembered your tendency to faint when overwrought."

Lottie sat on a sofa before the fireplace at Ferndown House, morning light filtering in through the windows.

The events of the evening before were all a blur. Like her come-out ball years before, she had fainted. A surfeit of nerves.

Vividly, she could still see Alex's stricken face right before the world went dark. The terror and horror in his gaze as her eyelids shuttered.

The affair was as embarrassing as it was shocking.

It had simply been . . . too much. The stuffy room. The weight of so many eyes. Her empty stomach and dizzy head.

And then seeing Alex again and knowing the sheer impossibility of *them*.

Love had washed over her, as visceral as it was horrific.

She loved this man.

Lady Charlotte loved Dr. Alex Whitaker.

She hadn't even dared voice such a thought to herself. Because the last time she thought she loved someone, she had committed to marrying him.

And she couldn't marry Alex. Not if she wanted to remain true to the promise she had given her father. Not if she wanted Freddie to have a bright future.

But in that moment, she could no longer deny it—

She loved him.

And the realization had caused her knees to lock and her chest to seize and blackness to swamp her vision.

Her world had gone dark.

"Father is out and about this morning to see what can be salvaged." Frank was pacing now. "Lords is already leaning so strongly toward *that man's* claim. And now Charlotte has packed their cannons with even more fodder to decide against our Freddie."

"Lady Gardner witnessed the entire affair with an almost unholy glee." Margaret clenched and unclenched one fist. "She is already making morning visits to spread the scandal."

"This is an utter disaster." Frank snorted. "Charlotte must be seen driving out with other gentlemen. Perhaps we should drop subtle hints that she is soon to be engaged to another."

"I am sure Nettlesby will be amenable to assist us," Margaret said.

Lottie's stomach dropped.

"Yes, he's a good sort." Frank paced. "But most importantly, Charlotte must give Dr. Whitaker the cut direct when next we see him. That is imperative!"

Frank continued his back and forth in front of the fire, venting his ire.

Lottie studied her hands, allowing her brother-in-law's words to wash over her.

However, it was the heavy weight of Margaret's nearly-silent censure that tore at her heart.

Her sister was trying to remain calm, but it was a testament to Margaret's frustration that she did not attempt to temper her husband's anger.

As for herself, Lottie feared her soul would quite literally rend in two.

Just as with Theo years ago, she was torn between her love for family and her love for a man.

She stared at Margaret's bent head. Her sister clenched her fist tightly, as if she could hold on to her son's future simply by willing it so.

How could Lottie do anything to deliberately hurt Margaret and Freddie? How could she be so selfish?

And yet . . .

A memory of Alex rose from the night before. The flash of panic in his eyes before she fainted, his arms already reaching for her.

And then waking up a few minutes later, her eyes slowly opening to see his beloved head bent over hers, his strong arm banded around her, cradling her to his chest.

She had nearly burst into tears.

The sheer *relief* of being with him again.

She wished to remain in his arms forever.

With Theo, the decision had been so obvious. How could she forsake her family for Theo? The very idea was laughable.

How very foolish she had been then. To assume that the weak emotion she felt for Theo was true love.

No. She had known nothing then of this sort of love. The romantic love that poets proclaimed and lyricists sang.

Alex hummed in her blood. How was she to face a life without him?

As Frank launched into a tirade about how Lottie *should* have behaved, she couldn't help but meet Grandmère's gaze.

Her grandmother did not seem upset. If anything, she appeared pensive . . . though with Grandmère's eyebrows, it was always difficult to say with any certainty.

AN HOUR LATER, GRANDMÈRE RAPPED on Lottie's bedroom door.

Lottie had been banished to her bedchamber, like a recalcitrant child. Frank and Ferndown were going to consult on a plan to somehow remedy this situation.

"How fare you, *ma petite*?" Grandmère asked, sitting on Lottie's bed and running a hand over her hair.

Lottie sat up, wiping tears.

"I have been better, Grandmère," she answered truthfully. "I never expected to be in this place. To be the one who caused a rift within our family."

"Ah." Grandmère studied her, those censorious eyebrows drawn down. "Gabriel was correct all those years ago to paint you as a collie."

"Was he though?"

"The most loyal of breeds. That has been you, *ma puce*."

"I do not feel particularly loyal at the moment, Grandmère." Lottie pulled her legs up and rested her cheek on her knees. "I have hurt Margaret and threatened Freddie's future and jeopardized their financial stability. I have been disloyal to Papa's memory."

"Mmmm. I fear you have a difficult choice before you."

"Choice?"

"*Oui.* It happens from time to time in life. *Une crise*, as we French say. A crisis point where you must choose between two impossible things. You love our Freddie and wish to see his future settled. You love Margaret and wish to remain loyal to her."

Lottie nodded, sniffling.

"But you also have come to care deeply for the doctor." Grandmère traced a finger down Lottie's cheek. "And . . . *loving* him comes at the cost of betraying Margaret and Freddie."

Lottie swallowed.

Loving him.

Of course, Grandmère would see the true state of Lottie's heart.

But even knowing this . . .

Even if she *were* willing to forsake Freddie and Margaret in order to unite her life with Alex . . .

None of it supposed that Alex wished something similar. Marrying her would mean accepting the marquisate, and she did not know where he stood on that point at the moment. She could not force his hand.

Was there any way forward that did not cause harm?

Oh, what a mess this was!

Tears tumbled down her cheeks

Grandmère pressed a handkerchief into her hand.

"Unfortunately, there will be no harmonious outcome with this situation," Grandmère continued, plucking Lottie's thoughts from her head. "You will have to sacrifice something. That is why it is called *une crise*. It is a crisis with painful consequences."

Lottie hiccupped.

They sat in silence for a few moments. Grandmère slid further onto the bed, pulling Lottie into her arms as she had when Lottie was little.

"Sometimes, *ma puce*, family is not only a thing of blood." Grandmère stroked her hair. "Sometimes, family are those who put your interests first. They are the ones who stand by you even when life becomes difficult. You are concerned about honoring your father's legacy and that is an admirable goal. He wanted his grandson to inherit. But do you truly believe that your father—were he here right now—would care if that son were Margaret's or yours?"

Lottie bit her lip, licking at the tears that continued to fall. "P-papa would not care. You are r-right. But *I* care. I simply cannot b-betray Margaret and Freddie. They are t-too much of my heart."

"Yes, your lovely loyal heart, as Gabriel was fond of saying. Your dedication to those you love is admirable. But I fear somewhere in your allegiance to family, you have begun to think of their future as having more weight than your own."

"But it feels so s-selfish to only think of my own wishes and desires."

"You love so fiercely, *ma puce*, but you need to extend a bit of that love to yourself. You need to stand firm in the knowledge of your own worth. In short, you have neglected a few important truths."

"Truths?" Lottie sniffed. "Like what?"

Grandmère smiled, continuing to run a hand over Lottie's curls. "Basic truths, *ma petite*. Such as . . . *you* are the only one who can live your life. Just as Margaret must live hers. Just as Freddie must live his. Your lives are not tethered together . . . not really. One of life's greatest ironies is this—we travel it alone. I have experienced enough loss to know this intimately. Even though others may surround us, in the end, the journey of life is a solitary one."

Lottie hiccupped, licking tears off her lip once more.

Grandmère pulled a handkerchief out of her sleeve and dabbed at Lottie's cheeks.

"Another truth—we do not choose the family of our birth. We do not choose the children that come to us." Grandmère tucked her handkerchief into Lottie's hand. "But in between those two points, we choose to make *one* person family. One person to tie to our side and walk the path of life with us. I know this truth feels dichotomous to my first point—that we are ultimately alone—but that is life, I suppose. Full of paradoxes."

Grandmère took Lottie's hands in hers.

"I don't know what to do, Grandmère," Lottie whispered. "I fear my heart will break in two."

"*Oui*, this *crise* will cause you pain. That is the way of things." Grandmère gave her a tired smile. "Several years ago, you faced a similar decision. Your family or marriage to Theo. In that instance, you chose family. And I do not think you have ever regretted that choice."

"No. I have not."

"So now, you face a similar decision. If you choose family, will you regret letting the doctor go? Will you mourn his loss like a death? Or will it be like Theo, a mild bit of heartache?" Grandmère gave a decidedly Gallic flick of her hand. "If, however, the doctor's loss threatens to tear you apart—if you realize you deeply love Dr. Whitaker, and he loves you in return—then perhaps it is time to *act*. To create a family that is wholly yours and shape a future that is uniquely your own."

25

Alex let himself into the front door of Andrew's townhouse. The hour was late. Far too late to be rousing servants or even the wee hall boy who lay asleep in the entryway.

The events of the night before haunted him—Lottie's eyes rolling back in her head and her body collapsing, a marionette with strings cut. The image looped over and over in his mind, like a perpetual-motion machine, winding him up tighter and tighter until he had to *do something* to release the pent-up energy.

He had taken to the gaslit streets of Mayfair, walking for hour after hour until his leg ached from the strain. But the physical pain was a welcome respite from the leaden weight of his heart.

How had he landed himself in this mire?

Part of him longed to hop on a horse tomorrow and head back to Edinburgh. To lose himself in caring for others and tamp down the jittery ache that rose whenever he thought of Lady Charlotte Whitaker's blue eyes.

The terror when she fainted . . .

He had faced, unutterably, the knowledge that he could lose her in an instant—

He shuddered.

As a medical man, knowing how to treat disease was generally a comfort. He understood what to do when faced with a crisis.

But when those he loved became ill, it was the precise opposite, as he knew only too well how a seemingly simple malady could quickly become lethal.

Och, bloody hell.

Those he *loved* . . .

He scrubbed a hand over his face.

He faced the truth directly.

Yes.

He loved Lady Charlotte Whitaker.

The emotion had flooded him weeks ago, more than likely beginning with that consuming kiss along the muddy lane. He had just been too terrified to admit it.

And now . . . what was he to do?

His life was spinning out-of-control.

The reports he received from Mr. Argent were dire. Lord Frank needed to be reined in immediately. The troubles plaguing the marquisate loomed large, eclipsing his resolve to not assume them.

He loved a lady who fought to remain loyal to her family.

McNeal and his patients awaited his care back in Edinburgh.

He limped for the staircase, but a glimmer of candlelight from the library to his left caught his eye. Pushing open the door, he spied a familiar dark head seated before the hearth, sipping whisky.

"Kieran!" Alex exclaimed, perhaps a bit too loudly for the hush of night.

His friend startled, sloshing his whisky and cursing loudly.

"Alex! Trust ye to scare me out of my wits." Kieran stood, teeth flashing in the dim light.

Alex limped across the room. Kieran met him halfway, giving him a tight hug, thumping his back.

What a relief! His friend had returned.

Moreover, a good blether was just what Alex needed to take his mind off his worries.

"How fare ye?" Alex asked, taking a seat opposite Kieran in front of the fire. He hefted his sore leg onto a tufted footstool and massaged his aching thigh muscles.

Kieran appeared . . . tired. He had lost some weight since autumn, his waistcoat loose around his middle.

"No' bad. Yourself?"

"Och. I'm fine."

Alex finally met Kieran's gaze, noting the haunted sadness there.

Kieran rolled his eyes, likely seeing a similar expression on Alex's face.

"A bunch of bloody eejits, we are, eh?" Kieran tossed back the rest of his whisky.

"Aye. Ignoring our troubles, I ken." Alex dug his fingers into the outside of his upper thigh, watching as Kieran set down the glass.

Was Kieran back to using the bottle to numb his pain?

"Dinnae worry about me, Doctor." Kieran settled back into his wingback chair, noticeably not reaching for the whisky bottle to fill his tumbler. "I'm finished with trying tae drown my sorrows in whisky. But a nip every now and again takes the edge off a lonely night."

Alex nodded, a tightness in his chest easing.

They talked about inanities, the long hand on the mantel clock moving past one in the morning. Kieran had arrived in London earlier in the day.

"Did ye find what ye hoped?" Alex asked. "This captain who said he had fished a woman from the ocean?"

"Aye." Kieran nodded. "I did. The woman he found even vaguely matched Jamie's description, but turns out, she was a Christian missionary. He returned her to the English missionaries working there—"

"Wait? Reverend Gillespie?"

"Aye. That's the man's name." Kieran raised an eyebrow. "Though I'm a wee bit surprised to hear it on your lips."

Alex sucked in a slow breath, his mind racing.

Here was confirmation then, was it not? A definite connection between the Reverend Gillespie and *The Minerva*. The S. Smith who had met Alex at the coaching inn *had* to be tied to Reverend Gillespie's missionary efforts. How else could he have known about Jamie? Smith was likely Gillespie himself. The coincidence was too great.

Alex continued to knead his leg, breathlessly telling Kieran everything he knew of Reverend Smith/Gillespie. The more Alex revealed, the more agitated Kieran became, until his friend was up and pacing the floor.

"But who is this person with memory loss that the reverend described?"

Alex shrugged. "A member of *The Minerva*'s crew, I assume. How many people did this captain save?"

"Just the one. Just the woman." Kieran's voice rose, his hands in his hair. "Did the reverend *say* this person was a man?"

Alex paused, searching his memory. Surely, the reverend had indicated as much. But the more he thought about it, the more Alex was uncertain.

"I cannae say for sure," Alex said.

"So . . . this person with the memory loss . . . she could be my Jamie." Kieran's voice bounded around the dim room in his excitement. "Think about it, Alex. It makes perfect sense. The captain fished Miss Eilidh Fyffe out of the water and deposited her with the only other group of British people in the South Pacific, the missionaries led by Reverend Gillespie. The missionaries cared for Jamie and brought her back when they returned to Britain. If Jamie lost some of her memories, no wonder she hasn't contacted us."

"It is within the realm of possibility," Alex agreed in a low tone, subtly encouraging Kieran to do the same. There were others asleep, after all.

"It makes sense, aye?" Kieran tempered his volume but still paced before the fire. "Jamie was increasing and didnae have a wedding ring on her finger. If she awoke and had lost her memories, it's plausible that she and the reverend would assume she had been ill-used. Reverend Gillespie contacted you specifically as he wished to take our measure, to ascertain what had truly happened to Jamie aboard the ship."

Kieran swallowed and looked back to the fire, his Adam's apple bobbing up and down.

Alex took in a slow breath.

This person with amnesia *could* be Jamie herself. It was certainly the most promising lead they'd had, to date.

But . . . what if he or she were not?

Alex had helplessly watched Kieran spiral into a morass of addiction and mental agony when other tantalizing reports came to naught.

And this bit of information was earthquaking.

If this person was not Jamie . . .

"Kieran, I agree that we should investigate this to its fullest," Alex began, "but ye must prepare yourself for it to come to nothing. I would hate for you to . . ."

Alex's voice drifted off.

Kieran shook his head, hands on his hips, head down, chest heaving.

"I know ye are concerned about me, but I cannae stop." He lifted his head, pale eyes glittering in the firelight. "I willnae stop until I suss it all out. I must find Reverend Gillespie. I'll speak with Andrew at first light and see if I can join his Runner in the hunt. I havenae said this tae anyone yet, but I feel it." He tapped his breastbone, his voice becoming hoarse. "I feel Jamie here, tucked into my heart, as if hers still beats, too. I think that's why I cannae accept the reality of her death . . . because she still feels so very *alive*."

Alex held his tongue. He understood Kieran's torment in ways that he hadn't a few months ago.

The thought of Lottie being lost somewhere, and Alex stuck in a never-ending limbo, wondering what had happened . . .

His hand clenched.

Something of Alex's thoughts must have shown on his face.

"You're not arguing with me? Trying to manage my expectations? That's uncharacteristic of ye." Kieran grinned. "Before he went tae bed, Andrew mentioned something about a fair lass who's caught your eye. I believe there was something about a marquisate, as well?"

Alex winced. "Aye. That's about the right of it, I suppose."

"Well, I have all night tae hear the story," Kieran sat down. "I cannae do anything about Jamie until first light, now can I?"

Alex shook his head but told him about Lottie. About her resilient spirit, clever mind, and innate goodness. About the marquisate tangle and both their wishes with regard to it. About Lord Frank's current path to squeeze profits from the marquisate, and Alex's recognition that he would likely have to assume the title. About the gossip running wild about Lottie and himself.

Kieran listened with eager attention, a wry smile appearing now and again.

"In short, I dinnae know what tae do, Kieran," Alex finished. "I fair adore the lass, but I cannae see how the situation resolves itself well for us. She is understandably loyal to her family. If I declare my intention to fight the attainder and assume the marquisate, she will feel betrayed. Lady Charlotte will not forgive me."

"Aye, but ye are a man of honor, Alex. I know ye. You cannae sit idle and watch Lord Frank pillage the marquisate. Ye must do something."

"I know. That's the worst part of it." Alex ran a hand through his hair. "I assume the marquisate but lose both of my loves in the process—Lady Charlotte *and* my medical practice."

"Look, Alex." Kieran leaned forward, eyes bright. "Ye worry. It's your job. Ye spend your life trying tae save everything and everyone—patients, a marquisate, a fair lass, even *myself* from time to time."

"Pardon?"

Kieran rolled his eyes. "Ye know what I mean. Ye have a wee tendency tae act like the Almighty himself sometimes, trying tae control the world around yourself. But ye have tae know by now that ye cannae do that. Ye cannae control even the smallest bit."

"Whatever are ye on about, Kieran?" Alex frowned. "I dinnae think myself tae be some godlike figure—"

"Do ye not?" Kieran laughed. "I've never seen ye eat even a gram of sugar. You're so concerned about the potential downside of alcohol that ye willnae touch the stuff."

"That's just common sense—"

"Before this trip tae London, when was the last time ye allowed McNeal tae take one of your patients? Or were ye too concerned that he would muck it up?"

"McNeal has his own case load. He doesnae need mine, too." But even as Alex said the words, he recognized that he had been reluctant to allow McNeal to take on more work. How many letters had he sent to the poor man over the last months? "Besides, what does any of this have tae do with the marquisate?"

"Just this—ye can be a bit black and white in your thinking. There is no middle ground for ye. No moderation. Ye can have Lady Charlotte as a wife, clearly and cleanly, or ye cannae have her at all. Ye are a doctor, so therefore ye cannae be a marquess."

"Kieran—"

"Nae—" His friend held out a staying hand. "—ye ken there is a grain of truth in my words. Life isnae so black and white. Winds turn, masts crack, sails have tae be jury-rigged. We make do until a new breeze comes and pushes us in an unexpected direction. Change is hard. It's often messy and hurts like bloody hell. But sometimes, ye have tae leave the past and move forward into an unknown future."

Silence rang with Kieran's words.

Alex pursed his mouth.

Yes, he did struggle to leave things to others, but that was only because he was a damn fine physician. He had worked hard to become such.

He didn't have a problem with letting things go that needed to be discarded. He had sold McPherson Farms, had he not?

Kieran watched him, surely noting the emotions flitting across Alex's face.

"I know ye, my friend," Kieran continued. "It's more than just rejecting things that are messy. Ye bury yourself in the things ye keep. Ye toss away the family farm because it holds pain for ye. And then ye use the excuse of your medical practice to run yourself to exhaustion every day. Of course, ye dinnae want tae give up your practice, Alex." Kieran stared at him. "It's an addiction for ye, as surely as alcohol was for your father. As sure as opium for Ian."

The truth of Kieran's words thundered through Alex's stunned brain.

Was work an uncontrollable force of habit for him?

Could work truly be an addiction?

His logical brain scoffed at the thought.

But the part of him that had been agitated and frustrated since coming to London recognized that there was truth in the idea.

Most days, he felt an almost overwhelming need to run, run, run. And without the endless tasks of a medical practice hanging over him—

with all the normalcy of his life stripped away—it was easy to see how incessant the feeling was. How pervasive.

"It's all right tae slow down. It's all right tae allow life to be chaotic and messy for a wee while," Kieran said, voice gentle. "It's all right tae allow others to carry the burden of care. I ken that life has dealt ye hard blows, vicious memories that would take any man down."

Alex swallowed, a tell-tale sting smarting in his eyes.

Blast Kieran and his unerring words.

"But I ken better than most that ye can only run so far and so fast." Kieran's eyes were too bright. "Eventually the pain of it all *will* catch ye. Ye've seen me at my worst. Dinnae allow yourself to land there, my friend. It's a terrible pit to crawl out of."

Silence for a moment.

Alex swallowed over and over. The pain of Ian's death would always linger. He could never escape it.

His lips trembled until finally a harsh breath escaped him.

Once.

Twice.

Damn and blast.

This was why he worked so hard. Because when he stopped there was simply too much to *feel.*

He dug a handkerchief out of his pocket and pressed it to his face, allowing it to soak his grief.

He could sense Kieran's eyes on him. No judgment. No pity.

Just the quiet understanding of a man who had already stared down the greatest pain life could hand him.

"Always trust ye to say a hard truth, Kieran," Alex said, mopping his cheeks. "My injury and unplanned holiday from my medical practice has been illuminating. But none of this automatically assumes that I should become a marquess, marry a bonnie lass, and give up doctoring for the rest of my days."

And yet, even as he said that, that very future opened up before him.

Lottie sitting with him before a fire such as this one.

Lottie smiling from across a breakfast room table, her eyes alight as she recounted a book she had been reading.

Lottie laughing hysterically, golden hair tumbling loose, as she chased two wee, equally blond children across the lawn.

Lottie grinning coyly as Alex tugged her into his arms, head bending down to claim her lips—

Abruptly, he understood with sharp clarity:

He had always assumed that it was the *doing* that gave life meaning—how many people he cured, how many he helped.

Such things were admirable, but without someone beside him, such acts lost much of their meaning.

Life was meant to be shared.

With Lottie, Alex only ever wanted to be in the present, to love and simply *be*.

"You love her." Kieran stated this as a fact.

Alex nodded.

"I love her," he whispered.

"Then what else matters?"

Alex snorted.

Everything else mattered, unfortunately.

She was committed to her family. He could hardly ask her to betray them in order to spend a life with him, could he?

He needed to respect Lottie's decisions.

"Knowing that I love her doesn't remove the obstacles to our union," Alex said. "She has very real concerns that I dinnae ken how to address."

"Here is my only piece of advice." Kieran sat forward. "Life is an endlessly shifting sand. If I were a poet, I would say that *change* is life's only constant. I set sail for one port only to arrive at another. One day you are a doctor; the next, you are a marquess. The injury that broke your leg could have easily killed you, or at the very least, rendered you an invalid for life. So why, when love arrives in the midst of all this chaos, would you turn away from it?"

"It isnae that easy, Kieran—"

"But, truthfully, it is, Alex. If your love for Lady Charlotte—and hers for you—doesnae lead ye to compromise a fair bit in order tae have one another, then perhaps what ye feel isnae quite love. But if ye do love her . . .Alex took in a deep breath, letting Kieran's unspoken words linger.

But if ye do love her . . . then act. Do something, even if it might end in chaos.

Och, he had been such an eejit.

How could he even contemplate a life without Lottie? How could he not fight for her?

The sensation nearly blinded him with its force.

Love.

Glorious. Overwhelming. Cleansing.

He loved her.

He was willing to sacrifice a great many things to be with her.

Would Lottie, with her fiercely loyal heart, be willing to do the same for him?

26

The ballroom was a crush of bodies.

Mrs. Sutton was likely pleased that her ball would be declared a raging success in drawing rooms across Mayfair tomorrow.

But for now, Lottie simply wished for a breath of fresh air.

It had been six days since Lady Montain's evening soiree. Six days of contemplating Grandmère's words and attempting to find a harmonious resolution—to envision a world in which she could marry Alex without injuring Margaret or Freddie.

So far, all she had received for her efforts was a sore heart and tired feet. Ferndown and Lord Frank had insisted that Lottie be seen all over Town, squired here and there by Nettlesby or some other eligible gentleman, all in an attempt to tamp down gossip.

Margaret was unsure if they had been successful.

Lottie simply wanted to return to Frome Abbey.

The ballroom was stifling. The adjoining series of drawing rooms were no better. Doors and windows had been opened to the dark garden behind the house, but as the evening was equally warm, the night air did little to alleviate the heat.

Once again, Lottie was fanning herself slowly, listening to the rumble of male voices around her. She was surrounded by men, all jockeying for her attention—Lord Nettlesby, Mr. Peterson, and others.

Men who had never worked. Who had never held a patient's hand as they lay dying. Who had never given a needed crutch to a poor tenant. Who had never welcomed a baby into the world with efficiency and tenderness.

How had she ever thought she would be content to marry a gentleman whose values were so disparate from her own?

The room swirled with silks and satins and perfume. Grandmère sat across the way, ensconced in the middle of a row of dowagers, chatting amiably with an old acquaintance while keeping an eye on Lottie. Frank and Margaret had disappeared into the crowd, currying favor for Freddie's case.

Two gentlemen, whose names she had already forgotten, were saying something to Lord Nettlesby. His lordship laughed and looked at Lottie.

"Whose side do you take, Lady Charlotte?" he asked her. "Mine or Carlton's here?"

Lottie blinked, turning her gaze to Lord Nettlesby.

"Pardon?" she said.

Nettlesby repeated himself, but Lottie was already distracted.

Her gaze flicked over the room and landed instinctively on a man who had stopped just inside the door.

Alex.

He was here.

He had come.

He surveyed the room, leaning on his cane with casual elegance, looking devastatingly handsome in a finely tailored evening coat and breeches.

As if seeking home, his head swiveled and his eyes unerringly found hers.

He gazed at her with an almost possessive interest. As if she were Laidronette, the fairy-tale princess from the story she had read him months ago. And he was the dragon prince, determined to claim her for his own. He even looked dragon-like; the green satin of his waistcoat glittered in the candlelight.

The walls tightened around her.

She needed to look away.

Lottie knew this.

But her treacherous heart pounded and leaped, desperate to reach him.

"Charlotte?" A hand touched her elbow.

Lottie tore her gaze from Alex to find Margaret beside her.

Oh, gracious!

Would her family expect her to give Alex the cut direct tonight? They hadn't discussed it specifically, but they expected her to at some point, did they not?

Nausea rose at the thought.

"Are you feeling unwell?" her sister asked. "I should hate for you to faint again."

As if to underscore her words, Margaret cast a pointed look toward Alex. The doctor skirted the edge of the ballroom, nodding to acquaintances. He neared the row of elderly dowagers where Grandmère sat.

Was Alex going to greet Grandmère? Would she return the greeting? Or would Grandmère give Alex the cut direct, as well?

Lottie couldn't bear to witness it, to feel the pressure of what her family might expect—

"I fear she is poorly," Nettlesby said to Margaret, not allowing Lottie a chance to speak. "She has seemed a bit vague tonight."

"The air is rather heavy," Lottie said, her mind seizing on the chance to escape. Anything to avoid being forced to confront Alex tonight.

Alex was drawing closer to Grandmère.

Lottie turned her back on the room.

"Come," Margaret said, placing a firm hand under Lottie's elbow. "Let us find you a fresh breeze."

Margaret tugged her through the crowd and out a pair of open doors into the slightly cooler night beyond.

Lottie took in a steadying breath of air, walking across the terrace to the stone railing and staring out over the large back garden. The Sutton's house was a recent property built on the newly-fashionable Belgrave Square, and as such, boasted beautiful, private gardens stretching deep into the night. Pathways were lit with torches, and guests strolled in the dim light.

"Lottie, what are we to do?" Margaret murmured, slipping her arm through Lottie's elbow.

"Does Grandmère intend to cut Dr. Whitaker tonight?" Lottie heard the tremble in her voice.

"I cannot say. But I fear Frank has the right of it. Regardless of what Grandmère does, you *must* give Dr. Whitaker the cut direct. If not tonight, then soon."

Lottie closed her eyes, swallowing back the emotion in her throat.

No. I cannot do it. Not yet.

Perhaps, not ever.

"Dr. Whitaker is a good man, and I consider him a friend." *More than a friend*, Lottie did not add. "I do not know if I have it in me to deliberately snub him."

The silence between herself and Margaret stretched thin.

"I do not know what more to do, Lottie." Margaret passed a weary hand over her face. "I feel I am on a knife's edge. I fear so greatly for Freddie's future."

"Margaret—"

"No." Her sister tightened her grip on Lottie's elbow. "Please, this is not the place to discuss it. We shall simply have to see what tomorrow brings. I will not press the issue of Dr. Whitaker tonight, but you cannot remain at this ball with him. The potential for disaster is too great."

Lottie nodded in weary agreement.

Margaret led her down the terrace steps and onto a path that circled the house and ended in an enormous glasshouse. The building was dark, but moonlight filtered through the skylights to illuminate the profusion of plants inside.

"Here." Margaret opened the door. "Mrs. Sutton is inordinately proud of her greenhouse. It's large enough to hide a regiment. Sit here." She pointed to a bench just inside. "I will fetch Frank, Grandmère, and our wraps."

Margaret turned to leave.

"Thank you." The words perhaps came out a bit more emphatic than

Lottie intended. But she felt much like a prisoner just reprieved from the guillotine. "Thank you for this."

Margaret glanced back at her, a wan smile on her face, shook her head, and then left.

Lottie took several steps into the greenhouse, passing by the bench Margaret indicated. The glasshouse was impressively large. Paths disappeared into densely packed trees and shrubs. She followed one a little farther into the building, finding another bench to sit upon.

The air inside the glasshouse was damp but refreshing, laden with the scent of exotic climes. As if the geraniums and camellia were settling in for the night and filling the air with a lullaby.

Lottie took in a deep breath. And then another.

Cleansing her lungs slowed the thump of her heart, but that, in turn, only highlighted the never-ending ache in her chest.

What was she to do?

She could not betray her family and choose Alex. Her loyal heart couldn't do it.

But it all meant living *without* Alex.

There was no choice that did not hurt.

Une crise, indeed.

The snick of the greenhouse door sounded.

Had Margaret returned so soon?

Lottie peeked through the plants to see two shadowy figures slip inside. Her startled shriek of alarm instantly morphed into a sigh of despair.

"Alex. Grandmère," she whispered as they walked around a large oleander bush to greet her. She stood. "Whyever are you here?"

Grandmère had her hand tucked into Alex's elbow. She patted his arm.

"The doctor insisted upon speaking with you, *ma puce*." Grandmère shrugged. "I felt it important for you both to clear the air. Margaret will be a moment, as she was waylaid by Lady Gardner, so you will have a few minutes. I shall make myself comfortable over here and ponder the foliage." She motioned toward a bench tucked a bit farther along a path and well out of sight of the door. "It will give you privacy to speak."

Grandmère moved to brush past Lottie and then paused.

"*Je t'aime, ma puce.*" Grandmère pressed a kiss to Lottie's cheek and then whispered in her ear. "Choose your own path and be happy."

Lottie sucked in a breath as Grandmère continued past her, taking a seat on the bench, her face politely turned away.

Lottie pivoted back to Alex, her mind buzzing.

"Forgive my maneuvering, but I had tae see ye, lass." He set aside his cane and reached for her gloved hands with his own. "I feared I was going tae have to scale the walls of Ferndown's house to be able to speak with ye. But the Dowager was accommodating when I asked for an audience with ye."

Lottie stared up at his face in the dim moonlight.

He was supposed to be her enemy. But all she could see was the outline of her dearest friend, her truest love.

Had it truly been over a month since she had last spoken with him?

A month since that afternoon along the lane, glorying in his kisses?

Abruptly, even spending another second outside his embrace was intolerable. This might be the last time she was ever (relatively) alone with him. She could not let the moment pass in polite inquiries after one another's health.

Lottie darted a glance at Grandmère and pulled Alex deeper into the drooping tree branches. She stepped closer, wrapped her arms around his shoulders, and popped up onto her tiptoes, pressing her mouth to his.

If Alex were surprised at all, his reaction did not show it.

His arms slipped around her, one around her waist, the other pressing into the center of her back.

Like that last day along the lane, Lottie ached to get closer still.

It was as if nothing would ever be enough.

She could spend the rest of her days loving this man, and it would still not be sufficient to purge the sheer *emotion* of him from her heart.

The thought made her kisses frantic. She trembled, hating the thought that he would leave her. That she might never see him again.

"I can't lose you," she whispered, her breath catching on a hiccup. "I c-can't."

He responded by holding her tighter.

Lottie lost herself in him. In the feel of his body pressed against hers. In the aching wish to keep him forever.

"Lottie. Lass." A husky groan escaped him as she continued to kiss his mouth. "All is well. I willnae leave ye."

"Whatever shall we do?" She continued to press kisses to his jawline. She felt his smile.

"I say we continue doing this. I am finding it a rather delightful way to spend an evening." He lifted her up, and Lottie lost her head once more, kissing her Alex.

Tears pricked.

Would that she could keep this man!

Finally, he pulled back, pressing his forehead to hers.

"Marry me," he murmured against her mouth. "Marry me, Lady Charlotte Whitaker."

Lottie gasped.

She jolted back onto her feet and rocked backwards, leaning against his arms that banded her waist.

"P-pardon?"

"Marry me." The simple words hung between them, their portent echoing as loudly as any gunshot.

"But—" Shock had forced air out of her lungs. It took Lottie a moment to remember how to breathe. "But . . . what about the marquisate? You don't want to be the marquess!"

"Ye have the right of it, lass. But the more I learn, the more I've accepted that the only way to solve the marquisate's ills is to remove it entirely from Lord Frank's control. That means I assume the title. There is no other solution. I've used these past weeks tae truly ponder my future. I dinnae go looking for a marquisate, but as a good friend pointed out, change finds us whether we want it or no—"

"But your practice in Edinburgh? You love being a doctor."

"Aye. But I figure I can still offer free medical care tae my tenants, so I shall not have tae give it up entirely."

She stepped back, forcing Alex to release her.

Her treacherous body protested the loss of him.

"Ye have any more *buts* tae throw at me?" he asked, hand open in supplication. "I'm happy tae argue all the reasons why I think ye should be mine."

Lottie pressed a hand to her stomach. It was almost painfully glorious to hear Alex say such words.

"Alex," her voice filled his name with such despair.

"I love you."

His words were a blow to her chest.

She could scarcely breathe.

"I love you," he repeated. "And once I realized that, nothing else really mattered. Having my practice in Edinburgh means nothing to me if I cannae have ye by my side."

"Alex." Lottie pressed a shaking hand to her forehead. "You know I can't betray my family. I *cannot.*"

"I ken that. It's one of the things I love best about ye. That your heart is so true, so loyal. Ye fight for those who you see as your own. Perhaps I'm selfish, but I want your loving heart turned on *me.*"

Lottie swallowed a sob.

It is! she longed to say. *Your heart is lodged in mine, and I will treasure it forever.*

"My father specifically wanted Freddie to inherit. And Margaret . . . Oh!" Lottie all but wailed. "It's just impossible, surely you see that?"

"Aye. And I can appreciate how the thought of hurting your family pains ye. It's to your credit, lass. But if *you* became the next Lady Lockheade . . . ye would still be honoring your father's legacy."

"Yes, Grandmère said as much, but I don't know that I can betray Margaret so." She pressed a shaking hand to her forehead. "How can I choose between two halves of my heart—"

A light appeared on the path to the greenhouse. Margaret, most likely, returning with a candle this time.

Lottie and Alex exchanged a panicked look, both understanding that her sister would not be as understanding of his presence here. Moving quickly for a man who still needed a cane to walk, Alex darted behind a large potted myrtle.

Lottie glanced toward Grandmère. Her grandmother shrugged and flipped her hand, motioning for Lottie to speak with Margaret.

The greenhouse door snicked open.

Lottie smoothed her hands down her ball gown and stepped toward the door, trying to calm her racing heart before facing her sister.

"Lady Charlotte?" a man's voice asked. "Are you here?"

Lord Nettlesby.

Oof!

Why was *he* here? How had he found her?

Of all the people Lottie least wanted to see at the moment.

She was inclined to remain silent until he left, but the light from his candle caught the sheen of her gown through the greenery.

"There you are," he laughed as Lottie stepped out.

She peered behind him. "Where are Lord and Lady Frank? They are to come and fetch me."

Nettlesby smiled and set the candle down on an obliging pillar. "I think it will be a few minutes before your family arrives."

"Oh." Lottie blinked.

Nettlesby appeared alarmingly smug.

Every hair on Lottie's arms instantly lurched to attention.

Abruptly, she realized that if Alex and Grandmère were not hidden in the shadows—if she did not feel Alex's eyes boring into her shoulder blades behind her—she would be horrifyingly alone with Nettlesby.

"Then why are you here?" she asked, proud of the steadiness of her voice. "Certainly you must know that you should not be here with me alone. It would not be proper."

"No." Nettlesby's grin turned almost malicious. "No, it would not do, would it. Why, Lady Charlotte, if we were caught out by the right people, some would say we would even have to marry, you and I."

A chill skittered down Lottie's spine.

He had come here on purpose to try to ruin her.

How could Frank and Margaret not see this man for the reprobate he was?

Never had she been so grateful for Alex's presence.

It gave her the courage to notch her chin higher and stare Nettlesby down. She could feel Alex's restlessness behind her.

What to do?

She began by sniffing and taking a few steps to the side.

As she guessed, Nettlesby turned with her. This put his back to the space where Alex and Grandmère were hidden by the dense foliage, allowing them to watch Nettlesby without Lottie in the way.

"I suggest you leave before Lord Frank finds you here." Lottie adopted her most imperious tone. "He will be seriously displeased."

"Who do you think directed me here, Lady Charlotte?" Nettlesby asked.

"Pardon?"

He leaned into her, forcing Lottie to take a step backward.

"Lord Frank *sent* me here," he said. "Deliberately."

Lottie froze, her mind racing.

No!

Familae primum semper cognosce.

Think first of family.

Frank would not encourage a man such as Nettlesby to compromise her. Margaret would never countenance it.

But . . . did Margaret know?

"You are lying," Lottie hissed.

He laughed. "You are far too naive and trusting, my lady."

Was he telling the truth?

No. No, it was a lie.

Even Frank would not stoop to such a low. Would he?

Nettlesby reached out and tweaked one of her curls, drawing it through his fingers. "Like silk, your hair."

Lottie slapped his hand away.

He snatched her arm and pulled her to him.

"How dare you touch me!" She yanked her arm free, staggering back.

Behind Nettlesby, Alex left the security of his hiding place, his gaze a thundercloud. Grandmère stood right behind him, her eyebrows ominous.

Lottie shook her head, warning them off for the moment. She didn't want Nettlesby to realize there were others present. Not yet.

There was information to be learned here.

"You are an opportunist of the worst sort, Nettlesby," she spat. "I shall ask Lord Frank to cut your friendship immediately."

Nettlesby laughed again. "Oh! Your defense of him is almost touching, my dear—"

"I am your *dear* nothing!"

"—but you clearly do not know your precious family as well as you think you do. Frank has grand plans, you see. But his debts are atrocious and piling up by the day. He needs the marquisate and its deep funds at his disposal. Of course, you panting after that wretched doctor threatens to derail everything. So he asked me to step in. Your sister may not have condoned her husband's plan, but she also has done nothing to stop it."

Was this true?

It couldn't be.

But what had Margaret said not an hour past?

I feel that I am on a knife's edge.

Was Margaret truly so desperate?

Nettlesby did not misread her stunned shock.

"I can see you are finally understanding the reality of this situation."

"Was Dr. Whitaker's accident not truly an accident either?" The question dropped from her lips.

Nettlesby shrugged. "Frank still insists it was, though I think he would have welcomed the doctor's death."

"How despicable!"

"It is the way of the world, my dear." Nettlesby snorted. "Never fear, however, I am a most willing accomplice in this. I am in need of a wife, and you—" He tugged on her curl again. "—are decidedly lovely."

Lottie's jaw dropped. She stepped back, looking Nettlesby up and down. And then, because she couldn't help it, she met Alex's eyes behind his lordship.

Nettlesby frowned and whirled, following her gaze.

He yelped in surprise to find Alex's angry glare and Grandmère's censorious eyebrows staring him down.

"This has tae be the most *glaikit*, numbskull thing I've heard in years!" Alex advanced on Nettlesby, causing the man to stumble back in retreat. Alex stopped beside Lottie.

"Indeed," Grandmère agreed, joining them. She raked Nettlesby from head to toe. "This news is most distressing."

Nettlesby swiveled his head between them all, eyes wide.

"How did you think this would play out, my lord?" Lottie asked. "Have you been reading Gothic novels?"

"Aye," Alex agreed. "Did ye suppose ye could simply be caught with a lady, perhaps even force a kiss upon her, and she would therefore *have* tae marry ye? That's absurd. The real world doesnae work like that."

"Or were you planning to actually assault me?!" Lottie shook her head. "No one can force me to marry where I do not wish. I would have to be foolish in the extreme to marry a man who had injured my person in an attempt to entrap me into marriage!"

"Now, see here, Lady Charlotte—" Nettlesby took a step toward Lottie and then thought the better of it when Alex growled and placed his walking stick in front of Lottie like a fence.

"Keep your distance," Alex warned.

Nettlesby glared at him and then turned back to Lottie. "Your family will not allow you to wed this man." He jerked a thumb toward Alex.

Grandmère coughed. "I would not be so sure of that. Our Charlotte is nearly four and twenty. We cannot prevent her from marrying where she wishes."

Lottie gave her grandmother a grateful look before looking back at Nettlesby.

The man had to be lying. Frank would never sanction this. She and her brother-in-law might not see eye to eye at times, but Frank would never be so callous, would he?

And even if Frank *were* so callous, Margaret would not permit Lottie to be bodily harmed in order to bolster Freddie's chances of inheriting.

"Well, *do* you intend to marry him?" Nettlesby asked, shooting a belligerent look at Alex.

"I don't—" Lottie began, but voices rose outside the greenhouse.

More people?

The door snicked open.

Through the foliage, Lottie recognized Frank with Lady Gardner.

"There you are wrong, Lady Gardner," Frank was saying. "Lady Charlotte holds no tendre for Dr. Whitaker. The man is a Scottish doctor, for heaven's sake. Can you imagine Lady Charlotte Whitaker married to one such as him?"

"Bah! Youth these days—" Lady Gardner broke off as Lottie, Alex, and Nettlesby came into view. "Oh! I say!"

Frank and Lady Gardner froze.

Lottie was quite sure they made a comical tableau.

Nettlesby, sulking and petulant.

Alex, stern and ready for battle.

And herself, wide-eyed and horrified.

"Lady Charlotte!" Frank's voice rose in outrage. "You are alone? With two gentlemen?!"

"Of course not, Frank." Grandmère took a step out of the shadows. "Our Charlotte is hardly so heedless of her reputation."

Lady Gardner nodded her head in greeting to Grandmère.

Grandmère returned the nod and then gave Frank a dramatically thunderous look.

Frank gulped. He had never been much of an actor; Lottie saw the truth clearly in his skittering gaze.

Frank *had* meant for Nettlesby to compromise her.

Given her furrowed eyebrows, Grandmère knew this, too.

Lottie's stomach swooped.

How . . . deplorable.

That her own brother-in-law would sell her like this.

That he would sanction *violence* against her person in order to bolster the chances of his son inheriting.

Before anyone could say anything further, the door burst open yet again.

"Lottie?" Margaret's voice called. "Are you here?"

Her sister rounded the corner and stopped beside her husband.

"Oh, heavens!" Margaret exclaimed, her gaze landing on Lady Gardner, Nettlesby, Grandmère, and finally Alex.

"Margaret," Lottie said.

Oh!

And there she saw it.

In Margaret's surprised gaze. In the quick flash of guilt and panic across her face.

Margaret perhaps had not known the specifics of Frank's plan. Lady Gardner's presence certainly was a surprise.

But . . .

Her sister had *known*.

She had known that Frank planned something.

And Margaret had done nothing to stop it. She had been silently complicit in the plan.

Lottie struggled to draw in a breath.

The weight of such betrayal . . .

After everything Lottie had done for Margaret and Freddie . . .

And if Alex and Grandmère hadn't been here . . .

Had Grandmère known that Frank plotted to compromise Lottie?

Or at least . . . suspected?

"Gracious," Lady Gardner's eyes lit with eagerness, as if attempting to unravel the currents of tension. "I feel there is a story to be had here."

Lottie didn't respond, her chest too tight, her eyes firmly lodged on her sister.

Did Margaret feel any guilt for her actions?

Would she have watched Lottie be forced to marry Nettlesby and spend the rest of her life bitterly unhappy?

And what if Lords sided with Alex in the end anyway?

It would have all been for naught!

Lottie could scarcely breathe.

Sometimes, family are those who put your interests first.

She closed her eyes and then opened them, meeting her grandmother's sympathetic gaze.

Yes.

Grandmère certainly had suspected something.

Her grandmother had recognized Margaret's desperation, her sister's increasing fears for her son. She had sensed that Margaret, like many a mother before her, would choose her child's future over her sister's.

And Grandmère had been correct.

No path led to a harmonious resolution here.

Not for Lottie. Not for Freddie.

It had never been a possibility.

Lottie had simply been too stubbornly set in her loyal course to recognize it.

"Lady Charlotte?" Lady Gardner wiggled her fingers. "I say, are you quite all right? Going to faint again?"

Lottie gave Lady Gardner a too-bright smile.

"I have actually never been better, my lady." She shot Margaret one final pained look. "I think I am finally seeing everything clearly."

And that was the truth.

"Lottie," Margaret began, gaze pleading, "I feel that perhaps you and I need to discuss—"

"I don't have anything to say at the moment, Margaret." Lottie's tone was terse.

She didn't trust herself to say more.

The wound was too new. Too raw.

Time and again, she had chosen Margaret and Margaret's needs.

Why had Lottie been so blindly loyal to Margaret and Frank and Freddie?

Loyalty, after all, was only good if those you were loyal to returned the sentiment. Otherwise, loyalty devolved into a sort of exploitation.

How had Lottie not seen that she was forfeiting her own life, her own heart, in exchange for theirs?

As Grandmère had pointed out, Lottie could only live her own life.

Create a family that is wholly yours and shape a future that is uniquely your own.

She could choose to make one person family.

Abruptly, the path she would choose was crystal clear.

She gave Margaret one last look, silently communicating all her anger and hurt, and then turned away.

Lottie smiled at Alex and placed a hand on his arm.

"Thank you for being here tonight, Dr. Whitaker," she said. "I shudder to think what might have happened otherwise."

"I am happy tae have been of service, my lady." Alex met her gaze.

Lottie drank in his dear face.

How had she ever thought him to be steel? He was warmth and kindness and everything she could have ever dreamed of.

"After some consideration," she said, "I have decided that, yes, I *will* accept your offer of marriage."

Alex gasped, head jerking back as if she had doused him with a glass of water.

"No!" Margaret gasped. "Lottie, please—"

"I say, Lady Charlotte," Frank hissed, "I cannot accept this."

"Silence!" Grandmère intoned. "This is Lottie's moment. You will not sully it."

Margaret took a step back, chastened. Lord Frank continued to scowl but said nothing more.

Alex and Lottie stared at Grandmère.

"Go on," Grandmère flicked her fingers toward them. "I would hear the rest of what you have to say to one another. Lady Gardner came to witness a spectacle. It would be a shame to disappoint her."

Lady Gardner nodded, eyes gleeful.

Lottie nearly laughed at the absurdity of it.

She looked back up at Alex.

"What did ye say, lass?" He reached for her hand, as if the need to touch her was utterly involuntary. "I fear I need a wee bit of a confirmation myself."

Lottie smiled.

This she could do.

It was as easy as breathing.

She squeezed his hand. "Dr. Alexander Whitaker, I, Lady Charlotte Whitaker—your distant cousin, sometime nursemaid, tutor in chess, fellow scholar, and most significantly, lover of your soul—" She pressed a hand to his chest. "—will happily accept the offer of marriage you extended to me not fifteen minutes past."

Alex laughed. "Are ye sure, lass? Ye dinnae want tae sleep on it? It seems that certain facts have come to light over these intervening fifteen minutes that might have some bearing?"

"They do. But only to show me how deeply I trust you. How deeply I l-love you." Lottie's voice broke at the end.

"Ah, lass."

"Marry me?"

"I dinnae mind if I do."

And without waiting for anyone's permission, Lottie threw herself into Alex's arms and kissed him most scandalously.

FROME ABBEY, WILTSHIRE
JULY 20, 1821
THREE MONTHS LATER

W hat will ye do today, Lady Lockheade?"
    Lottie smiled at her husband's question.

Her *husband*.

Lord Lockheade.

"Mmmm, must I do anything?" she replied with a laugh. "I'm rather enjoying having a long lie in with you."

"Mmmm." Alex cuddled her closer.

Lottie obliged, resting her head on that marvelous curve between his upper shoulder and neck, her nose pressed into his throat. He smelled of leather and wood smoke with an undercurrent of camphor.

They were snuggled together in the large bed where Alex had spent weeks recuperating. But now . . . it had become theirs—the bed they shared as husband and wife.

Lottie sometimes could not quite comprehend how thoroughly her life had changed from that January afternoon when she had watched Alex climb the front stairs to Frome Abbey.

She now wore his wedding band on her left ring finger. They had married three weeks ago in front of a large congregation of friends and family at St. George's in Hanover Square. Lottie had choked back tears as she recited her vows, and Alex's own voice had been suspiciously hoarse.

Bells pealed as they dashed through a shower of rice from the church to their waiting carriage. Passers-by had stopped to cheer and scramble for the copper coins Alex tossed from the open-top barouche.

After all, it wasn't every day that Lord Lockheade married.

A month before their wedding, Alex had been invested as the 8th Marquess of Lockheade. The Committee on Privilege had signed the necessary papers with a sigh of relief and washed their hands of the business.

Lottie knew that the transition from physician to marquess had not been an easy one. After all, Alex had spent nearly fifteen years of his life preparing and studying and practicing medicine.

Before his investiture as Lockheade, he had traveled to Edinburgh and seen his patients one last time, indulging in everything he loved about being a physician. Then he had deeded his share of the practice to McNeal, returned to London, and taken his seat in Lords.

Lottie's heart nearly broke for him.

But the situation lit a fuse of intense admiration in her heart for his dedication. Once his path was determined, her Alex fell into it with single-minded focus.

He studied and asked questions.

He rehired Mr. Argent as the marquisate's man of affairs, and Mr. Argent had been invaluable. Together, they had begun to set aright all that Frank had wrecked. Tenants' properties were being repaired. Wages were restored and additional laborers hired. Fields and farming methods were being modernized. They had also halted or reversed all the unsavory changes that Frank had made to the marquisate's other holdings.

Additionally, Alex had the advice of Lord Hadley. Hadley had taken Alex under his wing and acted as Mentor, helping him navigate the unfamiliar waters of the English aristocracy.

"Do you have a meeting this afternoon with Mr. Argent?" Lottie asked, kissing Alex's throat.

"Aye." Alex ran a hand up her arm. "But ye aren't quite convincing me tae leave ye, lass."

Lottie laughed, a soft breath of sound.

Yes, the marquisate and its people were already faring better under Alex's care. But Lottie still experienced a pang of betrayal whenever she thought about her sister and brother-in-law.

Margaret's actions had damaged their relationship, but they were slowly reconciling. It helped that Margaret had been decidedly contrite, apologizing repeatedly. Her sister had not condoned Frank's decision to have Nettlesby ruin Lottie.

"It was an absolutely appalling thing to do," Margaret said through her tears. "I gave a full account of the incident to Ferndown. His Grace was seriously displeased."

The duke's ire had rendered Frank penitent, and Lottie was working on forgiving him.

But Lottie *had* to do something for Freddie. After all, the poor boy had played no part in his parents' misdeeds.

All entailed properties of the marquisate had been devolved upon Alex, leaving very little to be divided between Margaret and Lottie. The Committee on Privilege had been eager to be done with the business and refused to break the entail.

But as a show of good faith, Lottie had deeded the small property she had inherited to Freddie when he came of age, ensuring that her nephew's future would be secure.

But in every other aspect, Lottie was focused on her own future with Alex.

"I didnae realize that love could be like this," Alex said, his fingers drifting up to run through her hair.

"Mmmm, like what? Blissful?" Her voice was teasing.

She felt more than saw him smile. "Something of the like." He paused, his fingers still tangling in her hair. "It's more like . . . I never grasped that marriage could be this place of affirmation and understanding."

"Like Wollstonecraft said, you mean?"

"Aye. I should have had better sense and listened to the woman properly in the first place."

"That is good advice for most situations in life." Lottie laughed and kissed his neck. "But I understand your meaning. I had no idea love could be so . . . accepting. That our love does not require me to give up pieces of myself or hide the bits that I fear you may not like—"

"Let it be said. I like *all* of you, lass."

Lottie pinched his side, causing him to yelp.

She raised up on an elbow, looking down at those steel eyes.

"I like all of you, too." She smiled and then pressed a soft kiss to his mouth.

In the end, Alex arrived dreadfully late to his meeting with Mr. Argent.

EPILOGUE

It was a dreich day in November when Alex received a letter from Andrew.

> *My Runner has finally tracked Reverend Gillespie to a town just south of Birmingham. We are planning on paying the reverend a visit—myself, Rafe, Ewan, and Kieran. Would you like to join us?*

Alex nodded his head.

Yes, indeed.

He would be honored to join them.

TWO WEEKS LATER, THE BROTHERHOOD OF the Black Tartan arrived in the wee village of Brawton just after luncheon. Andrew's Runner from Bow Street met them in front of The Three Bears inn, giving directions to a small cottage at the end of town.

The Brotherhood took off on foot, dodging puddles and mud along the cobblestone street.

As they turned off the High Street, Alex recognized Reverend Gillespie himself walking ahead of them up the lane. The reverend had changed little since their meeting at the coaching inn all those months ago.

The reverend's steps faltered as the Brotherhood quickly overtook him, Andrew on one side and Kieran on the other. But it wasn't until Ewan stepped in front of Gillespie that the reverend stopped entirely.

After all, Ewan was a mountain of a man—six-and-a-half feet of muscle and brawn. A former prizefighter who looked the part. Gillespie paused, audibly swallowing as he took in Ewan's height and stern expression.

The reverend spun in a circle, looking at them each in turn. Instead of being cowed, he met each of their gazes with a steady one of his own.

Alex had to give the man credit. He had gumption in spades.

Gillespie's eyes landed on Alex.

"Dr. Whitaker." The reverend nodded.

"That's Lord Lockheade to ye," Ewan rumbled.

Gillespie's eyebrows raised.

"My circumstances have changed since our last meeting," Alex said.

Kieran cracked his knuckles. "We're here because we ken ye to be the man who can answer our questions."

"I assumed you would find me eventually." Gillespie folded his arms, unshrinking before Kieran's not-so-subtle threat of violence. "You may ask your questions. But know this—my answers do not come cheap."

Alex snorted. At least the reverend was no longer pretending that avarice was not a motivating factor for him.

"We want to know everything you can tell us about *The Minerva*," Andrew said.

"Aye," Kieran nodded. "And every last wee bit about Miss Eilidh Fyffe."

The reverend nodded. "I receive money before I say a word."

"Or," Ewan leaned forward, "we give ye our word as gentlemen that ye shall be paid. Ye tell us what ye know. And then we decide what it's worth tae ourselves."

"One thousand pounds," Gillespie said, ignoring Ewan's words. "I will not accept a penny less."

Andrew snorted.

Alex raised his eyebrows. "That's an astronomical sum."

"Aye," Rafe agreed. "A lifetime of wages for a common day laborer."

"Precisely." Gillespie nodded. "Miss Fyffe was most vilely used. You cannot think that I will easily impart information to those I see as her abusers. You owe compensation for the wrongs you committed. Your debt to her remains unpaid."

Alex stilled, meeting Andrew's gaze across the group.

Your debt to her remains unpaid.

That was an all-too-familiar phrase.

"Ah. So you are the person behind those notices in the newspapers?" Alex asked.

"Yes," Gillespie nodded, at last confirming himself to be the author. "Atrocities were committed aboard *The Minerva*. I will see justice served. Miss Fyffe was ill-used. Someone should pay—"

The Brotherhood spoke over one another.

"Who told you these lies?!"

"Miss Fyffe was our dearest friend!"

"Is Miss Fyffe alive then?!"

"Miss Fyffe was my wife!" Kieran's voice cut through the noise. "No . . . she *is* my wife!"

"Wife?!" Gillespie frowned.

"Aye and I will hear all that you know." Kieran leaned toward the reverend, jabbing a finger. "I have been going mad not knowing what happened to her. I love my wife with my whole heart—"

The reverend frowned deeper, stepping back. "You and Miss Fyffe were married?"

"Aye," Kieran nodded.

"Witnessed the handfasting myself," Ewan agreed.

"Handfasting?" Gillespie rolled his eyes and folded his arms. "That is hardly a legitimate marriage."

"It is for a Scot," Kieran shot back.

"And were you married in Scotland then?" Gillespie asked.

Silence.

"I didn't think so," the reverend continued, shaking his head. "If the handfasting didn't take place on Scottish soil, then the marriage isn't legal according to English law."

"That's semantics," Kieran said. "Jamie and I considered ourselves married. If we need to formalize the union in a church, then so be it."

Gillespie opened his mouth, clearly determined to fight this.

Alex held out a staying hand. "As I said in our last meeting, we all loved Miss Fyffe—or Mrs. MacTavish, whatever you will—as family. We cared for and protected her. It is a testament to our care that we are all here today, desperate for information. You are a man of God. Please be reasonable. We shouldn't have to pay a King's ransom just to know if Miss Fyffe lives or not."

Gillespie stared at him. "The monies I request are not *un*reasonable. We are desirous to return to the South Pacific, my congregation and I, and continue our work there. You are clearly wealthy gentlemen." The reverend ran a scathing eye up and down Alex's expensive Garrick coat and darted a telling glance at the gold buttons on Andrew's waistcoat. "You can consider the funds a donation to my charitable cause."

"Again, any amount we pay ye will depend on the value of the information ye have. If ye do indeed have details about Miss Fyffe, we shall ensure that ye are rewarded handsomely." Ewan made a beckoning motion with his hand. "But first, ye have to tell us what ye know."

Gillespie paused. "Do I have your word as gentlemen that you will pay me the sum of one thousand pounds for the information at my disposal?"

"If you can direct us to the current location of Miss Eilidh Fyffe— whether alive or dead—the money will be yours," Alex said.

"Aye," Andrew agreed. "I give ye my word."

The others nodded.

Gillespie looked between them for a moment and then shrugged. "Very well. I shall tell you what I know."

THREE WEEKS LATER . . .

KIERAN STARED AT the cottage beyond the gate.

It was a typical English parsonage with a gabled roof and ivy growing over one window, the vine evergreen even in the crisp winter air.

At any other time, he might have even called the house quaint.

But the ache in his chest only focused on the end goal—

Find Jamie.

Find his wife.

Reverend Gillespie had told them quite the tale—one that led them to this small cottage in a forgotten corner of Yorkshire.

The Brotherhood waited at a nearby inn. Kieran had begged to come alone. To confront this without his friends as witnesses.

But now that he faced the house . . .

His heart galloped in his chest.

His hands tingled, nerves rendering him jittery.

He swallowed. Hard.

With a deep breath, Kieran squared his shoulders, walked through the wee gate, and rapped on the front door.

Silence.

He rapped again, louder this time.

Still . . . nothing.

No footsteps from within.

No low murmur of voices.

The turn of events was . . . anticlimactic, to say the least.

He had expected someone to be home.

A weight sank in his chest.

Had he, once more, been led astray?

Would he not find what he sought here?

No.

He had come too far, suffered too long. He would have answers.

Today.

Kieran took a step sideways and peered through the front window. The room within was dark.

But when he backed up along the front walk, he could see a thin wisp of smoke drifting from one chimney. Surely someone was at home.

Frowning, he doffed his hat and rapped once more on the door. This time the noise was loud enough to shake the window panes.

"May I help ye, sir?" A voice asked from behind him.

Kieran froze.

That voice.

He knew that voice.

It haunted his dreams.

All the air in his lungs left in an audible *whoosh*.

He slowly pivoted.

Oh!

And there she was.

Standing beside the gate, a basket filled with potatoes on her hip. A bright spot of color in the determined gray of winter.

"Jamie," he breathed.

His heart ballooned and swelled until it filled his throat, choking back any other words.

Bloody hell he had forgotten how much be adored the very sight of her.

A straw bonnet hid most of her dark curls, but her eyes still snapped with life. Freckles dusted her nose and cheeks.

She wore a heavy gray cloak over a printed muslin gown.

He had only seen her in a dress once before—their wedding day.

When aboard ship, she had dressed for her role as carpenter's mate.

But for their wedding—

"I want to feel pretty, Kieran," she had whispered to him, eyes glowing with love. "Just for today. Just for a wee while. I want to remember what it feels like to be Miss Eilidh Fyffe. I want to be a bonnie lass marrying her man."

He had purchased her a gown at a second-hand shop in Sydney—a pretty blue frock that clung to her figure and sent his thoughts tumbling. She had worn it for just a few hours, as they stood before Ewan, a cord wrapped around their hands, pledging their love.

The faded red gown she wore now showed signs of wear, the color bleached and uneven. Moreover, it was too large for her petite frame—a dress cast off by a taller, larger woman.

"Jamie," he whispered again, taking a step forward, reaching out, his arms aching to hold her.

She frowned and skittered back.

Kieran stopped, hand outstretched.

"Jamie?" he repeated, this time a question. "Jamie Fyffe?"

She shook her head, her brows drawing into a line. She continued to edge away from him, the picketed garden fence separating them.

Kieran paused.

"Jamie Fyffe was my brother." She licked her lips, darting a look past him to the cottage door, as if gauging the distance. "He is dead."

Kieran swallowed back the painful lump in his throat.

Gillespie had warned him this would be her reaction.

But . . .

He had hoped. That maybe if she saw him . . .

How could she have forgotten—

Oh, Jamie.

Where have ye gone, my love?

"Ye call yourself Miss Eilidh Fyffe, then?" he asked.

She nodded, inching back another step.

"Dinnae ye recognize me, lass?" Kieran had to ask it.

She continued to edge away from him.

Her hands holding the basket of potatoes had begun to shake.

"I think . . ." She swallowed. "I think ye be Master McTavish, my father's . . . protégé. Ye were to give Jamie a place aboard a ship."

"Aye. That is true, but—"

"My father is dead. Jamie is dead, too." Her voice trembled. "There is nothing here for ye."

Her words were a blow.

"I'm here for yourself," Kieran said. "If ye would listen—"

"No." She was shaking her head now, back and forth. "My father never properly introduced us. I don't know ye."

"Ye *do* know me, lass."

"No! I don't want to hear it."

He took another step forward. "Jamie, please—"

"I'm not Jamie!" she shouted. "I'm no one to you!"

She lobbed the basket at his head.

Kieran ducked, arms up to shield himself from the shower of potatoes.

When next he looked, Jamie was halfway down the muddy lane, running away from him as if Hell itself nipped at her heels.

AUTHOR'S NOTE

If you've made it this far, thank you!

I always love including some author notes at the end of my books, and this book is no exception. As usual, writing a Regency-era romance is an endless mix of historical fact and imaginative adaptation. I will attempt to separate the two for you here, though be warned, there are spoilers ahead if you have not yet finished reading *Making the Marquess*.

Most of the medical people and texts I refer to in *Making the Marquess* are based in fact. Rene Laennec invented the stethoscope in 1816, so I may have fudged the timeline by a year or two in how quickly it reached Edinburgh. Though as an avid student, Alex would be on the forefront of any medical invention. Chlorinated lime (which was basically bleach) was used as an early antiseptic, though doctors likely would not have called it that. The concept of bacterial and viral infections was not yet truly understood.

Along with this, I did a lot of research on limbs and what happened to people who broke them. Yes, amputation was a very real threat if the bone was broken badly enough. That said, Dr. Gooch with his wooden brace and Dr. Seutin with his starched bandages are real historical figures who furthered our understanding of how to effectively treat broken bones.

Mary Wollstonecraft likely needs no introduction, as she is a rather well-known historical figure. Her writings are largely considered the basis of modern feminist thought. As indicated, the quotes given here are taken from *A Vindication*, though I have condensed some sentences for readability. So yes, Wollstonecraft really said all those things in the late 18th century.

The *pons asinorum* is a very real thing the teenage boys dreaded learning.

Also, believe it or not, much of the story of Cousin Gabriel is based in historical fact. I got the idea for Gabriel as a character after visiting Drum Castle outside Aberdeen in Scotland. An enormous painting of a (mostly) naked winged Archangel Gabriel hangs in the library there. It is a self-portrait painted by Hugh Irvine, a younger son of one of the lairds of Drum. Around 1820, Hugh was living and painting in Rome and sent the enormous portrait home, as he didn't want his family to miss him too much. Basically, his mom looked at this enormous painting of her son—naked, with chiseled abs and an archangel's wings—and said, "It's marvelous! Hang it in the library for everyone to see." The painting has been hanging in the library of Drum Castle ever since.

Moving on.

Yes, I am aware that *grandmother* in French is hyphenated—*grand-mère*. I chose to alter that slightly for the character of Grandmère, as I wanted it to be her name, not just a noun.

Wow is actually an archaic Scottish expression that dates from the Middle Ages, but it didn't spread out of Scotland until the early 1900s. Consequently, it seems quite modern to us today. I always struggle to know how to include words and phrases from the past. I find that my language choices need to match what readers *presume* to be accurate, rather than the reality of what actually was.

I know I've mentioned this before, but for those reading one of my Scottish books for the first time, allow me to also comment on Scottish language and pronunciation. It's always a struggle to know how to write an accent, particularly in a historical novel. Scotland today recognizes three distinct languages: Scottish Gaelic, Scots, and English. Historically, Scottish Gaelic has been spoken in the Highlands. Most Lowland Scots in the early 1800s (i.e. those from Glasgow and Edinburgh) would have spoken a mix of Scots and English. (Sidenote: If you want to read some Scots, Wikipedia actually has an entire dictionary written in Scots—sco. wikipedia.org.)

Of course, I realized fairly quickly that a modern, primarily American, audience would struggle to understand Scots.

So, what to do?

After much consideration, I decided to go with a slightly more modern Scottish accent and syntax, simply to aid readability. I write novels, after all, not history texts. I've used modern spellings of Scottish pronunciations and, even then, restricted myself to a few key words to give a Scottish flavor to the text. So at times, the accent as written is not perfectly consistent; this was done to help readability. That said, I have continued to use more common Scots words wherever possible—e.g. *ken/kens/kent* (think, know), *eejit* (idiot), *glaikit* (foolish), *muckle* (enormous), *youse* (you all), *greit/greet* (to weep), etc.

I have created an extensive pinboard on Pinterest with images of things I talk about in the book. So if you want a visual of anything—including Hugh Irvine's painting, Gooch's brace, etc.—pop over there and explore. Just search for NicholeVan.

As with all books, this one couldn't have been written without the help and support from those around me. I know I am going to leave someone out with all these thanks. So to that person, know that I totally love you and am so deeply grateful for your help!

To my beta readers—you know who you are—thank you for your editing suggestions, helpful ideas, and support. And, again, an extra-large thank you to Rebecca Spencer, Annette Evans, and Norma Melzer for their fantastic editing skills.

I have to give an enormous shout out to Shannon Castleton. Thank you, my dear friend, for fielding my endless questions and for spending hours lending me insights from your brilliant brain.

Erin Rodabough also deserves another round of applause for her endless help. Thank you for being my writing *and* travel buddy.

Finally, thank you to Andrew, Austenne, Kian, and Dave for your endless patience and support.

And to all my readers, thank you for continuing to read and recommend my work!

READING GROUP QUESTIONS

Yes, there are reading group questions. I suggest discussing them over lots of excellent chocolate (solid, liquid, frozen, cake . . . I'm not picky about the precise state of matter of said chocolate; chocolate in any form is good chocolate).

Also—fair warning—there are definite spoilers inherent in these questions if you have not finished reading the book as of yet.

1. In the book, Alex recognizes that addiction runs in his family line. He gives himself essentially rigid rules to follow in order to avoid the pitfalls of addiction himself. How did you feel about that? Did you feel this was a reasonable reaction? Why or why not?

2. Alex has obvious control issues, as he is clearly a workaholic. Can working too hard be an addiction? Why or why not?

3. How did you feel Alex and Lottie were suited for one another? Did you truly feel like they had come to genuinely love each other? If so, what makes you believe that their marriage will be a lasting one?

4. Lottie is fiercely loyal to her family and refuses to even think about betraying them for most of the novel. This loyalty makes us admire her—as she is willing to sacrifice for those she loves—but it can also be frustrating, as Lottie does not immediately consider her own needs and wants. Have you ever felt this kind of loyalty to your family? Were you frustrated by Lottie's refusal to reach for her own happiness?

5. In order to marry, both Alex and Lottie had to sacrifice something important. Alex gives up medicine and Lottie dramatically alters her nephew's future (and by extension, her sister's). Should we sacrifice things we value for romantic love? Do you feel this is a reasonable expectation? Why or why not?

6. The story delves into the philosophies of Mary Wollstonecraft, one of the earliest feminist writers. Wollstonecraft claims that in not educating women, we deprive men of true companionship in marriage. We can see this idea echoed in the writings of Jane Austen, who surely had read Wollstonecraft herself. Austen took time to craft heroines who would be true companions to her heroes. Do you feel that Lottie will be a true companion to Alex? And what about the reverse, will Alex be a true companion to Lottie? Why or why not?

7. Toward the end of the book, Grandmère tells Lottie that we journey through life alone, but in that lonely journey, we can choose to "make one person family. One person to tie to our side and walk the path of life with us." How did you feel about this thought? Is this an accurate observation? Why or why not?

8. Clearly, this book contains a lot of information about Scotland and Scottish culture. Did you learn something new or unexpected? If so, what was it?

OTHER BOOKS BY NICHOLE VAN

BROTHERHOOD OF THE BLACK TARTAN

Suffering the Scot
Romancing the Rake
Loving a Lady
Making the Marquess
Remembering Jamie (Autumn 2021)

OTHER REGENCY ROMANCES

Seeing Miss Heartstone
Vingt-et-Un | Twenty-one (a novella included in *Falling for a Duke.*)
A Ring of Gold (a novella included in *A Note of Change.*)

BROTHERS *MALEDETTI* SERIES

Lovers and Madmen
Gladly Beyond
Love's Shadow
Lightning Struck
A Madness Most Discreet

THE HOUSE OF OAK SERIES

If you haven't yet read *Seeing Miss Heartstone,*
please turn the page for a preview of this
Whitney Award Winner for Best Historical Romance 2018.

SEEING MISS HEARTSTONE

. . . My lord, news of your current financial pressures has reached many ears. I know of an interested party who would be honored to discuss a proposed joint venture. They have asked to meet you along the Long Water in Hyde Park tomorrow morning, where they shall endeavor to lay out the particulars of their proposal . . .

—excerpt from an unsigned letter posted to Lord Blake

In retrospect, Miss Arabella Heartstone had three regrets about 'The Incident.'

She should not have worn her green, wool cloak with the fox fur collar, as Hyde Park was warmer than expected that morning.

She should not have instructed her chaperone, Miss Anne Rutger, to remain politely out of earshot.

And she probably should *not* have proposed marriage to the Marquess of Blake.

"P-pardon?" Lord Blake lifted a quizzical eyebrow, standing straight and tall, rimmed in the morning sunlight bouncing off the Long Water behind him. A gentle breeze wound through the surrounding trees, rustling newly-grown, green leaves. "Would . . . would you mind repeating that last phrase? I fear I did not hear you correctly."

Belle straightened her shoulders, clasped her trembling hands together, and sternly ordered her thumping heart to *Cease this racket.*

Swallowing, she restated her request. "After much consideration, my lord, I feel a marriage between you and myself would be prudent."

Lord Blake stared at her, blinking over and over. Belle was unsure if his reaction denoted surprise or was simply the result of the dazzling sunlight off the water behind her.

Silence.

Birds twittered. Branches creaked. Leaves rustled.

Eternities passed. Millennia ended and were reborn.

Belle gritted her teeth, desperate to bolster her flagging confidence. *You are strong and courageous. You can do this.*

In the past, her passivity over the Marriage Matter had nearly ended in disaster. So, Belle had set her sights on a more forthright course— propose marriage herself. Yes, she struggled to talk with people and preferred anonymity to attention, but her current situation was critical.

She needed a husband. Decidedly. Desperately. Immediately. As in . . . yesterday would not have been soon enough.

At the moment, however, her mental encouragement barely managed to convince the swarming butterflies in her stomach to not free her breakfast along with themselves. Casting up her accounts all over his lordship's dusty Hessian boots would hardly nurture his romantic interest.

At last, Lord Blake stirred, pulling a folded letter from his overcoat. He stared at it, eyebrows drawing down, a sharp "V" appearing above his nose.

"You sent me this message, asking to meet me here?" He flapped the letter in her direction.

"Yes." Belle bit down on her lip and darted a glance behind at her companion. Miss Rutger stood a solid thirty yards off, studiously facing the Long Water. "Well . . . uhm . . . in all truthfulness, Miss Rutger wrote the letter."

Lord Blake raised his eyebrows, clearly uncaring of the minutiae involved. "So you are *not* a gentleman interested in my business venture in the East Indies?" He unfolded the letter, reading from it. "'*I know of an interested party who would be honored to discuss a proposed joint venture. They have asked to meet you along the Long Water,*' et cetera. This 'interested party' is yourself?" He returned the letter to his pocket.

"Yes, my lord." Belle commanded her feet to hold still and not bounce up and down—the bouncing being yet another effect of those dratted nervous butterflies.

Lord Blake's brows rose further. "And you are offering . . . marriage?"

"Yes, my lord," Belle repeated, but she had to clarify the point. Apparently, she had no issue with being thought forward and brazen, but heaven forbid Lord Blake imagine her a liar, too. "Though . . . I *am* proposing a joint endeavor."

"Indeed," he paused. "Marriage usually implies as much."

Lord Blake shuffled a Hessian-booted foot and clasped his hands behind his back. A corner of his mouth twitched.

Was the man . . . amused? If so, was that good? Or bad?

And at this point, did it matter?

Belle soldiered on. "There would be significant advantages to both of us with such a match."

More silence. An errant draft of wind tugged at his coat.

"You have me at a disadvantage, Miss . . ." His voice trailed off.

"Heartstone. Miss Arabella Heartstone."

"I see." He removed his hat and slapped it against his thigh. "And why have we not met in more . . . uh . . . typical circumstances? A ball, perhaps? A dinner party where we could be properly introduced and engage in conversation about the weather and the latest bonnet fashions before leaping straight to marriage?"

"Oh." It was Belle's turn to blink, absorbing his words. *Oh dear.* "We *have* met, my lord. We were introduced at Lord Pemberley's musicale last month. We did discuss the weather, but not bonnets or . . . uhm . . . marriage."

She hadn't expected him to recall everything, but to not even *recognize* her? To not remember their brief conversation—

"How do you do, Miss Heartstone? It's a pleasure to make your acquaintance." Lord Blake bowed.

"The pleasure is all mine, my lord." Belle curtsied. *"Lovely weather we're having."*

"Indeed, we are."

It did not bode well.

The butterflies rushed upward, eager for escape.

"Right." Blake let out a gusting breath and shook his head, sending his hair tumbling across his forehead. The morning sun turned it into molten shades of deep amber, curling softly over his ears.

Lean and several inches taller than her own average height, Lord Blake was not classically handsome, she supposed. His straight nose, square jaw, and high forehead were all too exaggerated for classical handsomeness.

And yet, something about him tugged at her. Perhaps it was the breadth of his shoulders filling out his coat. Or maybe it was the ease of his stance, as if he would face the jaws of Hell itself with a sardonic smile and casual *sang-froid*. Or maybe it was the way he ran a gloved hand through his hair, taking it from fashionably tousled to deliciously rumpled.

Mmmmm.

Belle was going to side with the hair. Though sardonic smiles were a close second.

Regardless, her decision to offer marriage to him had not been based on his physical appearance. She was many things, but *flighty* and *shallow* were two words that had never been attached to her.

Replacing his hat, Lord Blake studied her, blue eyes twinkling.

Yes. Definitely amused.

That was . . . encouraging? Having never proposed marriage to a man before, Belle was unsure.

"Enlighten me, if you would be so kind, as to the particular reasons why you think this . . . joint endeavor . . . would be profitable." He gestured toward her.

Oh! Excellent.

That she had come prepared to do.

With a curt nod, she pulled a paper from her reticule.

"A list?" His lips twitched again.

"I am nothing if not thorough in my planning, my lord." She opened the paper with shaking fingers, her hands clammy inside her gloves.

"Of course. I should have expected as much. You arranged this meeting, after all." He tapped the letter in his pocket.

Belle chose to ignore the wry humor in his tone and merely nodded her head in agreement. "Allow me to proceed with my list. Though please forgive me if my reasons appear forward."

"You have just proposed marriage to a peer of the realm, madam. I cannot imagine anything you say from this point onward will trump that."

"True."

A beat.

Lord Blake pinned her with his gaze—calm and guileless. The forthright look of a man who knew himself and would never be less-than-true to his own values.

His gaze upset her breathing, causing something to catch in her throat.

Belle broke eye-contact, swallowing too loudly.

"Allow me to begin." She snapped the paper in her hand. The words swam in her vision, but she knew them by heart. The paper was more for show than anything else. She had done her calculations most carefully.

Taking a fortifying breath, Belle began, "Firstly, you have newly inherited the Marquisate of Blake from a cousin. Your cousin was somewhat imprudent in his spending habits—"

"I would declare the man to be an utter scapegrace and wastrel, but continue."

"Regardless of the cause, your lands and estates are in dire need of resuscitation." Belle glanced at him over the top of her paper. "You are basically without funds, my lord."

"As my solicitor repeatedly reminds me." He shot her an arch look. "It is why I am trying to fund a business venture in connection with the East India Company, as you are also undoubtedly aware."

"Yes, my lord. That is why I am proposing an enterprise of a slightly different sort. Allow me to continue." Belle cleared her throat, looking down to her paper. "My own family is genteel with connections to the upper aristocracy—my great-great grandfather was the Earl of Stratton—though we have no proper title of our own, leaving my father to make his own way in the world. I, as you might already know, am a considerable heiress. My father was a prominent banker and left the entirety of his estate to me upon his death three years past."

Belle clenched her jaw against the familiar sting in her throat.

Blink, blink, blink.

Now was *not* the time to dwell upon her father.

"Are you indeed?" he asked. "Though I do not wish to sound crass, I feel we left polite discussion in the dust several minutes ago, so I must enquire: How much of an heiress are you, precisely?"

Did she hear keen interest in his tone? Or was Lord Blake simply exceedingly polite?

"I believe the current amount stands somewhere in the region of eighty thousand pounds, my lord," she replied.

Lord Blake froze at that staggering number, just as Belle had predicted he would.

"Eighty thousand pounds, you say? That is a dowry of marquess-saving proportions."

"My thoughts precisely, my lord."

Her father had originally left her a healthy sixty thousand pounds, but she was nothing if not her father's daughter. Numbers and statistics flowed through her brain, a constant rushing river. She had used these skills to grow her fortune.

It was what her father would have wanted. Refusing to see her gender as a barrier, her father had taught his only child everything he knew—financial systems, probabilities, market shares—even soliciting her opinions during that last year before his death.

By the age of sixteen, Belle understood more about supply-and-demand and the mathematics of economics than most noblemen. Knowing this, the conditions in her father's will allowed her to continue to oversee her own interests with the help of his solicitor, Mr. Sloan. At only nineteen years of age, she currently managed a thriving financial empire.

She could hear her father's gruff voice, his hand gently lifting her chin. *I would give you choices, my Little Heart Full. A lady should always have options. I would see you happy.*

Belle swallowed back the painful tightness in her throat.

Now, if she could only land a husband and free herself from the guardianship of her uncle and mother.

Family, it turned out, were not quite as simple to manage as corn shares.

Her mother, hungry for a title for her daughter, was becoming increasingly bold in her attempts to get Belle married. She had all but forced Belle to betroth herself to a cold, aloof viscount the previous Season. Fortunately, the viscount—Lord Linwood—had asked to be released from their betrothal.

But the entire situation had left Belle feeling helpless.

She *detested* feeling helpless, she realized. And so she used that unwelcome sensation to suppress her inherent shyness and overcome her retiring personality.

Belle would solve the husband problem herself. She simply needed to reduce the entire situation to a statistical probability and face it as she would any other business transaction.

"Eighty-thousand pounds," Lord Blake repeated. "Are husbands—particularly the marquess variety—generally so costly?" He clasped his hands behind his back, studying her. "I had not thought to price them before this."

"I cannot say. This is my first venture into, uhmm . . ."

"Purchasing a husband?" he supplied, eyes wide.

Heavens. Was that a hint of displeasure creeping into his voice?

"I am not entirely sure I agree with the word *purchase*, my lord—"

"True. It does smack of trade and all polite society knows we cannot have *that*."

A pause.

"Shall we use the word *negotiate* instead?" she asked.

He cocked his head, considering. "I daresay that would be better. So I receive a sultan's ransom and your lovely self, and you receive . . ." His words drifted off.

"A husband. And in the process, I become Lady Blake, a peeress of the realm."

"Are you truly so hungry to be a marchioness? Surely eighty thousand pounds could purchase—forgive me, *negotiate*—the title of duchess." His words so very, very dry.

"I am sure my mother would agree with you, my lord, but I am more interested in finding a balance between title and the proper gentleman." She cleared her throat. "You come highly recommended."

"Do I?" Again, his tone darkly sardonic.

Oh, dear.

But as she was already in for more than a penny, why not aim for the whole pound?

"I did not arrive at the decision to propose marriage lightly. I had my solicitor hire a Runner to investigate you. I have armed myself with information, my lord."

Belle wisely did not add that, after crunching all the statistical probabilities, Lord Blake had been by far and away her preferred candidate. She was quite sure that, like most people, he would not appreciate being reduced to a number.

"Information? About me?" he asked.

"Yes. For example, I know you recently cashed out of the army, selling the officer's commission you inherited from your father. All those who served with you report you to be an honest and worthy commander—"

"As well they should."

"Additionally, you are a kind son to your mother. You send her and your stepfather funds when you are able. You visit regularly. Your four older sisters dote upon you, and you are godfather to at least one of each of their children. You are a tremendous favorite with all of your nieces and nephews. All of this speaks highly to the kind of husband and father you would be."

After her disastrous betrothal to Lord Linwood last year, Belle was determined to not make the same error twice. She learned from her mistakes. Her mother and uncle would not browbeat her into accepting one of their suitors again.

If nothing else, eighty thousand pounds should purchase—*negotiate*—her a *kindhearted* husband of her own choice.

Lord Blake shuffled his feet. "I-I really am at a loss for words, Miss Heartstone. I am trying to decide if I should be flattered or utterly appalled."

Belle sucked in a deep breath, her mouth as dry as the Sahara.

Stay strong. Argue your case.

She pasted a strained smile on her face. "Might I suggest siding with flattery, my lord?"

Visit www.NicholeVan.com to buy your copy of
Seeing Miss Heartstone today and continue the story.

ABOUT THE AUTHOR

THE SHORT VERSION:

NICHOLE VAN IS a writer, photographer, designer and generally disorganized crazy person. Though originally from Utah, she currently lives on the coast of Scotland with three similarly crazy children and one sane, very patient husband who puts up with all of them. In her free time, she enjoys long walks along the Scottish lochs and braes. She does not, however, enjoy haggis.

THE LONG OVERACHIEVER VERSION:

AN INTERNATIONAL BESTSELLING author, Nichole Van is an artist who feels life is too short to only have one obsession. In former lives, she has been a contemporary dancer, pianist, art historian, chore-ographer, culinary artist and English professor.

Most notably, however, Nichole is an acclaimed photographer, win-ning over thirty international accolades for her work, including Portrait of the Year from WPPI in 2007. (Think Oscars for wedding and portrait photographers.) Her unique photography style has been featured in many magazines, including Rangefinder and Professional Photographer. She is also the creative mind behind the popular website Flourish Emporium which provides resources for photographers.

All that said, Nichole has always been a writer at heart. With an MA in English, she taught technical writing at Brigham Young University for ten years and has written more technical manuals than she can quickly count. She decided in late 2013 to start writing fiction and has since become an Amazon #1 bestselling author. Additionally, she has won a RONE award, as well as been a Whitney Award Finalist several years running. Her late 2018 release, *Seeing Miss Heartstone*, won the Whitney Award Winner for Best Historical Romance.

In February 2017, Nichole, her husband and three crazy children moved from the Rocky Mountains in the USA to Scotland. They currently live near the coast of eastern Scotland in an eighteenth century country house. Nichole loves her pastoral country views while writing and enjoys long walks through fields and along beaches. She does not, however, have a fondness for haggis.

She is known as NicholeVan all over the web: Facebook, Instagram, Pinterest, etc. Visit http://www.NicholeVan.com to sign up for her author newsletter and be notified of new book releases. Additionally, you can see her photographic work at http://photography.nicholeV.com and http://www.nicholeV.com

If you enjoyed this book, please leave a short review on Amazon.com. Wonderful reviews are the elixir of life for authors. Even better than dark chocolate.

Made in the USA
Monee, IL
17 October 2024

67395293R00194